Praise for *The Secret Diamond Sisters*

"This quick and entertaining read is filled with glitz and glamour...get ready for one crazy and fabulous ride."
—*RT Book Reviews*

"Electrifying... *Gossip Girl* meets *The Princess Diaries* in a city that never sleeps."
—*Booklist*

"Highly addictive! Hold on tight, because *The Secret Diamond Sisters* throws you headfirst into the Vegas fast lane. A fun ride not to be missed!"
—Rachel Harris, author of *My Super Sweet Sixteenth Century*

"I opened *The Secret Diamond Sisters* and was transported to Vegas...there was never a dull moment! It's the helpless romantic's dream."
—*LitPick,* Five Star Book Review Award

"Michelle Madow has followed in the platinum heelsteps of Cecily Von Ziegesar *(Gossip Girl)*, Sara Shepard *(Pretty Little Liars)* and Ally Carter *(Heist Society)* in what seems like the first season of the Diamond girls' romantic, shocking and lavish lives."
—Nathan Siegel, *Goodreads* reviewer

"A never-ending rollercoaster from the very first page, with its intense drama and unique lifestyle."
—Nina Sachdev, 14, high school student

Books by Michelle Madow
available from Harlequin TEEN

The Secret Diamond Sisters series

(in reading order)

The Secret Diamond Sisters
Diamonds in the Rough

MICHELLE MADOW

DIAMONDS IN THE ROUGH

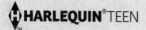

Recycling programs
for this product may
not exist in your area.

ISBN-13: 978-0-373-21136-4

Diamonds in the Rough

Printed in U.S.A.

To Molly Ker Hawn,
for believing in this series and taking a chance on it.

www.campusbuzz.com

First Day of School!
Posted on Tuesday 9/3 at 11:37 AM
I can't believe school starts tomorrow! Summer has gone by way too fast. I wish I could live in summer forever, gossiping about who's with who at what club, who has the best tan, and when we can stay out all night without having to wake up at dawn the next morning to sit in class all day.

Adrian Diamond's three daughters will be starting at Goodman this year, and since they supposedly grew up in some random town in northern cali, it'll be interesting to see how they adapt. They made a splash the first week they arrived, but since then they've been under the radar. Probably because they're nothing special and don't deserve any of the attention they got when they first arrived!

Anyway, I'm off to work on my tan and do some last minute back to school shopping. See you all bright and early tomorrow morning! ☹

1: Posted on Tuesday 9/3 at 12:56 PM
Savannah Diamond posted some YouTube vids singing and playing guitar (she's good, even though her vids are crappy quality on her laptop webcam and haven't gotten tons of views), but her and her sisters haven't been around as much since the first week they got here. Which sucks, cause they're HOT!

2: Posted on Tuesday 9/3 at 2:07 PM

I hear they're majorly behind on academics because their old public school sucked so they've been getting tutored so they won't be behind at Goodman. What a shitty way to spend summer!

3: Posted on Tuesday 9/3 at 4:21 PM

Nick Gordon's been MIA all summer too, and he was totally hanging with Savannah Diamond the week she arrived. Maybe they've been so involved with each other that they haven't had time for anyone else!!!

4: Posted on Tuesday 9/3 at 4:51 PM

Or she's been moping because Damien peaced out to travel all summer. Savannah was supposedly so obsessed with him that he left just to get away from her. Haha poor girl. Awkward, much?

chapter 1: *Savannah*

Savannah Diamond wanted her first day at her new school to be perfect, so she'd woken up extra early to get ready. But her nerves had her so on edge that she couldn't even sing into her hairbrush along with her favorite songs, pretending she was a pop star performing a show. Peyton used to get so mad at her for it every morning, since she, Courtney and Savannah shared a room, and Savannah woke up earlier than Peyton because she needed more time to get ready. Having a room to herself was the best.

If this were her first day of her sophomore year at Fairfield High, she'd have thrown on jean shorts, a pastel tank and sparkly summer flats. But The Goodman School was a fancy private school in Vegas, and since she and her sisters had found out last summer that billionaire casino owner Adrian Diamond was their father, and had moved into the penthouse next to his in The Diamond Residences, Savannah was supposed to be a sophisticated hotel heiress—not a girl who'd grown up in a poor neighborhood in a small town. She needed an outfit to fit the part. And since the only dress-code rules at The Goodman School were no ripped jeans and no belly buttons showing, she had plenty of options.

She settled on a metallic spaghetti-strap top by Young Fabulous & Broke, paired with a black flair miniskirt and strappy Jimmy Choo heels. She curled her hair to give it volume, put on a Swarovski crystal headband and went all out with makeup—deep purples and silvers from her Urban Decay Vice palette, winged black eyeliner with liquid gold sparkles, extra coats of mascara and shimmery lip gloss. As she walked to her jewelry box to decide what to match with the outfit, someone knocked at her door.

"Savannah?" Her sister Courtney peeked her head into the room. "Breakfast is here, and Adrian and Rebecca are on their way. Are you almost ready?"

"Are these earrings too much with the bracelets?" Savannah motioned to her dangly crystal earrings and Alex and Ani bangles.

Courtney examined Savannah's outfit. "I don't want you taking this the wrong way, but isn't it a bit much for school?"

Savannah pulled at her top and frowned. "The personal shopper from Saks said the outfit was perfect on me."

"It does look great on you." Courtney bit her lower lip. "But it seems better suited for a cocktail party or other nighttime event.... Not for school."

"I shouldn't have bothered asking." She played with her charm bracelets, shuffling her feet as she scrutinized the outfit in her full-length mirror. It *was* flashy. But she couldn't take fashion advice from Courtney, who had on jeans, flip-flops, a sky-blue T-shirt and practically no makeup. The only jewelry she wore was a practical watch and that boring old key necklace Grandma had given her for her birthday last year—

an heirloom from their great-great-grandmother. "Sure, it would have been too much for Fairfield High, but this is *private school* in *Las Vegas*. The first day is when everyone gets most dressed up, so I want to be ready."

"I was just trying to help, but whatever makes you happy." Courtney toyed with her necklace. "You're lucky you aren't nervous."

"You think I'm not nervous?" Savannah had tossed and turned all night, and her hands had been shaking all morning. "I don't know anyone in my grade. And I have no idea what'll happen if I run into Damien or Nick—which I'm assuming I will, since the school is small." She frowned, thinking about how stupidly optimistic she'd felt in the beginning of July at the Diamond Hotel grand opening, when Damien had apologized for kissing Madison, and Nick had given her attention all night. Because a week later, Damien had left on a month-long teen tour to Alaska and Hawaii, and Nick was always busy with work. "I'm worried that they'll see me and pretend they don't know me. Or that they've forgotten about me."

The pathetic part was that it had been weeks since she'd heard from either of them—aside from an occasional text from Nick that he felt bad about not having time to hang out—and she checked up on them daily on Facebook and Twitter. Nick had been inactive on both, but Damien had posted pictures on Facebook from his trip, of him with gorgeous, confident girls—the types of girls who made Savannah fade into the background. Girls like Madison Lockhart.

Which was why it was extra important that her first-day-of-school outfit was perfect. She needed to stand out, not fade away.

"You'll make friends," Courtney said. "And if Damien and Nick ignore you, they're not worth your time."

"Maybe." She knew Courtney was right, but that didn't mean it would hurt less if they pretended they didn't know her.

"I'm worried about the classes," Courtney said. "What if the tutoring this summer wasn't enough and we're behind? I could barely sleep last night thinking about it."

"You do look tired." Savannah observed the dark circles under Courtney's eyes. "Let me help." She applied concealer on her sister's face, pink blush to brighten her cheeks, and mascara so she looked like she'd made a *little* effort. "That's better. Now no one will know."

"Unless I fall asleep in class." Courtney laughed, wringing her hands together.

"That'll never happen," Savannah said. "You'll probably find class so fascinating that it'll keep you wide awake."

"We'll see," she said. "But let's head into the dining room. Adrian and Rebecca will be here any minute."

Savannah jingled her bracelets again at the mention of their father, Las Vegas hotel owner extraordinaire Adrian Diamond. He still didn't know her or her sisters deeper than surface level, even though they'd been living here for weeks. But he and his fiancée, Rebecca Carmel, had insisted they order room service so that they could have breakfast together before the first day of school. Adrian had been making small attempts like this to chat with them all summer, but he constantly traveled for work, and when he was in town he had business meetings, golf games or was locked in his office. He made time for Rebecca, but whenever he talked to Savannah and her sisters, there was a wall between them.

Savannah followed Courtney into the dining room. "Is Peyton up?" she asked.

"She was waging war with the snooze alarm twenty minutes ago, but I forced her awake," Courtney said. "She should be out of the shower soon."

"Sure she will," Savannah said. Peyton was notorious for her marathon shower sessions that stole all the hot water and made them late for school.

Her phone buzzed with a text message. It was from Evie, her best friend in Fairfield. Her heart warmed when she saw the text—texting before school had been something they did all the time before Savannah moved.

Good luck on your first day! You're so lucky your new school starts in Sep. Stupid fairfield high starting so early. #jealous ;)

thanks! I'm so nervous tho. wish you were here!!! <3

Fairfield high isn't as fun without you! <3 What'd you decide to wear?

Savannah snapped a picture of herself and sent it to Evie.

Cute! But isn't it too much for school?? I would totally LOVE it for a party, but you don't want everyone to think you're trying too hard...

it's fine for school in Vegas!!! ;)

Savannah's hands shook, and she paused before pressing Send. Could Evie be right? It was the same thing Courtney had said, and while Courtney didn't care about fashion, Evie did. Maybe she should switch out the skirt for jeggings, or match it with a more casual top, or wear shoes that wouldn't hurt her feet by lunch.

She was almost back to her room to change when the door to the condo opened, and Adrian and Rebecca strolled inside.

Adrian wore a navy suit—Savannah had never seen him in anything *but* a suit—and even though it was 7:00 a.m., his blue eyes were bright and his skin was glowing. The same couldn't be said of Rebecca, whose brown hair tumbled down her back in the most unruly way Savannah had ever seen it, and who was still in her pink silk pajamas. She poured herself a generous amount of coffee and cradled the cup as if it held the key to her survival.

"Is Peyton not ready for breakfast?" Adrian asked, pouring his own cup of coffee.

"I'll get her," Savannah said, glad to have something to do. Especially since this was the opposite of breakfasts back in Fairfield, which had usually been eaten on the go, because their mom had cared more about sleeping off her hangover than waking up so they could eat as a family.

"Peyton?" Savannah stepped into her sister's room and found her bent over, unraveling a towel on her head. "Are you almost ready for breakfast?"

"In a minute," Peyton mumbled, wrestling a hairbrush through her hair. Once finished, she flipped her hair up, giving a full view of her outfit.

"You're not allowed to wear jeans with rips in them," Savannah said. "It's against the dress code."

"Screw the dress code." Peyton marched to her vanity and lined her eyes with thick black liner. "These are the jeans I feel like wearing today."

"But you have so many jeans without rips in them," Savannah pointed out, knowing the only reason Peyton "felt" like wearing those today was *because* they were against the dress code. "Why don't you wear one of them instead?"

"Because I want to wear these." Peyton jutted out her chin and continued with her makeup. "And you apparently want to dress like you're going to a club instead of to school, but I'm not knocking your outfit and telling you to change, am I?"

"You just sort of did, but whatever." Savannah ran her hands over her skirt. Her clothes might have been more fashion forward, but they didn't break the dress code. Besides, what did Peyton know about what students wore at The Goodman School? No more than Courtney or Evie. "It's not my problem if you get in trouble. Are you coming to breakfast?"

"It's so dumb that we had to wake up thirty minutes earlier for this fancy breakfast," Peyton grumbled.

"I think Adrian's trying to be nice," Savannah said. "But you should see Rebecca. She's so not a morning person."

"I guess I have one thing in common with her." Peyton smirked. "And what about Adrian? Pristine, as always?"

"Of course," Savannah said. "You would think he doesn't need sleep."

"Maybe he's a vampire." Peyton laughed. "Like in those movies you like where they sparkle. They don't sleep, right?"

"I know you secretly like *Twilight*." Savannah's stomach rumbled, and she wrapped her arms around it. "But I'm starving, and the food smells amazing. Come on."

Room service had finished setting up breakfast, so the glass table had a white cloth spread on top of it, and the plates waiting at each seat were covered with silver domes like they were at a banquet. Adrian raised an eyebrow when he saw Peyton's jeans, but said nothing.

"Is Brett coming?" Savannah asked Rebecca.

"He had trouble waking up this morning, so he's still getting ready," Rebecca said.

Savannah wasn't surprised. Ever since Courtney and Brett's

public kiss at the grand opening, Brett avoided as many family meals as possible. Savannah had tried talking with Courtney about it, but her sister had shrugged it off, saying the kiss was a one-time thing, since Brett was off-limits as their stepbrother-to-be, and she needed to focus on school instead of guys. It was so typically *Courtney*—she was too much of a rule follower to rebel, and she was an expert at controlling her emotions. Savannah wished she could control her own half as well.

Still, she felt bad for Brett. He had a lot in common with Courtney, and they'd gotten along so well. But Courtney wouldn't budge—she'd had schoolwork and studying for the SATs on her mind all summer. Brett would have to get over her.

Just like Savannah would get over Damien. And Nick.

At least, she hoped so.

"Are the three of you looking forward to your first day of school?" Adrian removed the cover from his plate, and they all followed his lead.

"Yeah." Savannah poured syrup on her pancakes and took a bite. They were fluffy and delicious. "I'm excited to meet everyone." Her knees also bounced with worry about Damien and Nick, but she couldn't discuss her guy problems with Adrian.

"I'm nervous about the classes." Courtney cut her omelet, releasing the steam from inside. "I hope I'm not behind."

"Your tutor said you're ready to begin Goodman," Adrian said. "She was impressed by your work ethic."

"Thanks." Courtney took a bite of her food, although she chewed so slowly it was like she was force-feeding herself.

"What about you, Peyton?" Rebecca asked.

"The only thing I'm excited about is how this will be the

last first day of school I'll ever have," she said. "I can't wait to be done with classes forever."

"You don't know that," Rebecca said. "You might change your mind about college."

"No, I won't." Peyton huffed and poured herself a cup of coffee. "I can barely sit through high school classes, and I've heard they're *short* compared to college classes. No, thanks."

"You can make a decision about college when you find out which schools accept you," Adrian said calmly. "No one is forcing you to go, but it can't hurt to explore your options."

"Whatever." Peyton shrugged and focused on her food.

Once they finished eating, Adrian placed his napkin on the table and glanced at his watch. "Your ride will be waiting at the valet stand in fifteen minutes," he said. "Peyton, you need to change your jeans before you leave."

Peyton crossed her arms and glared at him. "Excuse me?"

"You have to change your jeans before you leave," he repeated. "I assume you put those on to disregard the school dress code. Your point has been made—you dislike following arbitrary rules—and while I understand your stance, it would be selfish to make your sisters late because you insist on fighting a battle you can't win."

Savannah couldn't stop a laugh from escaping, and Peyton's glare turned to her. She refocused on her food and took another bite of pancake, even though it was now cold and soggy, and she was full.

"It's almost time to leave," Adrian said, his eyes on Peyton. "If you would like, Rebecca or I can assist you in choosing a more suitable pair of pants."

"That won't be necessary." Peyton shoved her chair back, the metal shrieking against the marble floor. "I can dress myself."

"Glad to hear it," Adrian said as she slammed her door. No one at the table said a word, and the hint of a smile crossed his face. "I used to be the same way when I was a teenager."

Savannah couldn't imagine Adrian as a teenager, especially a teenager who was similar to Peyton. But his approach worked, because Peyton returned a few minutes later wearing black jeans with no rips or holes in them, her lips pressed into a pissed-off line. The jeans were so low-rise that a slit of skin showed between them and her shirt, but her belly button wasn't showing, so she wasn't breaking the dress code.

"Much better." Adrian nodded at Peyton's choice. "I have somewhere I need to be now, but I've made a reservation for dinner tonight so that you can tell Rebecca and me about your first day at Goodman."

They said their goodbyes, and Rebecca stayed behind, making sure their bags were packed with everything they needed. Instead of Savannah's ancient backpack, she had a new purple Longchamp tote—the same bag that many of the volleyball girls at Fairfield High had had and that she could never afford. Inside of it was her MacBook Pro. Apparently at Goodman, bringing a laptop to school wasn't begging someone to steal or vandalize it.

As Adrian promised, a limo was waiting for them at the valet stand. Savannah had been on many limo rides since arriving in Las Vegas, but it still didn't feel normal. Courtney's bodyguard, Teddy, drove them, and Savannah's and Peyton's bodyguards followed in a car behind. One of them would be on the Goodman campus at all times when they were at school. So awkward.

"It's dumb that Adrian won't let me drive us," Peyton said once they were seated. "What good are the Range Rovers he bought us if we can't take them to school?"

"He probably doesn't want us getting lost," Courtney said.

"And my car's been good for learning *how* to drive," Savannah pointed out. She couldn't wait to get her license when she turned sixteen in December. Along with the summer tutoring sessions, she'd taken an online drivers' ed class. Rebecca had been driving with her for the required fifty adult-supervised hours.

After fifteen minutes, the limo turned at a brick sign with The Goodman School engraved on it in block letters, and Savannah moved closer to the window. A long, scenic road led to sprawling stucco buildings that resembled a college campus. Where were the security guards, the threatening chain gates and the windowless, prisonlike buildings? The buildings here looked bright and airy, with large paned windows and groomed gardens surrounding them.

"Here's the Upper School." Teddy stopped the limo at a pink domed building with a stone fountain in front. "I'll be waiting here to pick you up at the end of the day."

Savannah stepped out of the limo and looked up at the building. Did people at Goodman actually say they were in "upper" school instead of high school? It sounded so strange.

"Where to now?" she asked Courtney.

Her sister glanced at her phone, where she kept notes about these details. "We have to go to the Upper School front desk, where we should find a lady named Betty. She'll give us our locker assignments."

They walked to the entrance, the students nearby watching them and whispering. None of the girls were dressed up—they mostly wore designer jeans, fashionable tops and flats. Savannah's hands shook, and she gripped the strap of her bag, focusing on not tripping in her three-inch Jimmy Choos. She should have worn her Tory Burch flats. Why had she worn such an over-the-top outfit, despite Courtney, Peyton and Evie's advice?

Oh, right—because she'd thought *everyone* at Goodman would dress up. And because she'd stupidly thought it would catch Damien and Nick's attention. Seeing as no one else was as dressed up, she might catch their attention…but not in a positive way.

Her throat constricted, and she wanted to run back to the limo and beg Teddy to drive her back to the Diamond so that she could change. But that wasn't an option. She would have to suck it up.

Betty at the front desk was an older woman with short gray hair—she looked like a grandma who baked cookies for her grandkids after school. She welcomed Savannah and her sisters and handed them their locker combinations.

"Here's the sheet you sign whenever you need to leave school, or if you arrive late," she said, pointing to a clipboard on the desk. "Seniors have senior privileges and can leave whenever they want. Everyone else has to say why they're leaving early."

"With a note from a parent?" Courtney asked.

"You don't need a note," Betty said. "At Goodman, we trust students to leave only when necessary. You're responsible for any missed material, so it's understood that attendance is crucial to earn high marks."

Peyton laughed. "And no one takes advantage of how easy it is to skip?"

Betty smiled. "The students here want to attend their classes so they can excel in their studies."

"It sounds nice." Courtney looked around in wonder at the well-lit, airy, carpeted building.

"What are senior privileges?" Savannah asked.

"As a sophomore, you won't have to worry about that for a while," Betty said, turning to Peyton. "Since you're a senior, you're allowed to leave campus for free periods and lunch, as long as you're back in time for class. There are a lot of restaurants nearby that students enjoy."

Savannah's mouth dropped open, and she closed it so she wouldn't look like a gaping fish. The seniors here went to *restaurants* for lunch? At Fairfield High, a good fraction of students were on subsidized lunches—including her and her sisters. They wouldn't have dreamed of going out to eat, or had the time, as Fairfield's lunch blocks were short and rushed. But with seventy-five minutes set aside for lunch, and credit cards connected to their parents' bank accounts, students at Goodman had no reason *not* to go to restaurants.

"What happens if we don't get back in time?" Peyton asked.

"If it happens more than three times, your senior privileges will be revoked," Betty said. "But that's rare, since students want to keep their privileges."

"You really trust the students here."

"It's the Goodman philosophy that everyone is capable of rational self-discipline," Betty explained. Then she told them to come to her if they had more questions, and they cleared out so that she could talk to the students in the line behind them.

"I guess this is where we part ways," Courtney said.

Savannah's stomach flipped. Goodman might as well have been in a different universe than Fairfield, she was dressed all wrong, and she had a terrible feeling that despite her summer tutoring, she would still be behind in her classes. Girls in a nearby clump were looking her over, smirking and whispering what Savannah imagined were mean comments. She pulled her miniskirt down to cover as much of her legs as possible (which wasn't very much), not wanting to leave her sisters' sides.

But they had no classes together, so she didn't have a choice.

Savannah arrived at first period early and situated herself in a seat in the middle of the U-shaped table configuration, then browsed YouTube on her phone to look busy. After putting her first video online—the one Nick had bought for her of her singing karaoke at Imperial Palace—she'd dreamed it would go viral and she would become an internet sensation. Instead, it had reached around three hundred views and plateaued off. She'd posted a few more videos since then, but despite her best efforts, she still hadn't cracked a thousand views on any of them.

Maybe she just wasn't that great and should stop trying.

"This is European History, right?" a short girl with long, dark hair asked from the door. She wore designer jeans and a fitted green T-shirt that looked like a Michael Stars, and the raised triangle label on her black tote was distinctly Prada.

The bag made Savannah regret her Longchamp. The girls at Goodman seemed to favor higher-end bags by Prada, Chanel and Givenchy, to name a few. After school, she *had* to go shopping for a new bag. She could use the Longchamp when she went to the pool.

"Yeah." Savannah placed her phone on the table and smiled, hoping to look friendly and approachable. "At least, I hope so. It's my first day. I'm Savannah." She moved her bag off the seat next to her so that the girl could sit there.

"I'm Alyssa." Instead of taking the seat next to Savannah, she left one between them.

Savannah's cheeks burned. Why did this girl not want to sit next to her? Was she really *that* overdressed? Or maybe

Alyssa had heard rumors about her and already didn't want to be friends? Savannah knew people talked about her online, but she'd hoped her new status as Adrian Diamond's daughter would make people *want* to be friends with her—not avoid sitting next to her.

"Sorry." Alyssa shrugged. "My two best friends are in this class, and I promised to save them seats."

"No problem." Savannah forced a smile. If she'd had a class with Evie and Evie had asked her to save her a seat, she would have done the same thing. She shouldn't take it personally. But that didn't stop her throat from feeling tight, as if Alyssa had purposefully insulted her.

"Did you go out last night and not have time to take off your makeup this morning?"

Savannah jerked at the question. "Um, no," she said. "Why?"

"You just seem really…done up for eight-thirty in the morning." Alyssa motioned to her own natural makeup, which was opposite from Savannah's purple metallic shadow and gold glitter liner. "I don't mean it in a mean way," she said. "I just guess Goodman is different from whatever school you transferred from."

"It's definitely different." Savannah sighed, not wanting to describe Fairfield High. It would probably make this girl judge her even more.

Then Alyssa pulled out her iPad, and Savannah saw something on the back of it that made her brighten—a sticker of a volleyball.

"You play volleyball?" she asked.

"Yep," Alyssa said. "I'm on the team here. Do you play, too?"

"I was on JV at my old school."

"Ohhh, okay." She nodded condescendingly. "Since Goodman's so small, we only have varsity."

"I was one of the best players on JV, and they subbed me in for varsity sometimes," Savannah said. "Maybe I'll have a chance."

All right, they'd subbed her in only once, when a stomach bug had made its way around school and a lot of the varsity players had gotten sick. And they'd lost that game. But Savannah *was* one of the better players on JV, and she would have been a serious contender for varsity this year at Fairfield.

"Maybe," Alyssa said, although she didn't sound like she believed it. Then other students filed in—including the girls Alyssa was saving seats for, Brooke and Jackie. The three of them gossiped like they hadn't seen each other in years, and Savannah brought out her laptop, pretending she was busy on it.

Being new and knowing no one in her grade really, really sucked.

She didn't fair better in her next class, so when it was time for lunch, she was on her own. Everyone else joined up with their friends, but Savannah hurried into the nearest restroom, waited for the door to shut, and burst into tears. Why did no one want to be friends with her? She ripped the stupid crystal headband that she'd thought was so cute this morning off her head and tossed it into her bag, along with the sparkly, dangly earrings. If only she could be like Superman and change her outfit, too.

She sniffed, grabbed a paper towel and fixed her makeup, trying to remove the glitter without making it look like more of a wreck. Then the toilet in the end stall flushed, and she froze, her hands propped on the sink. How had she missed that someone else was in the bathroom?

She wanted to dive into the nearest stall, but before she could, the girl opened the door and met her eyes. Luckily, this girl didn't look like the gossiping type. Her coarse brown hair was pulled back into a boyish bun. She wore thick-rimmed glasses and baggy cargo pants, and her fraying backpack had Japanese cartoon characters stitched into it.

She must be the school weirdo.

"Are you okay?" the girl asked as she washed her hands.

Savannah stared at her blankly. Of course she wasn't okay. But she wasn't about to confess her problems to this random girl, either.

"I'll take that as a no." She took a deep breath. "You're new here, right?"

"Yeah," she somehow managed. "Savannah."

"I'm Wendy," she said. "I was about to go eat with my friends, if you want to come with?"

Savannah's first day of school, and the only person who had reached out to her was the school weirdo. But she didn't want to be alone at lunch on her first day. And it was kind of Wendy to offer, especially since she knew nothing about her other than that she'd been crying by herself in the bathroom.

"Um, sure." She glanced at the mirror to make sure the mascara was off her cheeks, picked her Longchamp up off the floor and attempted a smile. "Thanks."

Goodman's cafeteria wasn't inside the upper school—they had a separate building just for eating. And they didn't call it the cafeteria, either. They called it the "dining hall," and *everyone* bought lunch. Not one person carried a bag from home.

"Upstairs are the normal daily foods—pizza, pasta, sushi, Chinese, salad bar and the hot meal special of the day," Wendy told Savannah as they entered the dining hall, which looked more like a restaurant than a high school cafeteria. The tables had chairs instead of attached benches, and the walls were covered with giant windows that had views of the swimming pool and the lake. "Downstairs is the deli bar where you can get made-to-order subs and sandwiches, and the grill where you can get hamburgers, hot dogs and fries and stuff."

"What do you normally get?" Savannah asked, still trying to process that they had *sushi* and *made-to-order subs*. That was nothing like the mystery mush at Fairfield High. Why did the seniors need to go to restaurants when they had all these choices at their school? Not that it mattered—she was glad the seniors went to restaurants, since it meant she wouldn't run into Damien.

"I get sushi almost every day," Wendy said. "Make sure to stay away from the pizza—it makes the frozen stuff from the grocery store taste like a delicacy. And Thursday is waffle fries day. They're the best, but you have to get to the grill early or the line will take forever. Anyway, I'm going to grab some sushi—want to come with?"

"I'm actually not a sushi fan," Savannah said. Well, she'd never tried it—the thought of eating raw fish weirded her out. "I'll just get a sandwich."

"The deli's downstairs." Wendy pointed at the steps. "I eat down there with my friends from anime club, and sushi is faster than sandwiches, so I'll save you a seat."

"Thanks," Savannah said. Her sisters were nowhere to be found, and sitting with Wendy would be better than sitting by herself. At least she seemed nonjudgmental and kind. But *anime club?* That was just…not Savannah's thing.

The line for sandwiches was long, and the last person in it was Alyssa from first period, who didn't acknowledge Savannah as she stepped into line behind her. Hopefully the line would move quickly, and Savannah could get away from her as fast as possible.

Then the last person she'd expected to see walked through the doors—Damien. He'd gotten tanner over the summer, probably from spending time outside on his teen tour, and his hair was longer—it almost hungover his dark brown eyes. Her heart pounded. Now she would find out whether or not he was going to ignore her and pretend like the time they'd spent together in July had never happened. She took deep breaths and played with the ends of her hair, praying he would notice her.

He waved when he spotted her, and she waved back, trying to keep herself from smiling like an idiot while her stomach flipped like crazy. Was he going to talk to her? At least he'd waved, so her fear of him ignoring her hadn't come true. This wasn't how she'd envisioned their first meeting since July—with her dressed wrong for school and her makeup smudged from crying—but he'd already seen her, so there was nothing she could do.

Alyssa was looking at Savannah, her eyes shining with a friendliness that hadn't been there that morning. "Did Damien Sanders just wave to you?" she whispered.

"Yeah." Savannah ran a hand through her hair and tried to play it cool, since Damien was getting closer. "We hung out a little bit over the summer."

Alyssa's jaw dropped, and Savannah couldn't help but feel victorious after the way the girl had snubbed her earlier.

"Savannah Diamond," Damien said, stepping into line behind her. "I've been wondering when I would run into you." Then he studied her closer, his expression morphing into concern. "Are you okay? Your eyes look red."

"It's just allergies," she lied, trying to sound upbeat. She'd never had allergies, but no way was she admitting to crying alone in the bathroom. "Anyway, how was the rest of your summer?"

"I did a Hawaii/Alaska teen tour," he said. "We cruised through Alaska, toured the Pacific Coast, and stayed at some resorts in Hawaii. It was pretty cool."

"Is that the tour by Rein?" Alyssa chimed in. "I'm looking into their Europe trip for next summer."

"That's the one."

Savannah nodded as if she knew what they were talking about, even though she'd never traveled beyond California and Vegas. "I saw your pictures on Facebook," she said. "It looked like you had fun." She tried not to sound bitter, but when she thought about the album he'd posted, she was reminded of the two tall, tanned girls in lots of pictures with him. Even though it had made Savannah feel like a stalker, she'd clicked on both girls' profiles. One of them lived in L.A., and the other in Miami, so they couldn't be a threat, but she hated seeing them draped all over him—even if it *might* mean he'd meant it when he'd said he was over Madison.

"It was fun, and everyone was cool, but it got old being around the same forty people all the time," he said. "I was glad to get home."

"Is everyone keeping in touch?" Savannah asked, thinking mainly about L.A. and Miami.

"For the first few days back we chatted on Facebook and stuff, but most of them are from California, New York, D.C. and Florida, so we've mostly split ways," he said. "But enough about me—what have you been up to while I've been gone?"

The real answer: doing mounds of work assigned by tutors to catch up on Goodman academics. But she wasn't telling Damien that.

"Hanging with my sisters at the pool," she said casually. She *had* spent a lot of time at the pool, but she'd usually brought her homework with her. "I've also been getting my YouTube channel started."

"How's that going?"

"It's going okay."

"Cool." Damien smiled, watching her like he really cared, and a thrill went up her spine. "I'll check it out tonight."

Her heart shrank at the realization that he hadn't seen her videos. "Let me know what you think," she said. Just because she'd been tracking (stalking?) him online all summer didn't mean he'd been doing the same to her. He'd been too busy traveling the country—and spending time with L.A. and Miami—to know her YouTube channel existed. Even now, he probably couldn't wait to get out of the lunch line to hang out with his real friends.

Savannah ordered and paid for her sandwich. "I guess I'll see you around," she said to Damien, gathering her plate in preparation to join Wendy and whatever friends of hers would be at that table.

"Hold up," he said. "Where are you sitting?"

Savannah's stomach fluttered at the idea that Damien Sanders cared about where she was eating lunch. But she didn't want to tell him she was sitting with the anime club.

"She was going to join me and some of the other volleyball girls at our table near the pool," Alyssa jumped in. "Tryouts are soon, and we heard Savannah plays, so we're hoping she makes the team."

Savannah glanced questionably at Alyssa, who smiled and tossed her long hair over her shoulder, as if none of this should be strange. Clearly she was being welcoming now only because of Savannah's connection to Damien.

But did it matter? It had broken the ice between them. Sure, things hadn't gone well in first period, but now that Alyssa wanted to be friends, she seemed like a fun girl. And Savannah would have more in common with the volleyball team than with the anime club.

"Do you and Alyssa want to eat with me and my friends upstairs?" Damien asked. "If her friends don't mind, of course."

"That sounds great," Alyssa said quickly. "I'm sure they won't mind."

"Okay." Savannah couldn't believe it. Sure, she was ditching Wendy, but when Savannah glanced around to find the other girl, a tall, lanky guy had joined Wendy at her table, so she wasn't alone. She would understand. After all, Savannah—a sophomore—had been invited to sit at a table with seniors. And not just *any* seniors—Damien Sanders and his friends. Which hopefully wouldn't include Madison, but it was too late to turn back now.

She tightened her grip on her water bottle to keep from shaking. "I thought the seniors went off campus for lunch?"

"We do sometimes," Damien said. "But since today's the first day back, most of us want to stay here and catch up."

He led them upstairs to a group at the center table in the cafeteria, and introduced them to his friends. Savannah recognized two of them from Myst over the summer, but the others were new to her. As they ate, Damien and Alyssa were the only ones interested in talking to her—the rest of them were too busy gossiping about their summers—but that was fine by her.

At least Madison wasn't sitting with them. But Damien kept glancing at the table where she was eating with Oliver and some of her other friends. Savannah's heart dropped at the realization that he still wasn't over Madison. But either Madison was oblivious to Damien, or she was an expert at ignoring him.

At the end of lunch, Savannah followed Alyssa to the trash cans. Alyssa was friendly and continued asking her questions—she was a completely different person from that morning.

Someone else called Savannah's name, and she brightened at the sight of Nick Gordon pushing through the crowd. He glowed as usual, but there were also huge bags under his eyes.

"Hey, Nick," Savannah said, relieved he wasn't ignoring her, either.

"How's your first day going?" he asked.

"It's different from my old school, but it's going well," she lied, since she didn't want to sound like a downer and tell him about how awful everything had been until she'd seen Damien in the sandwich line. "I met Alyssa in first period, and we both play volleyball. Do you two know each other?"

"We've seen each other around, but haven't officially met," he said, holding out his hand. "I'm Nick."

Alyssa nodded, as if she already knew who he was, and shook his hand. "Nice to officially meet you."

Nick smiled and turned back to Savannah. "Did your tutoring this summer pay off?"

"I hope so," she said. "But it's hard to tell on the first day."

"I'm sure you'll be fine," he said. "And I've been checking out your YouTube channel when I have time. Your latest videos are great."

"Thanks." Savannah shrugged. He was probably only saying it to be nice, otherwise wouldn't there be more people who agreed with him? "It's good to know that at least a few people like the videos."

"I bet one will go viral soon, and then you'll be an instant hit."

"That would be a dream come true."

His blue eyes were so focused on hers, and her breath caught at how electric the air felt around them. He opened his mouth to say something else, but then Damien joined them, and Nick took a step back.

"Hey, man," Damien said, as if he and Nick were friends. Which they weren't—especially since Nick used to date Madison.

"Hey." Nick slipped his hands into the pockets of his khaki pants. "Didn't see you around much this summer."

"I was doing some traveling."

"Bet that was fun." Nick held Damien's gaze steadily, and if Savannah didn't know better, she would have thought they were having a macho territory battle over her.

"I need to get to my next class," Savannah said, glad to have an excuse to get Damien and Nick away from each other. "Thanks for inviting us to sit with you," she said to Damien.

"You're welcome to join us whenever you want."

"And if you want a change of scenery, you can sit with me and my friends, too," Nick offered. "We sit out on the upper deck looking over the pool until it gets too cold."

"Thanks," Savannah said, not wanting to promise either of them anything. Were they really fighting over sitting with her? Or was she making this out to mean more than it did? "I'll see you guys around!"

Alyssa linked her arm with Savannah's as they left the dining hall. "I can't believe you know Damien Sanders and Nick Gordon and you didn't mention it!" she said, bouncing as she walked.

"I met them both this summer," Savannah said. "It's a long story."

"What are you doing after school today?"

"Nothing so far." Well, she was supposed to connect with Evie on Skype to tell her about her first day, but Evie wouldn't mind waiting.

"Good," Alyssa said. "You can come with me, Brooke and Jackie to Starbucks and tell us everything that happened this summer with you and two of the hottest guys in school. Judging from the way they just acted, I have a feeling this is going to be good."

chapter 2: *Courtney*

"Thanks for having lunch with me," Courtney said to Brett, taking a bite of her grilled cheese sandwich. The cheese was gooey and amazing—the dining hall at Goodman was a five-star restaurant compared to the cafeteria at Fairfield High. Brett had secured a table for them near the lake, beneath a tree and secluded from the main groups of students, which was just what Courtney needed.

"You looked like you needed a break from those girls in AP English." He hadn't sat with her in class—he'd been avoiding her since she'd told him they couldn't continue whatever was going on between them. Which was for the best, because every time she saw him, or *thought* about him and the incredible times they'd shared during her first week in Vegas, it felt like there was a hole in her heart. But when the group of girls discussing fashion, partying, celebrities and gossip about their "friends" had tried to drag Courtney with them to lunch, she'd looked at Brett for help. Luckily he'd stepped up and rescued her from their clutches.

"They had good intentions, but an hour and fifteen minutes of lunch with them…" Courtney placed her grilled cheese down and contemplated how to word it nicely.

"Would be mentally exhausting?" Brett supplied.

"Exactly." Courtney smiled and tried to ignore the electricity that arced between them. The best way to do that was to keep talking. "It was nice of those girls to reach out, but I didn't feel like I had much in common with them."

"It's only been half a day, and you can already tell that you're different from the girls at Goodman," Brett said, studying her. "And I mean that in the best way possible."

"They just haven't been exposed to much outside their little bubble." Courtney gazed out at the lake—anything to keep her from getting lost in Brett's forest-green eyes. Even if they weren't *together,* they could be friends, right? She just needed to get her heart in tune with her brain. Which would be easier if it would stop racing every time he looked at her. "But I'm going to the first Habitat meeting tomorrow during lunch block. Maybe I'll meet people I have more in common with there."

"You might." Brett nodded and took a bite of his sandwich. "I've never done Habitat, so I wouldn't know."

"I'm excited to find out what it's about," she said. "But I still don't understand why Adrian and your mom didn't want me working at the coffee shop at the Diamond. I thought they would be proud that I wanted to work."

"I understand why you'd think that." Brett scratched his head, as if figuring out where to begin. "But school *is* your job. Getting into a top college like Stanford or one of the Ivies takes more than good grades and a great SAT score. Everyone applying has those, so colleges want to see dedication and leadership in other areas, too. Were you part of any clubs at your old school, did you play sports, or were you involved in the theater?"

"I tutored once a week at the student tutoring center, and I'm going to the first student tutoring meeting after school today." Courtney's cheeks heated, and she broke off a piece of her sandwich. "I had to keep my grades up while working as many hours as I could to help out my family. I didn't have time for anything else."

"I get that." Brett placed his hand over hers, the heat from his skin sending electricity through Courtney's body. Her breathing slowed, her head spinning from his touch.

It took everything in her to pull away, and she sipped her water, as if it could wash away her feelings for him. It was unfair and unkind to lead him on when they couldn't be together.

Pain flashed across his face—she hated knowing that she'd hurt him. But it was gone a second later, and he continued with what he was saying, as if that moment had never happened.

"I know you could have written an essay about your situation that would have blown the admission councils away," he said. "But you're not in that position anymore. Now you're attending one of the most elite private schools in the state, and you'll be competing to get into the top colleges against students who go to similar schools all over the country. Out of the last graduating class from Goodman, twenty percent of the students went to Ivies, fifty percent went to top-tier schools that are almost as competitive, and the rest went to other selective schools. Adrian and my mom want you to be prepared."

"That makes sense," Courtney said, although it was a lot to take in. At least this conversation was keeping her thoughts away from how much she wanted Brett to put his hand on hers again, or how every glance at his lips made her flash back to when he'd kissed her at the grand opening. And how much she wanted him to kiss her again. "But I can't imagine those girls who were gossiping about parties and fashion going to Ivy league schools."

"They're shallow," Brett said. "But they're not stupid. They get good grades, and their parents will either donate to the college they want their kid to get into—like Adrian did for Goodman—or hire 'college admission strategists' to boost their applications and give them a better chance at being accepted to top schools."

The reminder of how Adrian had *bought* her and her sisters into Goodman by funding the new sports center made Courtney sad at the unfairness of it all. "What's a 'college admission strategist'?"

"What it sounds like," Brett said. "Someone who knows what colleges want and will sit down with a student and his or her parents, analyze the student's academic history and strategize how to create the most successful application possible. For a few grand, of course."

"And then that student has a better chance at getting into the school they want over someone who can't afford a strategist." Courtney shook her head. "That's not fair, is it?"

"It's not fair, but it's reality." He shrugged. "I'm not the biggest fan of everyone at Goodman myself, but not everyone here is shallow. You'll find your place."

Courtney wished she could feel as confident about that as he sounded. "I'm starting to understand why you liked your public school better."

"I preferred the *people* at my old school," Brett corrected her. "The teachers at Goodman are fantastic—they love what they do—and the classes are better, because they're smaller and discussion-based. Plus, I want to go to UCLA for their film program. If a college admissions strategist can help me get there, even though you're right that the system isn't fair, I can't turn the opportunity down. Wouldn't you do anything to get into Stanford?"

"I think so," Courtney said, although the realization that she would probably give in to such an unfair system made her stomach sink. "Sometimes it's hard to believe this is all happening. I always wanted to go to Stanford, but deep down I knew it wouldn't be possible."

"What do you mean?" He looked as if he genuinely cared about her response. She loved the way Brett listened because he wanted to hear what she had to say, and not because he was just waiting for his next opportunity to speak. It made him different from most people she knew. "Why didn't you think it would be possible?"

"Because if I left, who would take care of my mom and Savannah?" she said. "I probably would have ended up at the local community college so I could live at home and continue helping out. But now, to be talking about Stanford like it's a real possibility... I can't wrap my head around the opportunities I have now and what it means for my future."

"You would have realized it when Peyton gained access to her trust fund." Brett leaned forward, his eyes staring deep into her soul. "This was always bound to happen to you, Courtney. It just happened sooner than expected."

She was speechless, hardly able to think or breathe. Looking into each other's eyes was so personal, and it made it too easy for her feelings for him to fight their way to the surface when she needed to bury them.

"I don't think I'll ever understand why my mom refused help from Adrian," she finally said, her voice wavering. "She never spoke about him—it was like he did something so horrible that she wanted to pretend he didn't exist. I know she must have been worried out of her mind when I was kidnapped as a baby, and it sounds like she blamed Adrian for that happening, but I was returned home safely. There has to be more to it than that."

Brett's jaw clenched. "Now that the secret's out about Adrian being your father, she'll have to explain."

"Maybe," she said. "Or maybe she's being irrational. She never has been the most mentally stable person. Which isn't her fault, but it's still frustrating."

They ate in silence for a few seconds, and Courtney contemplated what she would say to her mom when she was released from inpatient treatment next month. They'd never been close—she'd always felt like her mom loved her least out of her sisters. It would be a difficult conversation, and she couldn't imagine how it would go. Her throat tightened just from trying.

"When did you say Habitat met again?" Brett asked, zapping her out of her thoughts.

"Thursdays during lunch block." Courtney ran a hand through her hair and tried to relax, glad he'd changed the subject. "Why? Are you thinking of joining?"

"I'll go to the first meeting with you and check it out. If I join, maybe I'll make a short video about the house we build."

"I would love that," she said, meaning it. His face lit up, and she wanted to grab his hand, to move her chair closer to his, to lean into him and rest her head on his shoulder and enjoy the view of the lake…but she had to stop these thoughts. If she wanted to continue being around him—which she not only did but wouldn't have a choice about once their parents were married—she had to make him believe she didn't see him that way. So despite every muscle in her body begging her not to, she leaned away from him and said, "It would be nice to have a friend join with me."

His face fell when she said the word *friend,* and the word tasted sour on her tongue. But then he sat up straighter and moved his chair closer to hers, and she knew he wasn't going to leave it at that. She couldn't back away, or get up in the pretense of having to be somewhere else, or do anything to discourage him.... She needed to know what he had to say. Not knowing would be positively painful.

"We both know that there's more than friendship between us." He rested his fingers on top of her hand, which she'd stupidly left on the armrest closest to him, and her skin heated, her breaths coming faster. "I know you're trying to fight it, but, Courtney...I can tell that you want to be with me as much as I want to be with you. And there's no reason for us *not* to be together. We could even be together in secret. No one has to know."

His eyes blazed, daring her to be honest with him. She yearned to say yes, to be brave and follow her feelings, no matter the consequences.

But she couldn't forget what Rebecca—Brett's mom and her soon-to-be stepmother—had told her after seeing her and Brett kiss in public. Rebecca had taken her to brunch at the Grande Café in the Diamond the day after the grand opening, just the two of them, so that they could talk about it....

"It seems like you and Brett are getting along well." Rebecca had been the one to start the conversation.

"We have a lot in common." Courtney fidgeted. *It wouldn't be long until Rebecca mentioned the kiss—the kiss with Brett that had been incredible, but that she'd given in to despite Adrian's rule that she and her sisters must not get romantically involved with their stepbrother-to-be.*

Rebecca nodded. "My son is a wonderful boy, and I would be proud of him dating someone as responsible as you."

Courtney's heart jumped. Maybe Rebecca wasn't going to forbid her from dating Brett?

"Thank you," she said, hoping the conversation would continue on this positive note. If Rebecca approved of Courtney being with Brett, she could convince Adrian to revoke his rule.

"However," Rebecca said, and Courtney's stomach dropped, her fork pausing midair, "while I know overcoming your feelings for Brett will be hard, Adrian and I have our reasons for not allowing this to continue."

Courtney placed her fork down, her appetite gone. "But you said you would be happy if Brett and I were together?"

"I said I would be proud if he dated someone as responsible as you," Rebecca repeated. "But we're about to become a family." She watched Courtney closely, as if begging her to understand.

But Courtney hadn't defied the rules just to be put back into place. If she wanted Rebecca to understand where she was coming from, she would have to be vocal about her feelings. It would be awkward, because she didn't know Rebecca well, but Brett was worth it.

"I've never felt this way about anyone before." She spoke quietly, looking down at her barely touched brunch. "The connection between us... It's real."

Pity shone in Rebecca's eyes. "I remember as a teen feeling like each relationship I was in would last forever, but unfortunately, it doesn't always work like that." She looked off into the distance, as if remembering something. "High school relationships end for various reasons, even if both people involved are fantastic individuals and have great times together. After those relationships end, it's healthy to put that person in the past and move on with your life. But if you and Brett dated and it didn't work out, you wouldn't be able to put each other in the past, because you would also be step-siblings. It would *strain the family, and it would put both of you through an incredible amount of pain."*

But it wouldn't be like that between Courtney and Brett.... They were different. She couldn't ignore her feelings for him because they might break up in the future.

On the other hand, Rebecca's logic was irrefutable. If they did break up, they would be forced to see each other often. They would be a part of the same family. Every time they were around each other would be incredibly painful. Courtney was already dealing with that now, and they'd only been "together" for a week. What if they were together for months, and then had to go through something similar to what they were going through now? It would be torturous.

The smartest long-term decision was to push aside her feelings for Brett to save herself from that hurt in the future.

So after talking with Rebecca, Courtney had had a similar conversation with Brett, during which she'd explained the reasons they couldn't date. He'd avoided her for weeks.

Now he was practically begging her to give them another chance. But despite wanting to give in—to say yes, she wanted to be together, and see how happy those words made him— she couldn't do it. She would disappoint the family, and the pain she would go through if it didn't work out between them scared her. Her sisters believed she was strong, that she could remain levelheaded in the face of anything, but that was only because she kept herself from making unwise decisions to begin with.

"What do you say?" Brett asked again. "Do you want to see where this leads?"

"We can't." Courtney pulled her hand away and laid it in her lap. Despite the desert heat, her skin felt cold where it had been touching his.

He sat back and scowled. "Is that really how you feel, or do you just not want to disappoint Adrian?"

"Not wanting to disappoint Adrian and your mom is part of it," Courtney said, her voice low. "But you know my main reason."

"How if it doesn't work out, we'll never get the space we need because we'll be in the same family." Brett repeated what she'd told him after that brunch with Rebecca.

"Yes." She nodded, her throat tight from forcing the word out. "We're not just two people who happened to fall for each other. In less than a year our parents will be married. If it doesn't work between us, it could get extremely messy. We would still have to see each other, and it would be painful. Like what we're going through now times a thousand."

"So you *do* still have feelings for me." His eyes gleamed triumphantly, and she couldn't lie to him and deny it. "I knew it. But there's another way to look at this…the way I choose to look at this. What if it *does* work out? Wouldn't it be worth it?"

For a brief moment, Courtney imagined pushing aside logic and acting on her feelings. She loved spending time with Brett, and trusted that whatever was between them was real and deserved a chance. Maybe it would work, and maybe it wouldn't. If it didn't work out, she could worry about it then. That's what Peyton would do. Sometimes Courtney wished she could be daring like her older sister, and let loose and enjoy the present without worrying about the future.

She could wish it all she wanted, but it wouldn't change who she was.

"We can't risk it." Courtney forced herself to sound strong. "Besides, if we dated secretly, I wouldn't be able to enjoy it. I would worry about Adrian and Rebecca finding out, and about how we would never be able to get space from each other if it didn't end well. I can't put myself through that."

"I can't imagine wanting to end things with you," he said, looking at her like he truly believed it. "So you have no reason to be afraid of that happening. I promise."

Her heart melted at how undeniably sweet that was, and she trusted that, in this moment, he meant every word.

"That's how you feel now." She blinked away tears. "But you don't know if you'll still feel that way weeks from now, or months from now. It's not a promise I could hold you to."

"You're right," he agreed, taking her by surprise. It was what she'd wanted him to say, but now that he had, she felt as empty as before—maybe more so. "Not that we can't be together," he clarified, "but that we can't know what will happen between us in the future. If we don't give this a chance, we'll *never* know. And I don't know about you, but I couldn't live with that. The only way to know is to try."

Courtney's heart raced; she wasn't sure how much more of this she could take before she caved. If he didn't stop pushing her, she would have only two options—give in and ruin whatever trust she was building with Adrian and Rebecca and risk putting herself through undeniable heartbreak, or distance herself from Brett and not even be friends with him. And as much as imagining them being only friends hurt, it had to be better than nothing. Right?

"You're making this so hard for me," she said. "But you know my reasons, and I hope you can understand and respect them."

"I understand them," he said, although the determination hadn't left his eyes. "But that doesn't mean I agree with them."

He dropped it after that, although she couldn't help feeling that it was only for now, and he wasn't giving up. Which *should* have frustrated her. She should make him promise to drop it completely, and not push her again.

But she couldn't do that. Because, while she wanted to believe everything she was saying, she still wondered what would happen if she could set aside her inhibitions and see what they could have together.

The student tutoring meeting started fifteen minutes after last period, but Courtney didn't want to be late, so she went straight there. One other person had the same idea: Madison Lockhart. Courtney didn't dislike many people, but she hadn't liked Madison since she'd kissed Damien in front of Savannah and made Savannah cry. Even worse, Madison hadn't seemed sorry about it.

Madison glanced at Courtney and draped her long dark hair in front of her shoulders. "If you're signing up to get tutored, you'll have to wait until Friday," she said, her voice so fakely sweet that it made Courtney want to roll her eyes. "This meeting is for the tutors only."

"Then I'm in the right place." Courtney sat down, leaving an empty seat between her and Madison, and dropped her bag onto the floor next to her feet. "I tutored at my last school, and I want to tutor here, too."

"You can't just decide to be a tutor," Madison said. "You need recommendations from teachers you've completed courses with at Goodman. Since you're new, that means you'll have to wait until at least next semester."

Courtney matched Madison's fake smile at the victory she knew was coming, which was petty, but she deserved it. "Over the summer I emailed the teacher in charge of student tutoring with recommendations from my teachers at Fairfield," she said. "She looked them over and said she would be happy to have me as an English tutor for lower classmen."

"Oh." Madison frowned. "Well, if you only tutor in English, you won't be working with your future stepbrother."

"Brett?" Courtney's heart leaped. "I didn't know you knew each other."

"I tutored him in bio." She tossed her hair back and smiled, as if enjoying a private joke. "We had one-on-one tutoring sessions in the private rooms all last semester, and let's just say we got to know each other pretty well."

"How well?" Courtney's chest tightened at what Madison was hinting.

But Madison couldn't have been involved with Brett. He would have said something, and besides, he would never be interested in Madison. She was the type of Goodman snob he didn't hang out with—the type of girl who was ignorant of everything outside of her one-percenter bubble. What could they have in common?

"I got to know him well enough," Madison said. "When two people spend that much time together, they form *some* sort of connection. We hung out a few times over the summer, too. I'm surprised he hasn't mentioned it."

Courtney's fingers clenched into fists, and she wanted to demand that Madison explain what she meant. But before she had a chance, three more girls walked in, followed by the teacher.

Throughout the introductory session, Courtney kept imagining Madison tutoring Brett in one of the individual rooms, the two of them getting to know each other until they couldn't keep their hands off each other. And Madison had more experience than Courtney—Courtney's only kiss had been with Brett at the grand opening. (There was also the time Oliver had *tried* to kiss her on the way home from the charity event held by his mom that she'd been forced to attend with him, but that didn't count.)

The images of Madison and Brett in a small room to-gether—using the table to study biology in a way quite different from reading about it in a textbook—made Courtney's mind fuzzy and unfocused through the entire meeting. She barely heard a word.

If Madison had said that stuff to distract her, it had worked. But Courtney wasn't having it. She also didn't trust Madison to be honest.

There was only one way to find out the truth: she had to ask Brett herself.

Once back at the Diamond, Courtney knocked on Brett's door. She needed to speak with him in person—this wasn't something she wanted to ask via text message or over the phone. And it wasn't a far trek, since their condos were across the hall.

Brett's eyebrows shot up when he opened the door. Then he smiled, as if he thought her being there meant she'd changed her mind about them being together. Her stomach twisted at how off guard he would be when he found out the reason for her visit.

Courtney took a deep breath to calm her nerves. Approaching Brett was the right thing to do—it was the only thing she *could* do to keep the what-ifs from driving her crazy and messing up her focus in school. She was here to make sure she stayed on track academically.

It would be easier to convince herself of that if her heart hadn't started pounding the moment she saw Brett.

"Hey." He opened the door wider and motioned for her to

come in. She did, keeping her hands gripped around the straps of her backpack so he couldn't see them shaking.

His condo was nearly identical to the one Courtney shared with her sisters—a foyer, living room with a panoramic view of the Strip, dining area, kitchen and a door to the master bedroom, all in a sleek contemporary style. The only difference was that his didn't have the extra hallway that led to the other two bedrooms.

"Are you busy?" Courtney asked.

"Just watching *The Walking Dead*," he replied. Courtney glanced at the ninety-inch television—the same size as the one in her and her sisters' living room—which was paused on an image of a fierce black woman swinging a sword at a bloodied, decaying monster. "I'm on season three."

"I've never seen it," she said. "Well, I've heard of it, but I don't know much about it. I never used to have time for TV." She glanced out the window and reminded herself why she was there: to ask him about whatever had happened between him and Madison.

But he spoke again before she had a chance.

"I have all the seasons on DVD. Now that you have more free time, we could marathon them from the beginning."

Her breath caught. Was he asking her as a date? Or as friends? Either way, marathon watching any show with Brett would be a bad idea. That would mean being alone with him for hours, and she couldn't trust herself to repress her feelings for him for that long.

She glanced at the corpse monster on-screen again and cringed. "It looks…violent. And gruesome."

"It definitely can be." He picked up the remote and powered off the TV. "But it's not bad when you remind yourself that it's makeup and effects. Plus, even though it's set in the zombie apocalypse, the essence of the show is about humanity—how people adapt and react in extreme situations, having to work together to survive with people they would have never encountered in their normal lives."

"It sounds like some of the dystopian books I read," Courtney said.

His eyes glinted with amusement. "So you don't have time for TV, but you do have time for reading?"

"Always." Courtney lowered her hands from the straps of her bag. "I borrowed books from the library at school so often that the librarian knew me by name. I can't fall asleep at night without reading at least a chapter, but I usually read more. And while I know I shouldn't, I sometimes read before doing my homework, to recenter my mind so I can focus."

"That's why I watch an episode of a TV show when I get home from school." Brett's voice rose, sounding so excited that they had this small thing in common. "But I should read more. Whenever I read a book, I usually enjoy it. But there are so many movies and television series I want to watch that I'll never have time for them all in my lifetime, so I go to those first."

"That's how I feel about books." Courtney smiled. "It's why I never read a book more than once—because the time spent rereading one book is one less new story I'll be exposed to in my life."

Suddenly Courtney realized she'd gotten off track from the reason she'd dropped by. "Anyway." She played with her hands, hating the turn this conversation was about to take. "I talked to Madison at the student tutoring meeting."

"Oh." Brett's face fell. "I didn't know you two were friends."

"We're not." Her voice shook at how she'd clearly struck

a nerve. "She happened to be there early, like me, and she… mentioned you."

"What about me?" He ran his hands through his hair, his eyes not meeting hers. She'd wanted to believe Madison was exaggerating, but after seeing Brett's reaction to the mere fact that Madison had *talked* to Courtney, she wasn't so sure.

"She told me she tutored you last year." Feeling shaky again, Courtney walked to the sofa and perched on the arm, dropping her bag on the floor. "In bio."

He joined her on the couch, keeping space between them, and took a few seconds to respond. "She did," he finally said. "I was behind in bio since I'd transferred into Goodman from public school, so I went to the tutoring center for help. Madison was the tutor assigned to me."

"Okay." Courtney forced herself to sound distant and detached—there was no other way for her to continue without risking losing control of her emotions. "She hinted that more went on between you than tutoring. That you were… involved. Over the summer."

Brett looked down, and Courtney's heart dropped. "It only happened once."

She reeled back, the thought of Brett and Madison together making her blood boil. How could she have not known about this until now?

"But it was before I met you," he said, his eyes blazing with intensity. "The night it happened, Madison and I both had too much to drink, and we kissed. It didn't go further than that, but she wanted it to. Afterward I told her it would never happen again. She refused to listen, but then I met you, and she finally got the message that nothing was ever going to happen with me and her." He scooted closer, and as much as Courtney knew she should put distance between them, his eyes pinned her in place. "Because after I met you, I knew you were the one for me. I've known it every day since. You're smart, caring, selfless, kind, understanding, and I can talk with you for hours. You're beautiful inside *and* out. No one else has ever come close to comparing to you, and to be honest, I'm not sure anyone ever will."

His words sent her head spinning and her heart racing—they were everything Courtney wanted to hear. She couldn't imagine anyone ever comparing to him, either.

But if they were meant to be together, why would fate have made it so they were about to be step-siblings? If she gave in to Brett and was with him in secret, it would eventually come out. Then she'd be a disappointment to Adrian and Rebecca, just like, for reasons she'd never known, she'd always been a disappointment to her mother. The only person who appreciated her for her, who had no expectations for her to be perfect, was Grandma. She touched the key necklace Grandma had given her for her birthday last year, hoping it would give her strength.

No matter what she did, she and those she cared for would end up hurt. So she fought the war waging inside her and focused on the one thing Brett had said that she found truly shocking.

"Madison Lockhart wanted to sleep with you, and you turned her down?"

Brett's eyes dimmed. "I just poured my heart out to you, and *that's* how you reply?"

"I'm sorry." Courtney bit her lip, hating how disappointed he sounded. "I do care about you, Brett. But we've already been through this—we can't be more than friends. Although I *am* glad to hear that you turned Madison down. I don't think most guys would have done that."

He watched her closely, but something in her eyes must have warned him not to push her any further. "I guess I'll take that as a compliment," he said. "But I don't think Madison wanted to *sleep* with me. She's a virgin. I think she wanted a relationship, but she wouldn't even say hi to me in front of her stuck-up friends, so I told her I wasn't interested. We haven't talked in weeks, and I still don't know why she fixated on me in the first place. Maybe because I don't worship her like most guys at school do."

"Madison's a virgin?" Courtney didn't like to gossip, but talking about Madison was a distraction from her own emotions. "No way."

"Yeah." Brett shrugged. "Guys are always joking about what they would give to be her first. I don't know what Madison hinted to you, but we only kissed once. If I'd already met you, it never would have happened."

Courtney's heart flipped at his confession, and every muscle in her body begged her to crush her lips against his, to feel his arms around her and to tell him to never let go. But then she would be a goner. And her ultimate decision would still be the same, so she would only be hurting both of them.

She stood from the sofa and grabbed her bag. "Thanks for being honest with me," she said, surprising herself by how levelheaded she sounded, when inside her emotions were tearing her to pieces. "You didn't have to tell me anything, since we're not dating, but I appreciate it. And I'm sorry we can't see where anything goes between us. I wouldn't blame you if you started avoiding me again. It might make all this easier...."

"I'm definitely frustrated." Brett stood and stepped closer so that he was right in front of her. He lifted his arm slowly and pushed her hair behind her ear, his finger brushing against her skin, leaving heat in its wake. "But that doesn't mean I don't still care about you. I meant everything I said to you. I know this is complicated, but I also know you care about me more than you're saying. Be with me, Courtney. We'll keep it secret for as long as we can, and then we'll deal with any consequences together. I promise."

Her heart pounded so hard she swore he could hear it. And he must have sensed that she wasn't going to move away, because he stepped closer, his nose grazing hers. Every molecule in her body urged her to give in; this felt so *right*. But then images passed through her mind—the disappointment that would surely be in Rebecca's, Adrian's, Peyton's and Savannah's eyes when they found out she'd been lying to them—and with a will Courtney didn't know she had, she pulled back.

"I can't." She shook her head, her cheeks hot, and she stumbled to the door. "I wish this wasn't so complicated, but it's about more than what you and I want. It's about my family, and the family that we're all about to become. If we were together in secret, I would have to lie to them. And as much as I care about you, I couldn't live with the guilt of doing that."

His hand dropped to his side, his eyes pained, as if she'd taken a knife to his heart. She turned away and hurried out into the hall, slamming the door shut behind her. Everything she'd said was true, but as she fumbled in her bag for her key, she wondered if she was making a huge mistake. Brett cared about her and wanted to be with her, and she cared about him, too.

But there were so many ways it could go wrong, and that positively terrified her.

chapter 3: *Peyton*

As much as she hated to admit it—and she still hadn't to Adrian and Rebecca—Goodman wasn't as awful as Peyton had anticipated. Back at Fairfield High, each school day had been excruciating, having to sit still all day and listen to teachers drone on and on from the textbooks, talking down to the students when they asked questions. But at Goodman, instead of listening to lectures all day, they had discussions. The teachers treated the students like equals, most of them even going by their first names.

Her favorite teacher was her English teacher, Hunter Sterling. He was in his mid-twenties, and with his shaggy brown hair and dark eyes, he looked startlingly similar to Damon from *The Vampire Diaries*. His Australian accent only added to his hotness. To impress him, Peyton even tried reading the books for class instead of looking them up on SparkNotes.

She still wasn't over Jackson, but her deliciously sexy bodyguard—who was also in his mid-twenties—had made it clear since the night they'd kissed in the elevator during the grand opening of the Diamond that they had to keep a professional distance. Peyton had tried to fight him on it—she knew she hadn't imagined the connection between them—but he refused to budge. And as her bodyguard, he was around her nearly all the time, which made it impossible to *not* think about him. A distraction like Hunter was just what she needed—for her own sanity, and to maybe respark Jackson's interest.

Which was why on a Saturday in late September, when she was walking through the Diamond after spending all day at the main pool, luck was on her side when she spotted Hunter sitting by himself at the bar. She reapplied her lip gloss and pulled down her sheer cover-up so that it showed off her cleavage. A glance behind her verified what she already knew—Jackson was on her tail. Perfect. This *had* to break his wall, or at least make a crack in it.

"Hi, Hunter," Peyton said, sliding into the seat next to her teacher. Her skirt rose up her thighs, and she crossed her legs toward him, not bothering to pull it down.

"Peyton," he said, clearing his throat. "I didn't expect to run into one of my students here."

"I live here," she said, figuring he already knew that. Most everyone at Goodman had known who she was from day one, since Adrian Diamond was famous around this city. "I was just coming inside from doing some reading at the pool." Strangely enough, it was the truth. If she *had* to do her reading, she might as well be outside instead of cooped up in her room. And sure, she'd only read for fifteen minutes before she'd gotten bored, but Hunter didn't have to know that.

"For class or for fun?" he asked.

"For class." Peyton never read for *fun* in her spare time—that was all Courtney.

"And how are you liking *One Hundred Years of Solitude?*"

"It's okay," she said. "There are parts that confuse me, but I'm doing my best." Not having much else to say about the book, and hoping Hunter wouldn't want to have some long, intellectual conversation about it, she was glad when Ramon, the bartender, came over to see if she wanted a drink.

"I'll have a strawberry daiquiri," Peyton said, wanting something refreshing after sitting out in the sun all day. Ramon knew she was underage and would give her a virgin daiquiri, but she was curious to see Hunter's reaction. Was he cool, or would he call her out?

Hunter raised an eyebrow but said nothing as Ramon placed the drink in front of her.

"What brings you to the Diamond?" Peyton asked, sipping her drink.

"It's slightly embarrassing, but I'll tell you if you promise not to judge me," he said in that ridiculously sexy accent of his.

"That's only fair." She smiled, trying not to bounce her legs in anticipation.

"I'm meeting someone from Match.com."

"No way." She laughed, but composed herself, since she'd promised not to judge him. "Why does someone like you have to use a dating website?"

"Someone like me?"

She gave him a once-over—tall, built, mysterious and a gorgeous Australian accent. "I would have thought you had a girlfriend, or at least would have no problem meeting girls at clubs and bars," she said. "They probably can't stay away from you."

"It's tough to meet people when you're new to a country, know nobody and most of your colleagues are twenty years older than you," Hunter said, taking a swig of his drink. "Plus, my best mate from home met his fiancée on Match, so he convinced me to give it a go."

"And where's your date now?"

"We're not supposed to meet for another twenty minutes." He glanced at his watch. "But it's my first time here, and these hotels in Vegas are massive—I didn't want to get lost. I've also never met someone from one of these sites before. I figured that grabbing a drink first might ease the nerves."

"Cheers to that." Peyton raised her glass, and he clinked it with hers. She smiled over the rim, her stomach flipping when he smiled back at her. "I hope you don't mind if I stay here while I finish my drink?" she asked. "I'll leave before your date gets here, of course."

"She's texting me when she gets to the entrance of the hotel, so you're free to save her seat until she arrives."

They chatted for the next fifteen minutes, and Peyton learned about life in Australia and how it was different from America. It sounded like the Australians were much more liberal and open-minded than Americans. Peyton thought she would like it there, and she told him so.

Then she spotted Madison Lockhart sitting across the bar with her short-haired blonde friend, Larissa. Peyton hadn't liked Madison since she'd broken Savannah's heart over the summer by kissing Damien—the guy Savannah had a crush on—in front of her, just to hurt her. It was cruel, and Peyton and her sisters had kept their distance from Madison ever since.

Madison had her phone out, the camera pointed at Peyton. Larissa glanced at Peyton, laughed at whatever was on the screen, and whispered something to Madison. Then Madison's eyes met Peyton's, and she lowered her phone.

Everyone at Goodman knew who Hunter was—the girls talked about him, because he was the only hot teacher in the upper school—but Madison wouldn't take pictures of him with Peyton and sell them out, would she?

Of course she would. Madison had already proven herself to be a bitch who hated Peyton and her sisters. If this was her latest stunt, there was no way in hell Peyton would let her get away with it.

"You could do a semester in Australia while you're attending university." Hunter's voice zapped Peyton's focus away from Madison and Larissa, reminding her she was mid-conversation with him. "Studying abroad is an excellent way to immerse yourself in another culture."

"I'll look into it," she said vaguely, since she didn't feel like getting into the I'm-not-going-to-college conversation. "Anyway, I see some people I know. I should head over and say hi to them."

She planned on saying a lot more to them than that, but Hunter didn't need to know the details.

"My date's almost here, anyway," Hunter said with what Peyton thought was disappointment. "Thanks for keeping me company while I waited."

"I enjoyed talking with you." She stood and straightened her skirt. "Good luck with your internet date. I hope she isn't too weird."

"Thanks." He chuckled. "I hope so, too. I'll see you on Monday."

Peyton hurried away, feeling bad about leaving so abruptly—but she had to reach Madison and Larissa before they paid their checks.

She held Madison's gaze as she approached, as if daring her to back down. The girl didn't flinch, not even when Peyton was close enough to notice that Madison's eyes were a similar vibrant shade of blue as hers and her sisters'. She must wear colored contacts.

"What do *you* want?" Larissa snickered, ending the stare-down. "You looked pretty busy throwing yourself all over Mr. Sterling. I mean *Hunter.*" She held her hands under her chin and batted her eyes dramatically. "He didn't reject you... did he?"

"Of course he didn't reject me." Peyton glared at Larissa. "But when I spotted the two of you doing something that looked suspiciously like taking pictures of us on Madison's phone, I had to make sure that wasn't what was going on. Because if it was, and those pictures got out, he could get fired." She turned to Madison, who was holding her phone on her lap. "So tell me—were you taking pictures of us, or am I just being paranoid?"

"Calm down," Madison said evenly. "No one's going to get fired."

"That wasn't an answer." Peyton reached forward and grabbed the phone out of Madison's hands.

"Hey!" Madison's mouth dropped, and she swiped for the phone, but Peyton held it out of her reach. "Give that back."

"Not until I make sure there aren't any pictures on here of me and Hunter." She clicked to go into the phone, and huffed when it was locked. "What's your password?"

"Seriously?" Madison said. "You expect me to give you my password? No way. Give it back."

She made a move for it again and missed, but not before Larissa got it in her grip. Larissa and Peyton held it tightly, glaring at each other like bulls in a ring, neither of them letting go. The hotel guests nearby were staring, but Peyton didn't care. She was *not* allowing those pictures to stay on that phone.

"Is there a problem here?" a stern voice asked from behind—Jackson. He must have looked intimidating, because Larissa let go of the phone, leaving it in Peyton's grasp. She turned to face him. He was business as usual, although she swore she saw a flicker of amusement in his hazel eyes. "Well?" he said, looking between Peyton, Larissa and Madison like they were all little kids.

Peyton raised her chin, refusing to be belittled. "I have reason to believe there are pictures of me on Madison's phone that were taken against my will and need to be deleted," she said, mustering as much snobby-hotel-heiress tone as she could manage without being over-the-top. "I was about to check, but Madison refused to give me her password."

Jackson took the phone from Peyton and handed it to Madison. "Enter your password, and then give the phone back to Miss Diamond. If she's mistaken and there are no pictures of her that were taken without her permission, then there's no harm done. If there *are* pictures, there will be serious legal repercussions initiated by Mr. Diamond if you don't allow them to be deleted. And if you refuse to cooperate by not entering your password, the phone will be confiscated under the assumption that you have something to hide. Do you understand?"

"And who exactly are you?" Larissa crossed her arms, although her nasally voice didn't sound as confident as it had earlier.

"I'm Miss Diamond's bodyguard." Jackson moved his suit jacket to the side, giving a glimpse of his gun. Larissa pressed her lips together and shrank back in her seat. "And I suggest that you cooperate. No need to make more trouble for yourselves than necessary."

Madison grudgingly entered her password and handed the phone to Peyton, who gladly took it from her. Peyton clicked into Madison's photo album, and sure enough, there were two pictures of her at the bar with Hunter, the two of them having drinks and flirting.

"And you told me to 'calm down'—as if I'd imagined you taking the pictures?" Peyton sneered and hit the trash can button beneath each one. "Good thing I'm not naive."

"I told you to calm down because I wasn't going to post them anywhere public," Madison said. "You and I might not be friends, but I don't want to get Hunter fired."

"So why take the pictures?" Peyton handed the phone back to Madison, feeling lighter now that the pictures were gone.

"Because you were drinking and flirting with our hot Aussie English teacher," Larissa chimed in. "Why *not* take pictures?"

Madison looked like she was going to add something, but she didn't have a chance.

"None of this matters, because the pictures are deleted," Jackson said. "Now, Peyton, I believe you need to get up to your condo to get changed for dinner. You're running late as it is."

"Right," Peyton said, although she knew as well as Jackson did that there were no dinner reservations that night. She stomped away from Madison and Larissa, not bothering to say bye, the sounds of their whispers and laughter coming from behind her. She would *not* give them the satisfaction of turning around and glaring at them.

As she made her way to the penthouse elevators, she reminded herself that despite what Jackson had done for her back there, nothing had changed between them. He wasn't going to open up to her again like he had for those few days over the summer. By intervening and making sure the photos were deleted, he was doing his job. Carl and Teddy would have done the same for Savannah and Courtney. She shouldn't get her hopes up.

She pressed the button for the elevator, and as always, Jackson appeared beside her. This elevator ride would surely be spent the same way as the rest of them since the kiss—either silent, with vague chitchat or with one-word responses from him when she attempted to have a real conversation. Not like she'd made any recent attempts. His barriers were impossible to break through, and eventually, she'd stopped trying. Being rejected over and over again was too painful.

The elevator was empty except for the two of them. She slid her key card into the slot, and pressed the button for the top floor.

"I could have handled those girls myself," she said, bracing herself for what would surely be a one-word, emotionless response.

"Not without causing a scene that might have led to people taking *more* unwanted pictures of you," he said, his jaw tense. "You need to be more careful."

She crossed her arms and watched the floor numbers on the display climb. That was worse than a one-word response—clearly he thought she was an impulsive kid. It was opposite from the way Hunter had treated her at the bar—as if she were an adult worthy of real conversation.

"Who was that guy you were talking to?" Jackson's voice broke through the silence. "The one your classmates took photos of you with?"

Her breath hitched at the realization that Jackson had asked her a *personal question*. And that seeing her with Hunter might have made him jealous. Could he still care about her?

"That was Hunter Sterling, from Australia." She tilted her

head toward Jackson, allowing her long hair to drape over her shoulder, and smiled. "Why are you asking?"

"Because he's too old for you," Jackson said, concern breaking through his normally impassive expression.

"He's only a little older than you," Peyton said playfully. "I would guess twenty-five or twenty-six. So he's not too old for me. We actually had a rather fascinating conversation."

"You want me to believe you walked up to this guy randomly and struck up a conversation?" Jackson asked. "I've been guarding you for months now, so I know that's not your typical behavior."

"And what's my 'typical behavior'?"

"You let guys come to you," he said, his eyes so intense that she forgot to breathe. "Not the other way around."

"Fine, you're right," she admitted. The truth was more interesting, anyway. "He's my English teacher. I saw him at the bar, and it would have been rude of me to not say hi."

"That guy was your *teacher?*" Jackson jerked his head to look at her straight on, his arm muscles flexing.

"Relax." Peyton kept her tone light. Jackson was *definitely* jealous—maybe all wasn't lost between them. "Like I said, it would have been rude of me not to say hi. I had a question about something we're reading for class, and he helped me out while he waited for his date to arrive. It's no big deal."

Jackson focused on the crack in the elevator doors, and Peyton chipped at her black nail polish, worried that the connection between them was gone again. "I hope so," he finally said, stepping aside so that she could leave the elevator first.

She walked into the hall, and he followed far behind, as if he'd never let his guard down to begin with. But that conversation was enough to give her hope. He still cared about her. They had a chance…. She just had to play her cards right.

And she was getting a distinct vibe not to push him anymore. At least, not right now.

Her phone buzzed with a text, and she took it from her bag, glad for a distraction. It was from someone she hadn't spoken to in a while: Oliver Prescott. She'd thought she was interested in him during her first few days in Vegas, but once she'd realized what a jerk he was—he'd stupidly bet he could sleep with her *and* her sisters before the end of summer—she'd moved on. She'd been the only one to sleep with him, and while she hated that she'd been played, better her than Courtney or Savannah. She was the only one of them strong enough to handle it, mainly because she was the only one who wasn't a virgin. To have your virginity taken by someone who was using you... Peyton shuddered at how awful that would feel. Someone would have to do something terrible to deserve that. Even the guy she'd lost her virginity to—her ex-boyfriend, Vince—had thought he loved her at the time.

She opened up the message from Oliver and read it.

Have u thought about what u want me to do for that bet, or are u gonna keep stalling?

Peyton rolled her eyes and threw her phone back into her bag. He didn't have to clarify what bet he was referring to. Over the summer, Oliver's parents had set him up on a date with Courtney. They thought she would be a "good influence" on him. At that point, Peyton and Oliver had already hooked up, and she'd been pissed that he'd agreed to go on the date with Courtney instead of bringing her. She'd told him Courtney would never be interested in him, but he'd claimed otherwise, going as far as turning it into a bet. Knowing that Oliver wasn't Courtney's type, and that Courtney would *never* fall for his games, Peyton had agreed. She'd won, and the terms of their bet stated that because Oliver had lost, he had to do any one thing Peyton asked.

Luckily they hadn't set a time limit, because she still hadn't come up with the perfect task.

Once she was inside her condo, she took out her phone and replied to the text.

Not yet. But once I do, don't worry—I'll let you know.

chapter 4: *Madison*

"Now that we're reaching the end of September—along with the end of our blood type unit—it's time for you to discover your own blood types," Madison's advanced genetics teacher, Mrs. Amy, said from the front of the classroom.

"Lab partners?" Madison's best friend, Oliver Prescott, asked from his seat next to her. He didn't normally take advanced classes, because he liked doing the least amount of work for school as possible, but Madison had convinced him that advanced genetics would be easier than chemistry or physics. Madison, on the other hand, was doubling up on her junior year sciences by taking both advanced genetics and AP chemistry.

"Of course," Madison said as Mrs. Amy passed out the supplies. She did most of the work when she did labs with Oliver, but she didn't mind. Science labs were fun, and this one would be easy. All they had to do was prick each other's fingers, put a few drops of blood on the card provided with the kit and analyze their results.

As they prepped for the experiment, they talked about their plans for the night. Their group was going to dinner at the Terrace restaurant at the Gates Hotel, and from there Oliver had reserved a center cabana at Luxe, the main club at the Gates, where Calvin Harris would be DJing. Cabanas at Luxe were one of the perks of Oliver's dad owning the Gates, although Madison had been best friends with him before his dad had built the famous Vegas hotel a few years ago. They'd become close in second grade, when they'd been assigned seats next to each other, and she'd helped him learn his multiplication tables. And here she was today, still helping him in science and math.

"Ladies first?" Oliver held up the lancet he would use to prick her finger, his eyes gleaming like he couldn't wait.

Madison held her hand out to him, turned her head and covered her eyes. "Warn me before you do it."

"You want to be a doctor and you're afraid of blood?"

"I don't mind other people's blood," she said. "But I hate when it's my own."

"I'm going to count to three," he said, holding her index finger in place. "One, two…" Then he pricked her finger, and Madison jumped, taking an audible breath inward.

"Way to not say three." She glared at him. He smirked, apparently amused, and she couldn't help but smile back.

"You survived." He held out his finger. "Now do me."

She grabbed the lancet and pricked him without counting off. "Payback," she said gleefully.

Oliver shook out his hand and cursed. "That hurt," he said, quietly enough to not draw attention to himself.

"Now for the experiment." Madison squeezed her finger to push out the blood, ready for the fun part of this lab. A few years ago she'd been watching a television show with her parents about a group of people lost on a deserted island, and one of the characters had needed a blood transfusion, but he hadn't known his blood type. Her dad had said the character needed a universal donor with O-negative blood, like himself, to make sure he didn't reject the transfusion. At the time, Madison hadn't thought to ask about her own blood type, but the current unit in class had made her curious.

She mixed her blood into the designated spots on the card and waited a minute for the results. Once it was ready, she picked it up and studied it.

"This can't be right," she said, mixing the blood some more. But the results didn't change.

"What do you mean?" Oliver glanced at her card. "It looks like you're AB positive. That's one of the rarest ones, right?"

"Mrs. Amy?" Madison raised her hand. "I need another card. There's something wrong with mine."

"Are you sure?" Mrs. Amy walked over from where she was helping another student, her eyebrows knitting in confusion. She picked up Madison's card and examined it. "This looks fine to me."

"It's not." Madison pushed back her shoulders and looked at her straight on. "May I please have another card? Just to double-check my results."

Mrs. Amy bit her lip like she was about to say no, but she must have seen the determination in Madison's eyes, because instead she said, "There are a few extras on my desk."

"Thank you." Madison rushed to the desk, picked up another card, and brought it back to the lab table. She squeezed the tiny puncture on her index finger, glad when fresh blood popped up.

"Are you sure there was something wrong with yours?"

Oliver sat on the table, watching as she redid the experiment. "I've never seen you mess up on a lab before."

"I didn't do anything wrong," Madison explained, mixing up the blood on the new card. "My first card was just faulty." She set it down and waited a minute for her *real* result.

But it was the same as before—AB positive.

She set her hands down on the table and glared at the card. They'd been studying blood types for a week, and she fully understood the unit. These results were impossible. She must be doing something wrong.

Mrs. Amy walked over to Madison's lab table. "Is everything okay?"

"I don't think I'm doing the lab correctly." Madison's cheeks flushed, and she could barely bring herself to meet her teacher's eyes.

"Let me take a look." Mrs. Amy picked up both blood type cards and examined them. Madison's heart pounded while she waited for her opinion, and she drummed her fingers on the table. "Nothing's wrong with your results," she said. "You did the lab perfectly, as always."

Madison's lungs squeezed so tightly that she could barely get any air. Normally, she expected her teachers to praise her in science class. But those results couldn't be accurate.

Everyone in the class was staring at her. Not wanting to cause a scene, she swallowed and forced herself to take a few steady breaths. "Thanks," she somehow managed to reply. Luckily, another student raised a hand and asked Mrs. Amy a question, which moved the attention away from Madison.

"Is everything okay?" Oliver asked once Mrs. Amy had walked away.

"I'm not sure." Madison's hand trembled as she picked up

the card and stared at it blankly. "But I think I'm going to have to cancel on our plans tonight."

Madison's parents were working at the hospital and wouldn't be back until later that night, so she watched movies by herself as she waited. She had what she called the Trifecta of Movies to Watch When in a Bad Mood—*Pride and Prejudice, Titanic* and *Moulin Rouge*. Whenever she watched those three movies, she forgot about her life and focused on the lives of the characters, drawn into their worlds and problems.

Her friends had texted to ask why she wasn't coming out, but they'd stopped bothering her once she told them she wasn't feeling well. Which was the truth, because her head had been pounding ever since she'd done the genetics lab. And when she'd gotten back home to the condo in the Diamond Residences—although sometimes it still felt strange to think of the three-bedroom penthouse as home, since they'd moved there a few months ago—she'd done something she'd resisted for months and ordered Dominos pizza. Sure, the condo had a room-service menu full of food from the five-star restaurants in the Diamond, but Madison loved Dominos.

After devouring the entire large by herself, she'd crawled into a baggy sweatshirt so that she wouldn't have to be disgusted by her bloated stomach rolling over her jeans. She would have to go on a fruit-and-veggie cleanse for the next two days to remove all that grease and fat from her body.

She'd finished watching *Pride and Prejudice* and was halfway through *Titanic* when her parents walked through the door, still dressed in their scrubs. They worked at the same hospital—her dad as the head of neurology and her mom as an anesthesiologist—and got similar schedules when they could. They were chatting as they walked inside but quieted when they saw Madison slouched on the couch with a movie on and an empty pizza box on the coffee table. She paused the movie, the food swirling inside her stomach as she thought how to begin the conversation she had to have with them. She felt so nauseated that she worried she might throw up—which, after how much she'd eaten, wouldn't be a bad thing.

"Madison," her mom said, placing her purse on the kitchen counter. "What are you doing home on a Friday night? Don't you have plans with your friends?"

"I canceled." Madison kept her voice steady. "I wasn't in the mood to go out."

"Are you sick?" Her dad's forehead creased in concern, which was understandable—Madison hadn't voluntarily stayed home on a weekend night since middle school.

"No," she said. "But I need to talk with both of you."

"Oh." Her mom pulled her long, dark braid over her shoulder and shared a worried look with her dad. "Okay."

They both seemed confused as they sat down in the living room, her mom on the armchair and her dad on the other end of the couch. Madison's head pounded harder as she looked at them, and she massaged the back of her neck in a failed attempt to relieve the tension.

"We did blood typing in genetics today." She took the card out of her pocket—once it had dried, she'd laminated it to take home—and tossed it onto the coffee table. "This was my result."

Panic flashed in both of their eyes, and neither of them looked at her as her mom picked up the card.

"AB positive." Her mom's voice shook, and she tugged on the end of her braid.

"But those results are impossible." Despite the tightening in her throat, Madison tried to remain calm. She'd learned early on that whenever someone raised their voice, they weren't perceived as rational and were less likely to get the results or answers they desired. Right now she needed answers. "I remember watching TV a few years ago and Dad mentioning he was the universal donor, O negative. But it's *impossible* for a child to have AB when one parent is O. The only scientifically possible blood types I could have are O, A or B, depending on Mom's, of course. I did the test twice, because I figured I got a faulty card the first time, but it was the same both times. AB positive."

She watched her parents closely, waiting for an explanation. But her dad twiddled his thumbs and refused to meet her eyes, and her mom twirled her braid, her face pale. Madison's stomach flipped, and she had to swallow down the pizza that was slowly rising up her throat.

Her dad finally looked up at her, his kind brown eyes shining with guilt. "I wish you hadn't found out this way."

"Found out *what?*" Her voice cracked. She couldn't say what she was thinking out loud—she had to hear it from her parents.

"Madison," her dad said slowly, curling his hands into fists. "You know that, no matter what, I am your father, and I love you very much and nothing will ever change that, right?"

"Right," she said, although suddenly it became hard to breathe, and her head spun, the world feeling like it was crumbling around her.

"But as you discovered today in genetics class, I'm not your biological father." He let out a long breath, his eyes pained as he waited for her reaction.

Madison blinked, a million questions running through her mind. It had been the answer she'd feared since doing the lab, but no imagining prepared her for hearing it said out loud.

She closed her eyes and laced her fingers through her hair.

"Am I adopted?" she finally asked. Although, looking at her mom, she didn't see how that was possible. She looked so much like her mom, with her blue eyes, full dark hair and smooth tanned skin. And she didn't look unlike her dad, either, with his dark hair and dark eyes. Sure, his skin had more of an olive undertone, his nose was larger and the possibility of inheriting blue eyes when brown eyes were dominant was slim, but she'd always assumed that for reasons of chance, she looked more like her mom than her dad. Plus, she'd seen baby pictures of her parents holding her in the hospital. How could she be adopted when they were there when she was born?

"You're not adopted," her mom said. "I'm your biological mother. But I hope you understand that this changes nothing. Your dad loves you just as much as I do."

"What do you mean, 'this changes nothing'?" Fire exploded through Madison's veins, and she slammed her fists down on the couch. "How could this not change anything? You and Dad have been married for over twenty years! But I'm not his biological daughter, which means you *cheated on him* and got pregnant. Then for some reason he took you back and you both decided to keep this all from me, raise me as if none of that ever happened, and think I would be okay with that." She pulled her legs up to her chest and wrapped her arms around them, burying her face in her knees and rocking back and forth. "This can't be happening."

"I know it sounds bad." Her mom reached for her hand, but Madison glared at her and pulled her arm away. Her mom flinched and brought her hand back to her lap. "But it's much more complicated than that."

"You *lied* to me for my entire life." She took a few shallow breaths, unable to get enough air, and tears rolled down her cheeks faster than she could wipe them away. She gave up trying and let them fall. Her dad handed her a tissue, and she blew her nose—it was a good thing no one but her parents could see her, because she must have looked a complete wreck. She focused on breathing steadily, and finally her lungs relaxed, and she was able to speak again. "No matter how 'complicated' it was, you chose to lie to me. Were you ever going to tell me the truth?"

Her parents looked uncertainly at one another. Finally her mom turned to Madison, her eyes set in determination. "You're right, and I'm sorry. You deserve the truth."

Madison used a clean tissue to dab away more tears and nodded for her to continue, bracing herself for more shock. No matter how hard it would be, she needed to hear this.

"About seventeen years ago, your dad and I were both stressed from our medical residences," her mom started, and Madison sat back to listen to the story, cradling the box of tissues to her side. "It was taking a toll on our marriage, so we separated for a few months to clear our heads and focus on our work. Your biological father and I had been friends since middle school, and during that time we…reconnected. That was when I got pregnant with you. But he already had a family, and soon after I found out I was pregnant, he found out he had another child on the way from his wife. I knew he wouldn't want to mess that up. As you also know, your grandfather—my father—is traditional with his religious beliefs. I worried he wouldn't fully accept a grandchild, especially a female grandchild, into the family out of wedlock. I feared he would never forgive me for having a child with a man who wasn't my husband—that he would never look at me with respect again. I didn't know what to do.

"The first person I went to was your dad. He helped me get through it, we resolved our marriage, and moved back in together. When I told your biological father I was pregnant with you, and that your dad and I wanted to raise you as our own, he didn't object, as long as he was still able to be a part of your life. His wife never knew his true relation to you. We made him your godfather, and he acted like one for the first year. He was involved as much as he could be, and you and your half sisters were around each other as much as possible, to ensure you would be close. But then something devastating happened to his family that tore them apart. He felt like it was his fault, so he made us swear to stay quiet about him. He had his reasons, and while it wasn't easy for anyone involved, we had your best interests at heart."

"My biological father." Madison shook her head, barely able to process everything her mom had told her. But there was one main question she needed answered. "Who is he?"

Her mom set her lips in a line. "You have a dad who loves you and has been there for you throughout everything," she said. "Your biological father stepped out of your life. He had his reasons, and while I'll never understand how he can live with his decision, your dad and I promised him that we wouldn't reveal his identity."

"You're *our* daughter, and that's all that matters," her dad added.

Madison stared hard at both of them. "If you don't tell me who he is, I will never trust either of you again."

"He doesn't want you to know," her mom insisted, her eyes begging her to back down. "It'll be easier for you if you don't know."

"You can't make that decision for me," Madison said. "He's my father, and I deserve to know who he is."

"*I'm* your father," her dad said, sounding hurt and betrayed. "Biology doesn't matter. I've raised you, and I love you. You're a gift to me. I know your mom and I are dedicated to our work and aren't home as much as some of your friends' parents, but it doesn't mean we love you any less."

"I know that," Madison said, and she did. Her parents got held up at work a lot, but they loved their jobs, and she respected them for that. They spent time with her when they could, and they went on family vacations twice a year where they spent every minute with each other. "But I have a right to know who my biological father is."

"You have to trust us on this," her mom said.

Madison glared at her. "You can't ask me to trust you after I found out you've been lying to me for my entire life."

Both of them were silent, and Madison stayed still, determined not to budge until they gave her an answer.

"Adrian Diamond," her dad said softly.

"What?" Madison heard him, but he couldn't have meant what she thought.

"Adrian Diamond is your biological father."

www.campusbuzz.com

The Volleyball Girls
Posted on Thursday 10/9 at 5:22 PM
Hottest team of the year award goes to the girls volleyball team. Who's going to the game tomorrow night?!?!

1: Posted on Thursday 10/9 at 6:13 PM
wouldn't be surprised if half the school showed up. i just like watching savannah diamond in those short shorts. her friend alyssa isn't bad either.

2: Posted on Thursday 10/9 at 6:47 PM
Hottest girls on the Volleyball team:
Savannah
Jackie
Brooke
Alyssa

3: Posted on Thursday 10/9 at 7:03 PM
Jackie's parents are gonna be outta town this weekend so she's throwing a RAGER at her house after the game tomorrow night! Bring your bathing suit. Or don't and we'll have more fun ;)

4: Posted on Thursday 10/9 at 8:16 PM
savannah's flying in her friend from cali for the weekend to come to the game. she's been posting on savannah's

facebook constantly about how excited she is, so i had to check out her page. she's not so bad looking herself. another reason to go to jackie's party tomorrow

---

5: Posted on Thursday 10/9 at 9:58 PM
could be a good pre-game before hitting up the strip...

6: Posted on Thursday 10/9 at 10:43 PM
Are you too cool for house parties? Must be Damien or Oliver or Madison or Larissa or one of their friends. #Losers

---

7: Posted on Thursday 10/9 at 10:56 PM
#jealous

8: Posted on Thursday 10/9 at 11:00 PM
You all DO realize this isn't Twitter, right? Hashtags don't work here.

9: Posted on Thursday 10/9 at 11:06 PM
#Whatever. They're #fun ;)

chapter 5: *Savannah*

"Thank your mom again for letting you leave school early today to visit?" Savannah asked Evie. The two of them sat in the back of her Range Rover—her bodyguard, Carl, was driving them—on the way to Jackie's party, and Savannah still couldn't believe her best friend was here. Evie had sat with Courtney and Peyton during the volleyball game, and now she would be with Savannah at the after-party. It was just like old times…but not really. Because in old times, Evie would have been playing on the team with her. And Savannah wouldn't already be thinking about how sad it would be when Evie left tomorrow morning. It was too bad her best friend couldn't stay all weekend, but Evie's dad's birthday was tomorrow, and she had to be back by dinner to celebrate it with him.

"I will, I promise." Evie smiled. "But I already told you how she said missing half a day of school wasn't a big deal, considering how you paid for my ride to the airport, the flight *and* are letting me stay with you. And I still can't get over where you live. I sort of knew what to expect from the pictures you've sent me, but it's different being there in person. You're the luckiest ever. I wish I suddenly found out I was related to a billionaire."

"It's all pretty amazing," Savannah said. "But I miss home sometimes. I wish I had a friend like you at school."

She'd already told Evie everything—how Alyssa was only nice to her *after* she'd seen that she knew Damien and Nick. Then she'd made the volleyball team, so the girls had no choice but to include her. But even though it was already October, and Savannah had been hanging out with them every day during school and practice for weeks, it wasn't the same. She didn't trust them like she trusted Evie.

"The girls on the team didn't seem that bad," Evie said. "And if you don't end up being close friends with them, you have your sisters, right?"

"Yeah," Savannah said. "But they're my sisters…they *have* to be nice to me. It's different."

"I wouldn't know." Evie shrugged.

"Right." Savannah felt bad for bringing it up. Evie was an only child, and while Savannah had always thought it was awesome that Evie had her own room *and* bathroom at her house, she'd always suspected Evie had been jealous of how close she was with her sisters. "Anyway, we should be there soon. You ready?"

"Of course." Evie checked her reflection, fluffed her hair while making a silly duck-face pose, and laughed. Her cheerfulness was contagious, and Savannah couldn't help laughing with her. "Let's rock this party."

The volleyball team was the first to arrive so they could set up, and Jackie gave them the grand tour. Her house was enormous—apparently her family had bought two lots in the community so that they would have room to build it. The living room, dining room and kitchen all had a two-story ceiling, and shooting off from the kitchen was a rec room with tables set up for beer pong and flip cup. Jackie's parents, who were out of town that weekend, lived in a first-floor suite with two walk-in closets, an exercise room and a sauna. Upstairs were five other bedrooms—even though Jackie had only two brothers—and a separate stairway near the kitchen led to another bedroom for their live-in housekeeper. They also had a huge library full of every issue of *Nevada Design,* the luxury interior design magazine Jackie's dad published.

It was the biggest house Savannah had ever seen. And judging by the way Evie walked around with her mouth dropped open, it was the biggest house she'd ever seen, too.

"Remember to keep everyone in the rec room, the kitchen and outside by the pool," Jackie instructed. "No one's allowed in my parents' suite. I don't care if couples go off into my brothers' rooms or the guest rooms, but my room is off-limits. Except for me and whatever guy I bring in there with me, of course."

"Brian Peterson was checking you out during the game," Brooke said.

"I know." Jackie winked. "And he was looking hot tonight. So who's ready to celebrate our win?"

They gathered into a circle, put their hands in the center, counted down to scream "Bruins"—their school mascot—and cheered. Then they did a round of shooters, and the party began.

Three hours later, the house was packed with most of the athletes from Goodman (freshmen not included except for a select few), and some randoms who showed up from other local private schools. The volleyball girls had given up trying to keep everyone in the "designated party areas" over an hour ago—they were too busy having their own fun. A group of guys had tried to teach Savannah and Evie how to play flip cup, but Savannah was failing miserably and slowing down her team, so they left the rec room and ventured outside to the pool.

"Cannonball from the balcony!" a junior guy Savannah recognized as one of Nick's football teammates yelled from Jackie's balcony, jumping into the pool with a huge splash. He emerged from the water, threw back his head and gave a Neanderthal roar with his fists in the air. Everyone watching cheered and clapped, screaming various versions of "Yeah, man!" and "That was awesome!"

"Savannah!" Brooke called from the shallow end of the pool, where she was hanging out with a few of the girls on the team and some guys who were flirting with them. They all had red Solo cups in their hands. "Come swimming with us!"

"I didn't bring a bathing suit," Savannah replied.

"You don't need one." Jackie laughed and threw back her long brown hair, which had reverted to its natural curly state in the water. "We're all in our underwear. Although Alyssa said she would get naked if Drew got naked, so things are about to get interesting!"

"We could do it," Evie said, soft enough that only Savannah could hear.

"I'm wearing a see-through thong," Savannah whispered. Even the drink she'd had since that first shooter wasn't enough to make her feel comfortable shedding her clothes in front of everyone. If Peyton was here, she would do it in a heartbeat, but Savannah wasn't as daring as her oldest sister.

"We're actually heading back inside," Evie said to the group in the pool, and Savannah smiled gratefully at her. "Just wanted to check out what the commotion was out here. Have fun!"

"Bye!" Brooke yelled before one of the guys dunked her underwater. She held her cup up high, and it miraculously escaped being submerged with her.

Savannah didn't know many people yet, and not wanting to look unoccupied, Evie had the brilliant idea to take pictures of themselves with the party in the background—probably because she wanted to show off to everyone at Fairfield High that she'd been to a party like this. They got every background they could, and there were a lot to choose from, so they were busy for a while. More people were jumping off the balcony and into the pool, a big group was smoking hookah on the porch and some guys—including Oliver Prescott, the son of Adrian's main rival and possible business partner, Logan Prescott—were gathered around the kitchen table, which was covered in lines of white powder that Savannah suspected was cocaine. She accidentally got a picture of Oliver doing a line, and she almost deleted it but stopped. This was the jerk who'd made a bet to sleep with her *and* her sisters over the summer. She would never put the picture online, but it might not hurt to keep it on her phone.

Once she and Evie had taken enough photos, she texted the best one to Nick.

are u coming to Jackie's party tonight? I was hoping to see u here...

Can't ☹ Busy w/family stuff. I'll cya in school on Mon

Savannah frowned, but she wasn't surprised. Nick was always too busy to see her out of school.

"We're about to play Survivor!" a senior guy yelled from the rec room. "Anyone wanna join?"

"Do you know what that is?" Savannah asked Evie.

"I have no idea." Evie grabbed her hand and pulled her toward the rec room. "But let's find out!"

When they got inside, Savannah saw the last person she'd expected to find standing around the cluster of tables—Damien. He and his friends normally hung out on the Strip, eating at the trendiest restaurants and seeing popular DJs spin at clubs. He rarely came to house parties with the sports crowd.

"Great game tonight," he said when he saw her, giving her a high five. Their hands connected, and a warm tingle rushed up her arm.

"Thanks." Her mind raced for something more to say to him. "I wasn't expecting to see you here tonight."

"Oliver and I decided to do something different for a change."

"Survivors ready!" the guy who had started the game yelled before Savannah could reply.

She quickly introduced Damien and Evie, then situated herself between them, trying to pretend like she wasn't clueless about this game. Damien picked up the pitcher of beer in the center of the table and poured a small amount in her and Evie's cups, and a little more in his.

"Have you played this before?" he asked.

"No, but we played flip cup earlier," she said. "Evie wasn't bad at it, but I was terrible."

"This is similar to flip cup, but everyone goes at once," he said. "Each round the last person to flip their cup is eliminated, until there's one person left."

"Doesn't sound too hard," she said. *Except for the flipping-the-cup part.*

"Go!" the leader of the game yelled. Savannah forced herself to drink the beer—it was from the keg and tasted gross—and prepared to flip her cup. Damien got his in one flip. Evie got hers soon after. They both cheered her on, but after multiple unsuccessful tries, everyone's cup was flipped but Savannah's, so she was the first out. Which meant she had to leave her spot around the table and stand off to the side.

Not having anywhere else to go, she watched the next round. Now that she was out, Damien and Evie were standing next to each other. They both flipped their cups quickly and gave each other high fives. Was it just in Savannah's imagination, or was Evie tossing her hair more than usual, purposefully letting her arm brush against Damien's and shooting him her trademark flirty smile that Savannah had seen her use on guys in Fairfield? And since Savannah was out of the game, all she could do was stand there and watch. Her blood boiled, and she crossed her arms. She didn't want to look pissed off, but she couldn't help it. She didn't want to see this.

Maybe inviting Evie this weekend had been a mistake. Savannah loved her best friend, but Evie had always overshadowed her in Fairfield. Why would she have expected any different in Vegas?

Damien glanced over at her, and she took out her phone, pretending someone had sent her a text. The next round started, and his cup-flipping skill somehow vanished. He was last and was kicked out.

"Have fun, guys." He high-fived the senior leading the game, then walked over to Savannah. "You looked upset, so I wanted to make sure everything was okay," he said so only she could hear.

Giddiness swirled through her body, and she put her phone away. "You got out on purpose?"

"You'll never know," he teased. "But let's find something better to drink—that beer tasted like ass."

"Glad I'm not the only one who thought so." She made a face, because the beer really was sour and warm. "But let me check with Evie first. I don't want her to think I've abandoned her." She walked over to where Evie was still playing Survivor and was now flirting with the senior leading the game. "Hey." Savannah squeezed Evie's arm to let her know she was behind her. "Damien and I are going to grab a drink that isn't beer in the kitchen. We'll be back soon. Are you okay here for a few minutes?"

"Of course." Evie smiled and thanked the senior guy, who had filled an inch of her cup with beer. "I'm rocking this game. See ya in a few!"

Savannah followed Damien into the kitchen, but the cheap beer and liquor in there didn't meet his satisfaction, either. After some exploration, they discovered a walk-in wine closet near the garage. He switched on the light, illuminating the rows of wine. It was more of a small room than a closet, with walls of granite, tiled marble floors and wooden refrigerated shelves. Savannah doubted Jackie would be pleased that they were considering raiding her parents' wine collection, but she was too happy to be there with Damien to say so.

She shut the door so no one would follow them inside and get the same idea. Jackie's parents wouldn't notice if one bottle was missing, right?

"This is what I'm talking about," Damien said, examining the rows of wine. "What're you in the mood for—red or white?"

"Whatever you want." Savannah wasn't as knowledgeable about wine as most of the people at Goodman seemed to be. Their families taught them about wine and allowed them to have a glass or two at dinner. Savannah's mom only kept the hard stuff in their apartment. It was cheap, and the few times Savannah had tried it, it had tasted vile.

Damien perused the rows, taking a few bottles out and reading the labels. He reached one in the middle, paused and showed it to Savannah. "Amarone," he said, pointing to the label. "One of my favorites."

"Sounds good," Savannah said, although she had never heard of it.

He found a wine opener, uncorked the bottle and poured the wine into the clean Solo cups Savannah had brought in from the kitchen. "Not the best way to drink wine, but it'll work." He handed her one of the cups. "Cheers."

Adrian had allowed Savannah and her sisters glasses of wine at dinner—although Courtney always declined—but Savannah was far from a connoisseur. They all tasted the same to her. She sipped the Amarone, and it was stronger than she'd expected, but good. Much better than the cheap beer and liquor in the kitchen.

"Like it?"

"Yes." Savannah flushed at the sudden realization that she was alone with Damien in a small space. And the way he was looking at her, his dark eyes so intense, as if he wouldn't have wanted to be in there with anyone else... It made her nearly forget to breathe.

"What's wrong?" he asked.

"Nothing," she lied. Then, deciding better of it, she said, "I guess I'm wondering why you're here with me instead of hanging out with everyone at the party. You were doing really well in Survivor—you probably could have won."

"You looked bored watching, so I thought you'd be happy to get away for a few minutes," he said. "Was I wrong?"

"No," Savannah said. "This is actually my first big house party. I've seen them on TV, and they looked so fun, so I've always wanted to go to one. But now that we're here…" She shrugged and sipped her wine while contemplating how to word it, not wanting to sound like a downer.

"It's not what you expected?"

"Exactly," she said. "People are either almost naked in the pool, playing drinking games in the rec room, doing drugs or pairing up. Even with Evie here, I feel out of place. Maybe I just haven't had enough to drink. I tried that beer, but…" She scrunched her nose as she recalled the taste.

"No explanation necessary." Damien laughed and raised his Solo cup. "We have Amarone to the rescue."

They sat on the floor and chatted while drinking the wine—after the first "glass," Savannah felt warmer and more relaxed. Midway through the second, she and Damien were talking as if they'd known each other for years. There were a few times when their skin would touch, but he didn't try to kiss her like he had in the Myst pool caves over the summer.

She should have been happy that he was respecting her request to take things slowly—he *had* tried to move too fast by putting his hand down her bathing suit bottom on the first night they'd met—but she also felt disappointed. Was he only paying attention to her out of pity because she'd looked bored during Survivor and Evie was too involved with the game to talk to her?

"What are you thinking about?" Damien asked. "You just got really quiet."

"Nothing," she said, taking another sip of wine. But her body felt warm and tingly now, and Damien *had* asked, so why not tell him what was on her mind? "Well, I guess I sort of feel like I'm never going to fit in with anyone here," she admitted. "The only reason Alyssa, Jackie, Brooke and the rest of them are being nice to me is because I know you and Nick, and because I made the volleyball team. They expect me to forget that first morning at Goodman when they wanted nothing to do with me. I'm trying, because they can be fun and it feels good to be part of a group, but I can't shake the feeling that they're not true friends. They're all so comfortable with each other. But even with Evie here, I feel like an outsider." Her cheeks heated, and she looked down at her wine, unable to believe she'd blurted that out to Damien.

He tilted his head, his forehead creasing. "You've been comfortable at clubs all summer, and it's a *house party* that makes you feel this way?"

"You thought I looked comfortable at those clubs?" Savannah laughed. He had to be saying that to be nice. "Because I felt like an outsider there, too. But the clubs are different—they feel like a fairy tale, not real life. It's easier to pretend that I'm what people expect me to be when I'm there. But being here, at Jackie's house… It hit home for me. This is how they've *lived* their entire lives—with pools, saunas, spare bedrooms, live-in housekeepers, wine closets and refrigerators full of more food than they could possibly eat. I don't belong here." She wrapped her arms around her legs and looked down, ashamed at what she'd admitted. Stupid Amarone, loosening her tongue.

"Hey." He used his index finger to force her chin up so her gaze met his. "You might feel that way, but you *do* belong here. I know it's a big change for you, and I can't imagine what it's like, but those girls aren't only friends with you because you're on the volleyball team. You're talented, and fun, and you say what's on your mind even if it's not the 'cool' thing to say. I like that, and if those girls don't, that's their problem, not yours."

Savannah's heart raced, and she stared up into his dark eyes, amazed by his kind words. "Thanks," she said, still embarrassed she'd admitted so much, even if it was apparently a trait he liked about her. He was watching her so intensely right now, his eyes traveling to her lips, as if he were about to kiss her again. She took another sip of wine to cool her nerves. Maybe he actually did like her?

Then she remembered when Madison had kissed him last summer, and how in that one instant he'd forgotten about her. How he'd gone on that teen tour and had those girls hanging all over him. And how Evie had flirted with him during the game, and he'd flirted back. Yes, he made Savannah's heart race and made her feel like he cared. But he was a player. What if he'd brought her in here because of some stupid bet, like the one Oliver had made over the summer about her and her sisters? The two of them *were* close friends, so it was possible.

"We should go back out there," she said, then finished her wine. "Evie's probably wondering where we are."

Disappointment flashed across his eyes. "If that's what you want," he said. "But before we go—what are you doing for dinner tomorrow night?"

"Evie's leaving in the afternoon, so nothing that I know of." She played with her bracelets. "Why?"

"I've been wanting to check out the new Italian restaurant at the Diamond," he said. "Want to go with me?"

She froze, her arm dropping to her side. Was he asking her on a date? Or did he genuinely want to check out this restaurant and was asking her out of pity after her embarrassing confession? *Or* was this the next move in his game, because she'd made it clear she wasn't falling for it tonight?

He watched her, waiting for an answer. "Sure," she said

quickly. After all, if she didn't go, she would constantly wonder what would have happened if she did.

"Great." He smiled, seeming truly happy that she'd agreed to go with him.

When she stood up, her head spun, and Damien reached out to steady her. "Thanks." She giggled and tried to focus. When had the room started tilting so much? "I didn't realize how strong that wine was until I got up."

"Amarone will do that to you." He held out his arm, and she took it, grateful for his help as he led the way out of the wine closet. "Come on, let's go find your friend."

They reached the living room, and Savannah spotted Evie sitting on the couch. Her arms were crossed over her chest, her lips curled in a scowl as she talked to Alyssa, whose hair was still wet from the pool. They both went silent when Savannah reached them.

"Where've you been?" Evie glared at her.

Savannah glanced at her watch and gasped—how had forty-five minutes passed since she'd left Evie in the rec room playing Survivor? "Sorry." She laughed, but it turned into a hiccup, which made her laugh more. Evie didn't laugh along—why didn't she lighten up? This was a party. Evie always had fun at parties. "I didn't realize how much time had passed. But you had fun playing that game with everyone, right?"

"The game ended thirty minutes ago, but I got out soon after you guys left for the 'kitchen.'" Evie's voice was flat. "I tried to find you, but you'd disappeared, and you weren't responding to my texts. So I was sitting here by myself until Alyssa came over."

"Sorry." Savannah shrugged, since there was nothing she could do. It was unlike Evie to get all mopey. "Do you want a shot or something?"

"No," she said. "I'm good."

"Okay." This was awkward. Especially since after all that Amarone, Savannah just wanted to have *fun*.

"Jackie and Brooke set up karaoke in the rec room," Alyssa said, breaking the silence. "You sing, Savannah, right?"

"Yes, I do!" She jumped and clapped her hands. "Does she have the *Frozen* sing-along? I totally have to sing 'Let It Go'! The Idina Menzel version, obviously."

"You can sing that?" Damien raised an eyebrow. "Don't get me wrong, you have a great voice, but it's a tough song."

"Um, yeah, I can sing that." Savannah laughed and rolled her eyes. "Follow me and I'll prove it!"

She pointed at the rec room, took a shot in the kitchen on the way there and the night was a blur after that.

chapter 6: *Courtney*

After a long morning of working at Habitat for Humanity, Courtney was ready for lunch break. She loved volunteering for Habitat, especially after meeting the family who would move into the house when it was completed, but she wasn't used to physical labor. She'd been assigned to painting the outside of the house, and her arms would be hurting tomorrow.

Once the pizza arrived, it was set up on tables, and everyone dug in. Courtney rarely took advantage of her Blamex—the Black American Express credit card that Adrian had given her and her sisters—but she hadn't hesitated to use it to buy the pizza lunch for Habitat volunteers. She'd also ordered extra pizza for the family who would eventually move into the house, so they could take it home for tomorrow. She understood what it was like not knowing if there would be enough food for every meal, or to have to stretch a loaf of bread and jar of peanut butter for as long as possible. Not a day passed when she didn't feel guilty for having so much now when most people had so little, and she was determined to give back.

Somehow, she'd ended up in front of Brett in the pizza line. He'd followed through with his promise to join Habitat with her—and despite Courtney's insistence that they not get too close, he always worked around it, like by sitting next to her in the meetings, or getting behind her in line right now. And despite her attempts to neutralize her feelings for him, her heart still raced every time he was near.

"Sit with me for lunch?" he asked after they grabbed their slices.

He looked so perfect with the sun reflecting off his green eyes, his hair messed up from working in the heat all day, and Courtney couldn't say no. She wanted to slap herself after agreeing. What was she *doing?* She should be joining a group to try making new friends, not going off with Brett. But her legs didn't want to listen to her brain, and she followed him to a shaded, secluded spot under a tree.

"Looks like you got more paint on you than on the house," Brett said as they set their plates down on the grass.

"Savannah's going to flip when she sees my jeans." Courtney took a long drink of water. The desert air was drying out her throat, and she finished half the water bottle in seconds. "But anyway, how's the roof work going?" She phrased it casually, as if she hadn't been subtly watching him work up there all morning.

"I sucked at first." He laughed. "But after a while I got the hang of it. I'm not the best, but I'm not as bad as Oliver. Poor guy almost fell off."

"I was surprised to see him here this morning," Courtney said. "He's never come to any of the meetings, and he didn't strike me as the type of person who voluntarily wakes up before noon."

Brett chewed a bite of pizza. "I have no idea why he's here, but he's hungover as hell. One of the other guys mentioned that Oliver was partying pretty hard at that volleyball party last night. He might be moved to painting so he doesn't almost fall off the roof again."

"That'll be good," Courtney said sarcastically. "A hungover person breathing in paint fumes. Hopefully he won't get sick all over a wall."

"That's some abstract art I *wouldn't* want to see." Brett finished his first slice and moved on to his second. "Anyway, what're you up to after this? The new Bond movie came out this weekend and I want to see it."

Had he just asked her out? Courtney froze, pizza slice in midair, unable to meet his eyes. She couldn't sit close to him in a dark movie theater. The tension that would build between them… She shook off the thought, not wanting to dwell on it. Because it couldn't happen.

"I'll probably take a long shower, then try to get some work done if I don't pass out from exhaustion first." She said the first excuse to pop into her mind. "Any energy I have left after today needs to be spent studying for the PSAT. I can't believe they're coming up next week."

"Haven't you been studying all summer?"

"Yes," she said. "But I want to review everything to make sure I'm ready."

"If you're not ready by now, that won't change in the next few days," he said. "And I'm sure you'll do great, but it's only the PSATs. The colleges don't see them. You can take a night off to go to the movies."

He might be right, but she didn't trust herself in a movie theater with him. And she really *had* planned on studying. "The colleges don't see them, but if I do well I can qualify for a National Merit Scholarship," she said. "I've been wanting that scholarship since freshman year."

"It's pretty competitive, right?" Brett polished off his second slice of pizza. Courtney had only just finished her first.

"Out of the 1.5 million juniors who take the PSAT every year, 8,200 of them get a scholarship." Courtney recited the facts she'd memorized. "It's competitive, but not impossible. With all the studying I've done on my own, along with my tutoring, I should score high enough to be in the top three percent of test takers eligible to compete."

"You've certainly studied hard enough," Brett said. "But you don't have to be nervous. Of course it's worth giving it a shot, but if you don't get a scholarship, Adrian will pay for you to go to college."

"I know." Courtney sighed. As much as she hated the idea of Adrian paying for her college, she wouldn't be able to refuse if that was the difference between going to Stanford or not going to Stanford. "But I've wanted this for over two years. I'm not going to give up now. Plus, receiving the National Merit Scholarship looks good on college applications."

"I'm sure it does," Brett said. "But don't stress too much. Try to relax. You've prepared enough that you'll benefit more by making sure you're well rested before the testing day instead of staying up late to study."

"That's a good point," she said. "Thanks."

"I mean it." He watched her closely, as if contemplating whatever he was thinking of saying next. "So if you're not up for the movie, why don't we study together?"

Her cheeks flushed, and she looked down at her half-finished second slice of pizza. "Maybe," she said, hating how he'd caught her so unaware. "But I probably won't be able to get much studying done.... I'll be so exhausted after working in the heat all day that it'll be impossible to focus. Anyway," she said before he could figure out another way to ask her out, "the teachers started cleaning up the lunch area. I'm gonna go help out with that." She moved to stand up, fumbling to take her empty water bottle and plate with her.

"Courtney?" Brett said, and she paused, her breath stopping in her chest. "Are you planning on finishing that?" He glanced at the half-finished slice of pizza on her plate, and her heart fell to her stomach. What had she *wanted* him to say?

Certainly not that.

"No." She thrust her plate at him and stood up. "Enjoy it. I'll see you around."

She tried not to glance back at him as she walked away, but she couldn't help it. He must have been waiting for it, because he gave her a wave with what was left of the pizza, and she felt terribly guilty for running away.

If suppressing her feelings for him was the right thing to do, then why did it feel so wrong?

As Brett had predicted, Oliver got moved from working on the roof to painting the outside of the house. He positioned himself next to Courtney—probably to annoy her. And he showed every sign of being hungover. He had circles beneath his eyes, his dark shaggy hair was a mess and his face took on a greenish hue every time he bent down to dip his brush into the paint. Courtney would never say it out loud, but after he'd bet he could sleep with her and her sisters over the summer *and* had tried to kiss her when she'd told him she wasn't interested, she couldn't help enjoying seeing him so miserable.

He wiped sweat from his brow, leaving a streak of paint in its place. "One more hour of this torture," he complained, taking a break from painting to sip his water.

"I don't mean to be rude, but why are you here?" It was the most she'd said to him since they'd started painting. "You never expressed interest in Habitat until today, and it seems like you hate it."

"Princess Courtney deigns to speak to me." He smirked.

She rolled her eyes. "Never mind. Let's just keep painting." She turned away from him, planning to ignore him for the rest of the day.

"I'm here because of my parents." Oliver surprised her by seriously answering her question. "A few of my teachers gave me academic warnings, so my parents are pissed. They said I have to get my grades up, join extracurriculars and make sure there's no more publicity about my partying and gambling. If I can't do that, they want to send me to boarding school. No way am I letting that happen. My sister's in boarding school, and from what she says, it sucks."

"I didn't know you have a sister," Courtney said.

"Half sister," he said. "Brianna. We have the same dad, and my mom prefers to pretend that she doesn't exist. But there's no way I'm leaving Vegas to go to some strict-ass school in the middle of nowhere. How lame would that be?"

Courtney thought boarding school might be good for Oliver, but she doubted he would react well if she said so, and she didn't want to pick a fight while doing charity. "Why'd you choose Habitat?" she asked instead, genuinely curious about how, out of all the clubs offered at Goodman, he'd chosen the one that involved hands-on work on Saturday mornings.

"I figured it would be easy," he scoffed. "No papers, no homework—all I would have to do is show up and build stuff. But waking up early and working in the heat all day blows."

"It's definitely not something you want to do while you're hungover."

He raised an eyebrow. "I'm surprised you know what a hangover looks like. I didn't think you drank."

"I don't." She focused on the spot she was painting. Because she was more than familiar with what a hangover looked like—knowing had been inescapable when growing up with her mom. Sometimes Mom was curable with a few glasses of water and an aspirin. Other days it was worse, with her throwing up until late afternoon, lying in bed moaning and clutching her stomach, swearing she would never drink that much again. Last year, when it had gotten really bad, Courtney and her sisters had gone a month living on peanut butter sandwiches because their mom had spent all the grocery money on alcohol. So, yes, Courtney knew what a hangover looked like.

"Why not?" Oliver stepped closer to her, and she moved away. "Maybe a few drinks would help you loosen up."

"I don't need to loosen up." Courtney focused on painting, refusing to look at him. The predatory way he was watching her made her feel like there were snakes crawling under her skin.

"You'll never know unless you try," he said. "We could have had fun this summer. It sucks you found out about that bet, because I made it before I met you. After we hung out at my mom's event, I actually liked you. Who knows what would have happened if you'd given me a chance instead of going for your emo soon-to-be stepbrother?" He laughed and glanced up at Brett, who was hammering the roof so hard that Courtney worried he might break it. "And that got you nowhere, since, from what I hear, the two of you aren't 'allowed' to date. Although you looked pretty cozy at lunch…"

"We're not dating." Courtney splattered paint against the wall. She wanted to dump the bucket of it over Oliver's gelled hair. Instead she took a deep breath and glanced up at Brett, whose warm eyes met hers.

He climbed down the ladder and joined them, claiming to need another bottle of water. "How's everything going down here?" he asked, looking back and forth between Courtney and Oliver.

"Fine." She didn't want to tell Brett what Oliver had just said. The last thing they needed was a rematch of the scuffle they'd had at the grand opening last summer. Given Oliver's hungover state, Brett would win the fight, and Courtney didn't want him getting in trouble on their first Habitat build day.

"Are you sure?" Brett leaned closer to her and said softly, "Because you looked like you wanted to break Oliver's nose with the hard end of your paintbrush."

Her grip tightened around the handle. "Then I'll have to work on making my feelings not as transparent."

He eased the paintbrush from her hand and placed it next to the bucket. Her skin tingled where it touched his, and she made no effort to move away. "Since the day's almost over, let's see if we can help with cleanup," he said.

"Okay." She didn't want to be around Oliver for a second longer.

Brett led the way, and she followed.

"What was that asshole saying to you?" he asked once they were far enough from Oliver that he couldn't overhear.

"Nothing important." Courtney shrugged. And it really *wasn't* important, because she didn't believe a word that Oliver said. He'd never "actually liked her"—and by bringing up Brett, he'd just been trying to get a reaction from her. To see if she still had feelings for Brett after they'd kissed over the summer.

She hated that it had worked.

"Come on," Brett said. "I saw the two of you talking. You looked livid. He obviously said something to piss you off."

"He was just saying how he's only doing Habitat because his parents are forcing him," she said. "He doesn't care or realize that by being here, he's helping to change the lives of an entire family by giving them a home when they wouldn't have had one otherwise. He's so ignorant. I don't think I could have taken listening to him for much longer."

"Well, I'm glad I was able to help you get away," he said. "Especially after you admitted to wanting to smack him with your paintbrush. It wouldn't have been right for you to get in trouble on our first build day because you were giving Oliver what he deserves."

She paused midstep. Hadn't that been similar to what she'd been thinking, but about not wanting *Brett* to get in trouble?

"Everything okay?" he asked. "You're not thinking of going back there and starting a fight with him, are you?"

"I just…" She ran her fingers through her hair, unsure how to phrase it. It warmed her heart that, just by looking at her, Brett could tell what she needed. She'd never had someone other than her sisters and Grandma care about her like that. "I'm glad you came down when you did. Thanks for saving me."

"Does this mean you've changed your mind about that study session tonight?" He raised an eyebrow. "Or a movie. We wouldn't have to go out. We could watch at my place— I'm sure I can find something you'll like."

Her eyes locked on his, and she wanted to say yes. But Oliver had given her a hard time about having *lunch* with Brett. It had been obvious even to him that every time she and Brett were around each other, she had to battle to control her feelings. She doubted a movie at his place would remain strictly friendly. And if anything more were to happen between them, and anyone—mainly Adrian or Rebecca—were to find out, it would mean losing their trust and disappointing them. Courtney couldn't do that.

"I don't think so." Her heart dropped at the disappointment in his eyes, and she hurried to the teachers to offer to help clean up.

No matter what she did, it seemed impossible to make everyone happy.

chapter 7: *Peyton*

On Saturday afternoon, Peyton was in her room, trying and failing to concentrate on homework. Figuring a break was in order, and with Courtney at the Habitat for Humanity build and Savannah grabbing lunch with Evie before Evie went back to California, she journeyed to the main pool at the Diamond by herself.

The Diamond Residences penthouses included access to the exclusive rooftop pool, but Peyton preferred the main pool because it was busier—filled with people to watch and potentially meet. It was surrounded by palm trees and manicured hedges, with the golden towers of the hotel and condo overlooking it all. People swam in groups, talking and laughing, and it was late enough in the day that it was nearly impossible to find an open chair.

Luckily Peyton had reserved a VIP cabana that morning. After applying tanning oil—with SPF 15 since Courtney insisted she protect her skin a *little*—she laid back on her lounge chair, readjusted her blue plastic-framed sunglasses and listened to her iPod. She tanned for thirty minutes, and then took out the book she was supposed to be reading for class, although instead of reading, she looked around to people watch.

That was when she spotted Hunter Sterling, lounging with friends, wearing only a bathing suit. And wow, did he work out when he wasn't teaching. He had the chiseled body of an Abercrombie model—he might even give Jackson a run for his money. Not like Peyton had ever seen Jackson shirtless, since he always wore his professional suit around her, but he had to be superfit to be a bodyguard.

Hunter's friends appeared to be around his age, and the five of them were drinking beers and talking. She wanted Hunter to see her, but not have it be obvious that she was looking for his attention, so she got up for a dip in the pool, right near where they were hanging out. When she pulled herself out of the water, Hunter's gaze met hers and he waved.

Taking that as an invitation, she strutted over, knowing she looked hot in her barely-there black bikini, her skin glistening from the water. She glanced over her shoulder, trying to see if Jackson was watching, but as always, her bodyguard was hidden within the masses of tourists. Oh, well. She might not be able to see him, but she knew he was watching.

She smiled when she reached Hunter and his friends. "I've never seen you at the Diamond pool before," she said, trying to act like running into him was normal and had happened more than once.

"My best mates are visiting this week, and they wanted to stay at the best hotel in Vegas," he said, motioning to his friends and introducing them.

"Naturally, you brought them here," Peyton said.

"This *is* the best hotel in Vegas, isn't it?"

"I only moved here this summer, so I'm no expert." She

flipped her long hair over her shoulder. "But that's what I hear."

"Then it looks like I'm in the right place." He grinned, and it was like the teacher/student separation was gone. But there were no open seats around them, and she felt awkward standing.

"I've got a cabana over there." She pointed to her cabana, which was empty except for her stuff on her chair. "If you want the best of Vegas, you *have* to hang out in a poolside cabana."

"What do you say, boys?" Hunter raised his beer and looked at his friends. "To the cabana?"

"To the cabana!" they repeated, clinking their beers together and standing up.

Peyton led the way through the maze of chairs draped with white-and-gold striped towels. The cabanas were separated with dark wood dividers and spiral hedges. Each had a cushioned bench and a few lounge chairs in front of the entrance, which had a white curtain for privacy.

"Now this is what I'm talking about," one of Hunter's friends said, a blond who was heavier than the rest of them. He situated himself on the couch and turned on the plasma-screen TV, flipping channels until arriving at ESPN. "Americans and their football." He scoffed. "I'd like to see them take that padding off and play a proper game of rugby."

Peyton had never been into watching sports—and she didn't know what rugby was—so she had nothing to say to that. "There's beer in the minifridge." She pointed to the cabinet under the television. Guys never turned down free beer. "Take whatever you'd like."

Hunter was still standing near the entrance, so Peyton pulled a Carlsberg out of the minifridge, popped it open, and walked over to him. "This is what you were drinking before, right?" she asked. "If you want something else, the cabana wait staff will be over soon."

He stared at the beer as if she were handing him poison instead of a drink. "If anyone sees us here, I could get in serious trouble."

Peyton frowned; she was enjoying forgetting that Hunter was her teacher. But she didn't want him to be uncomfortable, so she pulled the rope to the curtain so no one could see inside the cabana. "There." She smiled, perched her sunglasses on top of her head and widened her eyes, as if she hung around the pool with her teachers every day. "Is that better?" But despite her calm appearance, worry fluttered in her stomach—there was a chance Hunter would leave. That would be so embarrassing, since Jackson had to be watching.

He scanned the cabana, where his friends had already settled into the couches, enjoying their drinks and ESPN. "You can't tell anyone," he said, reaching for the beer. "This stays between us. Got it?"

"Done," she said triumphantly.

"But, Peyton—"

"How do you two know one another?" his blond friend on the couch interrupted.

"My father owns the Diamond, and I live in the Residences with my sisters," Peyton said, grateful for the switch of topic. "Hunter hangs out here sometimes, so I've seen him around."

"Hanging with socialites?" His friend cocked an eyebrow and raised his beer. "Cheers, mate."

Peyton hardly considered herself a *socialite*—a few months ago she'd been a nobody from Fairfield, California—but whatever they wanted to think was fine by her. It was better than them knowing she was one of Hunter's students.

They hung out in the cabana for a while, chatting about Vegas and the places they had to visit while on vacation—or as they called it, "on holiday." Peyton shared a couch with Hunter, and they all laughed, drank beer and had a good time. His friends were cool. If Peyton ever visited Australia, she would hit them up so they could show her around.

Thirty minutes into the conversation, her iPhone lit up from inside her pool bag. She grabbed it to see who had texted her.

Jackson. They'd exchanged numbers that summer, when he'd first been assigned to be her bodyguard, but he never sent her texts. Her heart beat faster in anticipation of what it could say. She clicked to the message, and smiled when she saw he hadn't sent one text—he'd sent four.

1: Why are you bringing your teacher and his friends into your cabana?

2: Do you know how much trouble he could get into if he's caught drinking with a student?

3: If Adrian finds out about this, he's not going to be happy. Think, Peyton. Is this worth it?

4: If you don't get them to leave, I'm coming in after you.

Peyton imagined what a scene it would cause if Jackson stormed in here, dressed in his intense bodyguard suit, and she couldn't help it—she laughed.

"What's so funny?" Hunter asked.

"Nothing." She bit her lip, her fingers hovering over the screen. "Just something a friend sent me."

We're just hanging out having a few drinks...no one will find out. No need to come in after me. Unless you want to join in the fun ;)

She pressed Send and tossed the phone back into her bag without waiting for Jackson's reply. Let him wonder...or better yet, let him come in.

The phone lit up a few more times, and as much as she itched to see his response, she ignored it.

"Someone's texting you," Hunter said, motioning toward her phone.

"It's just my bodyguard." Peyton shrugged, careful not to show how the thought of him distracted her from everything else. She needed to have fun with Hunter and his friends—not pine over Jackson. "He can be overprotective, but he'll back off."

"Why do you need a bodyguard?"

Peyton leaned forward, her elbows on her knees. "So I don't get kidnapped," she said, lowering her voice so she sounded mysterious.

"I guess that's something you have to worry about when your family has heaps of money," Hunter's short friend on the other side of him, who was named Eddie, said. "You must have loads of interesting stories."

Peyton wasn't sure if she should share anything personal about her family, but these guys would be back in Australia soon, so what would it matter? "One of my sisters was kidnapped as a baby and held for ransom." She paused for dramatic effect and looked each of them in the eye, as if she were telling a ghost story around a campfire. "My father got her back safely, but ever since then, we've had bodyguards. Mine can be a real pain. He's practically my age, but he's always trying to tell me what to do." She rolled her eyes, since if she acted like Jackson irritated her, they wouldn't see that she had feelings for him. "So annoying."

"Sounds like it," Eddie agreed. "You don't seem like the type who likes being told what to do."

"You got that right," Peyton agreed.

"What's he so uptight about, anyway?"

"He doesn't like that I closed the door to the cabana," she said, because she couldn't exactly say he was upset that she was drinking with her teacher. "He gets antsy when he can't see me. As if there aren't enough eyes in the sky in this town."

"Eyes in the sky?" Eddie scratched his chin and looked up.

"The cameras." Peyton pointed to the black glass half circle lodged into the ceiling. "They're everywhere, especially in the casinos. You haven't noticed?"

"I saw them, but I didn't know what they were." He shrugged. "Now I do."

Hunter shook his head at Eddie, as if he thought his friend was missing a few brain cells. "If your bodyguard is worried about the door being closed, maybe my mates and I should be on our way," he said, moving to get up from the couch. "We wanted to play some poker today, anyway."

"My bodyguard is fine," Peyton said calmly, although she was pretty sure Jackson was worried about her—which she kind of liked. Really liked, actually. "Like I said, he gets overprotective. I'm not going to get kidnapped right now—unless one of you isn't telling me something?" She looked at his friends mischievously.

"Let's stay here a little bit longer," one of Hunter's other friends—Thomas, with slicked-back hair, who Peyton thought was a little sleazy—piped in as he grabbed another beer from the minifridge. "How often do we get to hang in poolside cabanas with hot Vegas hotel heiresses? Wait—don't answer that, Hunter. I'm sure you do this stuff all the time, but for us plebs it's a luxury." He turned to Peyton, a predatory gleam in his eyes. "Are your sisters planning on joining us?"

"They're busy." Peyton shrugged, glad it was the truth. She wouldn't want Thomas within fifty feet of her sisters. "But if you all want to play poker, there's a deck of cards around here somewhere."

"What're we playing for?" Eddie asked.

"Money, a round of drinks, lunch," Peyton suggested. "Unless you have anything else in mind?"

"I've got a few things in mind." Thomas ran his eyes up and down Peyton's body, which made her shudder.

"We keep this PG, or I'm going into the casinos to play, and you're all coming with me," Hunter insisted. Peyton smiled at him in thanks. She'd played strip poker before with friends, but the way Thomas was looking at her made her want to put her cover-up back on. Plus, the friends she'd played with were people she knew, who were her age. This was different. She might be daring, but she wasn't stupid.

She'd just grabbed the deck of cards when the curtain flew open, revealing a very pissed-off Jackson. He stood in the entrance, looking out of place in his uniform amongst the bathing suits everyone else had worn to the pool. His arms were crossed, and the vein in his forehead looked about to burst.

"Apologies for the intrusion, but Miss Diamond's father needs to see her immediately," Jackson said, his voice clipped.

"'Miss Diamond' is an adult, and can see her father when she's ready," Thomas said, clearly after one beer too many, since he appeared unaffected by Jackson's commanding presence.

Jackson stared him down, the anger in his eyes so intense

that Thomas averted his gaze. "I would hardly consider a seventeen-year-old to be an adult."

"Seventeen!" Eddie laughed, coughing on a mouthful of beer. "Hunter, she could be one of your students!"

Hunter looked down at the floor and shuffled his feet. Peyton must have looked guilty, as well, because understanding crossed over Eddie's face.

"No way." Eddie gasped. "You're not *actually* one of his students, are you?"

Peyton's face heated, her throat so tight that she couldn't bring herself to answer. "I've gotta go." She grabbed her bag and hurried to the exit of the cabana. "You all can keep the cabana—it's on me. Have fun!" She barely met Hunter's eyes as she stomped after Jackson. Jackson refused to turn around to look at her—this was bad. She had to say *something* to fix this.

"Why does Adrian want to see me now?" she asked him once they were inside. She hadn't realized her father was back in town—he'd left for business in Macau a week ago. He was supposed to be there for another few days.

"He doesn't," Jackson said, still not turning around. "He's not back in town yet."

Peyton stopped walking, which got him to stop and face her. His expression was so cold, and he was giving her that awful look, like he thought she was an immature kid. Like he was *disappointed* in her. It made her feel like crap. If she were a year older, there would be nothing wrong with her talking and playing cards with Hunter and his friends in the cabana. There were so many worse things she could be doing. It was stupid of Jackson to get riled up about this.

"If Adrian doesn't need to see me, then why did you burst into the cabana, call me out and pull me away from my friends?" she snapped. "We were having fun, if you know what that is."

The moment the words left her mouth, she felt bad. Maybe that was too harsh. Jackson was only trying to do his job. But it was already said, so there was no taking it back.

"Those weren't your friends." Jackson stepped closer to her, his eyes blazing, which made her pulse race and her limbs go numb. "That was your teacher and *his* friends. Do you have any idea how much trouble he could get in if anyone knew he was drinking with you? And do you understand how angry Adrian will get if pictures leak to the public? Tabloids would have a field day with that story."

"Tabloids don't know I exist," Peyton said.

"Don't you ever look yourself up online?"

"No." Peyton laughed. "Unlike Savannah, I don't browse the internet for hours. Especially not to look myself up."

Jackson took out his phone, typed something into it and handed it to Peyton. Curious, she took it to see whatever he wanted to show her. It was Google, with her name written in the search bar and the results listed below:

Las Vegas casino owner Adrian Diamond's daughters—Peyton, Courtney and Savannah—move to the Strip to live with him in his newest luxury hotel.

Peyton, Courtney and Savannah Diamond attend the grand opening of the Diamond Hotel and Residences.

The real-life fairy tale of Peyton, Courtney and Savannah Diamond: The secret heiresses to Diamond Resorts Worldwide.

And the list went on. Tons of popular websites had heard of, and written articles about, Peyton and her sisters' return to Vegas. Google Images had pictures of her, too. People who had never heard of her a few months ago now not only knew her and her sisters' names, but what they looked like. Something about that was weirdly creepy.

"Adrian's kept you and your sisters out of the spotlight, so everything out there about you is mild so far," Jackson said, taking his phone back. "But if reporters find out about your Saturday afternoon cabana party with one of your teachers, they'll destroy you *and* him. I'm sure Adrian has made it clear that all your privileges would be taken away, too."

"I've lived without these 'privileges' for most of my life," Peyton reminded him.

"I know," he said. "But you've changed since then. You certainly seem used to your Saturday afternoon cabanas. Do you know how much those cost?"

Peyton shook her head, dreading the answer. Last summer, the first time she'd mentioned wanting to go to the main pool, Rebecca had reserved a cabana for her and her sisters. Ever since, Peyton had done the same. She'd assumed the cabanas were free for her because her father owned the hotel.

"One cabana is four hundred dollars a day on the weekend," Jackson said. "If the tabloids find out about your escapades with your teacher, I'm guessing Adrian will take away your credit card privileges. That means no more cabanas."

"Oh." Peyton followed Jackson back to her condo, feeling like an idiot. She'd just been having fun with Hunter and his friends—it hadn't crossed her mind that hotel guests might recognize her and take pictures of her to send to reporters. No wonder Hunter had been so antsy. "I closed the curtain door of the cabana," she said, even though, listening to herself now, it sounded lame. "No one could see what was going on inside, so you didn't have to barge in and embarrass me."

"I was trying to protect you," Jackson said. "You have no idea what you're getting yourself into."

"I can handle myself fine." She clenched her fists, half wanting to march back to the cabana and resume the game of poker with Hunter and his friends. But she didn't want to get Hunter fired. And she remembered the looks on his friends' faces when Jackson had spilled her age—discomfort. In seconds she'd gone from someone they wanted to spend time with to a kid.

Hopefully it wouldn't be awkward when she saw Hunter on Monday morning.

"I know you can handle yourself," Jackson said. "And I'm sorry it conflicts with your fun, but I have to do my job."

With that, he closed the door to the condo, leaving her inside and alone.

chapter 8: *Madison*

Madison glared at the numbers on her scale and wrapped her arms around her bloated stomach. How had she gained seven pounds?

Ever since her parents had told her about Adrian Diamond being her biological father, with strict instructions that she tell no one, the secret had been suffocating her. She couldn't go out with her friends without feeling like every word to them was a lie, so she'd barely gone out at all. Her weekdays consisted of going to school, doing homework and marathon-watching *The Vampire Diaries* until she was tired enough to go to sleep. Weekends were the same, although instead of school she had SAT prep class on Saturday afternoon.

She couldn't get motivated to go to the gym anymore, and her diet had gone out the window. Luckily it was fall, so she could wear sweaters to hide her stomach. But if she kept eating so much pizza, fried food, carbs and cheese, it was going to be impossible to lose the weight for the annual Lockhart family winter break trip to the Caribbean.

Assuming there would still *be* a Lockhart family winter trip. She couldn't look at her parents anymore without being reminded of their betrayal. How was she supposed to enjoy a week in the Caribbean with them?

She stepped off the scale, glad when the number disappeared from the screen. She should stay off it until she got back on track with her diet. Seeing the numbers going up was making her feel worse. Her twenty-six-inch True Religion jeans that had been loose in the summer barely zipped up now, and she hated the idea of having to buy a pair of twenty-seven-inch "fat jeans." After this weekend, she *had* to get back on track.

The doorbell rang—dinner had arrived. Her parents didn't cook, so when they were home for dinner—which had been happening a lot more since the Adrian-Diamond-is-your-biological-father bomb had been dropped—it consisted of going out, ordering in or reheating leftovers. Tonight, they'd ordered room service. Her mom opened the front door, and Madison stayed in her room while the servers set up the meal in the dining room.

"Madison!" her mom called. "Dinner's ready."

"Coming!" she yelled back, glancing in the mirror. She hadn't showered, since the only place she had to be today was her semiprivate SAT tutoring session. Her hair was flat, and she had no makeup on, but it didn't matter. She wouldn't be seeing anyone tonight besides her parents.

She threw on a sweatshirt she hadn't worn since middle school and headed to the dining room. Her parents were already seated, and she took her place in front of her cheeseburger (with extra cheese) and fries. Her wineglass was full, and there was a half-empty bottle of Cakebread Chardonnay on the table, one of her favorites. Her parents usually ordered it as a celebration or a consolation.

Madison suspected tonight was the latter.

"How was SAT class today?" her mom asked, cutting into her mahi-mahi. Grilled fish and vegetables was normally what Madison ordered, too, since it wasn't fattening. But her cheeseburger and fries looked much more delicious.

"Fine," Madison said, taking a huge bite of her burger. It was absolutely heavenly. "We did a practice run of the math section and I scored better than the other three kids." She forced the excitement into her tone that she *would* have felt before her world crashed down on her two weeks ago, but she could tell it sounded fake.

"That's good," her dad said in between bites of filet. "Do you have plans with your friends tonight?"

Did she *look* like she had plans with her friends tonight? Madison wanted to say something snarky, but instead replied with a simple, "I'm just staying in. I have a lot of homework, with it almost being the middle of the semester and everything."

"But it's a Saturday night," her dad said. "Homework has never stopped you from enjoying a weekend night. You've always been great at getting everything done on Sunday."

"Junior year is harder than sophomore year," Madison lied. "We get more homework over the weekend, and I won't be able to keep up my 4.0 if I wait until Sunday to do it all." Besides, now that she'd gained weight, her form-fitting dresses would make her look like a cow.

"We understand that." Her mom put her fork down and took a sip of wine. "But, Madison, you've barely left the condo in two weeks except for school. Your dad and I are worried about how you're handling the situation."

The situation. That was what they'd been calling the *truth.* Ever since that day, she'd felt like they were strangers. She was pissed at them for lying to her, and she hated that she couldn't tell anyone about how her entire life had fallen apart in the blink of an eye. They'd made it especially clear she couldn't tell Adrian what she knew.

What would he do if she marched up to him and told him? And why did he not want to be part of her life, but he was welcoming Peyton, Courtney and Savannah into his?

It was more reason for Madison to hate the Diamond girls, even if they technically were her half sisters. She hadn't liked them from the moment she'd seen them. Peyton was a slut, Courtney a holier-than-thou Goody Two-shoes and Savannah a wannabe who was desperate for attention. How could she be *related* to them?

"Your mom and I think you need to talk with someone about this," her dad said. "A professional."

"Like a psychiatrist?" Madison looked at him as if he'd lost his mind. What if someone from school found out she was seeing a therapist? The rumors would make everything worse. "No way."

"We're worried about you." By the concern in her mom's eyes, Madison could tell that she meant it. But that didn't make her less angry about how she'd been lied to. "When you're home, it seems like all you're doing is watching TV," her mom continued. "You've stopped going to the gym, and you've been eating greasy, fatty food at a rate that, if continues, will have a negative impact on your health."

Madison shrugged and took another bite of her cheeseburger.

"What we had to tell you was hard to hear, and we're sorry you found out the way you did," her mom continued. "Your dad and I have been supportive in every way we can, and we want you to realize that we're still the same family we've always been. You have to figure out how to accept that and move forward. A professional can help."

"I don't need a professional." Madison dunked a few fries into ketchup and shoved them into her mouth. Why did her parents expect everything to go back to how it was? Nothing could ever be that way again. "I'm doing fine, really. My grades are as good as ever, so you have nothing to worry about."

"But you haven't gone out in weeks," her mom said. "You can't avoid your friends forever."

"I'm not avoiding them," Madison insisted, although she'd taken to "accidentally" misplacing her phone around the condo so she could "miss" seeing her text messages. Like that one from Oliver yesterday asking if she wanted to go with him to Jackie's volleyball party last night, and the one from Larissa this morning about meeting with their friends for lunch. "Anyway, what's the big deal? Most parents would be happy if their kid went to school, did homework and didn't go to parties."

"We know you, and this isn't your normal behavior." Her mom's voice was strained; she sounded desperate now. "Your dad and I are only trying to help. The last thing we want is for this to ruin the relationships you have with your friends."

"I'm actually going to the pool with some people tomorrow." It was a huge lie, and Madison didn't know why she said it. It might get her parents off her case, but she shuddered at the thought of wearing a bathing suit in public. She would look like a repulsive blimp.

"Good for you." Her mom smiled. "You'll feel better once you get back to a normal routine. But if you feel like you need to talk with a professional, I can make that appointment for you, okay?"

"I'll keep that in mind." She picked up the remaining half

of her cheeseburger, but knowing she had to go to the pool tomorrow made it unappetizing. She would have to keep her cover-up on. And because, despite what she'd told her parents, she wasn't meeting any friends there, she would bring her iPad for company. She could watch a few episodes of *The Vampire Diaries*.

Hopefully her parents wouldn't discover she was going alone, and more important, that no one she knew would see her there.

www.campusbuzz.com

The Hottie from Down Under is hooking up with PEYTON DIAMOND!
Posted on Saturday 10/11 at 12:41 PM

Have you all seen the pictures of our new English teacher, Hunter Sterling, with Peyton Diamond? There are two of them having drinks at the Lobby Bar in the Diamond, and two MORE of her talking with him and some of his friends at the Diamond pool, and of them following her into her private cabana. <u>CLICK HERE</u> to see them all!

I already knew Peyton was a slut—she screwed Oliver Prescott, and who knows how many other guys this summer. Now she can add Hunter to her ever-growing list. She's such a dirty hoe, I don't want to know how many STDs she has. It goes to show: just because she moved from her shitty, rundown trailer park town to a penthouse in the Diamond, she's still total trash. And gross trash, at that. She cakes on so much makeup that it's impossible to tell what she really looks like. Not like guys care, as long as they can get with her.

Her sisters are no better. Courtney Diamond pretends to be holier-than-thou, but everyone knows about her public makeout session with Brett Carmel, her soon-to-be-stepbrother, over the summer. If she's anything like her older sister, I would bet they slept together. And it wasn't only Brett she hooked up with that first week, but Oliver, too. Yeah, you heard me right. Courtney and Oliver went to Mrs. Prescott's charity event over the summer, and they left together. Courtney might be worse than her sister—at least Peyton doesn't hide that she's a dirty slut.

Lastly, there's Savannah. Every time I see her, I want to wring her neck. Not only is she trash, but she's an idiot, too. She actually believed Damien Sanders was interested in her. Newsflash, Savannah: Damien doesn't give two shits about you! He's still leading her on (they disappeared together at that volleyball party last night and couldn't be found for over an hour) and when they got back her cheeks were so flushed, you could tell that they were having sex. Stupid, dirty slut. As if Damien would be interested in an idiot like her. But she makes it so easy for him that you can't blame him for using her. She's pretty much asking to be screwed over—in more ways than one!

Plus, Savannah's so stupid that she actually thinks her youtube channel can make it big. But have you all seen <u>THIS?!</u> In case your ears can't stand it, it's Savannah trying to sing and BUTCHERING Let It Go. Maybe Savannah will finally get a reality check and stop thinking she's hot shit with her youtube channel that's clearly going nowhere. Delete it, bitch, for all our sakes!

1: Posted on Saturday 10/11 at 12:59 PM

any girl (or guy) would have to be blind to not notice how hot hunter sterling he is. and with his sexy australian accent, listening to him speak makes early american puritan stories interesting (and that's saying a lot, because that stuff is sleep inducing.)

it's one thing to LOOK, but from those pics, obviously peyton's hooking up with him. you're right about her being a dirty hoe. out of all the girls hunter could get with, why pick HER?! GROSS.

PS: Listened to Savannah "singing." OMG MY EARS HURT TURN IT OFF!!!

---

2. Posted on Saturday 10/11 at 1:13 PM
wow, you really hate the diamond girls, don't you? if you listen to Savannah's songs on her channel, she has an amazing voice. she's a natural talent. she was just drunk at that party and that song is hard to sing sober, let alone wasted. and no way do i believe for a second that Courtney hooked up with Oliver. She HATES him.

3: Posted on Saturday 10/11 at 1:20 PM
Courtney hates Oliver cause he hooked up with her and ditched her!

---

4. Posted on Saturday 10/11 at 1:23 PM
it's hard to NOT think Peyton's hooking up with Hunter from those pics. And she didn't only bring him into the cabana with her, but those guys that were with him, too! She probably showed them a good time in there...

5: Posted on Saturday 10/11 at 1:27 PM
hell yeah she showed them a good time...between her legs!!!

---

6. Posted on Saturday 10/11 at 1:32 PM
As a guy who's in one of his classes, I've seen Hunter Sterling peek down the hot girls shirts. Larissa, Madison, and Kaitlin, to name a few. The guy's a perv.

7. Posted on Saturday 10/11 at 2:08 PM

If Madison keeps gaining weight, he won't be checking her out for long!!! She's easily put on ten pounds since school started. She was TOO thin this summer, so she looks healthy now, but it would suck for her if she keeps gaining, especially since she talks shit about fat girls all the time...

8. Posted on Saturday 10/11 at 2:17 PM

I can't be the only one who remembers Madison was chunky in middle school, right?

9: Posted on Saturday 10/11 at 2:34 PM

You're definitely not the only one who remembers. Karma's finally giving that bitch what she deserves!!

10: Posted on Saturday 10/11 at 3:14 PM

Wow. There are some terrible things said on this site, but this takes the cake. I've never posted on here before, but whoever started this thread needs a reality check. Because sure, those pictures do make it seem like Peyton and Hunter have crossed the line of what's professional for a student/teacher relationship. But you know what those pictures are NOT? Proof that they're sleeping together. Even if they *are* sleeping together, you don't know the full story. I don't know Peyton or her sisters, and I'm not going to pretend like I do, but it sounds like you don't know them, either. All you're doing is fueling rumors. And judging someone because of where they're from is flat-out LOW. I just hope that most people who read what you posted know better than to assume it's true.

11: Posted on Saturday 10/11 at 3:28 PM
Preach! <3

12: Posted on Saturday 10/11 at 3:58 PM
Poster #10 has a point. But I mean, come on. Look at those pictures. You can't blame someone for assuming Peyton and Hunter are hooking up???

13: Posted on Saturday 10/11 at 4:15 PM
She (or he??) does have a point, but apparently it's one you missed...

chapter 9: *Savannah*

Savannah straightened her last section of hair and checked the time on her iPhone. Thirty minutes until her date with Damien. Her stomach fluttered, and her body felt tingly and on edge. This was the first time a guy had asked her out to dinner just the two of them. And it was *Damien Sanders,* one of the most popular, confident, hottest guys in school.

With nothing else to do while she waited, Savannah brought her laptop over to her bed and browsed Facebook. Then she clicked her YouTube channel. That afternoon, after Evie had left to go back home, she'd recorded and uploaded an acoustic cover. She was curious whether anyone had watched it.

The video had almost one hundred views. Not bad, but nowhere near what she'd hoped for when first making her channel. There were also a few comments, so she scrolled to see what they said.

The one on top, with the most "thumbs-ups," made her stop cold.

Want to see something funny? Check out this AMAZING

video of Savannah Diamond BUTCHERING "Let It Go" from *Frozen!*

Savannah stared at the comment for what must have been minutes, afraid to click the link. Karaoke at Jackie's party last night had been fuzzy, but at the sight of the comment, some memories came back to her. The way she'd been so confident that she'd insisted multiple people record her singing. But then, she'd had so much to drink that it was impossible to focus on the words that went along with the karaoke track without them blurring. And even worse, the song had been much more difficult to sing than she'd anticipated, and the drinks had made her lose control of her voice, so the notes hadn't come out right.

Unable to resist, she clicked the link and cringed while she listened and watched herself. Whoever had posted that was right—she'd forgotten words and missed notes—she *had* butchered the song. And she looked like a giggling idiot while doing so. But hadn't she asked everyone to delete the videos after it happened? They'd all said they would, and after so many drinks, Savannah had just *believed* them. And who was "them" anyway? She vaguely remembered Evie being there, and Alyssa, Jackie, Brooke and Damien, and a bunch of other volleyball girls and football guys.

Which of them had taken videos?

She couldn't remember. It could have been *anyone*. To make it worse, whoever uploaded it had included a comment linking people to the horrible clip under every one of Savannah's videos.

Who hated her enough to do that? Evie had been angry after Savannah had disappeared with Damien, but Evie was her best friend. And, yes, Evie had still been upset when she'd left to go back to California that morning. But she would never do something that cruel…would she?

Savannah wanted to text her to ask, but she couldn't. Because if Evie hadn't posted the video, she would be *more* mad that Savannah suspected her. Plus, why would anyone ever admit to it?

She leaned back in her bed, banging her head against the headboard. She would probably *never* know who'd posted the video. And it was all her fault for drinking too much and singing drunken karaoke. She'd *encouraged* people to record her. How much stupider could she get?

She stayed like that for a few more minutes, hoping that when she opened her eyes again, she would realize she'd dozed off and this had all been a bad dream. But the video was still there. There was no escaping this awful mess.

She had only five more minutes until her date with Damien. They were meeting outside the restaurant, but after seeing that video, Savannah didn't want to go out anymore. She wanted to stay in her room and wallow about her YouTube dreams being crushed because of one mistake at a party.

But Damien was waiting for her, so she dragged herself off the bed and out the door.

As promised, he was waiting by the new Italian restaurant, Adagio, when Savannah arrived. It was packed with people dressed in designer clothing and expensive jewelry, and everything gleamed with sophistication: polished wooden floors, glossy red armchairs and glowing brown walls. Damien hadn't seen her yet, and he looked so at home there, leaning against the railing near the hostess stand. Eating at the finest restaurants was normal for him; Savannah doubted he'd ever been inside a chain like Olive Garden or Chevys, both of which had been special-occasion restaurants when Savannah had lived in Fairfield. And the Diamond placed Adagio in the "casual dining" category.

After living in Vegas for a few months Savannah was growing more comfortable with eating at places like this, but she still looked around in wonder. Sometimes she felt like Cinderella—one day the clock would strike midnight and this Las Vegas fairy tale would end.

She greeted Damien, who was wearing a navy button-down that complemented her royal-blue dress, and the hostess led them to their table—a two-top in the front corner of the restaurant where the ambient noise wasn't quite as loud. They ordered their drinks—a cherry Coke for Savannah and a Sprite for Damien.

"You look beautiful," Damien said after the drinks arrived.

Savannah's cheeks heated, and she looked down at her place setting. "Thanks," she said, taking the silverware out of her napkin and placing it on her lap. She should be acting bubbly and excited to be there with him, but she couldn't bring herself to do it. Not after seeing that awful video online. Instead she studied the menu as if it was the most interesting thing on the planet.

"Is everything okay?" Damien eventually asked, sounding genuinely concerned.

Before she could tell him about the video, the waiter came over. "A selection of artisanal cheeses, to welcome Savannah Diamond to Adagio." He placed a platter of fancy cheeses on the table and told them about each one, although afterward Savannah couldn't remember a word he'd said. "My name is Eduardo and I'll be your server for this evening. Do you know what you'd like to order?"

Savannah went for penne with meatballs—she never could resist classic Italian food—and Damien got veal marsala. Eduardo took away their menus, and Savannah's stomach dropped. No more pretending that she was focusing on the menu and making chitchat about the food.

"Do you remember when I did karaoke last night?" she said, since there was no way she could pretend she wasn't upset. Better to just let Damien know what had happened.

"Yeah." He cleared his throat and sipped his Sprite. "You saw the video, didn't you?"

"You know about it?" Savannah's mouth dropped.

"I saw it just before I left tonight," he said. "I was hoping you hadn't seen it yet. I knew you would eventually, but I wanted to warn you first."

"Do you know who posted it?" Savannah's heart raced, and she sat up straighter. If he knew, maybe they could convince whoever it was to take it down.

"No." He shook his head. "I wish I did, but you asked everyone in that room to record you. And whoever posted it made an anonymous YouTube account."

"Damn it." Savannah rarely cursed, but a non-swear word wouldn't cut it for how angry she was. "This sucks. Maybe I should delete my channel. No one cares about it, anyway."

"That's not true," Damien said. "What about that video of you singing at Imperial Palace? You got great comments on that one, right? And a bunch of views?"

"That was the first video I posted," she said. "Since then, it's gone downhill. I record covers, but barely anyone watches them, and if they do, they don't comment." She sighed and leaned back in her chair. "I should take a hint."

"Don't do that." He sounded alarmed that she was considering it. "You have an incredible voice."

"So why aren't my videos doing well?"

He paused, as if contemplating how to continue. "Do you want the truth?"

"Sure," she said, although from the way he phrased it, she doubted it would be something she wanted to hear. "Why not? Nothing can be worse than having the worst video ever of me singing posted online just so someone can make fun of me."

"All right." He took a deep breath, and Savannah braced herself. "That video of you at Imperial Palace showed off how awesome your voice is. It was just you on stage, focusing on singing, and the recording was high quality because it was done professionally. The rest of your videos are just you playing guitar while singing, using your laptop camera to record, right?"

"Right…" Savannah nodded. At least he'd taken time to check out her channel.

"I don't want this to come off the wrong way," he said. "Because I meant it when I told you you're talented and have an amazing voice. But have you ever taken a guitar lesson?"

"No." Her cheeks heated, and she took a sip of her soda. "It wasn't something that was exactly available to me back in California. And now, with catching up on the Goodman curriculum, volleyball and going out, I haven't thought about when I would have time to fit it in. My guitar playing isn't *that* bad, is it? I can play a few chords and strum songs. Anyway, I'm on YouTube for singing, not to become a famous guitarist."

"Your guitar playing isn't bad," he said. "I don't play, so anyone who can is impressive to me."

"Why do I feel like there's a 'but' to this?"

"When I watch your videos, it seems like focusing on playing guitar distracts you for what you're on YouTube for— singing," he said. "When you're not playing, like in that one video at Imperial Palace, your voice is awesome, you hit every note and it sounds perfect. But when you play guitar and sing at the same time, it gets kind of…off sometimes. It doesn't sound bad, but it might be stopping you from singing at your full potential. And you're using your laptop camera, so the sound isn't as good as it could be. I don't know what it is—maybe the angle you're facing the computer—but the guitar drowns out your voice."

"Wow." Her throat tightened, and she blinked away tears. "Just throw it all at me. My videos are a lot better than a lot of the ones posted on YouTube, you know."

"I don't watch a lot of singers on YouTube, so I wouldn't know, but I trust you on that," he said. "But don't you want to be the best?"

"Yeah." She shrugged. "But according to you, I suck at guitar, so that's not going to happen."

"I never said you sucked at guitar," he said gently. "Just that it might not hurt to take some lessons. But your voice is incredible. And I think I know how you can make your channel awesome."

"Oh, yeah?" she asked, doubtful. "Because no offense, but what do you know about any of this?"

"Just hear me out," he said, and she sat back, motioning for him to continue. "Goodman has a great recording studio in our arts building. Last year I took an elective in recording—I thought it would be easy. It was harder than I thought, but now I know my way around the studio. So I've got two main ideas. The first is that we find someone to play guitar—the artsy kids hang out around the studio all the time, and I'm sure one of them will want to do it—and practice a few songs with them. We'll pick the best ones, then record you singing using the professional equipment, with someone filming it. The other is that we first make a studio recording of you sing-

ing to a karaoke track, and then get your stepbrother, Brett—
he's into filming, right?—to edit a video of you dancing and
singing along in a cool location. Or we can do both, depending on what works best for the song."

She sat back, amazed. Who knew Damien was creative?

"So…what do you say?" he asked.

"Those are good ideas," she said. "But can anyone just walk
into the recording studio and use it?"

"As long as you sign up for an open time slot," he said.
"And it's not usually busy. I know you've got volleyball after
school, so I was thinking we could do it during lunch block."

"You would give up lunch with your friends to help me
with this?"

"You bet I would," he said. "Whoever posted that video
from last night deserves for you to post an awesome video of
you singing to prove how wrong they are about you. So, are
you in?"

"I don't know." She rested her elbows on the table, even
though it was something Rebecca repeatedly told her not to do
at dinner. "Now that the video from last night is out there…
I'm not sure if people will ever be able to forget it. This is
probably a waste of time."

"They *will* forget it, once they see a newer recording that
shows how talented you are," he said. She was about to say
how he was wrong, but he continued before she had a chance.
"Come on, Savannah. Whoever posted that video was trying
to tear you down. You're not going to let them win, are you?"

Something about his tone made her realize he wasn't going
to accept no for an answer.

"I guess it can't hurt to try," she said, which earned a smile
from him. "If you want to help me with recording, then,
sure, I'm in."

Dinner arrived, and throughout the meal they brainstormed ways to use social media to make Savannah's YouTube channel more popular. The food was amazing, of course, but secondary to the conversation.

"You're really good at this stuff," Savannah said once they'd finished their meals. "Are you going to major in marketing or publicity in college?"

"I haven't thought about it much." He shrugged, his eyes distant, and then he snapped back into focus. "I've heard most people start college planning on doing one thing and end up doing something completely different, so I assume I'll figure it out eventually. But a lot of my friends think I have no direction."

"Who told you that?" Savannah asked. After the way he'd gotten so excited brainstorming how to turn around her YouTube channel, she couldn't imagine him having no direction.

"Madison."

"Oh." Savannah played with the remains of her food. "What's going on between you two?" She tried to sound nonchalant, but she hoped more than anything that he was over her.

"I don't know," he said, and Savannah's heart dropped. "She's been acting really weird for the past few weeks."

"How so?" Savannah didn't particularly want to talk about Madison, especially on a date with Damien, but she was curious about this "weird behavior." Especially because lately, whenever Savannah walked by Madison in school, Madison watched her like she was trying to figure her out. Then if their eyes met, Madison would glare and walk away.

"She's stopped going out with her friends," he said. "We've called and texted her to find out what's wrong, but she rarely responds. I've seen her get upset before, but this is different.

She still follows the motions of being social at school, but I can tell it's hard for her, and I'm worried about her."

"That's strange." Savannah couldn't think of anything else to say. After the awful way Madison had treated her over the summer, Savannah thought she deserved to have something go wrong in her perfect life. But she wasn't going to say that out loud—after what Damien had told her, it would sound pretty nasty. "I hope she's okay."

"Me, too," he said. "Hopefully whatever's bothering her is just a phase and she'll snap out of it soon. But enough about Madison. What do you say we check out the new vodka bar? I hear they make a great cotton-candy martini, and I'm curious about the bacon-flavored vodka."

"Bacon-flavored vodka?" Savannah wrinkled her nose. "That sounds disgusting!"

"They have peanut-butter-flavored vodka, too."

"You got me there," she said. "Peanut butter is my favorite. Well, maybe not my *favorite* favorite—that would be chocolate. Or pancakes. But I have to wake up early tomorrow. My grandma wants to chat on Skype with me and my sisters before she leaves for church."

Which was true, but Savannah had withheld the important fact about that Skype call: her mom had just started outpatient treatment and had moved in with Grandma, so they would be talking to her, too.

The thought of the upcoming conversation made Savannah queasy, and she regretted eating so much pasta. She hadn't spoken to her mom since before the move to Vegas—before she'd realized how much had been kept secret from her and her sisters. She wished she could see her mom in person, but her recovery was a slow process, and they had to take it a step at a time. She and her sisters weren't supposed to bombard her with too many questions. It would be hard, since Savannah had so much she wanted to ask, but she loved her mom and wanted to see her get better.

"Are you okay?" Damien asked.

"I'm fine," she said, forcing the thoughts of her mom out of her mind. "Was just thinking about family stuff. And honestly, I don't think I'm fully recovered from last night."

"We can call it a night," he said, placing his napkin on the table. "Want to meet outside the recording studio on Monday during lunch? We'll see which music kids are around and recruit them to our cause."

"Our 'cause'?" Savannah repeated. He was really getting into this.

"Yep," he said. "Our cause to make you famous."

chapter 10: *Courtney*

Habitat had been so exhausting yesterday that Courtney had fallen asleep at seven-thirty on a Saturday night. But she'd tossed and turned, because all she could think about was the Skype conversation with her mom this morning. It had been easy for her to wake up at six-thirty—she'd always been a morning person—and she finished her Cheerios as she waited for Savannah and Peyton to join her in the dining room, where she'd set up her laptop. Her stomach swirled as she thought about talking to her mom for the first time in months, and she regretted eating when she was nervous.

Savannah pranced into the dining room still wearing her pink pajamas, singing the newest One Connection song. As always, each note sounded perfect. Courtney couldn't help dancing along. If Savannah was nervous to speak with their mom, she didn't look it.

"How was your Habitat build yesterday? Did you have fun with Brett?" Savannah emphasized his name and raised her eyebrows. "I was so bummed when I came back from dinner and you'd crashed already. I wanted all the details!"

"You know nothing can happen between me and Brett," Courtney repeated for what felt like the billionth time. "Adrian and Rebecca were clear that he's off-limits. Brett and I are friends—nothing more." Maybe if she kept saying it, she would start believing it. Plus, she wanted to be a good influence on Savannah, which meant not breaking the rules. "And Habitat was great until I got stuck painting next to Oliver in the afternoon. He actually had the nerve to hit on me. I couldn't believe it, since he knows that we know about that stupid bet he made over the summer. As if I would *ever* be interested in him. Ugh." She shuddered.

"Oliver woke up early on a Saturday morning to build houses?" Savannah asked, pouring herself a glass of orange juice.

"He wasn't happy about it," Courtney said. "And he was all too proud to tell me why he *was* there—he's in trouble with his parents for partying too much. They're forcing him to join extracurriculars, so he chose Habitat, thinking it would be easy. If he's caught in any more scandals, they're threatening to send him to boarding school."

"That's interesting," Savannah said thoughtfully, glancing at her phone.

Courtney didn't have time to ask what she meant, because Peyton came stomping out of her room, her hair unbrushed and her eyes half-closed. "I need coffee *now*," she grumbled, stumbling to the Keurig and brewing a cup. "Whose brilliant idea was it to do this so early on a Sunday again?"

"Grandma's," Courtney reminded her. "She's getting Mom on an early rising, early-to-bed schedule, and they have church at nine."

"It'll be so strange to talk to her," Savannah said, curling into a ball on the chair.

"I know," Courtney agreed. "But we have to remember what Grandma told us. Even though we're upset and angry at Mom for keeping so many secrets, she's in a fragile state and she's nervous about facing us—more so than we are about talking to her. We don't want to upset her and trigger a relapse. It's going to be hard, but we have to act as normal as we can while talking to her, okay? No yelling or attacking her about how she lied to us for all our lives."

Despite Adrian telling them that her parents' decision to keep them away from him had been for the best, Courtney couldn't help sounding bitter. She and her sisters deserved to have known him before now. Their mom shouldn't have kept them separated for so long.

"Since we're only supposed to say nice things, I'll stand in the background and say nothing," Peyton said while inhaling her huge cup of coffee.

"If that's what it takes for you to be civil to Mom, then fine," Courtney said. "Are you both ready?"

Savannah nodded, and Peyton shrugged—which Courtney took as a yes—and she initiated the Skype call. She'd used her credit card to buy and deliver the newest Apple computer to Grandma, and they'd been chatting on Skype for the past few weeks, so they were both familiar with the program. Grandma accepted the call, and a picture of her and Mom popped up on the screen. Courtney took a sharp breath inward, looking closer to verify that the woman next to Grandma was *Mom*.

Her skin, which used to have red blotches on the cheeks and fine lines on the forehead, was fair and smooth. There were no baggy dark circles under her blue eyes, and she'd lost enough weight so that her face, which used to be round and puffy, was defined and glowing. Even her dark blond hair looked healthier, with the scraggly split ends trimmed into a layered below-the-shoulders cut. She looked…healthy. And young. Like the clock had been rewound ten years.

"Wow, Mom," Savannah was the first to speak. "You look amazing."

"Thanks, baby." Their mom smiled, and her teeth looked whiter, too. "And you look so sophisticated and grown-up. Your hair got so long!"

"They're extensions, Mom." Savannah pulled her long blond hair in front of her shoulders and twirled it around her fingers. "I got them over the summer."

"Of course." She continued smiling, but it looked forced now. "Have you all been settling into your new place? And liking your new school?"

"It's nice, but different," Courtney said. "I miss being home sometimes." It was silly, since their penthouse in the Diamond was a palace compared to their cramped, run-down apartment in Fairfield, and the Goodman School was a far superior learning environment than Fairfield High, but sometimes Courtney missed the familiarity of the life she'd left behind.

Once the initial awkwardness disappeared, their mom told them about how much better she was doing now, and apologized for not seeking treatment sooner. She swore she wouldn't relapse. Courtney hoped she was right, but she'd witnessed her mom saying she would never drink again so many times that she had trouble having complete faith that this would stick.

"I know it'll take time for you to trust me again, and I take full responsibility for that, but hope the three of you can one day forgive me for what I put you through, and that we'll be able to move forward and create new, better memories," their mom eventually said. "I don't expect it to be now, or even soon, but hopefully in the future it will be possible." It sounded rehearsed, as though her therapists had helped her craft what to say to them, but she was trying. That was more than they'd gotten from her before.

"Thanks, Mom," Courtney said. "I appreciate it. And Adrian told us about what happened when I was a baby, so we understand why you were scared to keep us in Vegas."

The smile disappeared from her face. "He told you?" she croaked. "But he promised…"

"What did he tell you?" Grandma asked Courtney, wrapping an arm around their mom's shoulders.

"He told us that I was kidnapped for ransom, and my nanny was killed," Courtney said, playing with her key necklace. What had she said wrong? She thought Mom would be happy that she understood how scary the kidnapping must have been for her. "And how once you got me back, you and Adrian agreed Vegas wasn't safe for us, and it wasn't safe for us to be around him, either. Which was why we were raised without him in our lives?" She said the last part as a question, because it had always sounded like a stretch. Yes, Adrian was worried about them, but letting that worry keep him from his daughters sounded so extreme.

Their mom let out a breath. "Yes," she said, relaxing into her chair. "What happened was extremely hard on Adrian and me, and we did what we thought was right at the time."

At the time. Not what was *actually* right. But Courtney held her tongue, keeping her promise to not say anything that might upset Mom.

"Anyway, how would you girls feel about visiting for Thanksgiving?" Grandma's voice was overly perky. "Adrian insisted on buying me a new house large enough to accommodate myself, Aunt Sophie, your mom and the three of you if you choose to visit."

"I thought you hated taking charity," Peyton said in distaste.

"I do dislike handouts," Grandma said. "But he was insistent, and his points on why it was for the best were so sound that if I had refused, it would have only hurt everyone I care about."

Courtney wanted to ask how Aunt Sophie was doing, but she stopped herself. Whenever Aunt Sophie was having a good day, she made an effort to say hi during their conversations. Which meant this morning must not be a good one.

Ever since Aunt Sophie had been diagnosed with terminal cancer last year and moved in with Grandma, it had been hard on their grandmother. Courtney couldn't imagine knowing you were losing a sister, let alone a twin. The tough way Grandma carried on with life inspired her.

"Do you think we can visit over Thanksgiving?" Savannah asked Courtney, her eyes wide.

"As long as Adrian's okay with it, we'll visit over Thanksgiving," Courtney said to Grandma. She disliked needing his permission, since she was adult enough to make decisions like this on her own, but he was their legal guardian now.

"Perfect." Grandma smiled. "If we talk any longer we'll be late for church, but I'm glad we got to catch up."

"And I'm glad to see you girls, even if it's only on the computer," their mom said, reaching for the screen. "I can't wait to see you over Thanksgiving. I love you."

"Love you, too," Courtney said, Savannah echoing her. Peyton said a simple bye, and Courtney closed out the conversation.

"That wasn't as hard as I thought," Savannah said. "And

Mom looked amazing, like she was ten years younger. I really think rehab is going to stick."

She sounded hopeful, so Courtney nodded, trying to look just as optimistic.

"What's wrong?" Savannah asked. "Don't you think rehab will work?"

"It's not that," Courtney said. "I agree that Mom looks better than ever."

"So, what is it?"

"It was Mom's reaction when I mentioned the kidnapping," she said. "She was so worried, as if I knew something I shouldn't. But when I told her what Adrian told us, she was relieved. Almost like there was something more to the story that they're keeping from us."

"What could they be keeping from us?" Savannah asked. "Adrian told us what happened."

"He did, but he looked so sad," Courtney said. "The ending to the story was happy—he got me back safe, and hired us bodyguards so it wouldn't happen again. It seems like an extreme reaction to cut us out of his life until now."

"Maybe he just wasn't interested in being around little kids," Peyton said, finishing off the last of her coffee.

Savannah crossed her arms and narrowed her eyes at her.

"What?" Peyton said. "Some people don't like little kids. I have trouble imagining Adrian playing tea party with a two-year-old."

"I don't think that's it," Courtney said, although she couldn't picture Adrian playing tea party with two-year-olds, either. Their mom also lost patience easily. It was probably why they'd had a nanny. "I don't know if I'm reading into things too much, but whenever I mention the kidnapping to anyone who lived through it, they get this scared look, as if I've heard something I shouldn't. I get a sense that there's something they're not telling me—something big that I should know."

"I haven't noticed," Peyton said. "But if you're convinced there's more, you could try seeing your secret records."

Courtney whipped her head to look at Peyton. "My *what?*"

"Your records," Peyton repeated. "This summer, Jackson told me that there are records kept on all of us, for our personal security. Maybe there's something in them about the kidnapping."

"Are we allowed to see these records?"

"Don't think so," Peyton said. "I think Jackson slipped when he mentioned it to me. I asked him if I could see mine, and he said no way."

"Great." Courtney crossed her arms and leaned back in her chair. How was she supposed to hack into secret records that were most likely kept on Adrian's computer, guarded with a password in his office surrounded by security men and cameras?

That was a task for the people in that *Ocean's Eleven* movie—not her.

She didn't have much time to worry about it, because someone knocked on the door. She answered it, and found Adrian and Rebecca waiting in the hall. He'd returned from his trip to China today, and had promised he would stop by. He was dressed casually, in a navy button-down and black dress pants; and Rebecca looked like she was on her way to the gym, in yoga pants and a draping black shirt, her brown hair pulled back in a ponytail.

Adrian, as usual, got straight to the point. "Have you finished the Skype call with your mom?"

"Yeah." Courtney motioned for them to come in.

"How's she doing?"

"She looks really good," Courtney said. "Much healthier, and she sounds happier, too."

"And Grandma invited us to visit over Thanksgiving," Savannah said. "Is it okay if we go?"

Adrian paused and looked at Rebecca, as if she knew the answer.

"I don't see why not," Rebecca said.

"Do you girls want to go?" he asked.

"Yes," Savannah said, nearly bouncing out of her chair. Courtney agreed, and Peyton shrugged, which was her way of saying *sure*.

"Then you can visit your grandma and mom over Thanksgiving," Adrian said. "On one condition."

"What's the condition?" Courtney's stomach knotted.

"That you spend Christmas with me."

"Here, in Vegas?" Savannah asked.

"We could do that," Adrian said. "Or we could go to New York to see the Christmas tree at Rockefeller Center and the Rockettes show at Radio City, St. Kitts to spend Christmas relaxing on the beach, Rome to see the Pope speak at the Vatican or whatever other ideas you have. We'll figure something out. But I want to spend Christmas together, as a family." He put his arm around Rebecca's shoulders, and the two of them shared a smile.

"We could extend the trip through New Years," Rebecca added. "I've heard the fireworks over the Coliseum are spectacular."

"That sounds fair," Courtney said, although it was hard to imagine Christmas not at home, with Mom and Grandma. Grandma always cooked dinner on Christmas Eve at her place, and they listened to her cheesy CD of Christmas carols while they ate. When they got home, they watched Christmas movies on TV until the clock struck eleven-thirty, and then their mom forced them to bed so they wouldn't be awake when Santa came through the window. (They didn't have a chimney, so Mom insisted Santa entered through the window.) In the morning, there would be a present-opening frenzy.

When Courtney was younger, she'd thought the presents came from Santa, but as she'd gotten older, she'd wondered where Mom got the money to buy the gifts. Now she suspected that for that one day every year, their mom had accepted financial help from Adrian.

"Perfect," Adrian said. "I'll have your travel arrangements for Thanksgiving arranged. I'm glad your mom is doing better."

"She is," Courtney said. "But there was something about the conversation that struck me as strange."

Peyton and Savannah looked surprised—apparently they hadn't expected her to bring it up to Adrian. But Courtney was too curious to let this go.

"And what was that?" Adrian asked.

"At one point, I mentioned the kidnapping," Courtney started, playing with her hands. "Mom was shocked that I brought it up, like she didn't want me to know. But then Grandma asked me to tell her what you told me, and after I did, she was relieved. It...made me feel like there's something you aren't telling me." She felt bad accusing Adrian of lying, but she couldn't let this slide.

Adrian's face hardened, and Rebecca toyed with her pearl necklace—something she did when she was nervous. Was Rebecca in on this, too?

"I've told you everything you need to know," Adrian said smoothly. "Your mom must have been worried that you were going to get angry at her for keeping the kidnapping from you, and relaxed once she realized that wasn't the case. Anyway, I'm jet-lagged from the trip, so I'm going to get some rest and get caught up on some work. I'll see you all for dinner tonight. Seven-thirty at the Five Diamond."

"And I'm going to the spa this afternoon, but I have some time before my appointment if you girls want to join me for brunch," Rebecca said.

Savannah and Peyton said they could go, but Courtney had a lot of homework and studying. Yesterday she'd been too tired after getting back from the Habitat build to focus.

But when she brought her laptop back into her room to work, her mind kept wandering to what Adrian had said. Telling her "everything she needed to know" wasn't the same as telling her *everything*. And her mom's reaction was more than relief that Courtney wasn't going to yell at her over Skype.

What was everyone hiding? And how would Courtney get them to tell her the truth? It had been clear from Adrian's response that her suspicions wouldn't be enough to get him to budge.

Whatever the secret was, she would have to uncover it herself.

chapter 11: *Peyton*

"And in the gift bags for the kids, we can include the latest iPod," Rebecca suggested, writing the idea down in her iPad.

"Good idea," Savannah said. "We can load it with my Sweet Sixteen playlist."

All through brunch, Peyton had been listening to Rebecca and Savannah plan Savannah's Sweet Sixteen party for her birthday in December. It was becoming an all-out extravaganza. When Peyton had turned sixteen, her mom had taken her and her sisters to a Tex-Mex restaurant, where she'd been forced to wear a sombrero while the wait staff sang "Happy Birthday" in Spanish. When it was time to leave, her mom had been so sloshed on giant margaritas that Peyton had driven the family home. Then she'd snuck out—which was easy to do when Mom was passed out—to meet up with friends. They'd seen some guys from a band they knew play a local show and had hung out at a diner until sunrise, where they'd talked, laughed and gorged themselves on pancakes and milk shakes.

Savannah's party, on the other hand, would be at Abandon

Nightclub, two weeks before the club officially opened in the Diamond Residences. It sounded like it would be bigger than a wedding. The theme of the party was music, and Savannah and Rebecca had been discussing the details of centerpieces, color schemes, food options and gift bags for the past hour.

But Peyton had been unable to focus on the conversation, because she was seething about an incredibly awful Campus-buzz forum post that a girl from one of her classes had linked her to last night. Peyton didn't spend much time online, but apparently someone had posted something "so terrible about her and her sisters" that she had to see it. So she'd clicked the link.

The first two images on it were the ones of her and Hunter at the Lobby Bar—the pictures she remembered *deleting* from Madison Lockhart's phone. Madison must have backed them up. There were more photos of her and Hunter around the pool—photos that Madison easily could have taken, since she also lived in the Diamond Residences.

Madison had obviously written the post.

Not unexpectedly, the things Madison had written about Peyton were downright cruel. Every sentence made her angrier than the last, until Peyton had gotten so pissed that she'd wanted to punch the computer screen. But despite all of that, she might have been able to let it go…if Madison hadn't continued on to insult Courtney and Savannah. The section about Courtney was all lies, and the one about Savannah linked to an awful video of her singing drunken karaoke. Savannah was trying so hard to make her YouTube channel a success. When she saw what Madison had posted about her, it would crush her.

Madison was a cruel, hateful, jealous bitch.

So while Savannah and Rebecca were chatting about party

ideas, Peyton was brainstorming ways to knock Madison off her pedestal. She had a few thoughts, and was leaning toward one of them. If she could pull it off, Madison would get what she deserved.

Finally the brunch/party planning session ended, and Rebecca went to the spa while Peyton and Savannah headed to the pool. Peyton had been so distracted by the forum post and the Skype call with Mom and Grandma that she'd forgotten to reserve a cabana at the main pool that morning, and they were all booked, so she and Savannah went to the exclusive Diamond Residences rooftop pool instead. It was smaller than the main one, more for wading than swimming, but there were plenty of open chairs. They laid down their towels and situated themselves for a day of soaking up the sun.

"How was your dinner with Damien last night?" Peyton asked Savannah as she sprayed on her tanning oil. "You went to bed so quickly after coming back that I didn't get a chance to ask."

"Sorry," Savannah said. "I had a rough night, so I went to bed early."

"What happened?" Peyton stopped midspray to look at Savannah. "Damien didn't do anything to you, did he?"

"No!" Savannah's eyes widened. "Dinner went well. But right before we left, I saw this video someone posted of me singing…." Her voice shook, and she took a few sips from her water bottle. "It was so awful. I was at that volleyball party on Friday night, and I had too much to drink, and people were doing karaoke. So I stupidly decided to sing a really hard song without any practice. A bunch of people recorded it, then someone created a fake YouTube account and posted the video, and I have no idea who did it. I talked with Damien about it

last night, and he had ideas to help my YouTube channel…
but I wish I knew who posted that video."

"I know who posted it." Peyton ground her teeth, her
body tense.

"What?" Savannah gasped. "How could *you* know?"

"You found the video through that Campusbuzz post,
right?"

"No…" Savannah shook her head. "Someone linked it in
a comment to my videos. What Campusbuzz post?"

Crap. Savannah hadn't seen it. And now that Peyton had
mentioned it, she couldn't keep it from her sister.

"This one." Peyton took out her iPhone, brought up the
post on the website and handed it to Savannah. She hated
knowing what her sister was about to read. "Prepare yourself—it's harsh."

It took Savannah a few minutes to read, and she occasionally glanced up at Peyton, saying "Omigosh," "I can't believe
someone wrote this" or something of the sort.

"Wow," she said once she was finished, her eyes still locked
on the screen. "Whoever wrote this *hates* us."

"Yeah," Peyton agreed. "You could say that."

They sat in silence as Savannah read it again.

"I know the stuff about me isn't true, and neither is the
stuff about Courtney…but you didn't hook up with Hunter
Sterling, did you?"

Peyton laughed. Out of everything in the post, *that* was
the first thing Savannah asked? "No," she said. "I've seen him
around and talked with him, but that's all."

"Okay." Savannah handed the phone back to Peyton. "But
how do you know who posted the video?"

"Because I know who posted *this*." Peyton pointed to her

phone. "And the person who wrote it has to be the same person who uploaded the video."

"It seems like it," Savannah said. "But you can't know who wrote the forum post. It's all anonymous."

"I *do* know, because I know who took those pictures of me and Hunter at the bar." With that, Peyton summarized what had happened that day with Madison—how she'd caught her taking the pictures, approached her about it, been reinforced by Jackson and deleted the photos from her phone. "She must have backed them up before I deleted them," she said. "Because I remember what the photos looked like, and they're the same ones that are on that forum post. And since Madison lives at the Diamond, she could have been at the pool that day to get the other photos." She paused to see if Savannah was going to disagree, and when she didn't, she continued, "Did you see Madison at Jackie's volleyball party on Friday?"

"No." Savannah shrugged. "But I drank a lot, so everything's blurry. Damien and Oliver were both there, and Madison's close friends were with them, so it's possible she showed up by the time karaoke started."

"It's more than possible," Peyton said. "I would bet she was there. And we know she isn't fond of us. She *has* to be the one behind the post."

"It makes sense," Savannah agreed. "I knew she was mean, but wow, this takes it to a new level. I just wish there was a way we could…" She paused and glanced at the sky, as if searching for the right word.

"Get back at her?" Peyton supplied.

"Yeah," Savannah said. "To make her stop being so awful to us."

"Well…" Peyton took a deep breath and chipped at her nail polish. "I have an idea of how we can do that."

"What is it?"

"It stems from something that happened last summer." Peyton sipped from her water bottle, contemplating how to word it so she didn't sound like an awful sister. "I didn't mention it because I wanted to forget it happened, but...I slept with Oliver."

"*What?*" Savannah said so loudly that some people turned to look at her. She lowered her voice and continued, "You had *sex* with Oliver? When? And *why?* Especially since you knew he had that stupid bet about trying to sleep with all of us."

"Yes, I had sex with Oliver." Peyton fidgeted, wanting to get past this part of the story and on to the part about getting back at Madison. "I'm not proud of it, which is why I didn't tell anyone, but it's done. When it happened, I didn't know about the bet."

"And we found out about the bet the night of the grand opening, so you had to have hooked up with him the first week we were in town."

"Yep." Peyton nodded, waiting for her sister to piece it together.

"But Oliver was interested in Courtney that week. He went to that charity event and to the grand opening with her. So it had to have been *before* he asked Courtney out, because you wouldn't sleep with him if you thought Courtney was interested in him...right?"

"Of course it was before he asked Courtney out." Peyton couldn't believe Savannah would consider otherwise.

"Omigosh." Savannah's eyebrows shot up, and she ran her hands through her hair. "It wasn't the first night you met him, was it? The night we got here—on the Fourth of July?"

"It was," Peyton admitted, unable to look at her sister. "It was the only one-night stand I've ever had, and it was stupid.

I was so angry about everything—about Mom putting her drinking before us, about us getting shipped away and about her lying to us about Adrian, that I wasn't thinking straight. Oliver and I started dancing, and he was hot, and one thing led to another. There were a few days when I thought I was interested in him...but it all went to hell that night he asked Courtney to his mom's charity event instead of me."

"Wow," Savannah said. "I remember that dinner, when Oliver's mom encouraged him to ask Courtney to that event, but I had no idea about what was going on with you and Oliver. Courtney didn't, either. She wouldn't have gone with him if she did."

"I know," Peyton said. "I never blamed Courtney."

"Oliver's such a jerk." Savannah huffed and crossed her arms. "It was probably part of his stupid plan to try sleeping with all of us."

"His mom did seem intent on him taking *Courtney* to the event, but I thought I liked him at the time, and I was pissed about it," she said. "I was going to tell Courtney that night, but she didn't come to Luxe with us because she wasn't feeling well. But Oliver was there, so I asked him why he didn't ask *me* to the event, and we got into a big fight. He was a total ass—he said he wasn't interested in me, but that he might be interested in Courtney, and he gloated about how he could easily get her to fall for him. I said there wasn't a chance in hell that Courtney would be interested in him, especially once I told her how he'd already hooked up with me."

"What did Courtney do when you told her?" Savannah asked. "And why didn't either of you tell me about this?"

"I never told Courtney. I haven't told anyone until now."

"What?" Savannah's eyes bugged out. "Why not?"

"Because Oliver...made a bet with me." Peyton chewed the inside of her cheek—this was the part Savannah might take the wrong way. "He said if I didn't tell Courtney about our conversation and I was right about her not falling for him, he would do any one task I asked of him. If Courtney *did* fall for him, I would have to do one task he asked of *me*. But I knew Courtney wouldn't go for him, so I took him up on it."

"Then Courtney kissed Brett at the grand opening," Savannah said. "So Oliver lost the bet. But why didn't you tell Courtney afterward?"

"If she'd known that Oliver and I had a thing first, she would have felt bad about going out with him," Peyton said. "But it was over—Courtney wasn't interested in Oliver, and I wasn't interested in him anymore, either. So I let it drop."

"If I were in Courtney's place, I would want you to tell me." Savannah bit her lower lip. "What if he says something to her first?"

"Oliver wouldn't brag about losing a bet," she said. "Besides, you're not asking the important question."

"What question?"

"I won the bet. Aren't you curious about what I asked Oliver to do?"

"Sure," she said. "What was it?"

Peyton paused for dramatic effect, then said, "I haven't asked him to do anything yet, because I've been waiting for the perfect moment. And that time is now. I can use my winning the bet to get back at Madison."

"How?" Savannah scrunched her forehead. "Are you gonna ask Oliver to do something to Madison? Because they're really good friends… I can't imagine him turning on her."

"Just wait and see—I have a plan."

Peyton picked up her phone and took a deep breath—could she really do this? Then she glanced at the Campusbuzz post again, and fresh anger surged through her veins. Madison couldn't say that crap about her and her sisters without any consequences.

She opened her messages and texted Oliver.

I know what I want you to do for the bet.

His reply came seconds later.

finally. care to share???

Meet me at the rooftop pool at the Diamond residences and I'll tell you...

be there in 15. looking forward to hearing what u got planned ;)

She placed her phone beside her and smiled. He wouldn't be happy when he realized what she had in store for him. But if he had the balls to follow through—which she suspected he did—Madison would get the payback she deserved. She would learn she couldn't publicly bully the Diamond sisters and get away with it.

"Are you going to tell me this plan, or leave me wondering?" Savannah asked.

"Oliver will get here soon," she said. "Once he does, you'll see for yourself."

Fifteen minutes later, Oliver strolled through the pool entrance in his Ray-Ban Wayfarer shades, a towel thrown over his shoulder like he owned the place. He smirked when he saw them, tossed the towel onto the chair next to Peyton's and peeled off his T-shirt to reveal his toned, tanned chest. It was impossible not to watch his every move. The waitress came over to take his drink order, and he flashed his fake ID and asked for a mojito.

"Put it on my tab," Peyton said, and the waitress hurried off to get his drink. She smiled at Oliver, reminding herself that *she* was the one in charge. "Glad you could make it."

"It's been a while," he said. "I guess you told Little Diamond about our deal?"

Savannah frowned, her petite features pinched. "You're only one year older than me."

"Feisty." Oliver laughed. "I like it." The waitress came back with his mojito, and he took a long sip.

"I did tell Savannah." Peyton settled into her chair, enjoying how carefree Oliver was right now. She couldn't wait to see his shift in attitude once she told him her plan. "And I have the perfect task for you."

"What'll it be?" He rubbed his hands together, looking ready to take on anything. "It's taken you long enough, so this better be good."

"I want you to have sex with Madison."

"Whoa." Oliver put his hands out. "Madison and I have been friends since lower school. She doesn't think of me that way, and I don't think of her that way."

"That makes you one of the few guys at school who doesn't." Peyton knew that Madison and Oliver were only friends—it was part of what made this task perfect. "But you like to brag about how you can get any girl to fall for you. If that's true, then Madison will be your biggest challenge yet."

"Look, Peyton, seriously now." Oliver's voice shook, and he ran his hand through his hair. "This is about more than that. Madison would kill me if she knew I was telling you, but she's a virgin. She wants her first time to be special or whatever. I can't take that from her because of a bet."

Peyton nodded, since she'd only been in Vegas for a few months, and even *she* knew that Madison was a virgin. Everyone at school knew.... People talked about it on Campusbuzz. It was the fact that Madison's first time would be because of a bet—and the heartbreak that would follow when Peyton spilled the truth to her afterward—that would make this revenge perfect.

But her breath hitched at the reminder of what she was taking away from Madison. For the rest of Madison's life, she would have to live with having lost her virginity in this awful way. Was it *too* extreme? Maybe. But it never would have come to this if Madison hadn't hated Peyton and her sisters for no reason and posted all that crap online about them. Who was to say she would ever stop the cruelty towards them...and to others? Unless someone did something, she probably wouldn't, and she shouldn't be able to keep getting away with it.

"Maybe you're the best person to take Madison's virginity," Peyton said, surprising herself by how calm she sounded. "If you're such great friends, then you trust each other. It's better that you're her first than some guy who will use her and forget about her."

"Clearly you don't know Madison if you think she would let anyone use her like that," Oliver said.

"Maybe not," Peyton said. "But we had a deal, and this is the task I've chosen for you. I didn't expect you to be so resistant. I mean, I'm asking you to sleep with one of the hottest girls in school. Don't tell me that in all your years of friendship, you haven't fantasized about her at least once."

"It doesn't matter what I've thought," he said, although he couldn't look at Peyton. "I would never hurt Madison like that, or risk ruining my friendship with her. What are your other ideas?"

Peyton was surprised; she hadn't thought it would take this much convincing. Oliver didn't have the reputation of being the most moral guy around. She'd originally thought of this only to get back at Madison, but now she realized it would also be payback to Oliver for the bet he'd made about her and her sisters. And despite the sinking feeling in her stomach about how awful it sounded when said aloud, she was determined for him go through with it. "No other ideas," she said. "This is your task."

"What if I say no?" Oliver leaned back and sipped his mojito. "This has been entertaining, but you can't *make* me do anything."

Peyton frowned. He was right—she couldn't force him. She'd just assumed he would follow through because he loved to gamble, and he didn't seem like the type to turn down a challenge.

His smirk sent fire through her veins.

"Courtney told us about your conversation with her yesterday during Habitat—about how your parents are going to send you to boarding school if you get in any more trouble for partying," Savannah chimed in.

"What's it to you?" Oliver asked.

"Remember Jackie's party Friday night?" Savannah asked, which was clearly rhetorical, since that was only two days ago. "My friend Evie and I took a bunch of pictures for her to share with our friends back home. Does this look familiar?"

Savannah brought out her iPhone, tapped on the screen a few times and handed it to Peyton for her to show to Oliver. Peyton checked it out and smiled triumphantly. It was a perfectly timed action shot of Oliver sitting with a group of friends around a table, doing a line of coke. She sent the photo to herself for backup and handed it to him.

His nostrils flared, his hands shaking. "This proves nothing," he finally said. "It could be Photoshopped."

"But it's not, and that won't be anyone's first thought if it shows up on Facebook. And if we tag your parents in the picture..." Peyton tsked and shook her head. "Off to boarding school you go."

Oliver tapped the screen and handed the phone back to

Peyton. "Well, that's not going to happen, because I deleted it. Nice try, though."

"As if I didn't send myself a copy first." Peyton rolled her eyes and gave the phone back to Savannah.

"And while you two were talking, I emailed it to myself for backup," Savannah added.

Oliver glared at both of them. "You would really destroy my life over this?"

"We made a deal," Peyton reminded him, although this *was* going further than she'd imagined. But now she was irritated that Oliver was being so resistant—especially because the bet he'd made over the summer involved him taking Courtney *and* Savannah's virginity without caring. Why should Madison's be different to him? "I won our bet, so you have to do any task I want. I'm sorry you don't like my choice, but I'm not changing my mind."

"Why do you hate Madison so much?" he asked. "I know she hasn't been welcoming to you and your sisters, but isn't this an extreme way to get back at someone for not wanting to be friends with you?"

"I have my reasons, and they're more than Madison 'not wanting to be friends with me.'" Peyton held his gaze, remembering the awful things Madison had said about her and her sisters on that forum. And it wasn't only that one post that she *knew* Madison wrote—there had been other cruel posts about them since they'd moved here. Peyton had browsed them last night. Who knew how many Madison was behind?

"You're going to make Madison fall for you, and then you're going to take her virginity." Peyton swallowed back the bitter taste in her throat, trying to ignore how harsh this sounded. "You can do it. And if I don't think you're trying…then that picture goes online, and off you go to boarding school."

"Fine." Oliver set his jaw. "But I have one condition."

Peyton blinked—was he actually agreeing? But despite her doubt that this might be too extreme, she couldn't back down now. "Name it."

"I'll try to get Madison to *want* to sleep with me, but if she refuses, that's it. I won't make her do anything against her will. You might think I'm an ass, but I have never and will never go that far. Got it?"

"I never asked you to physically take advantage of her," Peyton said, surprised he thought she wanted him to do *that*. Knowing he'd believed that made her shudder. "The task is to get Madison to fall for you and to sleep with you because she *wants* to. But you can't tell her about the bet and get her to play along. If you do, I *will* find out, and the picture will be online before you know it. This task shouldn't be a problem for you, though. You're infamous for getting who you want—I have faith you can pull it off."

"Maybe," he said. "But I tried with Madison in middle school, and it didn't work out for me then."

"I've seen Facebook pictures of you in middle school, so I know how much you've changed," Peyton said. "You got hot, and you know it. The entire *school* knows it. Isn't it time you made Madison notice, too?"

It was hard to tell what he was thinking behind his sunglasses, but he tensed up, his hands gripping his drink and his lips pressed together. Peyton had a feeling she'd gotten to him.

"And what great timing," Savannah said, finishing up the last of her water. "Because here she is now."

Sure enough, Madison Lockhart had just strolled out the door, her flowing black cover-up blowing in the breeze. She spotted them and scowled. Peyton thought she would turn around and go to another pool, but instead she walked to the corner farthest away from them, situated herself in a lounge chair under an umbrella and pulled her iPad out of her bag. She plugged in her earbuds and focused on the screen—probably checking the comments under her Campusbuzz post.

"I'm not surprised Madison doesn't want to hang out with me and Savannah, but I thought she was your best friend," Peyton said to Oliver.

"She is." He rubbed the back of his neck. "But something's been off with her lately. She's been distant. Not only to me, but to everyone."

Madison *did* look miserable, her forehead creased and her lips turned down as she focused on her iPad. But Peyton shrugged it off. Madison's personal issues weren't her problem.

"Well, now's the perfect time for you to start your task," Peyton said, wanting to end this conversation. She was feeling worse and worse about it. And she didn't *want* to feel badly, because Madison had asked for it. "It sounds like Madison needs someone to talk to—someone she can *trust*. Like you. And who knows where *that* will lead?"

"I'm going over there, not because *you* want me to, but because *I* want to." Oliver stood and grabbed his towel. "I would rather spend time with her than you, anyway."

"Good luck, Romeo." Peyton smiled and blew him a kiss, making sure he couldn't tell she was having second thoughts. He flung his towel over his shoulder and swaggered over to join Madison.

Once Oliver was out of earshot, Peyton said to Savannah, "That went better than I'd expected."

Hopefully her sister would validate what she'd done, because Madison looked so sad and vulnerable that Peyton was feeling guiltier by the second.

"I guess." Savannah pulled her hair over her shoulder and tugged on the ends. "I feel bad, though. Are we taking this too far?"

"No." Peyton tried to sound confident. "Should I show you that website again as a reminder of what Madison said about us? About how she called us trash, sluts, and posted that video to humiliate you?"

"No." Savannah played with the ties of her bathing suit. "I don't want to see it again."

"Good," Peyton said. "Because neither do I."

"But was it too much with the picture?" she asked. "Yeah, Oliver's a jerk, but I would feel awful if he got sent to boarding school because of me."

"It wasn't too much," Peyton assured her. "After the way he treated me—the way he would have treated you and Courtney, too, if he'd completed that bet—he deserves whatever's coming to him. That photo convinced him to go through with the deal. But if it makes you feel better, even if he doesn't go through with it, we won't put up the picture. Okay?"

"Okay," Savannah agreed, although she didn't sound sure.

Peyton jittered her legs, not sure herself. But she forced herself to be still. This was *Madison* they were talking about—the girl who'd been determined to bring Peyton and her sisters down since they'd moved to Vegas. Madison might be a virgin—for now—but she was far from innocent. She couldn't keep getting away with the crap she was pulling. Besides, Madison and Oliver might *call* each other friends, but there was definite chemistry between them.

Once they hooked up, Peyton would tell Madison the truth. Then Madison's heart would be broken, and her friendship with Oliver would be ruined.

They would both get what they deserved.

chapter 12: *Madison*

When Madison saw Savannah, Peyton and Oliver relaxing on lounge chairs by the pool, she wanted to leave. She'd come to the rooftop pool because it was never as crowded as the main pool, but then three of the people she wanted to avoid most were here. It was like she was cursed.

Her second thought was: Why's Oliver with Peyton and Savannah? He'd told her about his one-night stand with Peyton, but as far as Madison knew, they hadn't spoken since Peyton had found out about his bet to sleep with her and her sisters. Now he was hanging out with them?

But it would be cowardly to duck out, so Madison situated herself at the opposite corner of the pool, purposefully not facing them. She wouldn't have minded spending time with Oliver—she missed seeing him out of school—but she didn't want to go near the Diamond girls. Her half sisters. They were a reminder of the lies her parents had told her for her entire life. And she wasn't allowed to tell them the truth, so every second around them would be spent pretending ignorance.

She kept her cover-up on—no need to display her newly acquired seven pounds—and watched *The Vampire Diaries* on her iPad. One episode, then she could leave. But then her parents would wonder why she hadn't spent much time with the "friends" she was supposedly hanging out with. Two episodes should be enough.

She'd watched a few scenes when a shadow fell over her. She pressed Pause, removed her earbuds and looked up to see Oliver. The muscles in the back of her neck tightened. It wasn't that she didn't want to see him—she just didn't have the energy to pretend to be the person she'd been before her world had come crashing down.

"Mind if I join you?" he said, laying his towel on the chair next to hers.

"As long as those Diamond girls don't follow you." She turned her iPad off and placed it on the side table. "Why are you hanging out with them, anyway? I thought you didn't like them."

"My parents want me to be friends with them, so I figured I would play nice."

"You never cared about pleasing your parents before."

"I still don't," he said. "But my grades have been slipping, and some of my teachers gave me academic warnings, so my parents have been on my back about it. After all those tabloid articles this summer, they think I'm going out too much and that it's interfering with school. They threatened boarding school if they don't see an improvement."

"I knew you wouldn't be able to get away with barely doing your homework forever," she said.

"Junior year blows." He sounded casual, but by the way he leaned his head back and exhaled, Madison could tell he was troubled. "I won't stop going out or anything lame like that, but I'm also not spending the next year and a half at some strict boarding school in the middle of nowhere."

"You know, I happen to be a student tutor," she reminded him, trying to ignore the "being lame by not going out" comment, since that's exactly what she'd been doing lately. "I can help you if you want."

He would probably say no, like he always did when she offered to help with his grades, but it sounded serious this time. The Goodman School was intense about keeping its 100 percent acceptance rate of students to four-year colleges. The school would probably be lenient on Oliver since the Prescott family donated a lot of money, but if he failed to live up to academic expectations, he could still be asked to leave.

He stirred his drink, even though it was mostly ice now, as if considering her offer. "You know, I think I'll take you up on that," he said. "Thanks."

"Really?" Madison blinked, unsure she'd heard him correctly.

"Why so surprised?"

"You've never been interested in being tutored before. What gives?"

"I need to get my grades up if I want to stay at Goodman," he said. "And you're the best student tutor around. What do you say—are you up for the challenge?"

The way he was watching her, like he wanted her to say yes more than anything, made her mind so hazy that she nearly forgot the question. *Tutoring,* she reminded herself. *He wants me to help him get his grades up.* Anyway, why was she getting flustered? This was *Oliver.* They'd been friends forever. It was normal for him to come to her for this.

"I think I can handle it." She smiled for real for the first time in a while, and they spent the next twenty minutes figuring out what classes Oliver needed the most help with.

"So, where've you been hiding for the past few weeks, Mads?" he asked once they finished coordinating schedules.

"I've been busy," she lied.

"Too busy to see your friends?"

She shrugged. "Junior year is harder than I thought."

"Everyone else is still managing to go out and have fun," he said. "And you're smarter than all of them. Ever since that day in genetics, when you freaked out during that lab, it's like you've disappeared."

Because that was the day her life had changed forever. She wished she could tell him everything. If there was one person she trusted more than anyone else, it was Oliver. It would make her feel better if she shared the secret with him—with a true friend who cared about her and would sympathize with the betrayal and anger she was feeling. He would keep it secret. And her parents *did* want her to talk to someone. They meant a professional, but talking to Oliver would be better than keeping it bottled inside. Right?

But Savannah and Peyton were lounging at the opposite side of the pool, and Madison couldn't talk about it with them so close by. She was being paranoid, because they were *probably* out of listening distance, but what if they heard? They would ask Adrian if it was true, and Adrian would be forced to acknowledge Madison as a daughter, which he had no interest in doing.

She was unwanted by her biological father. The reminder made her stomach turn. He'd taken in Peyton, Courtney and Savannah, so why didn't he want her? What did they have that she didn't?

"Hey." Oliver placed his hand on top of hers. "Is everything okay?" He watched her with so much concern, as if she were about to break. Which she supposed she sort of was.

"Not really." She kept her hand under his, liking how warm and safe he made her feel. He was one of the few people who cared about her. Who'd never lied to her. She could trust him. And if she spoke quietly enough, Peyton and Savannah wouldn't overhear. "You're right about that day in genetics. I freaked out during that lab because—"

"Do either of you want a drink?" A cocktail waitress interrupted the conversation, and Madison jolted back, realizing how close she'd come to being overheard.

"Just water." Alcohol sounded tempting—maybe it would help her relax—but Madison needed to watch her calories. Oliver ordered another mojito.

"What were you saying about the lab?" he asked once the waitress had walked away.

"It's nothing." Madison snapped back into focus. Had she really been about to tell him the truth? With the Diamond girls so close by—with other *people* so close by? What had she been thinking? That was *not* a conversation she should have in public.

Oliver squeezed her hand, watching her as if he didn't believe her. "When you're ready to talk about it, let me know, okay?"

"It's not a big deal," she lied again. "I'm sure I'll be over it in a few days."

He pressed his lips together, looking like he disagreed. "I know you, Mads, and I've never seen you isolate yourself like this," he said. "Whatever's going on is really bothering you." She opened her mouth to deny it, but he continued before she had a chance. "You don't have to talk about it now, but I'm not going anywhere, so you can stop shutting me out. The group isn't the same without you. Without you around…" He paused and scratched the back of his head, as if searching for the right word. Then he refocused on her, his expression so intense it made her body turn to jelly. "I've missed you. And I mean it—whenever you're ready to talk about what's going on, I'm here for you. I just hope you know that."

"Thank you," she said, holding his gaze. "That means a lot."

"Well, it's just the truth."

"I know," she said. "But I'm glad you told me."

The waitress dropped off their drinks, and Madison took a sip of her water, watching an older lady wade in the pool. Had she just had a *moment* with Oliver? No, she couldn't have. They were friends, nothing more. But he was acting differently right now. He was being uncharacteristically verbal about his feelings. Letting her in more than ever before.

What had changed with him?

She shook it off, since clearly the change had been with *her,* not Oliver. She'd been so out of sorts recently that he was treating her like she was about to break. He must think she was pathetic. *Everyone* must think she was pathetic.

"I guess I was so caught up in the pressure of junior year, with making sure my grades and PSAT scores are perfect for when we take the SAT and apply to college next year, that it took over my life," she said. " But you're right—I should start hanging out with everyone again. And I will. Starting now."

"That's what I like to hear." Oliver clinked his glass with hers and smiled. "Glad to have you back."

If only she could be happy to *be* back, then everything might be on the path to being normal again.

www.campusbuzz.com

High Schools > Nevada > Las Vegas > The Goodman School

Trick or Treat or PARTY!
Posted on Thursday 10/30 at 4:23 PM
Who's excited for HALLOWEEN tomorrow night?! And how lucky are we that Halloween is landing on a Friday? We get to celebrate on the real deal, in the city with some of the biggest and best costume parties in the world.

Where will you be partying? There are so many options: the Fetish & Fantasy Halloween Ball at Hard Rock, Night of the Killer Costumes at the Palms, Angels and Devils at the Gates, Fairytale Masquerade at the Diamond, and more.

I already have plans, of course, but it's fun to hear what you all have in mind ☺

1: Posted on Thursday 10/30 at 5:13 PM
Apparently the volleyball girls and football guys have a major takeover planned for Myst, with multiple tables on the VIP level reserved for them. I overheard some of the girls talking about how they're on a special list so they don't get carded. Lucky.

2: Posted on Thursday 10/30 at 5:46 PM
Those tables START at $5K each, but getting them reserved and not being carded is what happens when Savannah Diamond is one of your teammates. Her father bought her way into the school, and now he's *trying* to

buy her way into popularity. But her so-called "friends" are using her for her money and connections, and she has no idea. So pathetic.

3: Posted on Thursday 10/30 at 6:08 PM

A girl from Palo Verde is having a blow out while her parents are out clubbing all night. So we can hang out with people *our own age.* I don't get why so many of you are into the club scene. It's mainly people in their upper 20s and 30s who don't want to hang out with high schoolers, and tourists who party with you and then go home and forget about you. What's the point?

4: Posted on Thursday 10/30 at 6:59 PM

which is why we go out with big groups of our FRIENDS and hang out with each other. we live in one of the best party cities in the world and we like to take advantage of it!!!

5: Posted on Thursday 10/30 at 7:19 PM

I want to go PARTY TRICK OR TREATING. Knock on doors, but instead of bite size candies, you get shots of alcohol! Why has no one thought of this before?!?!

6: Posted on Thursday 10/30 at 7:28 PM

...that already exists. Haven't you ever been to an Around the World party?

chapter 13: *Savannah*

"This is amazing!" Jackie said to Savannah as the hostess led them to their tables at Myst on Halloween night. "I can't believe you got us in."

"Of course," Savannah said as they situated themselves around the center table in their section. She'd arrived early with Jackie, Alyssa and Brooke, since she wanted to be there when the rest of their group showed up. Each table had two bottles of sparkling cider chilling in buckets, the flutes on a silver platter, and a selection of juices—which would get spiked with the alcohol the guys were bringing in their flasks. But after what had happened at Jackie's party, Savannah intended to stick to cider.

She poured herself a glass and looked around in wonder. Myst had been decorated in the theme of the night—"Fairy Tale Masquerade"—and it truly did look magical. Thick vines with twinkling stars wound around the walls and ceilings like an enchanted forest, a layer of mist coated the ground and the lights shining on the three-story waterfall turned the water a variety of greens, blues and reds.

Savannah and her friends had dressed to the theme, each of them wearing mesh fairy wings of various colors, short sparkly dresses to match their wing color and glittering tiaras. Savannah had picked the color that always looked best on her—blue.

Alyssa glanced over the balcony at the stage, where the opening DJ was mixing to the crowd of costumed people dancing on the second floor. It was busy, but not as packed as it would get later. "When will Calvin Harris come on?" she asked.

"Probably not until after one," Savannah said.

"Wow." Alyssa looked at her watch. "Glad I'm sleeping at your place tonight."

"You can always sleep over if you need to," Savannah said. Alyssa's parents were strict with her curfew—she couldn't get home a minute after midnight—but they turned the other way when she slept at a friend's. Savannah had never had a weekend curfew. Her mom had never enforced one, and Adrian didn't give her one because her bodyguard protected her at all times.

About an hour later, more of their group arrived—the usual sports crowd that Savannah had been hanging out with since school started. She'd invited Damien, but he'd already had plans with Madison and Oliver and their crowd at Luxe, the main club in The Gates. She hated that Damien was spending Halloween with them instead of her, but that was his close circle. He'd known them since lower school.

Besides, she'd been spending a lot of time with Damien at the recording studio at school. He was now acting as her "manager" for her singing. Since Goodman had a great arts program, it had been easy to find a guitarist, bassist and drummer who wanted to work with them, and Brett had been happy to help them make videos. Their first few covers were acoustic and laid-back, with Brett recording them from multiple angles in the studio. They'd gotten a few hundred views on YouTube, and a bunch of positive feedback, but nothing major.

She wanted that to change with their most recent cover, which was their most elaborate one yet. It was One Connection's latest song, and it was cute and fun, with Savannah singing and dancing around her condo. She'd worn all her favorite sparkly outfits, and Damien and Brett had bought cardboard cutouts of the One Connection guys for her to mess around with while dancing. She'd put it up on her channel last night. Hopefully it would rack up views, and the awful video from Jackie's party would be forgotten.

Savannah itched to pull out her phone and check her You-Tube channel, but she forced herself to focus. She needed to be present at the party. Three more football players joined their table, dressed as knights to fit the fairy-tale theme. Savannah did a double take when she realized Nick was one of them—the golden curls peeking out under his helmet were unmistakable.

Her hands shook, and she gripped her cider. Nick hadn't been to any parties since summer, and since she was spending lunch in the arts building, she'd barely seen him in weeks. Every time she'd asked him if he was going to a party, he'd said he was busy. She'd eventually taken the hint that he wasn't interested. So she smiled and waved, like she had with a bunch of the guys she knew, and then focused extra hard on the conversation with her friends.

She continued to pretend to be involved with talking to them, although she fidgeted with the straps of her fairy wings—which were already getting annoying—unable to think of anything but Nick. She tried not looking at him, although thinking about *not* looking at him was making her do exactly that. What did it mean that he'd come out tonight? Maybe he wanted to talk to her? But then wouldn't he have come over and said hello?

Focusing on her friends was impossible, so Savannah took a restroom break to recenter herself. Maybe when she returned to the table, she could switch seats so her back was to Nick. It might be awkward, but whatever. Better than accidentally staring at him all night.

But on her way back, a hand touched her shoulder, and she turned around to come face-to-face with none other than Nick.

"Hey," he said casually, as if they hadn't gone weeks without speaking.

Staring into his blue eyes, with the beat of club music in the background, Savannah was reminded of the first time she'd met him—when she was leaving Luxe in tears after Madison kissed Damien. That night had ended up being fun—they'd gone to karaoke, and the video of her singing was the first one she'd put online. Her chest panged at the memory. That had been the last week they'd seen each other outside of school. Sure, they'd seen each other at lunch a few times and around the halls, but if he was interested in her, wouldn't he have made more of an effort?

"Hi." Savannah played with the straps of her wings. "I wasn't expecting you to show tonight."

"I have to be up early tomorrow, but Halloween's my favorite holiday, so here I am," he said. "Thanks for the tables.... It seems like everyone's having a great time."

Why would he be waking up early on a Saturday morning? It probably had to do with football practice. But now that she was closer to him, she could tell how tired he looked, even in the dim light. He had dark circles under his eyes, and his skin had lost the glow it'd had over the summer.

She wanted to ask him if everything was okay. But he'd been so distant recently—he wouldn't want to talk with her about whatever was going on. He was just being polite because he ran into her.

"I'm glad you were able to make it." She smiled, and not knowing what else to do, she said, "We should head back to our friends—I don't want them wondering where I am." With that, she turned away, feeling like she should say more, but not knowing what. How had they gone from clicking so well to barely speaking?

"Wait, Savannah," he called.

She faced him again, somehow managing to be graceful despite the clunky fairy wings. "What?" she asked hopefully.

"I'm sorry I haven't been able to see you much since summer."

"I just don't get it," she blurted, feeling bolder than normal—maybe because it was Halloween, and she was in a costume. "One day everything between us was great, and then suddenly you were busy all the time. I don't understand what happened."

"Things have just been hectic recently." He took his helmet off and ran his hands through his hair. "I wish it didn't have to be this way. But I promise—none of this was your fault. It's all on me."

"That's the oldest line in the book," she said, surprised by her anger. She had liked Nick—she'd trusted him. What had happened to the Nick she'd met her first week in Vegas? Did he exist, or was that a front for girls he was pretending to be interested in? "If something was bothering you, you should have talked to me, not ignored me. I'm going back to find my friends."

"Hold on," he said, and the hurt in his eyes made her stay put. "You're right—you deserve a real answer."

"Okay." Savannah waited, hoping that this "real answer" would clear everything up.

"I'm not supposed to talk to anyone about this." He moved closer to her as a drunk guy in a dragon costume stumbled past. "But it's a long story, and the hall leading to the restrooms at Myst isn't the best place to tell it."

Savannah glanced at her watch. "Calvin Harris isn't going on for two hours," she said. "If you want to go to the Lobby Bar to talk, we've got time."

He hesitated, and she prayed he wouldn't back out of telling her whatever he was about to confess. "Your friends won't mind?"

"They'll survive without me for a little while."

He nodded, and together, they headed out of the club.

"So, what's going on?" Savannah asked once they had situated themselves at a table in the back of the bar.

Nick glanced around, as if he was worried someone would overhear.

"No one's paying attention to us," Savannah said. "So, what's this long story that supposedly explains why you've been ignoring me for months?"

"What I'm about to tell you has to stay between you and me," he said, his eyes blazing with intensity. "I mean it. No one else besides my family knows—not even my friends from the team, and I've known them since lower school. They suspect something's up, but they don't know the full story. So, can you promise you won't repeat any of this, not even to your sisters?"

"I promise." She was so curious that she would have promised anything.

"Okay." He took a deep breath. "Remember the week we met, how my credit card was turned down at the poolside restaurant?"

"Yeah." Savannah had ended up putting their meals on her own card, and the waitress had brought out a complimentary dessert when she saw Savannah's name and realized she was Adrian's daughter. It was one of the first times Savannah had gotten special treatment because of her last name. She would never forget that moment.

"I tried to make it seem like it wasn't a big deal, since we'd just met and I didn't want to embarrass myself," he said. "But it kind of was."

Savannah didn't know much about Nick's family besides that his dad owned a commercial real estate company. She hadn't considered that they could have money problems, but she had a bad feeling about where this was headed. "What happened?" she asked.

"I don't know the full details, but earlier in the summer my dad got in trouble with his latest building. It didn't follow the right codes." Nick shrugged, as if this wasn't a huge deal, although it clearly was. "He got sued big-time, and taken for all he had. For all our family had."

"Wow." Savannah gaped, unsure what to say. And here she'd thought Nick had been distant because *he wasn't interested in her.* It sounded so childish and self-centered next to the truth. Savannah had seen what it was like for Courtney when she was balancing school, tutoring and work—she'd had no time to date anyone. And Courtney didn't play a varsity sport, too. So, strangely enough, Savannah got it. Nick didn't have time for a girlfriend.

But everyone always needed a friend.

"I'm sorry," she finally said. "You know you could have told me the truth before now…right? If anyone at Goodman understands what it's like to have money issues, it's me. Well, obviously not me right now, but me before moving here."

"I know," Nick said. "But things got crazy the week you moved here. My mom blames my dad for getting us into this mess, and she moved out, bringing me with her. It's why I'm living at those crappy Harbor Island apartments now."

"They can't be too bad, right?" Savannah pictured the dreary two-bedroom apartment she'd shared with her mom and sisters before moving to Vegas, with the worn floors and the stained furniture crammed inside. Nick's new place couldn't be worse than that.

"Compared to where I used to live?" He raised an eyebrow. "It's a big adjustment. My mom got a job to pay rent and electric bills and stuff, but she married my dad right after college and her unused communications major couldn't get her anything more than a receptionist position. Goodman's tuition is forty grand a year, and we can't afford it anymore, so I've been working to save up."

"Goodman costs *forty thousand dollars* a year?" Savannah's mouth dropped open. She knew private school cost money, but she didn't realize it was that much. That was over one hundred thousand dollars for her and her sisters—way more than her mom ever made in a year, let alone could spend on education.

"Yep." Nick nodded. "The sad part is that, before all this happened to my family, I never thought twice about it."

Savannah did the math in her head. As a high school junior, Nick couldn't be making more than minimum wage. Even if he worked all summer, he couldn't make enough to pay for Goodman. But he was still a student there, so he must have found a way. "How did you save up forty grand in a few weeks?" she asked.

"My mom talked to the headmaster, and they're giving me half the tuition in scholarship, since I'm the best quarterback they have and they don't want to lose me. But even covering half the cost is rough. I worked two jobs all summer—one selling shoes at Finish Line in the mall and the other bussing tables. I started the week after we met, but over the summer I didn't make half of what I need, so the headmaster's letting me pay in installments. That's why you've barely seen me this year. When I'm not at school, doing homework or at football practice, I'm selling shoes." He looked down at the table, his eyes refusing to meet hers.

"Working hard for what you want is nothing to be ashamed of," Savannah said, amazed he even needed to be told that. "It's admirable. I was applying for summer jobs in Fairfield before my sisters and I moved here. It was the first summer I was old enough. Courtney didn't want me working during the school year because of volleyball, but I probably would have anyway, to help our family."

"I get why Courtney would say that," Nick said. "Working while being in school *and* playing sports is impossible. Any semblance of the social life that I used to have has gone out the window. The guys don't get it—they give me a hard time about not coming out anymore. And I can't tell them the truth without breaking my family's trust. My dad made it clear that I'm not supposed to tell *anyone* about what happened, and I promised him I wouldn't. You're the only one who knows."

"I won't tell a soul."

"Football's all that's keeping me sane right now," he said. "But I haven't had much time for homework, so my grades haven't been great. And if I drop football for more time to study, I'll lose my scholarship, since football's the reason I have it to begin with. I'm stuck in a never-ending cycle, and it's exhausting."

Savannah nodded, understanding exactly what he meant. She'd seen enough of the students at Fairfield vs. Goodman to know how unfair it all was. How the students at Goodman were given every opportunity to succeed and cruised through life, and how many students at Fairfield slipped through the cracks because of the tough circumstances they'd been born into. Sure, they were lucky to live in a country that gave them an education at all, but was it an *equal* opportunity? No way. It sucked, but there was no getting around it—life just sucked and wasn't fair sometimes.

But she might be able to help Nick.

"How much more money do you need?" she asked.

"Ten thousand." He buried his fingers in his hair, letting out a long breath at the mention of that much money. "It's funny, really. Before all this happened with my dad, that would have been nothing. Now it feels impossible."

"It's easy to get lost in the fantasy world of Vegas," Savannah said. "But I get it. Ten thousand dollars is a lot of money."

"If I didn't have school, and homework, and football practice, it wouldn't be as bad," he said. "But since school started, I can get in sixteen hours of work a week without crashing, if I'm lucky. That's about a grand a month. If I take extra shifts over winter and spring break, I'll be able to cover it all, but I'm pretty burnt out. This year has been rough."

He looked lost, and Savannah wanted to help him so badly. "I don't want this to come across the wrong way, but if you have a credit card reader for your phone, I could help you out. My dad doesn't glance at charges that are less than five figures."

"I don't need charity," he said. "I've got this handled myself."

"It's not charity," Savannah insisted. "It's a friend helping a friend. Don't you see that trying to balance school, work and sports is too much? I've always known it was—I was prepared to quit volleyball once I got a job sophomore year, because my family needed my help. And Fairfield's academics are nowhere *near* as intense as Goodman's. You said yourself that your grades are slipping, you look exhausted and quitting football isn't an option. So can you do me a favor and let me help?"

"No." He rubbed his eyes, and Savannah wondered just how sleep-deprived he was. "It's too much."

"When's your birthday?" she asked.

It took him a second to think about it. "February ninth," he said. "Why?"

"I was hoping it would be around now." Savannah frowned. "For a reason to give you a birthday present. How about a belated half birthday present?"

"I really appreciate that you want to help." He laughed for the first time since they'd sat down, and finally there was a hint of a sparkle in his eyes. "But I haven't celebrated my half birthday since I was ten. Anyway, I'm not taking your money, Savannah. Well, Adrian's money. My parents would be humiliated if they found out. Trust me—I've got this covered. I'm just glad you heard me out."

"Okay, fine," she said, since she didn't want to push it. "Just don't forget my offer. It's there if you change your mind."

"I'll remember it," he said. "But I'm not going to take it."

"I do have one request, though."

"Oh?" He raised an eyebrow. "And what's that?"

"No more avoiding me. I know you don't have much time to hang out anymore, but an occasional text message to let me know you're hanging in there would be nice. Also, make sure you're not working on December thirteenth, because that's the night of my Sweet Sixteen party. It's going to be awesome, and I want you to be there."

"All right," he said. "I think I can handle that."

Once that was over, the walls between them were finally broken down again. And for the first time since the start of the school year, Savannah's life was—for the most part—going the way she wanted. She had a fun group of friends, her You-Tube channel was slowly doing better, she was spending every lunch period with Damien and she was on good terms with Nick again.

So why did she have a strange feeling that it was all too good to last?

chapter 14: *Courtney*

Halloween had always been one of Courtney's favorite holidays. She loved the decorations, the movies, the excuse to eat foods that were bad for her and the costumes. She also loved how her mom used to get excited about Halloween, too—when they were younger, she'd helped Courtney and her sisters pick out the perfect costumes. She'd had a rule that they could never be the same thing twice. Before drinking had taken over her life, she'd taken them trick-or-treating, and then when they'd gotten home they'd watched old slasher movies like *Scream* and *Friday the 13th* while seeing who could eat the most candy.

In more recent years, her mom had gone out partying instead, and Peyton had gone out with her friends, too. Courtney had told herself that it didn't matter, since they were too old for trick-or-treating. But she couldn't dispense with celebrating altogether, so she and Savannah had kept up the tradition of watching the Diamond Halloween slasher movie lineup.

This year for Halloween, Courtney was alone. Savannah had reserved a few VIP tables for her friends at Myst—she had invited Courtney, but it wasn't Courtney's scene—and Peyton was getting ready for some party at Hard Rock that was supposedly the "wildest Halloween party in Vegas." It was the first year ever that Courtney didn't have a costume.

But not getting dressed up on Halloween felt sad, so she took out a fringed black dress from the back of her closet and tried it on. If she paired it with long pearls, she could be a flapper at one of Gatsby's parties in the Roaring Twenties. She did her makeup heavier than usual, imitating the smoky eyes and bright red lips that came up when she Google-searched "flapper makeup." All that was off was her hair, but since she wasn't cutting her long blond locks, she left it down, letting it fall in its natural waves. It wasn't the best costume ever— she needed a sparkly feather headband and gloves to make it perfect—but it passed.

She didn't want to stay in when she was dressed up, and she was curious about what people in the Diamond had chosen as costumes, so she headed out of the condo to grab dinner at one of the restaurants downstairs. She didn't mind eating alone, as long as she had her Kindle with her.

"Going partying tonight?" her bodyguard, Teddy, asked. He was older than Adrian—he looked like he could be a young grandfather—and Courtney always wondered how he would protect her in an extreme situation. But he must be able to, otherwise Adrian never would have entrusted her safety to him. From his tone, she could tell he didn't expect her to be going partying—he knew well enough from guarding her that she wasn't into that scene.

"Just grabbing some dinner." She held up her Kindle. "And getting some reading done."

She requested a table in the front of the Grand Café so that she could watch everyone pass by in their costumes. People had been dressed up all day—some even all *week*—but the craziest costumes had come out tonight. The "Fairy Tales" party was at the Diamond, so there were tons of people in barely-there princess, prince, fairy, knight and dragon costumes. Angels and devils were also popular, along with various superheroes. Courtney's favorite was a girl who had dressed like Daenerys from *Game of Thrones.* The outfit was intricate, and most likely handmade, complete with the white-blond wig necessary to portray the *Khaleesi.*

Courtney had ordered her food and had settled into reading *Remembrance,* the first book in the Transcend Time Saga, when her phone buzzed with a text message. It was from Brett.

Mind if I join you?

That was a strange way of asking to hang out. Unless he knew where she was? She looked up and found him standing outside the perimeter of the casino. Their eyes met, and he waved, which sent her stomach flipping in a million directions. Then he glanced at his phone and held a hand out in question, as though waiting for her to respond.

As if she could say no. Anyway, it was just dinner. In a public place. Nothing could *happen* between them because of it.

Of course you can join me ☺

She put down her Kindle as he walked over. "You're not getting dressed up for Halloween?" she asked as he sat down next to her.

"I haven't dressed up for Halloween since elementary

school," he said. "You look great, though. Where are you headed tonight?"

"Honestly?" Courtney said, although of course she would be honest with Brett. "I threw this together last-minute. My plans don't go further than dinner."

"That's a shame," he said, perusing the menu. "Why not?"

"Because my sisters are going to Halloween parties at clubs," she said. "But I would rather have a *Scream* or *Friday the 13th* marathon."

"A *Friday the 13th* fan?" he asked, smiling. "I didn't expect you to like those kind of movies."

"Only on Halloween," she said.

"Tell me, then." He pressed the pads of his fingers together, as if he were about to ask a serious question. "If you're a fan of the *Friday the 13th* series, who's the killer in the original movie?"

"Jason's mom," she said without a beat. "That's easy— especially since it's the same question the killer asks Drew Barrymore's character in the first scene of *Scream*."

"Correct," Brett said. "But the real test was seeing if you caught the *Scream* reference. You passed."

Courtney shared a smile with Brett, and their eyes locked, leaving her tongue-tied. She realized she was staring at him, but before she could think of something to say, the waitress came over to take their order.

While Brett placed his order, Courtney watched the people in crazy costumes parading around the casino. Her mom would have loved this—there was enough variation to give her ideas of fresh costumes for years.

The thought of her mom made Courtney remember the Skype conversation they'd had earlier that month, which reminded her of something she wanted to ask Brett.

"Do you know if we can see the records Adrian keeps on us?"

He scrunched his eyebrows. "How did you get from slasher films to your personal records?"

"So you do know about them?"

"Only that we have them to help our bodyguards protect us," he said. "Not much else. Why?"

She took a deep breath. "You know how when we first met, I mentioned I thought my family was keeping something from me?"

"About the kidnapping?"

She nodded. "I let it go, thinking I was being paranoid. But I chatted on Skype with my mom earlier this month when she moved to outpatient treatment. I told her that Adrian had told me everything, and she seemed worried. Then when I told her what he *had* told me, she was relieved, as if there was something more about the story she didn't want me to know. I asked Adrian about it afterward, and he told me I knew everything I needed to know...but it felt like an indirect answer. I can't shake the feeling that there's something big being kept from me, and I want to find out what it is."

"And you think your personal records will tell you." It was a statement, not a question.

"They might," Courtney said. "Although Peyton asked her bodyguard if she could see hers, and he said we're not allowed to. Have you ever seen yours?"

"Nope," Brett said. "I've never tried. The point of them is so our main bodyguards and night bodyguards can keep up-to-date on what we've been doing. They're probably pretty boring. Especially mine, since it starts about a year ago, when my mom and I moved into the Diamond."

"If only we could sneak into Adrian's office and search for

them on his computer..." Courtney laughed, unable to believe she was contemplating this.

"I would love to see that." Brett smiled. "But Adrian's office is guarded by people, cameras and who knows what other technology. You would have to be a skilled criminal to pull that off."

"So much for that idea." She sighed.

The waitress came over with their food, and Courtney took a bite of her vegetarian pasta. It was delicious—everything at the Grande Café was wonderful, since the chef was the *Iron Chef America* champion. Courtney had never seen the show, but from tasting his food, she understood why he'd won.

"From everything you've told me, it definitely sounds like there's more to the story," Brett said. "We won't be able to break into Adrian's files, but we'll find another way."

His optimism gave her a surge of hope. "You have an idea?"

"Not right now," he said. "But I believe you, and I'll keep thinking about a way to get answers. Between the two of us, we'll come up with something."

"Thanks," she said softly. "It means a lot that you believe me."

"Of course I do." He placed his fork down, focusing only on her. "You're the most honest, trustworthy person I've met since transferring to Goodman and moving to the Diamond. If there's any way for me to help, I will."

She couldn't look away from him, and it was like her entire body had caught fire as she replayed the compliment in her mind. No one had ever said anything that sweet to her before.

"Thanks," she said. "I would like that. For you to help, I mean. That would be nice of you." Her face heated—she must sound like a bumbling idiot—and she took another bite of her pasta. But she'd already eaten half of the huge portion and wasn't hungry anymore, so she asked the waitress to box it up.

Brett finished his hamburger, and he grabbed the check when the waitress placed it down.

"I can get that." Courtney reached for it, but he held it away from her.

"Don't worry about it," he said, seeming to enjoy this. "I've got it."

"I was here first," she said. "You weren't going to have dinner here before you saw me. Let me do it." She had to pay for her half. It didn't matter that both their credit cards went to Adrian's bank account—if she let Brett pay for dinner, it would feel like a date.

"Our credit cards go to the same place." He slid his card into the slot. "It's no big deal."

"Fine." She couldn't do anything else without causing a scene, and she didn't want him to think she was overanalyzing the situation. This *wasn't* a date. He was only being pragmatic.

She leaned back and crossed her arms, as if she could demonstrate through body language that this was *not* a date, but he smiled at her, apparently entertained. She crossed her legs away from him, banging her knee against the bottom of the table, and he looked *more* amused. She huffed and sipped her water. This was so ridiculously frustrating.

"I know you didn't plan on going out after dinner," he said, and she tensed, since the only continuation for that sentence had to be asking her to do something with him. "But have you heard about the *Titanic* ghost exhibit?"

She smiled and widened her eyes, unable to help it—she loved the *Titanic*. "I know about the *Titanic* Artifact Exhibit," she said. "I found it when I was looking up things to do in

Vegas, although I haven't gotten around to seeing it yet. But I didn't know it was a *ghost* exhibit."

"It wasn't designed to be a ghost exhibit." Brett's voice lowered, as though he was telling a scary story around a campfire. "But they have real artifacts from the ship, and since the exhibit opened, strange things have happened there. Some say that the previous owners of the objects in the museum haunt the tourists who walk through. The picture of the ship's designer, who made the decision to lower the number of lifeboats, has been taken off the wall as if those who died didn't want to display it. Then there's the Lady in Black, a ghost wearing a black dress and her hair in a bun, who walks around not speaking to anyone. One staff member claims she disappeared in front of his eyes."

He told the story so dramatically that Courtney had unconsciously moved closer to him as he spoke. Once he was finished, there was so much electricity between them that she could barely breathe.

"Sounds creepy," she finally said, shivering at the thought of ghosts of the *Titanic* passengers haunting the exhibit. "But you don't believe any of that's true, right?"

"Who knows?" he said. "I've only been once, a few years ago on a school field trip. We didn't see any ghosts. But on Halloween night, the tour guides dress up as dead passengers and give a special ghost tour. I've always wanted to check it out."

"Let me guess," Courtney said. "You want to go now?"

His eyes lit up. "Are you agreeing to come?"

She bit her lip. The *Titanic* ghost tour sounded fun. Then again, this reminded her of earlier in the summer when Brett had taken her to hotels around Vegas, which had eventually led to them kissing on the night of the grand opening of the

Diamond. Her eyes traveled to his lips, and she couldn't help it—she wanted him to kiss her again now.

"You're thinking too hard about this." By his confident tone, he knew he'd won. "You don't have plans tonight, I don't have plans tonight, and we both want to find out if the *Titanic* exhibit is haunted. Why shouldn't we go?"

Courtney could think of a few reasons—mainly that being around Brett made her feelings zigzag out of control—but she'd told him why they couldn't date enough times, and she didn't feel like rehashing it again. Anyway, this didn't have to be a date. Just two friends hanging out when they had no other plans.

Plus, she wanted to see the ghost exhibit, and she didn't want to go by herself. If she said no, she would have to wait until next year.

"I'm in," she said.

It was against her better judgment, but she couldn't turn back now.

chapter 15: *Peyton*

Peyton's friend Jill was coming over in an hour so they could go to the Fetish & Fantasy Halloween Ball at the Hard Rock, and she still wasn't sure what to wear. She'd ordered a few costumes online and couldn't pick between her three favorites. Usually she would ask her sisters' advice, but Savannah was at Myst, and Courtney was downstairs getting dinner. Which left one option. Well, she had other options—like texting Jill pictures and asking her opinion—but the option she had in mind had more interesting possibilities.

She brought the three costumes into her bathroom and checked herself out in the mirror, adjusting her push-up bra to show off maximum cleavage. Then she picked up her phone, chewing the inside of her cheek as she stared at the screen. What if she got rejected…again?

Deciding to take a chance, she opened a new text message.

I'm having an emergency and need your help. Come to my room??

She pressed Send. Her heart pounded as she waited at the end of her bed, crossing her legs to show them off at their best angle. Was she about to make a fool of herself?

She didn't have much time to worry before Jackson burst through her door. His suit was perfectly in place, and his hair was sheered so close to his head that he could pass as a soldier. He reminded her of a blond Channing Tatum.

"What's the emergency?" He stood straight, concern in his hazel eyes. But that concern gave her hope. Maybe all wasn't lost between them.

If she was doing this, she might as well go all out. She walked to the door and locked it. "It's a Halloween emergency." She kept her voice low and calm so her nerves wouldn't show, but she gripped the doorknob to remain steady. "I need help deciding which costume to wear."

The worry in his eyes shifted to annoyance. "You brought me in here for a *fashion* emergency?"

Peyton's throat tightened, and she swallowed down the panic. Had this been a mistake? But he was still here, so she might as well make the best of it.

"My sisters aren't around, so I figured you could help since you were standing outside the condo anyway." The words came out so fast that she needed to pause to catch her breath. "Unless you're busy doing something else?"

"This isn't professional, Peyton." He clenched his jaw, his eyes not meeting hers.

Unbelievable. If she'd told any other guy that she wanted to give him a private show of three assumedly barely-there costumes, they would have jumped at the opportunity. But not Jackson. He always had to be so damned stoic.

"Whatever." She rolled her eyes. "At least this is in private and doesn't involve you publicly dragging me out of a cabana."

"You're lucky I got you out of that cabana when I did," he said. "If I hadn't, those photos posted online might have been worse."

"You know about the photos?" Peyton's stomach sank. "Does that mean Adrian saw them, too?"

"Yes, I know about them, but Adrian doesn't," he said. "The photos were posted in a high school forum, not a major website or tabloid."

"Well, that's a relief," she said. Although if Jackson had seen the photos, it meant he'd seen every cruel thing Madison had written about Peyton and her sisters. He had to know none of it was true. Well, almost none. She shuffled her feet and glanced down at the floor, hoping he wasn't thinking about the part that had mentioned Oliver.

"At least you had a daiquiri at the bar—no one can prove it wasn't a virgin drink," he said. "But you *were* drinking with Hunter in the cabana, and if the Goodman administration found out, it wouldn't be you who got in trouble—it would be him. He could get fired, and with a mark like that on his record, he might never get a teaching job again. His career would be ruined."

Peyton ground her teeth together. She hated it, but Jackson was right. "I can't change what happened," she said. "But you saw me delete those photos from Madison's phone. And the second time I hung out with Hunter, the cabana doors were closed."

"You shouldn't be 'hanging out' with him at all," Jackson said, his voice rising. "He's a teacher, you're a student."

"I'm almost eighteen," she said. "He's not *that* much older than me."

"You turn eighteen in March." Jackson's voice revealed no emotion, and Peyton's chest panged. Would she ever be able to reach him again…like she had that first week? "Even after your birthday, Hunter will still be an authority figure," he continued. "Any relationship with him beyond that is inappropriate."

Peyton's eyes tingled, and she blinked away tears. She refused to let Jackson know he was getting to her. Because it wasn't *Hunter* she suspected he was thinking about, but himself. Would he ever see her as something beyond an assignment—as a person worth getting to know?

"I actually had a good conversation with Hunter that day at the bar," she said. "Did it cross your mind that maybe he was enjoying hanging out with me?"

"He should be adult enough to know better than to lead you on." Jackson didn't miss a beat.

"Or maybe he just hasn't forgotten how to have fun." She sucked in a frustrated breath. "But if it makes you happy, I won't talk to him again outside of school."

"Thank you," Jackson said, his shoulders relaxing. "That does make me feel better."

"Good," she said, although she felt anything but.

"Does this mean I can resume my position outside your condo?"

"Well, now that you're here, I really would like your help," she said. "I'm leaving soon for Halloween, and I still don't know what to wear. It's only three costumes."

"Fine," he gave in. "Where are they?"

"In my bathroom." She bit her lip and smiled. "I'm going to give you a fashion show."

He raised an eyebrow. "I thought you were rushed for time?"

"It's impossible to tell how something looks unless it's off the hanger," she said. "And if I'm running a little late, it won't be the end of the world."

He said nothing, which she took as him giving in, and she hurried into the bathroom. She studied the costumes on the counter. Which one first? They all looked hot on her, but she started with the one that covered the most skin. Not that it covered a *lot* of skin—just more than the other two options.

She reentered the bedroom and posed, expecting a visible reaction from Jackson. But his bored expression didn't change.

"You don't like it?" she asked.

He shrugged. "It's the same as all the other dresses you wear, but with cheetah all over it."

"It's not cheetah." She pulled at the bottom of the form-fitting minidress. "It's leopard. And the headband with the ears makes it obvious it's a costume."

"It's unoriginal," he said. "Half the girls in Vegas will be dressed like a jungle animal tonight."

"Fine." So much for the leopard dress. It was also her least favorite of the three options—for the same reason Jackson had said—so she wasn't bummed by his lack of enthusiasm. Just wait until he saw the other two costumes.

Back in the bathroom, she put on the next one—a "sexy princess slave" costume she'd found online. The top was a golden bikini with snake patterns on it, and the matching bottom had two pieces of brown fabric in front and back with enough space between them so they didn't cover her legs. The model wearing the costume on the package had her hair in a side braid, so Peyton quickly braided her hair and stepped out into her room.

Jackson's eyes widened, and he smiled. *That* was more like it.

She placed her hands on her hips to draw his attention to her bare stomach. "I take it you like this one?"

"I do, but it's unexpected," he said. "I didn't know you were a *Star Wars* fan."

"*Star Wars?*" She scrunched her nose. "I've never seen *Star Wars.*"

"Then how did you find that costume?"

"Online." She shook her hips so the fabric danced around her legs. "In the Sexy Costume section. It's a 'princess slave girl' costume."

"And did this 'princess slave girl' have a name?"

"I don't know." Her eyes narrowed. "I think she did, but I didn't pay attention to it."

"She did." He sounded so obnoxiously full of himself. "Does Princess Leia sound familiar?"

Peyton scowled. "Please, don't tell me she's a character from *Star Wars.*"

"You'll be attracting nerd boys all night." Jackson chuckled, and even though Peyton was annoyed, she loved hearing him laugh. "Beware of Luke Skywalkers and Han Solos breaking out in light-saber duels for your attention."

"There will be no light-whatever duels, because I'm not dressing up as someone from a weird sci-fi movie."

"*Star Wars* isn't weird." Jackson stood straighter, looking honestly offended. "If you gave the movies a chance, you might like them."

"Whatever." Code for *no way in hell.* "Hopefully you'll like the next costume."

"Change away, princess."

She ignored his sarcasm and went back into the bathroom. The final option was the hottest of the three—a costume no straight male could refuse. If Jackson didn't like it…well, then Peyton knew some bars in San Francisco that might cater more to his taste.

She walked back into the bedroom, placed a hand on her waist and popped her hip. "What do you think of this one?"

Jackson stared at her, his eyes so intense that Peyton could barely breathe. "I like it," he finally said. "What's it supposed to be?"

"A nurse," she said slowly.

"In what world do nurses wear leather miniskirts, crop tops and fishnets?" His voice was calm and controlled, but Peyton had seen enough of his initial reaction to know he wasn't unaffected. Could her plan actually be working?

Not wanting to break the mood, she touched the red stethoscope draped over her neck and sauntered toward him, until their bodies were nearly touching. "The world where it's Halloween, and they're at clubs." She looked up at him through her eyelashes, her heart pounding when he didn't move away. "And since you have to go everywhere I go, you'll be there, too. Maybe you'll even dance with me." She circled her hips to demonstrate, and his eyes dilated as he watched, his hand twitching forward as if to touch her.

Then he stepped back, putting ample space between them. "I actually have the night off. The night guard will be taking over at ten."

"But you're always my guard on the weekends." Her lungs deflated, and she tried sounding annoyed to mask her hurt. "The night guard is for when I'm sleeping."

"As you know, it's Halloween." Jackson motioned to her costume and smiled. "You're not the only one who wants to spend the night with your friends."

"You have friends?" Peyton said. "I thought you hung out with Teddy and Carl." Those were her sisters' bodyguards, and once she'd said it, she regretted it. Of course Jackson had a life outside of watching her. He did have Monday and Tuesday off. Why had she never asked him what he did when he wasn't working?

Probably because he insisted on keeping a "professional distance" and rarely talked to her like she was a real person instead of an assignment.

"Yes, I have friends," he said. "Hard to believe, but I have a few of them."

"Of course you do." Peyton attempted to laugh it off, but it came out as an awkward, girly giggle. She winced at what an idiot she sounded like. "You'll have fun with them tonight. And it's probably better that you're not there, anyway, because Jill and I are meeting up with her friends from UNLV. Seniors. In a fraternity."

Jackson's fists tightened. "How does your friend know senior fraternity guys?"

"They're friends with her brother." She shrugged. "No big deal."

"And they want to spend Halloween with a high school girl and her friend?"

"Yes." Peyton somehow waved it off, even though his words stung. "Why do you care? Unless you're jealous? Because there are ways you could convince me to stay. We could spend your night off together." She tilted her head, and stepped forward to close the gap between them.

His eyes burned with emotion, his lips inches from hers, and heat rushed through her at the possibility that he was about to pull her toward him and kiss her. She wanted him to press her against the wall and rip the sexy nurse costume right off her. Her body thrummed with anticipation, and unable to resist any longer, she brushed her lips against his.

"No." He shook his head and pulled away, his eyes flashing with irritation, and anger…and what Peyton could have sworn was desire. "I've said it before and I'll say it again—this can't happen."

"But you want it to," she challenged, frustrated that she'd come so close and been pushed away again. "You should stop being such a 'can't' person and try being more of a 'want' person."

"What does that mean?" he asked.

"Just that you're always so concerned about what you 'can' and 'can't' do that you don't do what you *want* to do."

"You have no idea what you're talking about."

"I think I do." She forced herself to sound confident, despite her palms sweating so much that she had to wipe them on her skirt. "You just don't want to admit I'm right."

"Well, I *wanted* to have the night off tonight, and that's what I'm doing." He stomped away from her and opened the door. "I'm guessing you have to finish getting ready, so I'm going to wait out the rest of my shift in the hall. Have a fun night, Peyton. And try to stay out of trouble…if you can manage it."

And with that, he left her alone.

chapter 16: *Madison*

Madison wasn't in the mood to go out for Halloween. But she'd been keeping her word to be more social, so when Oliver offered her and their friends a cabana at Luxe, she agreed to go. The theme was Angels and Devils, and while it didn't leave much room for unique costumes, Madison had dressed as a "dark/fallen angel." Her black minidress flowed enough so it didn't show the weight she'd gained, and she'd topped off the outfit with fluffy black wings and a halo she'd found at the Halloween store, along with heavy black eyeliner. The costume fit her dark mood perfectly.

She was trying to have fun with her friends, but since she couldn't tell anyone about Adrian Diamond being her biological father, there was a gap between them she couldn't close. She felt distant from *everyone*. Especially from Oliver. They'd been spending more time together recently because of the tutoring sessions, and every day he reached out made her feel worse about keeping this secret from him.

"Hey." As if he knew she was thinking about him, Oliver

plopped into the empty space next to her. He was dressed as a devil, with a red smoking jacket and fake horns. "You look bored. Is everything all right?"

"Of course." Madison forced a smile. "I was just checking out everyone's Halloween costumes."

"There are some crazy ones out there." He looked over the balcony of their cabana as a bodybuilder walked by with every inch of his skin painted red, his only piece of clothing a tight red speedo.

"Thanks for getting the cabana and convincing me to come out," she said. "I don't want you to think I haven't noticed how much you've been there for me these past few weeks. Because I *have* noticed, and I appreciate it." Madison was rarely so open about her feelings, especially in a place this public, but Oliver deserved to know that his reaching out wasn't going unnoticed.

"Of course, Mads," he said. "I know you'll get through whatever's going on, but even the strongest person can't do it alone." He looked into her eyes so intensely, as if she were the only person in the club, and placed his hands over hers. A bolt of warmth shot through her body, and Madison's breathing slowed. She recognized the look in his eyes—it was the look guys gave her when they wanted to kiss her.

Strangely enough, the thought of his lips pressed against hers made her heart race. Feeling barely in control of her actions, she held her gaze with his and leaned forward, as if daring him to do it.

"Hey, guys." Larissa broke into their conversation, and Madison jolted away from Oliver, shaking herself out of the daze. Had Oliver really been about to kiss her in front of everyone? And had she been about to *let* him? Her cheeks heated. What had she been doing?

"Hey, Larissa." Oliver sounded annoyed. "What's up?"

"I was about to take a restroom break and was seeing if Madison wanted to join me," she said, shooting Madison a look that said *If you don't come with me, there will be hell to pay later.*

This must be about Oliver. He and Larissa had been "friends with benefits" over the summer, but the "benefits" part had ended in August. Larissa had claimed Oliver was too much of a player for her to take seriously, and she'd moved on to Harrison. But judging by how she looked like she could shoot fire out of her eyes—which was amplified by the red corset, matching miniskirt and devil horns she was wearing—she was pissed.

"Sure," Madison agreed, standing up and trying to shake off whatever had just happened between her and Oliver. She and Oliver had always occasionally flirted, but she'd never allowed their friendship to become anything more because she didn't want to be another one of his conquests.

But was that all she would really be to him? She hoped that if anything happened between them, it would mean more than that—to both of them. And she had no idea what to think about that.

They finished washing their hands, and Larissa hurled her paper towel into the trash. "What the hell was that all about?" she said, her eyes blazing.

"What do you mean?" Maybe if Madison played clueless, Larissa would drop it. Because she wasn't quite sure what had just happened, either.

"You and Oliver." Larissa grabbed Madison's arm and pulled her to the corner of the restroom, stumbling and leaning against the wall. Now that Madison was closer to Larissa, she could smell that her friend reeked of alcohol. She had to get out of there, fast. Larissa had a notorious temper when she drank while upset. "Are you two secretly seeing each other? Is that why you've been acting so weird lately?"

"There's nothing going on between me and Oliver," she said, her voice shaking.

"Oh, please." Larissa rolled her eyes. "The two of you looked like you wanted to rip each other's clothes off right where you were sitting."

"We did not," Madison insisted, although her cheeks heated at the image of them doing just that. She shouldn't be thinking of Oliver that way...but the intense way he'd been watching her, as if she were the only person in the club—in the *world*—that he cared about, refused to leave her mind. "Anyway, what does it matter? I thought you were dating Harrison."

"Harrison and I have a thing now, but I was with Oliver all summer," she said. "And now I find out that you've been screwing him behind my back? How long have you been lying to me?"

"Whoa, there." Madison choked back laughter. "Oliver and I have been friends since lower school. Nothing has ever happened between us. And you know that the moment *that* happens for the first time—with *anyone*—you'll be one of the first people to know."

"Do I really?" Larissa shot back. "Because since you moved into the Diamond, you've become a completely different person."

"No, I haven't." Madison could barely force the words out, since she knew they weren't true.

"Yes, you have," Larissa said. "I barely know you anymore. First I thought you needed time to adjust to living on the Strip, and you did start returning to normal in August and September. But then you got weird again. You rarely hang out with us outside of school anymore, and when you do it's like you don't want to be there. But after seeing you with Oliver I put it together. You two are sleeping together and keeping it from everyone. I suppose it explains the weight gain. Now that you and Oliver are together, you must not be concerned with keeping a perfect body to make sure every other guy at school is pining after you, too." She laughed, bitter and resentful. "It must have been the reason he ended things with me. I always knew you were selfish, but I never thought you would be such a bitch to *me*."

Madison clenched her fists, every muscle in her body tight. Larissa might only be saying those things because she was drunk, but this was going too far.

"Until now, you said that you and Oliver 'mutually agreed' to end your friends-with-benefits thing from the summer," she said, her tone laced with venom. "You acted like you were happy about it because he was too much of a player for you, so I couldn't have known otherwise. And stop assuming all this crap about me. Because I'm *not* sleeping with him, but if I were, he would care more about me than he ever could for you."

Madison was shocked after it left her mouth—she hadn't meant to be that mean. But Larissa was looking at her like she was the most horrible person on the planet, and the words had already been said—she couldn't take them back.

"You are such a bitch." Larissa pushed Madison aside and hurried out of the restroom. A group of women nearby must have been listening, because they'd stopped chattering and were gaping at Madison like she was the Wicked Witch of the West. Madison stared them down, and they went back to their business.

A few months ago, she would have strutted back into the

cabana and made the rest of the night extra fun, not letting a stupid fight get to her. But a few months ago, she never would have *had* a fight like that with Larissa. She wouldn't have been so confused about her feelings for Oliver. And she'd had no idea what her parents had been keeping from her—that her entire life had been a lie.

She didn't have the energy to pretend everything was okay anymore. She just wanted to go home.

Luckily there were enough taxis from people arriving to the party that it was easy to catch one back to the Diamond. She settled into the backseat, and relaxed as it headed home. She couldn't wait to take a sleeping pill and pass out for the night.

Then her phone buzzed with a text. Oliver.

Where did u go?

Wasn't feeling well, so I'm going home.

Want me to come over?

She chewed her lower lip, her thumbs hovering over the keyboard. She was pretty sure Oliver had been about to kiss her, and if Larissa hadn't interrupted, Madison would have let him. Would he expect them to continue where they'd left off? And more important, was that what she wanted?

She imagined what it would have been like if he *had* kissed her, and her heart fluttered. What was happening to her? Oliver was her *friend*. If they kissed, it would change everything. But people said the best relationships started as friendships. Could that be happening to them?

Possibly. But if this was going somewhere, she didn't want it to start on a lie. Nothing could happen between them until she came clean to him about her father. And since he'd been drinking since dinner, now wasn't the right time for that. Plus, she wasn't sure if she was ready to betray her parents' trust—despite how they'd betrayed hers.

I'm just going to go to sleep. Don't leave the party on my account. Have fun tonight! ☺

She pressed Send and shoved her phone into her bag. She might not be ready to tell him everything, but the secret had become a parasite eating away inside her, turning her into a shadow of the person she used to be.

It wouldn't be long until it came pouring out.

www.campusbuzz.com

Oliver Prescott and Madison Lockhart??
Posted on Saturday 11/1 at 11:47 AM

I was in the bathroom at Luxe last night and overheard a massive fight between Madison and Larissa. Oliver and Madison have been sleeping together behind Larissa's back for MONTHS and Larissa only found out about it last night. Madison was so nasty to Larissa and all but admitted it was true. It goes to show that Madison is a huge bitch, and not worth being friends with. If you're friends with her (or *think* you're friends with her, since Madison doesn't care about anyone but herself), run far, far away. You'll thank me later.

1: Posted on Saturday 11/1 at 12:19 PM
i thought Madison was a virgin?

2: Posted on Saturday 11/1 at 12:33 PM
Madison's a bitch and a liar. She probably lost her virginity before any other girl in her grade, but lied to cover it up so people wouldn't think she was a slut.

3: Posted on Saturday 11/1 at 12:52 PM
she's probably been hooking up with oliver since middle school. wouldn't be surprised!

4: Posted on Saturday 11/1 at 1:07 PM

She got a hotel room with Damien at the Gates over the summer, too. I'd bet she's been with him AND Oliver for who knows how long. What a slut-whore.

5: Posted on Saturday 11/1 at 1:18 PM

The proper term is "slore."

But really, people. Here you go again gossiping about situations you know nothing about. Let's back up and think about this logically. Like every student at Goodman, I know that Madison and Oliver have been close friends since lower school. If they *did* sleep together—which you can't assume from this site—it's probably because they care about each other. But whether or not that's the case, it's their business, not yours. And it makes no sense to go from Madison hooking up with Oliver to her being some slut who sleeps around. She might not have the reputation for being the nicest girl in school, but the lot of you are no better.

6: Posted on Saturday 11/1 at 1:34 PM

your missing the point: madison and larissa were supposed to be friends, and madison was hooking up with oliver when larissa had a thing with him! which makes madison a BITCH!!

7: Posted on Saturday 11/1 at 1:49 PM

*You're

8: Posted on Saturday 11/1 at 1:57 PM
really? correcting grammer? this is the *internet*, not an essay for school...

9: Posted on Saturday 11/1 at 2:02 PM
*grammar

10: Posted on Saturday 11/1 at 2:13 PM
This wouldn't be getting so out of control if Madison just owned up to what she did. I mean, she led Damien on the moment he showed interest in Savannah, so clearly Madison just doesn't like other girls getting their hands on her boy-toys. But the way she and Oliver went behind Larissa's back for so long makes her even more of a slore. One good thing comes from this: Now that the secret's out, she'll have no friends, which is what that bitch deserves.

11: Posted on Saturday 11/1 at 2:28 PM
and she's been gaining weight, so if you want to bang her while she's still hott, get on it now!!

chapter 17: *Savannah*

"Abandon will be opening in mid-December, but it'll be ready to go by the end of November," Rebecca said as she led Savannah, Alyssa and the party planner through the double-door entrance and into the club. "I can't think of a better way to test it out than having it be the location for your Sweet Sixteen."

Abandon was on the main floor of the Diamond Residences tower, and even though it wasn't finished yet—the walls were still bare, the tables were piled in a mountain in the center and the pool was empty—Savannah knew from the design plans that it would be beautiful once it was ready. Opposed to Myst, which had a vertical feel with its three floors, Abandon had low ceilings and was spread out through multiple rooms on the same level. The main room featured a long bar with mirrored walls behind it and a DJ stage overlooking a dance floor. Behind that, an elevated platform held VIP tables and booths. Farther back, on the other side of the platform, was a smaller bar and gambling tables. And parallel to everything was an outside area with a huge wading pool with large round cushions in the middle, palm trees, two floors of cabanas creating the outside wall and, of course, another bar.

Photos weren't allowed since the club hadn't opened yet, so Rebecca had Savannah and Alyssa leave their phones with the bodyguards who were waiting at the entrance. Rebecca and the party planner were deep in discussion about the design details, so Savannah and Alyssa explored.

"This place is amazing!" Alyssa said, her eyes wide. "Your Sweet Sixteen is going to be the best of the year."

"It is going to be pretty great," Savannah agreed. And she *was* excited, but at the same time, this would be the first birthday she would celebrate without her mom there. Every year, the two of them had gone to Dunkin' Donuts for breakfast and stuffed themselves with doughnuts. For dinner, she, her sisters, Mom and Grandma had gone to Macaroni Grill, which used to be Savannah's favorite, and for dessert they'd gone to Grandma's, where they would eat the cookie or brownie cake Grandma had made that day with vanilla bean ice cream on top.

A lump formed in Savannah's throat, her eyes prickling with tears. She cared more about celebrating her birthday than Courtney and Peyton did theirs, so everyone had gone out of their way to make her day special. They'd even been allowed to skip school if her birthday landed on a weekday. Now this would be her most extravagant birthday yet, and Mom and Grandma wouldn't be there to see it.

"Are you okay?" Alyssa played with the end of her long, dark ponytail. "You suddenly looked really sad."

"I'm fine." Savannah blinked away the tears. "I was just thinking about how this will be the first birthday I'll celebrate without my mom and grandma."

"You're visiting them over Thanksgiving, right?" Alyssa

asked, and Savannah nodded. "I thought you were going to celebrate both Thanksgiving and your birthday when you were there?"

"We will." She shrugged. "But it's not the same as celebrating on the actual day. A birthday is special because it's the *one* day of the year that's yours. If you celebrate on days that aren't that day, it's no different than any of the other three hundred and sixty-four days of the year that aren't your birthday."

"I guess," Alyssa said. "There's no way they can come here?"

"Nope." Savannah shook her head. "My Grandma needs my mom home to help her take care of Aunt Sophie."

No one knew her mom had been in rehab, so Aunt Sophie's cancer was the excuse Savannah used about why her mom never visited. But really, her mom wouldn't be at her sixteenth birthday party because Vegas was a terrible place for a recovering alcoholic. There would be an open bar at the party for the adults, although, since it was a private party, those under twenty-one would probably get served anyway. The temptation would create a rough environment for her mom, especially combined with the stress of seeing Adrian for the first time in years.

They walked outside to check out the pool, and Savannah imagined what it would look like when it was filled with water and people were lounging near the bar and inside the cabanas. There was even a retractable roof if it was too cold for outdoor swimming, which it probably would be at night in December.

"So, who are you inviting?" Alyssa asked.

"The entire team, and everyone in our grade," Savannah said, glad the conversation had veered away from her mom. "Courtney and Peyton also get to invite some people. And, of course, Adrian and Rebecca are inviting a ton of their friends.

Which unfortunately includes the Prescott and Lockhart families." Savannah hadn't been thrilled when Rebecca had broken that news, but since Adrian was close with both families—and was paying for the party—she couldn't say no. "Rebecca is apparently best friends with Madison's mom, and promised her that she would invite some of Madison's friends, too. So Madison doesn't feel 'uncomfortable.'" Savannah rolled her eyes, unable to picture Madison being uncomfortable *anywhere*.

"It'll definitely be an…interesting group," Alyssa said.

"There you are, girls," Rebecca said, walking up with the party planner behind her. "What do you think of Abandon?"

"It's perfect," Savannah said, smiling. "I'm just worried that it's so huge that there won't be enough people to fill it up!"

The party planner, Gail, glanced down at her clipboard. "There will be so much going on, you won't need as many people as you think to fill up the space," she said. "We're going to have the seated dinner in the middle section, and the appetizer and dessert bar will be in the back. I gave Rebecca a list of food options, so the two of you can sit down later and discuss what you want. Out by the pool we'll have various entertainment stations set up, like henna tattoos, photo booths, psychic readings, massages, a caricature artist, a cell phone bling station and more. And the gambling area will be open to all ages, since every guest will receive three chips upon arrival, and the proceeds from all further chips purchased will go to a charity of your choosing."

"You're officially going to have the best Sweet Sixteen ever," Alyssa said, breathless.

"Don't spoil the plans to anyone, though," Savannah told her. "I want everyone to be surprised."

"Speaking of a surprise," Rebecca said, "I put in an inquiry a few weeks ago, and recently heard back from the producers with the go-ahead. How would you feel about having your party featured on *My Fabulous Sweet Sixteen?*"

Alyssa squealed, but Savannah froze, at a loss for words. She'd watched the show a few times with Evie, and the girls on it were spoiled brats. One of them had thrown a temper tantrum because the BMW her dad bought her wasn't the exact model she'd wanted. Savannah was nothing like that.

She would *appreciate* her party. But maybe that would put her in a good light? And she did want recognition from the entertainment industry. It could spread word about her YouTube channel.

"How does Adrian feel about it?" she asked. "I know he does everything he can to keep us from bad publicity, and those shows aren't known for presenting the girls positively...."

"I've already discussed that with the producers," Rebecca said. "They were so excited to have us on the show that they signed an agreement with our lawyer to only air footage we approved. We can also buy back the rights to the episode if we don't like the finished version, so the producers are going to make sure we're happy with it. All we need is your consent, and we're good to go."

"You can't turn this down," Alyssa chimed in. "It's the opportunity of a lifetime. Your party was already going to be the best of the year, but with it being on *My Fabulous Sweet Sixteen,* it'll be the best *ever.*"

"Okay, okay," Savannah said, her head spinning. "I'll do it."

"Great," Rebecca said. "Now that you've agreed...some of the camera crew is here now. They want to get preliminary footage of you seeing the venue for the first time, your excitement about the party and some more small things for the show. Tomorrow they'll be interviewing you and the rest of the family, next week they'll come along with us when we go dress shopping and more."

"But I thought we weren't allowed to take photos of the club right now," Savannah said.

"You're not," Rebecca said. "But the producers are contracted not to let the footage release until the club opens. So... shall I bring them in?"

"Sure." Savannah took a deep breath. "Let's do it. And... thank you. It was pretty cool of you to make this happen."

"I know moving away from home hasn't been easy, and I want you to be happy here." Rebecca squeezed Savannah's hand and went to fetch the camera crew. She would obviously never replace Mom or Grandma, but she was trying so hard to be welcoming. Savannah had always been grateful for that.

It didn't take the crew long to set up, fix Savannah's hair and makeup and get things rolling. They must have been doing this for so long that they had it down to a science. It felt so unreal. The film crew of *My Fabulous Sweet Sixteen* was here, to feature *her party* on the show. Her brain felt so jittery and jumbled she could hardly think.

"Let's start with you introducing yourself and letting the viewers know where you are," the director, Carson, said. "Start talking at one, two...and *go!*"

The lights blasted in Savannah's eyes, and she blinked a few times to try and see. Everyone was watching her, expecting her to say something brilliant. She swallowed and played with her bracelets, unsure what they wanted to hear.

"Hi." Her voice shook, and she waved awkwardly at the camera. "I'm Savannah Diamond, and I'm turning sixteen on December thirteenth. We're all here at Abandon nightclub...." She motioned around the club. "And, um...this is where the party's going to be!" Her voice sounded overly perky at the end, and she did a little dance, wincing at how incredibly awkward that all was.

From the blank expressions on the camera crew's face, it was worse than she'd thought.

She shielded her eyes from the lights. "Do you want me to try again?"

"Yes, let's try again," Carson said. "This time, speak louder and relax. Be confident. Let the viewers *feel* your excitement!"

"Okay." Savannah bounced her knees, thinking *excitement!!!* and the camera started rolling again.

"Hi!" she said so loudly that she felt like she was screaming. "I'm Savannah Diamond! I'm turning sixteen soon, and this is where my party will be!" She held her arms wide, then realized she'd forgotten to say the name of the venue. "The party will be at Abandon nightclub," she said, stumbling at the scared look on Carson's face. "The club's going to be awesome for the party...and it's not opening for real until after my party...so everyone will be partying here for the first time...." She forced a bright smile, gave a double thumbs-up and added, "I can't wait for the party!"

The red recording light went off, and she clenched her fists, stomping her foot on the floor. How many times had she said the word *party* in the past few seconds? And giving a *thumbs-up?* This was nothing like singing on camera, when the words were already written and she was around people she knew, instead of total strangers.

"Sorry." She shuffled her feet, unable to meet anyone's eyes. "That was awful."

"You're just warming up," Carson said. "Take a minute to think about what you're going to say, and then we'll try again."

Each take was one disaster after another. They tried filming in different spots around the club, with Carson asking her questions to lead what she was saying, and even with him feeding her lines, she messed up every time. She was so frustrated she wanted to throw something. Each take was getting worse, not better.

Finally, Carson said, "We're not getting anywhere with this today. For now, let's get basic footage of you walking around with everyone, chatting about party plans. We'll interview Rebecca and your party planner, and we'll try again with you tomorrow."

They struggled through a few takes of Savannah walking around the club, pretending to talk party details with Gail and Rebecca. Finally, the camera crew packed up to get B-roll of the Diamond, saying they would see her again tomorrow. Savannah didn't miss the warning in Carson's tone—that she'd better be prepared.

"I was awful, wasn't I?" she said once the production crew was gone.

"It wasn't that bad," Alyssa said, although she hardly sounded convincing. "But my parents better sign these release papers, because I *need* to be on the show with you. And maybe it'll be easier when you're filming with friends."

"You just weren't ready," Rebecca said. "It was my fault. I wanted it to be a surprise, but I should have given you warning so we could prepare. We'll practice tonight so you'll be ready for tomorrow, okay?"

"Okay," Savannah said, although there was an awful pit in her stomach. What if she was terrible at acting and couldn't get them the footage they wanted no matter how much she practiced?

She tried to push aside her worries as they discussed more party details. After what felt like forever, they headed out, reclaiming their bags from the guards at the entrance. Right after picking hers up, Savannah's iPhone buzzed. She took it out to see who was texting her.

Her screen had blown up with alerts. Texts, missed calls, Tweets, Facebook, Snapchat—the red alert circles on the top right of each icon were in the double digits. What was going on? Had another embarrassing thing been posted about her online? Savannah's stomach sank even further, and she opened her texts, bracing herself for whatever she was about to see.

Evie had texted her most recently, and she saw the last of the long series of messages first.

OMG I can't believe this is happening! You are soooo lucky! CALL ME BACK ASAP!!

Savannah's pulse quickened, and she scrolled up to read Evie's texts from the beginning.

I'm listening to the Ryder Garrison Weekend Top 40 Count-down on Top Hits and he has this Net Watchers thing where he talks about YouTube artists he finds who have amazing covers and this week he PLAYED A CLIP OF YOUR MOST RE-CENT COVER SONG!! The One Connection one! He's play-ing it every three hours for THE ENTIRE WORLD TO HEAR!!! And he announces your YouTube name, too!!

"Omigod." Savannah could barely breathe as she checked the rest of her texts, Tweets and other alerts. Everything confirmed that her song was being broadcast on an international radio show. People she'd never met were Tweeting her that they loved her music and had subscribed to her channel. She wanted to reply to them all, but there was no way she could do it on her cell. She had to get to her computer.

"What happened?" Rebecca fiddled with her pearls. "Is everything all right?"

"Hold on." Savannah had to see her YouTube channel. She clicked on her profile and took a sharp breath inward when she saw that her number of subscribers was up by the *thousands*. And the number of views for her recent video had passed the five-digit mark—in less than one day. "Omigod," she said again. "I can't believe this." But when she blinked, it was all still there.

"You're killing us here." Alyssa twisted her ponytail, and she leaned forward to see Savannah's phone. "What's going on?"

Savannah repeated what Evie had said in her text, each word coming out faster than the last. "Now I have over five thousand subscribers and my video views are over seventy thousand. And it's still going up!"

Alyssa took her own iPhone out of her bag and tapped the screen. "Wow," she said after a few seconds. "This is amazing, Savannah! I can't believe it."

"I can't believe it either!" The words were coming so fast that it hurt to breathe. "Do we have Sirius radio anywhere?"

"I'm sure we can find it somewhere." Rebecca's face glowed. "Come on."

Which was how Savannah, Alyssa, Rebecca, Peyton and Courtney found themselves in Savannah's room twenty minutes later, gathered around Courtney's MacBook Pro, listening to Top Hits through their newly purchased subscription of Sirius radio. Ryder Garrison's *Weekend Top 40 Countdown* was on a three-hour loop, which took ages when you were waiting for a specific part.

They would have used Savannah's computer, but she was too busy replying to the comments on her YouTube and Twitter. She loved talking to everyone who had watched her video, but the coolest part was that they seemed even happier that Savannah was taking the time to talk to *them*. As if she wouldn't? Before now, no one had heard of her channel. Savannah wanted to make sure to reply to every single person who took the time to message her so they knew how grateful she was for their support.

Peyton brought in her computer, and they used it to chat on Skype their mom.

"Hey, girls," Mom said after picking up. Her hair was pulled back in a ponytail, and she was dressed in what looked suspiciously like gym clothes. "Sorry I missed your earlier phone calls—I had my yoga class at the gym. What's up?"

Once Savannah got over the initial shock of her mom going to the gym—her mom *never* worked out—she shared the news.

"Oh, honey, that's wonderful." Her mom beamed. "I have a doctor's appointment in an hour, but I'll stay on the line and listen with you until I have to leave, okay?"

It wasn't the same as her being in the room with them, but it was the best they could get. After a few minutes of chatting, Savannah stepped aside to call Damien, since he'd done so much for her to make this happen.

The moment she told him the news, he said he would be right there and hung up. He also lived in the Diamond, so he was at her door in a minute. She let him inside, and he picked her up and swung her around in a circle in the middle of the living room—she felt like a princess in a fairy tale.

"I can't believe this is happening!" Savannah said once he put her down.

"Believe it," he said, his dark eyes shining down on her. "I Tweeted Ryder telling him about your video right after you'd put it online, and I'd hoped he would give it a listen, but... wow. I can't believe it made the show."

"*You* made this happen?" Savannah said, realizing that this entire time they'd been talking, Damien's hands had been wrapped around hers. And she didn't want him to let go.

"No," he said, giving her hands a squeeze. "*We* made this happen. You made the decision not to delete your channel after that video of you at the party was posted, and to persevere and get more songs out there. I only tried to let people know about you."

He was looking at her with so much admiration, and Savannah's heart raced, her head dizzy. There were no words to get across how grateful she felt. She wanted more than anything to kiss him again, like she had over the summer, before everything had blown up with Madison. But despite their almost-kiss in the wine closet, she wasn't sure Damien was interested in her as more than a friend. She was afraid of making the first move and getting rejected. Also, her family was nearby.

So she wrapped her arms around his neck, her cheek brushing his. "Thank you," she said softly, her lips close to his ear. "You have no idea how much this means to me."

He took a sharp breath, and for a second, she dared to think that being close to her was having an effect on him. That the feelings he'd claimed to have for her that summer had been real.

"Savannah!" Peyton yelled, interrupting the moment between her and Damien—if there had been at moment at all. "Ryder's coming back on…. This might be it!"

Savannah dragged Damien into her room, and like everyone had done multiple times, they paused whatever they were doing to listen.

"This is Ryder with a *Y,* bringing you the Sirius XM Top Hits *Weekend Top 40 Countdown.* Now here's your weekly *Net*

Watchers! I was blown away by this fantastic cover on YouTube, and I wanted to share it with you all, so listen to this clip."

Savannah squealed and bounced on her bed as a few lines from the chorus of her recent cover played for the entire world to hear. Her heart beat faster, and her eyes filled with tears of happiness. People were sitting around at their homes, or driving in their cars, and they were listening to *her*. On the *radio*. This was un-freakin'-believable.

"If you want to hear more from this talented new artist, go to YouTube.com/SavannahDiamond," Ryder said. "And now, for the next song on the *Weekend Top 40 Countdown*. Up ten spots from last week, give it up for your five favorite boys from the UK, One Connection!"

"Wow," Savannah said for what felt like the millionth time this afternoon. "I can't believe it."

"Well, you should, because we all just heard it!" Alyssa said. "You're totally on your way to YouTube stardom."

The words sent chills down Savannah's spine.

"It is pretty incredible," Peyton said. "I've always known you're talented, but when you started putting your videos online I never thought *this* would happen."

"It's amazing," Courtney said. "Of course I've always believed in you, but stuff like this rarely happens. Even the most talented people sometimes never get discovered. But this..." She shook her head, running her fingers through her hair. "*Wow* is right. I'm so proud of you, Savannah." From the tears in her eyes, Savannah could tell she meant it.

"I'm proud of you, too," their mom said, looking so healthy and radiant on the computer screen. "When you visit for Thanksgiving, we'll do something special to celebrate."

"That would be great," Savannah said. "I can't wait to come back home and see you."

"And I can't wait to see you," she said. "But I don't want to be late for my appointment, so I have to run. I'm so glad to have been there with you to hear that. I love you girls."

"Love you, too," Savannah and Courtney chorused, at the same time as Peyton said, "See you soon."

Their mom's face disappeared from the screen, and there was silence for a few seconds.

"I'd say a celebration is in order," Rebecca said. "Are you all up for ice cream? Serendipity has the best on the Strip, and this is the perfect excuse for a splurge."

Every one of them said yes, and they gathered to leave. Savannah couldn't believe this was all happening. Her body thrummed with excitement, but she was nervous, too.

She didn't want to do anything to mess this up.

chapter 18: *Courtney*

The rest of November slipped by in the routine of school, homework, tutoring, Habitat, SAT practice and a more-than-usual amount of reading for pleasure. The camera crew for *My Fabulous Sweet Sixteen* was also around sometimes, but Courtney did her best to avoid them. She'd had one interview, but that was it. Luckily, the show was focused on Savannah. Who, as much as Courtney hated to admit it, was a much better singer than actor. The director was pretty frustrated with her. But Rebecca had hired Savannah an acting tutor, which would hopefully pay off soon.

At the end of school on the Monday before Thanksgiving, Courtney grabbed popped chips from the vending machine and headed to the student tutoring center, like she did every Monday and Wednesday after school. Madison was already there, sitting on the couch nibbling on apple slices, along with Dani and Lizzie, who tutored in history and French. Courtney sat at the opposite side of the room and checked her email and Facebook until Mrs. Ely came in to give them their tutoring assignments.

"I have Dani in room one and Lizzie in room two," Mrs. Ely said, glancing at her clipboard. "Madison and Courtney, I don't have anyone for you today. Things usually get slow around here with a vacation approaching. If you like, the two of you can stay here and use this time to do your homework. I'll count it toward your tutoring hours for the semester."

They both thanked her, and she went to her office, presumably to get work done herself.

Courtney was glad to have the time to do homework, but not so happy to be stuck in the room with Madison. If Mrs. Ely hadn't specifically told them to stay in the tutoring center, she would have beelined for the library so she wouldn't have to be around the girl.

She reached for her planner and read over her assignments, praying that Madison would ignore Mrs. Ely's instructions and leave. Instead, she sat back and made herself more comfortable on the couch.

"Do you have any plans for Thanksgiving break?" Madison asked casually.

As much as Courtney had no interest in befriending Madison after what she'd pulled on Savannah over the summer, she was clearly talking to her, and she had to reply.

"My sisters and I are going to California to visit our mom and grandma," she said. "What about you?" It was her natural instinct to ask in return.

"Just hanging out here," Madison said, as if "here" was the most boring place on Earth.

"Cool." Courtney took a textbook out of her backpack and opened it.

"You and your sisters are all so close in age," Madison continued on, either oblivious to Courtney's desire to get to work or not caring. "What's that like? I've never had any siblings. I imagine it's fun having girls close to your age around all the time, who have to like you no matter what."

"We certainly don't *like* each other all the time." Courtney laughed. "But we do love each other, which is what matters."

"Really?" Madison asked. "You three seem to get along so well."

"I wouldn't say we *don't* get along," she said. "But we're all very different. We get in fights over stupid things, but at the end of the day, we'll always be there for each other."

"It must be nice." Madison's eyes misted over. What was going on with her? She'd never wanted to be friends with Courtney—quite the opposite, actually.

"Yes." Courtney took out her calculator to get started on the math problems. "It is."

"How's it going with Adrian?" Madison crossed her legs, apparently not planning on doing her homework. Or letting Courtney do hers. "You hadn't spent much time with him until you moved here, right?"

Courtney lowered her pencil. "I don't mean to be rude, but why are you asking me all these questions?"

"I was just trying to be nice," she said. "Since we're stuck here together for the next hour."

Courtney didn't buy it. She hadn't forgotten how Madison had hurt Savannah, and how she'd been so snide about what had happened between her and Brett that summer. They had nothing in common and they were *not* friends. "We're supposed to be doing homework."

"You're starting with math?" Madison pulled out her textbook. They shared a lot of classes since they were both juniors and in advanced levels in nearly every subject, but they never sat anywhere near each other.

Courtney nodded and focused on the first problem in the set of thirty due tomorrow.

"Do you want to do the odd problems and I'll do the even?" Madison asked. "Then we can trade answers when we're done."

Courtney chewed on the eraser of her pencil. "Isn't that cheating?"

"No." Madison laughed. "It's being pragmatic. I understand the concept of what we're doing, and I'm sure you do, too. If we do it this way, it'll take half the time."

"And if our teacher notices that we got the exact same questions wrong...?"

Madison raised an eyebrow. "We have unlimited time, and the instructions are in the pages beforehand. How often do *you* get homework questions wrong?"

"Not often," she said. If she struggled with a question, she worked on it until she got it right. She aced practically all of her math homework assignments.

"I thought so." Madison smiled. "So, what do you say? You take the odds and I'll take the evens? Or the other way around. It doesn't matter to me."

Courtney glanced at her planner. She had a lot of homework due tomorrow—blame it on teachers wanting to cram everything in before break. And the book she was reading for fun right now was amazing, and she was dying to know what would happen next, but she wouldn't allow herself to read until her homework was completed. Plus, she understood the math unit, so it was practically all busywork. The logic in Madison's plan was undeniable.

"Fine," she agreed. "I'll take the odds, you take the evens."

They worked on their homework, and luckily, Madison stopped asking Courtney questions about her life as they completed the problems. They finished within five minutes of each other.

"Now we take pictures of each other's homework and copy it when we get home," Madison said, picking up her notebook and joining Courtney on her sofa.

"Okay." Courtney took Madison's notebook, her legs bouncing at the reminder of what they were doing. What if they got caught?

"Don't be so worried," Madison reassured her. "We're working together, not cheating. We didn't need to do double what we did, anyway."

What they'd done wasn't *right*, either. Still, Courtney handed her notebook to Madison and snapped a picture of Madison's notebook with her iPhone.

"So, how are things going between you and Brett?" Madison asked, handing Courtney's notebook back to her. "You two hang out sometimes, right?"

"Our parents are engaged, so, yes, we hang out sometimes." Courtney wasn't giving Madison more than that. "He told me about what happened between the two of you over the summer."

"Yeah, well, that was months ago." Madison shrugged and flipped her hair. "I'm over it now. It was his loss, right?"

"Sure," Courtney said, although she thought staying clear of Madison was the right decision for Brett.

"Anyway, you never answered my question about Adrian," she said. "What's it like having him as a father? He honestly never struck me as the paternal type.... No one even mentioned he had children until you and your sisters moved here."

Since when had Madison become so nosy? And why did

she think any of this was her business? "He just didn't want us growing up in the spotlight." Courtney pulled out her history textbook, uncapped her highlighter and started reading the assigned chapter. Hopefully Madison would get the hint and let her complete her homework in peace.

"Wow." Madison's eyes flashed with hurt. "You really don't want to talk to me, do you?"

Courtney threw her highlighter into the crease of her book. "You've been unwelcoming to me and my sisters since we got here. Do you blame me for not wanting to confide in you about my personal life?"

Madison jerked backward—apparently she hadn't expected Courtney to be so blunt. Courtney hadn't expected it, either. It just sort of came out.

But she wasn't sorry.

"You're right." Madison bit her lower lip, in a rare moment of what appeared to be self-doubt. "I guess I'm trying to apologize."

"Seriously?" Courtney couldn't hide the suspicion in her tone. But she leaned forward, curious about where this would go.

"Yeah," she said. "As the only girl besides you and your sisters who goes to Goodman and lives in the Diamond, I should have reached out when you moved here. But I didn't, and I feel bad about it, so I was hoping we could start over."

It was a decent start. But it didn't begin to cover the main reason Courtney hadn't trusted Madison since week one. "Thanks," she said. "But the person you need to apologize to isn't me—it's Savannah. You weren't interested in Damien, but you knew she was, so what you did to her at Luxe was downright cruel."

"How do you know about all that?"

"Because Savannah's my sister," Courtney said, amazed that Madison could be so clueless. "Of course she comes to her sisters when she needs to talk. And she's friends with Damien now, so she knows all about the way you treated him."

Madison paled—this conversation must not have been going the way she imagined. "You're right," she finally said. "I should apologize to Savannah."

"Yeah." Courtney nodded, although if Madison followed through with that, it would shock her. She readjusted her textbook in her lap to return to her work but couldn't stop herself from saying, "If you don't mind me asking, what brought on this change of heart?"

Madison looked at Courtney intensely, like she was about to tell her something serious. "It's been a rough few weeks for me," she said, her voice wavering. "Some stuff happened with my family that I didn't expect, and I learned that people I thought were my friends aren't truly there for me, after all. And it just really... Well, it sucks pretty badly." Her eyes glazed over, as if she were about to cry, which was the last thing Courtney expected from Madison.

"I'm sorry to hear that." Courtney tried to remain diplomatic, although she didn't feel *too* bad for Madison, since she'd brought it on herself. But it sounded like she needed a sister right now, and since she was an only child, she had no one.

Madison brightened. "So you accept my apology?"

"If you apologize to Savannah, and if *Savannah* accepts your apology, then I will, too."

"I'll do my best." She smiled and walked back over to her couch. "And, Courtney?"

"Yeah?"

"Thanks for listening."

"No problem," Courtney said, giving her a small smile in return.

But even if Madison apologized to Savannah, and if Savannah accepted it, it didn't mean Courtney thought they would ever be friends.

chapter 19: *Peyton*

Peyton walked down the emptying hall to drop off a paper before Thanksgiving break, unable to believe she'd made it through three months at Goodman. When she'd made the deal with Adrian last summer that she could leave after two months if she hated it and go to public school instead, that was what she'd planned on doing. But if she ignored the entitled attitudes of most of the students at Goodman, the actual school part wasn't so bad.

At Fairfield High, they crammed thirty or more students into each room, and the teachers lectured in monotones, just as bored as the kids they were teaching. Peyton had only paid attention to the clock, which moved so slowly that it might as well have been moving backward. It had been prison, and being trapped behind a tiny desk made her feel like she could explode.

But at Goodman the classes were small, with an average of eleven kids, and instead of rows of cramped desks, they had tables in a semicircle. The teachers enjoyed their jobs and led classes in a discussion format instead of lecturing. A bunch of them even went by their first names, to create an environment of equality and positive energy.

When Peyton had started at Goodman, it all had sounded bogus. But now—and she'd never admit it to anyone—she enjoyed some of her classes. There would always be some she hated—like math—but English, history and even science weren't torturous anymore. Which was why, when the two-month mark passed, she'd said nothing to Adrian about switching to public school. He never asked, so they both acted like the deal they'd made in the summer didn't exist.

Since it was the day before break, it was a half day, and most everyone had bolted out of the building the moment the clock hit twelve-fifteen. If Peyton hadn't needed an extension on her English paper—just because she didn't hate school as much anymore didn't mean she was now the best at getting assignments completed on time—she would have been out of there, but she had to drop the paper off at Hunter's office.

She turned the corner to the teachers' hall and ran straight into Oliver Prescott.

"Hey," she said casually, not wanting to give him a chance to scurry away without talking to her.

His eyes darkened—apparently she wasn't on the top of his list of favorite people right now. "Shouldn't you be on your way to California?"

"We're leaving in a few hours," she said. "Just have to drop off this paper first. What're you doing in the teachers' hall?"

"Had to talk with a teacher." He stepped away from her. "But I'm on my way out—I'll see you around."

"Wait." She wasn't letting him get away that easily. "How's it going with that task I gave you? It's been over a month. I thought you'd have completed it by now."

"These things take time," Oliver said, smooth and confident. "But don't worry. I've got this."

"Do you?" Peyton raised an eyebrow. "Because I'm starting to feel like you're stalling."

"This isn't something that can be rushed." He smirked. "Besides, we never agreed on a deadline, so I can take as long as I want."

She clenched her fists; he had the annoying talent of making her blood boil. "If you can't get this done by the end of the year, you're seriously losing your game."

"I'm not losing my game." He looked around, as if making sure no one was listening. Then he leaned forward, lowered his voice and continued, "She was all over me on Halloween. I would have had her if Larissa hadn't showed up and ruined it."

"And Halloween was, what…three weeks ago?" Peyton laughed. "Come on. What've you been doing since then? Don't tell me you're second-guessing yourself. Or maybe Madison's not your type and you're just not attracted to her? I would have a hard time believing that, but, hey, then it makes the task even better."

Oliver gritted his teeth. "I'm plenty attracted to Madison," he said slowly, as if restraining from yelling. "But something's up with her. She's going through something tough, and she won't open up to anyone about it, not even me. So have some compassion and give me time."

Peyton exhaled and crossed her arms. "It's sweet that you care so much about Madison, but I don't care about her feelings. So get it done by New Year's, or who knows what pictures I'll post online when the clock strikes midnight…." She let the threat hang—even though she meant it when she'd promised Savannah they wouldn't post that photo—and Oliver glared at her.

"What do you have against Madison, anyway?" he asked. "I know you're not friends with her, but why do you want to hurt her like this?"

"It's none of your business," Peyton said.

"You *made* it my business when you used our bet as a revenge plan on her."

"Fine," she said, since it wouldn't matter if he knew. "You've seen that Campusbuzz site, right?"

He nodded. "Once or twice."

"I don't really go on it, either," she said, since no one admitted to spending time on it, even if they were addicted. "But a few weeks ago there was a particularly nasty post about me and my sisters. Someone linked me to it, and I checked it out—only to find that one of the pictures on it was one I caught Madison taking of me earlier in the year. I forced her to delete it from her phone, but apparently she'd backed it up first, because I would recognize that picture anywhere."

"So you think *Madison's* behind the post?" Oliver said, as if it were the most unlikely possibility ever.

"Um, yeah, I think she's behind the post," Peyton said. "I'm sure of it. I *saw* her take that picture, and I saw it on her phone. It would be one thing if she'd attacked only me—I would get over it—but she targeted my sisters, too, making up awful lies about them. I won't let her get away with it."

"So now you're using our bet from the summer to get back at Madison for what you *think* she wrote about you and your sisters, and threatening to blackmail me if I don't follow through," he said. "That's pretty devious."

"You're one to talk." Peyton rolled her eyes.

"I never said *devious* was a bad thing." He smirked. "But even if you're right and Madison wrote that post—which I don't think she did—what you're doing is pretty shitty. It's worse than what you think she did to you."

"Whatever." Peyton faltered, because, yes, what she was asking him to do to Madison was awful. But she didn't care how much Oliver doubted it—Madison took those pictures and wrote that post. Who else could it be?

"I have to drop off this paper," she said, since this conversation was only making her feel worse. "Have a fun break. Maybe you can use it to make progress."

With that, she flipped her hair over her shoulder and strutted down the hall, not glancing behind her. She'd already set this in motion—she wasn't backing down now.

She reached the door to Hunter's office, knocked and let herself in without waiting for him to reply. Instead of sitting at his desk, like she imagined most teachers did, Hunter was lounging on his couch, the footrest up as he graded papers. If Peyton hadn't known better, she would have assumed he was a college student finishing the last of his homework before break.

He looked up at her, smiled and dropped his pen onto the stack of papers. "Hey, Peyton," he said, his lazy tone reminding her of when they'd hung out in the cabana. "I was starting to worry you wouldn't show."

She shut the door behind her. "And risk not getting this paper in after you gave me an extension?" She joined him on the couch and offered it to him. "Never."

"Great." He took the paper, and his fingers brushed against hers, sending a warmth shooting through her body. He stared at where their skin had touched, but then he glanced away, adding the paper to the pile. "One more paper for me to grade while you and your friends are enjoying your break," he joked.

"I'm visiting my family in California," she said, crossing

her legs in his direction. "Leaving town in a few hours. But you should try to take *some* time to relax over break. Hang out at a pool...maybe even in a cabana?" She couldn't help it—even though she'd promised Jackson she wouldn't see Hunter anymore outside of school, she wanted to remind him of the time they'd hung out. She wanted to know if he still thought about it. About *her*.

Especially since, after Jackson had rejected her on Halloween, he'd put the wall up between them again. Peyton wasn't *that* forgettable, was she? That easy to push away?

"I don't think I'll be renting any cabanas on my salary." Hunter laughed. "But thanks for letting my friends and me use yours that one day. We had a blast."

"Anytime," she said. "If you ever find yourself at the Diamond pool again, let me know. Maybe I can call in a favor and get you a cabana."

"That's a tempting offer," he said. "But, Peyton, you know we can't see each other outside of school like that again, right? I didn't say anything, because I didn't want to put you in an awkward spot, but the headmaster knows about those pictures. There was nothing in them to prove anything happened—especially since you live at the Diamond, and it would make sense to run into you there—but I did get a warning. If anything else like that pops up online again, I could get in serious trouble."

"The *headmaster* saw those photos?" she asked, and he nodded. "Which I guess means you did, too. You didn't see that entire post that went along with them, did you?"

His eyes flashed with guilt, and he didn't have to say anything to confirm that, yes, he'd seen it all.

Her cheeks heated, and she buried her face in her hands. Why hadn't she thought that Hunter might have seen it? The forum wasn't a huge tabloid or anything, but it was notorious throughout Goodman. And the things that had been written about her—that *Madison* had written about her—it was so humiliating. How much of it had he believed?

She couldn't bring herself to look at him, dreading that his expression would confirm what she feared—that he thought the post was true. That he, along with everyone else at Goodman, agreed with every horrible thing said about her.

"Hey." He pulled her hands down from her face, forcing her to look at him. "Yes, I saw it. I was hoping you hadn't, because whoever wrote it... Well, whoever wrote it is clearly a miserable person. But we both know that none of it was true. That's what matters, okay?" He stayed where he was, his gaze locked with hers, and Peyton's heart beat so fast she felt like she could barely breathe.

So she did the first thing that crossed her mind—she leaned forward and kissed him.

His mouth opened, his tongue brushing softly over hers, and her pulse quickened at the realization that this was actually happening. She was kissing Hunter Sterling. And he was kissing her back. Had she locked the door behind her? Whatever—it didn't matter. She ran her fingers through his hair, pushing her body against his, not wanting this to end.

Then he pulled away and shot out of the couch, his face twisted in horror.

"You need to leave." He pressed his thumb against his forehead, unable to meet her eyes. "If anyone ever found out about this...I could lose my job. We need to forget that ever happened."

Her heart fell. For a moment—for one stupid moment—she'd thought he cared about her.

But she was wrong.

"Fine." She stood up and straightened her top, maintaining as much dignity as possible. "Have a good break."

His only response was to nod and look at the door, as if he couldn't wait for her to go.

She darted out of the room, slammed the door behind her and hurried out of the school. She couldn't wait to go to the airport and get a break from this town. Although that meant seeing Mom and Grandma again, both of whom she hadn't seen since summer. And she wasn't particularly close to either of them. But seeing them had to be better than the rejection she'd been getting at every turn in Vegas…right?

Unfortunately, given her mom's track record, she knew to brace herself for anything.

chapter 20: *Madison*

Since Halloween, Madison's life had been hell. Larissa had convinced their friends that she was a deceitful, slutty bitch, and they'd stopped hanging out with her. The only person who spent time with her outside of school was Oliver. He was the one keeping her sane.

So when Madison got back to her condo on the first day of Thanksgiving break, she wanted to sulk, order pizza and watch season two of *Downton Abbey,* her latest television obsession. But she was five pounds away from losing the weight she'd gained last month, so instead of succumbing to the temptation of Dominos, she stuck a VitaPizza (190 delicious calories!) into the microwave.

Her parents wouldn't be home until that evening, so when her pizza was ready, Madison settled in front of the television for some quality time with Lady Mary and the rest of the *Downton Abbey* crew. It was a great show, and Madison loved historical fiction, but it also kind of tortured her, because it was about three sisters. Which reminded her of the Diamonds and the guilt from keeping the secret from them. Every time she saw one of them in school she felt worse. The secret kept building up inside her, and she would eventually break down from keeping it to herself.

If she hadn't broken down already.

Maybe if she confided in *one* person, she would feel better. Then she could piece herself back together and make sure the second half of junior year wasn't as awful as the first.

Since she'd lost all her other friends, Oliver had to be that person. She trusted him more than she trusted anyone.

But there was that lingering memory of how they'd almost kissed on Halloween. And if she and Oliver had kissed…it would have changed everything between them. Because Oliver hooked up with girls—he didn't *date* anyone—and he eventually broke their hearts. So Madison couldn't let anything happen between them, even if whenever she was around him recently, her stomach fluttered, and her skin tingled when he touched her.

Those feelings couldn't be real. They were a strange reaction to her life falling apart. Plus, they hadn't had another almost-kiss since Halloween. It had been an "in the moment" thing…they were both in costume…they weren't themselves. It was best to forget about it. And she needed her best (only?) friend right now.

She picked up her phone and clicked on her texts with Oliver.

What're you up to right now??

woke up from a nap…about to order lunch. u?

Just finished eating. Do you mind if I come over? There's something important I want to talk to you about.

She stared at the text without sending it. Telling Oliver would change everything. She would be betraying her parents' trust, but it would feel so much better to share this with someone. Oliver would keep the secret.

She took a deep breath and ran her fingers through her hair. Was it fair to drag him into her drama? But she'd been feeling like such crap recently, like a shadow of her former self. She couldn't go on like this any longer.

She pressed Send.

Half an hour later, Madison stood outside the towering double doors of the Prescotts' villa at The Gates. Oliver knew she was coming, so he'd left the doors unlocked, and she let herself in.

She'd been to the villa a lot, but every time she walked inside she was amazed that it looked more like a museum than a home. Unlike the modern penthouses in the Diamond, the villas at the Gates were palatial. Oliver's reminded Madison of the Vatican, with its high ceilings, dark wood, ebony floors and silk-paneled walls. The furniture was thick and carved, with a masculine feel. Oliver had mentioned that the Prescott villa was nearly ten thousand square feet. It also had a back-yard with a pool and hot tub. Many scandalous parties had happened in that backyard—until the middle of sophomore year, when the Prescotts had forbidden Oliver from having large groups of friends over.

Madison found Oliver in the kitchen, eating lunch at the wooden table that looked fit for a small medieval banquet.

"Hey." He dropped his sandwich and sipped something that could have been water, although, judging from the short crystal glass, it was probably vodka. "Is everything okay? You seemed worried in your text."

"You have no idea," she said, joining him at the table. She'd thought about this moment the entire way over. Now that it was here, her throat felt thick, and she could barely get the words out. "A few weeks ago I found out a huge secret, and it's been eating away at me and I can't take it anymore." Her eyes filled with tears, and she buried her face in her hands, swallowing away the sobs that were trying to force themselves out. It wasn't the first time Oliver had seen her cry, but breaking down in front of people made her feel so weak and helpless.

"What'd you find out?" He spoke faster than normal. "Nothing to do with me, right?"

"Why would it have anything to do with you?" She looked up, surprised at how he'd jumped to the edge of his seat. "You're the only person who hasn't ditched me since I found out."

"No reason." He relaxed and sipped his drink. "Sometimes it just feels like everyone blames things on me when they're not my fault. Guess I'm an easy target." He smirked—clearly he didn't care *that* much about people gossiping about him. "Anyway, do you want a drink? I can open up a bottle of wine. It might make whatever's going on easier to talk about."

"Yeah." Madison somehow managed a smile. "That'd be nice."

He went to the wine closet and came back with a bottle of red. "Is Brunello Pinot Noir all right?"

"Your parents won't get mad at you for drinking it?" Madison knew how intense Oliver's parents had gotten about trying to control his drinking—and how much they loved their wine collection. She didn't want to be the reason he got in trouble.

"They have so many wines in there, and this one isn't from the rare section, so they won't notice it's gone," he said. "Besides, they know wine isn't my drink of choice. But you like it, so I'll have a glass or two with you. Or you can have the bottle and I'll stick with vodka. Whatever you'd like."

"We can split it." Madison eyed the bottle—with the way her temples were throbbing, she wouldn't mind finishing off the entire thing. But that would be way too many calories. Not to mention that she'd be wasted.

He poured them both a glass, and since the kitchen felt so impersonal, they went to his room. Thanks to the cleaning staff that came to the Prescott villa every morning, Oliver's room was perfectly neat, his king-size bed crisply made. Madison took her shoes off and situated herself on it next to him, both of them leaning on the mound of pillows propped against the headboard. The memory of the almost-kiss on Halloween still lingered in her mind, so she left about half a foot between them. She couldn't allow herself to get distracted.

"So." Oliver played with the stem of his glass. "What's going on?"

Madison sipped her wine. The pinot could have used time to breathe, but she needed the liquid courage, so she took another long drink. "Remember the day in advanced genetics when we did blood typing?" she asked. "Around the end of September?"

"Of course," he said. "I'll never forget that day. You got upset because you thought you messed up the lab, and you've been on edge ever since."

"Yeah." Her heart warmed to hear he'd noticed it had been that exact day that everything had changed for her. Which only confirmed she was right in telling him this. "Except I didn't mess up the lab. I did it right both times. Which was what made me even more upset…"

And from there, she spilled the entire story.

★ ★ ★

"Wow," Oliver said once she'd told him everything. Saying it out loud hadn't been easy—Madison had cried so much that her eyes were dry and her cheeks had to be puffy, and half the bottle of wine was finished. Her body was warm and her head felt fuzzy in that tingly buzzed sort of way, and she poured herself a third glass, filling it high so she wouldn't need to reach for the bottle again soon for a refill.

"Adrian Diamond is your father." Oliver shook his head, his eyes wide. "Peyton, Courtney and Savannah are your *sisters*."

"*Half* sisters," she corrected.

"It doesn't matter," he said. "Brianna's my half sister, but it doesn't make her half as important to me than if we'd had the same mom. I just… This is crazy. I'm still wrapping my mind around it."

"There are still times when I wake up in the morning and wonder if it's all been one long nightmare." Madison closed her eyes and took a long sip of wine, the silky texture of the pinot making its way down her throat and warming her stomach. Then she opened her eyes again and balanced her wineglass on her knees, holding on to it to keep it steady. "But it's not a dream—it's real. And these past few weeks have been hell."

"I can't imagine." He exhaled and looked at the ceiling.

"My parents told me not to tell anyone, because Adrian doesn't want anyone—even me—to know. But I couldn't keep it to myself any longer. I mean, what kind of man doesn't want to be involved in the life of his daughter? He gave my mom the deal on our condo, and he lives so close to us, but he hasn't bothered getting to know me. And to keep from me that I have *sisters*? It's so messed up that I can't get it through my head. I needed to tell someone—I felt like I would explode if I didn't. And you're the only person I can trust. But you can't tell anyone." She looked at him straight on, her breath catching at the intensity of his gaze. "Okay?"

"I promise." He stirred the ice around in his vodka—he'd stopped drinking the wine after his first glass, saying that she needed it more than him. "But this isn't a secret you have to keep," he said, the anger in his voice surprising her. "Your parents and Adrian are the ones at fault, not you. You shouldn't have to feel this way."

"I know." Her eyes watered again, and she took another sip of wine, willing the tears away. "The worst part is that Adrian claimed Peyton, Courtney and Savannah as his daughters, but he has no interest in me. I don't get it. He wants them, so why doesn't he want me?" The tears rolled down her cheeks, and Oliver wrapped an arm around her, pulling her closer. He felt so warm and comforting, and she buried her head in his shoulder, squeezing her eyes tight as if it could make this entire mess go away.

"There's no excuse he could have." Oliver's voice was low and controlled, his body tense, as if he might explode at any moment. "The only reason I can think is that the Diamond sisters never had a father figure around, so their mom must have told them about Adrian being their father. You have a dad—who loves you as much as he would any biological daughter—so it was easier for your parents to keep secret. But that doesn't make any of it okay. Was he ever planning on telling you?"

"Apparently he has a trust set up for me, so my mom was going to tell me when I got access to the money." Madison sniffed. "Whenever that would be. She said some bullshit about not wanting me to know until I was older because Adrian said it would be 'safer' that way. Which makes no sense, because he's letting Savannah, Courtney and Peyton into his life *now*. Why does he want them around if he never wanted to be a father? And why continue keeping me in the dark?" She pounded a fist into the bed, which only made the tears come faster. "I don't think they were *ever* going to tell me the truth. Apparently Adrian's my godfather, so I'm guessing they would have used that as a reason why he gave me the money. This is just all so wrong and I hate it. I hate not being able to tell Adrian that I know, or to tell Savannah, Courtney and Peyton that we're sisters."

Oliver nodded, his eyes solemn, and handed her a tissue from the box on his nightstand. "I guess that explains why you've stopped talking shit about them all the time."

"Yeah." Madison sat up and wiped away her tears. Oliver didn't move his arm from around her, and she remained nestled against his shoulder. "I mean, obviously I didn't like them when they got here. But now I know they're my *sisters*." The word sounded so strange when spoken aloud. "So I've been avoiding them, because I couldn't imagine talking to them and not telling them. But the day before break, I was in the tutoring center with Courtney and had a conversation with her— she's actually pretty nice. And I don't want them to hate me anymore. I want them to know the truth, but my parents told me not to tell anyone. It's been ripping me apart every day."

"I can't imagine," Oliver said. "So you wouldn't have posted anything about them on a website a few weeks ago, would you have?"

"A website?" Madison tilted her head, confused about where this was coming from. She was confessing a huge secret, and he was bringing up a *website?*

"Yeah," he said. "That Campusbuzz site where everything's anonymous."

"No." She took another long sip of wine and snuggled more into Oliver's arms—the world was feeling floaty now, and she liked it. "I mean, I know the site, but I haven't looked at it since summer. People with nothing better to do were making up stuff about me. I don't have time to look at that crap. Especially now that I stopped going out with everyone... I can't imagine what people must be thinking. And it's all because I can't be around our friends and pretend to be happy and carefree, as if nothing's changed."

"You shouldn't have to pretend," he said. "Is the only reason you've been keeping this to yourself because your parents told you to?"

"And because of Adrian," she said. "He didn't want me before, and I doubt that's going to change because I stumbled on the truth and forced my parents to tell me about him."

Oliver's eyes lit up. "You know what I think?" he said, continuing before Madison could ask what. "I bet your mom *wants* the secret to come out. If it's been eating you up for weeks, can you imagine what it's been like for her, keeping it from you for sixteen years? She didn't *have* to tell you that Adrian was your biological father, but she did. Maybe she wants you to do what she couldn't, and fix this."

"So you think I should confront Adrian?" Madison's stomach jumped at the thought.

"What other option do you have?" he said. "Continuing on like nothing's changed is making you miserable. How long do you think you'd be able to keep this up?"

"Until I go to Stanford and won't have to see my parents every day." She shrugged, knowing how unrealistic that was.

"We have over a year and a half until we go to college," he said, pointing out what she already knew. "It's only been two months so far. No offense, Mads, because you're one of the strongest people I know, but I don't think you can handle keeping this secret for so long. And you shouldn't *have* to."

"But what if I tell Adrian, and he tells me he wishes I never found out?" She could barely get the words out; it hurt too much to think about. "Or that when my mom and dad discover I spilled the secret, they never forgive me? Or that Savannah, Courtney and Peyton hate that we're related and tell me that, no matter what genetics say, I'll never be a sister to them?"

"I don't think they'll do that." Oliver moved some hair off her face and pushed it behind her ear. "But thinking about the worst-case scenario is only going to make it harder for you. You owe it to yourself to tell the truth and find out how they'll *really* react. They might surprise you, but you'll never know if you don't come clean."

Which made sense, but it was easier said than done. "So if you were in my position, you would tell Adrian what you knew? Even if you thought he didn't want you?"

"If I found out someone else was my father besides my dad, and my parents had been lying to me for my entire life?" His eyebrows creased. "Hell, yeah, I would tell him. If Adrian doesn't want to be in your life, then he should have the balls to say it to your face. But whatever he has to say about it, you have a right to hear it from him."

She stared at the remaining wine in her glass, as if the answers were there. Then she finished it in one gulp and reached across Oliver's chest to place it on the nightstand. "I hate that no matter what I do, someone's going to get hurt."

"True." He nodded. "But if you don't tell anyone, you'll be the one who's hurt. And you don't deserve that."

"Thanks," she said. "Although I'm not so sure about that."

"What do you mean?"

"I haven't been the nicest person since starting high school," she began. He tried to protest, but she stopped him. "You know it's true. I've snubbed so many hopefuls out of our group of friends, I've dissed Brett in public, cheated on Nick with Brett, talked about people I claimed were my friends behind their backs and went out of my way to be mean to the Diamond sisters the week they got here. I even used Damien's crush on me to hurt Savannah, which ended up hurting him." She picked at her cuticles, unable to look at Oliver as she admitted all these awful things. "Maybe I deserve what's happening to me. It's karma's way of getting me back."

"No." Oliver lifted her chin, forcing her eyes to meet his. "Yes, it sounds bad when you say it that way. But we're in high school, Mads. Shit like that happens. You've stepped on some people's toes, but it'll blow over. In the meantime, I've got your back. But this—Adrian being your biological father and your parents lying to you about it—is bigger than high school drama. So don't for a moment think that anything you've done has made you deserve this. What you deserve is to be able to tell Adrian, Peyton, Courtney and Savannah what you know. Your parents might not be happy about it at first, but they love you and they'll forgive you. Besides, you have more reason to be pissed than they do, right?"

"Yeah." Madison nodded, her heart racing. "And I *am* pissed at them. I can't believe they could lie to me about something so huge. It's like I don't know who they are anymore. I don't even know who *I* am anymore." She groaned and buried her face in his shoulder. "This is all so messed up. I wish I could go back to how things were before, when I had no idea about any of this. It was so much easier."

"You would rather be ignorant than know the truth?" he asked, running his fingers gently through her hair. "That doesn't sound like the Madison I know."

"You're right." She sighed. "I was just being dramatic. Of

course I would rather know the truth. What I wish is that everything was how I always thought it was and my dad was my biological father, or that my parents and Adrian had been honest with me from the beginning. Then I wouldn't be in this position in the first place."

"But this is the way things are," he said.

"I know," she said. "I don't like it, but trust me, I know." She stared at her empty wineglass on the nightstand, her body tingling from the alcohol, her head spinning. Should she finish off the bottle and pour herself another glass? No. A fourth glass of wine would put her over the edge. And while a part of her wanted to get to the point where she forgot about everything that was bothering her, she'd learned what a bad idea that was after the getting-drunk-and-making-out-with-Damien incident last summer.

"Are you going to tell Adrian that you know?" Oliver asked.

That was the question of the past two months, wasn't it? After Oliver's pep talk, she wanted to say she planned on marching into Adrian's condo today and confronting him. But in her heart, she knew she wouldn't do that.

"I want to," she said. "But it's more complicated than that. You're right that I need to tell him, but I don't want to do it behind my parents' backs."

"So, first you're going to tell your parents that you're going to tell Adrian, and then you'll talk to Adrian?"

"Yep." Madison wished she felt as confident as she sounded.

He took another sip of his drink—the ice had all melted now. "That sounds like a good idea in principle," he said. "But what if they tell you that you can't tell Adrian? That they'll kick you out or something if you do?"

"They might get angry, but they're not going to kick me out," she said. "If they did, I could crash with you, right?"

She laughed, but it didn't help her feel any better. "But, yes, I'm going to tell them first. Then they can't get angry at me for going behind their backs. I'm waiting until after Thanksgiving, though. I don't want to ruin the holiday."

"Just promise me you'll go through with this." He traced circles on her shoulder with his thumb, reminding her that his arm had been around her this entire time. The amount that he cared about what happened to her took her breath away and warmed her heart, making it beat so fast that she wondered if he could feel it. "I've hated seeing how miserable you've been these past few weeks," he said. "You *have* to do this for yourself. If you need anything, you know I'm here for you, right?"

His dark eyes were intense with concern, his lips so close to hers that she couldn't help watching them as he spoke. She wasn't sure what made her do it—maybe it was the wine, or the way he was looking at her like he cared more about her than anything in the world—but she leaned forward and kissed him.

For a second he froze, and she panicked. Had she read into his feelings too much? But then he pulled her closer, burying his fingers in her hair as he kissed her back with so much passion that she couldn't breathe. His lips were so full and soft, and they moved perfectly in time with hers, as if they were made for each other. This was right. *They* were right.

Needing to be closer to him, she climbed on top of him, her legs straddling his hips. He trailed kisses down her neck, and she leaned her head back, enjoying every second of his touch. She wrapped her arms around him, pushing her hips into his. A groan escaped his lips, and as he kissed the sensitive spot under her ear, tingles exploded through her body. She crushed her lips against his again, running her hand up his shirt to explore his chest. His shirt came off within seconds, and she pulled hers off as well, throwing it onto the bed next to them, savoring the sensation of her skin against his.

His fingers traveled to her back, expertly unhooking the clasp of her bra, and the reality of what she was doing came crashing down on her. This was *Oliver*. Her best friend. Best friends weren't supposed to make out and rip each other's shirts off…at least, not if they wanted to stay best friends.

Nothing between them would ever be the same.

She pushed his hands away and redid the clasp of her bra, her cheeks heating from how close she'd come to allowing him to take it off entirely.

"Are you okay?" he murmured, his lips giving her chills as they moved against her neck.

"Yeah." Madison looked up at the ceiling and took a deep breath. "Maybe. I don't know." She rolled off Oliver's lap, grabbed her shirt from where she'd flung it next to them and pulled it back on. This was turning into one big mess. She ran her hands through her hair, unable to bring herself to look at him. "Honestly, I have no idea what I'm doing. My life's been falling apart, and you're the only person who's been here for me, and it's making me really…confused."

"Okay." He breathed out. "I get that."

Madison's face heated; she wanted to erase the past ten minutes. Did Oliver view her as more than a friend, or was that in her imagination because of how low she'd been feeling recently? She couldn't bring herself to ask. It was too pathetic, especially after the way she'd just thrown herself at him.

There was only one way she could protect herself from being hurt even more: pretend what had happened was a mistake. "I shouldn't have done that." She spoke softly, her throat so tight she was barely able to force the words out. "I was upset, and I had all that wine, so I wasn't thinking clearly.

You're my best friend, and I don't want that to change. I *can't* have it change. Because if I don't have you…then I have no one."

She hung her head, her hair hiding her face, hating how needy she sounded. But it was true. And she couldn't risk Oliver acting like Damien had after she'd kissed him, how he'd told her she was a bitch and that things between them could never go back to how they were. She'd already lost Damien; she couldn't lose Oliver, too. She pulled her knees to her chest and wrapped her arms around them. The thought of how alone she would be if that happened made her feel so empty that it hurt to breathe.

"It's not going to change," he said, steady and calm, resting his hand on her shoulder. "I'm not going anywhere, Mads. I promise."

She forced herself to look back up at him, and the honesty in his eyes made her heart jump. "Really?" she asked, her voice cracking. She needed him to confirm that he meant it—that all wasn't lost between them.

"Really," he said. "After everything you told me about your family, I could never leave you to handle it on your own. And about what just happened between us… You've been on my mind a lot recently, and I've been hoping that would happen for a few weeks now. But if it's too much for you on top of everything else, or if you don't feel the same, I understand. Our friendship is the most important thing to me, and I don't want us to lose that."

"You have no idea how happy I am to hear that," she said, smiling for what felt like the first time since she'd gotten to the Prescott villa. She also had to remind herself to look at Oliver's face and not his chest, which was still bare, since she'd thrown his shirt somewhere on the floor. Yes, she'd seen him in a bathing suit countless times, but this was different. It took all of her self-control not to reach out and touch him again. "And since you were honest with me... I've been feeling like there might be more between us for a few weeks now, too," she admitted. "But it all happened around the same time that my parents told me the truth about this whole mess, and I don't know if I'm just trying to find something to hold on to while my entire world crashes around me."

"That makes sense." Oliver reached for her hand, but he pulled back at the last second, resting his arm by his side instead. Her heart plummeted, but she understood why he'd done that. He probably didn't want to confuse her even more. "The fact that you've been keeping that secret for so long amazes me. I wish you'd told me sooner. Then you wouldn't have had to go through this alone."

"I haven't been completely alone," Madison said. "Even though I'm angry at them, I still have my mom and dad."

Oliver's eyes hardened. "But they want you to pretend nothing's changed. You can't do that anymore."

"I know," she said, her voice shaking. She pressed her tongue to the roof of her mouth to stop the tears—she'd read somewhere that would work. She didn't want to cry again. She *couldn't* cry again. Shouldn't her tear ducts be in a drought by now? "After Thanksgiving is over, I'm going to tell them that I'm done keeping their secret."

"If you want me to be there with you when you talk to them, I will," he offered.

"No," she said. "This is something I should do alone. But thank you."

"Anytime." He smiled, but it felt forced, like there was more he wanted to say. Her stomach flipped under his gaze, and she had the all-encompassing urge to kiss him again and melt into the protection of his arms.

"I should go." She got up, grabbed her purse from where she'd dropped it earlier and spun to face him. He still hadn't moved from where he was sprawled shirtless on the bed, and it took her a few seconds to focus. "But I'm glad things aren't going to change between us…after what just happened."

"Like I said, your friendship is too important to me to let anything mess it up." He looked and sounded so sincere, but Madison thought she spotted a trace of guilt in his eyes. He must feel bad for letting things get so heated between them when she was feeling vulnerable.

"I'll let you know how things go after I talk to my parents." She tried to sound resolved, but her hands shook as she let herself out of the villa, unsure if, when the time came, she would have the strength necessary to go through with it.

She also knew that while Oliver might claim otherwise, things between them would never be the same again.

www.campusbuzz.com

Savannah Diamond's Fabulous Sweet 16!
Posted on Tuesday 11/25 at 5:26 PM
By now I guess everyone knows that Savannah Diamond's sweet sixteen party will be on that show "My Fabulous Sweet 16!" A friend who has a parent who's a teacher at school said that after school shut down for break, a camera crew came in to film. So cool!

1: Posted on Tuesday 11/25 at 5:38 PM
they filmed a little bit during and after volleyball practice and they had to do like, ten takes! I'm no actress, but from what I saw, Savannah SUCKED on camera! a friend and i watched from the sidelines and it was soooo funny :D

2: Posted on Tuesday 11/25 at 5:47 PM
invitations are apparently going out this week—crossing my fingers i get one!

3: Posted on Tuesday 11/25 at 5:59 PM
Hate to burst your bubble, but if you have to "cross your fingers" for an invite, you're probably not going to get one. The save the date thingies were sent out a while ago. If you didn't get one, then it sounds like you're not invited!

4: Posted on Tuesday 11/25 at 6:11 PM

she invited everyone in the sophomore class and the volleyball team, along with some juniors and seniors.

5: Posted on Tuesday 11/25 at 6:23 PM

woohoo, another chance for the Diamonds to show off how awesome they are. i'll pass.

6: Posted on Tuesday 11/25 at 6:29 PM

#jealous

7: Posted on Tuesday 11/25 at 6:37 PM

The party's gonna be at the new club at the Diamond, Abandon. Apparently they're going all out and it's gonna be the party of the year!

8: Posted on Tuesday 11/25 at 6:48 PM

The girls on that show are all portrayed as such brats. I would hate to have my life on display like that. Savannah Diamond must be one hell of an attention whore.

9: Posted on Tuesday 11/25 at 6:57 PM

With the party being broadcast on national TV, it'll be harder than ever to decide what to wear! Time for my mom's personal stylist to come to the rescue...

10: Posted on Tuesday 11/25 at 7:10 PM

#FirstWorldProblems

11: Posted on Tuesday 11/25 at 7:24 PM

#OnePercentProblems!

chapter 21: *Savannah*

Adrian was using the Diamond jet for a business trip to Macau, so Savannah and her sisters flew to California in a chartered private plane. It wasn't as big as the Diamond jet, but it was still far more luxurious than anything Savannah could have imagined traveling in a few months ago.

Savannah was so excited to see Mom, Grandma and Aunt Sophie that she could barely sit still, and she was also relieved to get away from the cameras that had been following her around Las Vegas for the *My Fabulous Sweet Sixteen* special. Despite the private acting coach, she'd barely improved since that disastrous first day of filming, and the production crew was getting frustrated with her—which only made her mess up more. She was fine in practice, when barely anyone was watching, but once the cameras started rolling, she overanalyzed what she was doing and clammed up.

Maybe this break was what she needed to relax and get in the right mind-set.

The flight wasn't long, and when they landed, a limo waited

on the tarmac to drive them to Grandma's new home. The house was in Napa Valley, and it was nothing like the cramped one-bedroom condo in Fairfield that Grandma had previously shared with Aunt Sophie. All gray stone and dark wood, it was in a gated community where each house was surrounded by tons of land. It was built into a hill with lots of trees behind it, and while it at first appeared to be only one floor, at closer look it clearly had a large basement. With the sun setting behind it, it was absolutely picturesque.

"Grandma forgot to mention that the new house was in Napa and not Fairfield," Peyton said as she stepped out of the limo. "She's getting all fancy now."

"You know Grandma," Courtney said. "She's probably trying to be modest."

Napa and Fairfield bordered each other, but they were completely different worlds. Napa was full of renowned vineyards owned by upper-class families, and was known for luxury. Fairfield's claim to fame was being the home of the Jelly Belly candy factory and the Anheuser-Busch brewery.

It was hard to picture Grandma living anywhere except her practical no-frills condo, but before the limo had a chance to come to a stop, she stepped out the front door of the stone-and-wood house and hurried to greet them, a huge smile on her face.

"I've been waiting for you girls all day," she said, giving them each a hug and pausing to look at them. She'd gained weight in the past months. Before she'd been so frail that Savannah had worried she would knock her over with a hug, but now she was sturdier and healthier. "I hope you're all hungry, because your mom has quite the feast waiting for you. She's in the kitchen doing the finishing touches now, and she can't wait to see you."

"Mom's cooking?" Savannah couldn't imagine her mom preparing a meal more complicated than peanut-butter-and-jelly sandwiches.

"Yes." Grandma nodded. "It's a hobby she's taken up since moving in. She's still learning, but she's proud of what she's made, so be sure to compliment her and at least *pretend* you like it. She insisted on making it on her own, but she did allow me to take charge of dessert."

"Warm apple cobbler and vanilla bean ice cream?" Savannah's mouth watered at the thought. No apple cobbler came close to being as good as Grandma's—not even the one at the Diamond.

"You'll have to wait and see." She winked and led the way up the long sidewalk. "But let's get you girls settled in. When your father first insisted on buying me a house, he wanted a place with six bedrooms, so you would each have a room when you visited. But I couldn't imagine what I would do with six bedrooms for the rest of the year, so I convinced him that four bedrooms were sufficient. Aunt Sophie and I have the masters on the main floor, and your mom's bedroom, along with the guest room where the three of you will stay, is in the base-ment—although, since the house is built on a hill, it doesn't feel like a basement at all. I figured you'd shared a room for most of your lives, so you could manage while you're here, especially since this room is triple the size of your old one."

She opened the door and motioned for them to go in. The inside of the house smelled like barbeque, and Savannah and her sisters found their mom in the kitchen, her back toward them as she stirred what looked like pulled pork.

"Guess who just got in," Grandma said.

Their mom turned around, holding a wooden spoon in one

hand, a burgundy apron tied around her waist. Savannah was speechless—she'd never seen Mom in an *apron*.

"Hi, girls," she said, playing with the spoon as she looked at each one of them. She spoke softly, like she was afraid one wrong move would send them running back to Vegas. "I'm so glad you're here for Thanksgiving. I've been getting dinner ready for hours… You're hungry, right?"

Savannah nodded, her eyes filling with tears. She'd known her mom looked better from their Skype conversations, but seeing her in person made it much more real. She'd lost the weight she'd gained from drinking, her skin was creamy and smooth instead of blotchy and red and her eyes sparkled with energy. Savannah ran to her and hugged her, squeezing her eyes shut as her mom wrapped her arms around her.

"I've missed you, too, baby," she said, holding her so tightly that Savannah thought she would never let her go. Finally she did, and she held her at arms' length, her hands resting on Savannah's shoulders as she took in her designer jeans, Louboutin ankle boots, fitted top and leather jacket. "You look so different from last time I saw you. Your hair is beautiful. And your clothes… You look so grown-up!"

"You look great, too," Savannah said, her stomach grumbling from the delicious smell of the pork. "And the food smells amazing. I didn't realize you knew how to cook."

"I'm learning," she said. "Dinner will be ready in ten minutes.… Why don't the three of you bring your stuff downstairs and get settled in, then we'll catch up while we eat? I know you've already told me a bunch over Skype, but I'm sure there's much more to talk about."

"I'll show you your room," Grandma said, and they grabbed their bags from the foyer and followed her down the steps. The house was airy and spacious—a perfect countryside retreat. "Aunt Sophie's having a good day today, so the two of us are going into town for dinner," she continued. "We'll be back for dessert, but I thought you would appreciate the time alone with your mom. Here's your room." She motioned to the door. "Get yourselves settled, and when I'm gone, please, go easy on her," she said, more to Peyton than to Courtney and Savannah. "I know she hasn't always been easy to live with, but she's recovering so well, and I would hate to see her have any setbacks."

"Of course," Savannah said.

"Good." Grandma smiled. "I'll see you after dinner."

"That was actually really good," Savannah said, polishing off her pulled pork sandwich. Who knew Mom could cook?

"Your grandma did help a bit," Mom said. "We wanted to make sure you girls enjoyed it."

"The veggie burger was good, too," Courtney added.

"And I take it you liked your sandwich, Peyton?" Mom played with her fork, so hopeful when she looked at Peyton, who had barely spoken throughout the meal.

"It was okay." Peyton shrugged, even though she'd finished her sandwich before Savannah.

No one said anything for a few seconds, and Savannah focused on eating her veggies. The dinner talk so far had been mostly chitchat, and while she liked having a peaceful meal like a normal family, she had a feeling it wouldn't last.

"More lemonade?" Mom picked up the pitcher and filled up their glasses.

"Did you make the lemonade, too?" Courtney asked.

"No." She smiled. "I bought it at the grocery store. It's one of those all natural, high-end brands. Isn't it delicious?"

"Okay, I can't take this anymore." Peyton threw her napkin on the table and looked straight at Mom, who froze mid-sip of lemonade. "How could you think it was all right to not tell us anything about our father? When you had us believing he was a no-good criminal, I understood why you wanted to keep us away from him. But he's Adrian-fucking-Diamond. We went our entire lives struggling to pay rent, to pay for food. When you couldn't keep a job for the past year, do you have *any* idea how hard Courtney and I worked to keep our family afloat? We put our academics and social lives on the line because you were too wasted to take care of us, and once Savannah was old enough, she would have done the same. Then we find out that Adrian could have *helped* us. How the hell could you think cutting him out of our lives was in our best interest?"

Savannah dropped her fork and stared at Peyton, shocked at her sister's outburst. It was so different from what Peyton had thought when they'd first moved to Vegas—but she was right. And despite what Grandma had said about Mom being fragile, how she'd asked them to be gentle with her, their mom seemed healthier than ever. Savannah and her sisters had gone *months* without answers. Didn't they deserve some now?

"It's more complicated than you know." Mom's eyes watered, and red blotches popped up on her cheeks—which Savannah knew meant she was stressed. "Adrian is a danger to you. Yes, life was never easy for us, but with no ties to him, the three of you were safe and able to *have* your lives at all. Do you have any idea what it was like for us after Courtney..." She choked up and took deep breaths, her eyes blazing with pain. "After the kidnapping, our lives fell apart. *I* fell apart. I couldn't look at Adrian without hating the danger he'd put you in. I had to get the three of you away from him, and when I left, he didn't put up a fight. He knew I was doing the right thing. He let the three of you go…. He let all of us go. He tried to give me money, but I wanted *nothing* from him. I wanted nothing that could trace him to us. It was all a reminder of…" Her voice cracked, and she took another sip of lemonade. "It was a reminder of how he destroyed our family."

"But something doesn't add up." Courtney remained still, somehow keeping her voice calm. "Yes, the kidnapping was awful, but I got back home safely. And afterward, Adrian got us each a bodyguard. It must have been terrifying when it happened, but I don't see how anything can justify you keeping him from us, and him allowing you to do that."

"It's all too much to explain." Mom blew out a breath and sank into her chair. "After it happened, I blamed Adrian. I *still* blame Adrian. I wish you could trust that I did what I did for a good reason." She glanced at Savannah, as if begging for support. "You believe me, don't you, baby?"

Savannah looked down at her plate and moved her vegetables around with her fork. "I believe you didn't do anything to purposefully hurt us." She chose her words carefully. Why had Grandma thought it was a good idea to leave them alone with Mom so soon?

Mom smiled for the first time since this conversation started. "Everything I did was because I love you," she said. "Because I want to protect you."

Peyton crossed her arms and glared. "For wanting to protect us, you did a shitty job. We would have been better off with Adrian than we ever were with you."

"I did the best I could!" Mom stood up so abruptly that her plate fell off the table and shattered on the floor. "You think you know what you're talking about, but you have *no idea* what I had to go through. I did everything the doctors at that facility wanted me to do, all for *you*. I thought you would see that I'm different now, that I'm better, and that this could be a fresh start. But I knew it wouldn't be long until you started attacking me. Well, I'm done listening to this. Have fun cleaning up." She stomped out of the kitchen and down the stairs, the door to her room slamming shut so loudly that they could feel it through the house.

"Well, that went well." Peyton eyed up the mess on the floor. It didn't end there—dirty pots and pans were all over the counters and the stove. Mom apparently hadn't mastered the art of cleaning while she cooked.

Part of Savannah wanted to go downstairs and apologize to Mom for what Peyton had said. But when she started yelling and screaming and throwing things, no one but Grandma could get through to her. When Savannah was younger, she used to hide in her closet when Mom's temper came out. She would go behind the clothes, shut her eyes and sing softly to herself to drown out the banging, wishing her closet was magical like in that book series Courtney liked, and that it would bring her to another world. But of course that had never happened. All that would happen was that Mom would start drinking, which would make her yell more.

Savannah hoped that what Peyton had said wouldn't trigger a relapse. But there was no alcohol in the house. They just had to give Mom space until Grandma got home.

"Maybe you should have waited until Grandma was back to ask Mom about Adrian," Courtney said softly.

"So Grandma could cover for her and make it sound like what she did wasn't as awful as it was?" Peyton said. "No, thanks. We were sitting around the table passing around the lemonade, and it was so fake it made my skin crawl. I couldn't pretend everything was all right anymore—like she hadn't *lied* to us for our entire lives. And I was the only one who had the guts to bring it up, so I did. Don't tell me you both weren't wondering exactly what I asked."

"I was," Savannah said. "But I didn't want her to melt down on our first day here. When we were eating and chatting, she seemed so happy. Was it terrible for us to be nice through one meal?"

"Yes," Peyton said. "It was. It was all so *fake*. You might have been fine smiling through it, but I couldn't sit there and pretend everything she did—everything she kept from us—never happened."

"I wasn't being fake." Savannah clenched her fists, wanting to strangle her sister. "I was being nice. There's a difference."

Peyton rolled her eyes and brought her dishes to the sink. "At least I spoke my mind."

"And where did it get you?" Savannah asked, happy when Peyton's only response was to shrug. "That's right—nowhere."

"We don't know that," Peyton said. "Maybe now she'll apologize for lying to us. Because I don't know if you've realized, but she hasn't said anything close to an apology yet. All we get are excuses after excuses. Is it so hard for her to admit she messed up? She might not be drinking anymore, but beyond that, nothing's changed. She's as irresponsible and selfish as ever."

"You both need to stop this," Courtney said, her fingers pressed against her temples. "What's done is done, and arguing is getting us nowhere. Grandma will help us smooth this out when she gets back. For now, let's clean up this mess."

She handed Savannah a broom and a dustbin, and they got to work.

Cleaning the kitchen didn't take long. Once they were done, Grandma still wasn't home and Mom remained locked in her room. The apple cobbler was in the oven staying warm, but none of them felt right eating it without Mom, Grandma and Aunt Sophie. So while they waited for them to get back, Savannah took her phone to the outside deck to chat on Face-Time with Evie.

Her best friend's freckly face and red hair popped up on the screen after one ring. "Hey, girl!" Evie said. "I take it you've arrived back in CA?"

"Got in late this afternoon," Savannah said. "My grandma and mom live in Napa now.... Check it out." She reversed the camera to show Evie the sprawling deck and back of the house. When she was done, she switched back to the front camera. "This house is like a resort. It's amazing."

"Looks nice." Evie's eyes flashed with longing, but it disappeared a second later. "I obviously can't visit tomorrow because of Thanksgiving, but my mom said she'll drive me over on Friday so we can hang out. Does that work?"

"Yeah." Savannah smiled at the thought of seeing her best friend for the first time in weeks—especially since the last time they'd seen each other, Jackie's volleyball party, hadn't ended well. "Sounds great."

"So, how's everything with your mom?" Evie asked.

Savannah gave her the rundown on what had happened since she and her sisters had arrived. "Now my mom's locked in her room, Grandma's not home yet, Peyton's watching TV and sulking and Courtney's reading. But enough about that. Have you gotten an answer from your mom yet about coming to Vegas for my Sweet Sixteen?" Savannah had invited both Evie *and* her mom, since Mrs. Brown had always been like a second mother to her, driving her to volleyball practice and letting her sleep over practically every weekend.

"She said as long as you're sure the hotel room will be free, we can come!" Evie squealed. "But the flights are my Christmas present, so we better have tons of fun."

"Trust me, we will." Savannah made a mental note to buy Evie the best Christmas present ever to make up for the flights. "I'm so excited you'll be able to come! The party's going to be amazing."

"I can't wait," she said. "How's it going with filming for *My Fabulous Sweet Sixteen*? I still can't believe your party will be on the show."

"It's going okay." Savannah shrugged.

Evie raised an eyebrow. "You sure about that?"

"No." Savannah sighed and slumped in the chair. "I'm terrible on camera. I don't know why Rebecca thought I would be any good at this. Just because I can sing and record videos for YouTube doesn't mean I can act."

"It can't be that bad…." Evie said.

"Trust me," she said. "It's *that* bad. Every time the camera starts rolling, I freak out. And everyone thinks I'm going to mess up, which makes me mess up more. It's an awful cycle. And the other day I heard the director telling Rebecca…" She swallowed, a lump forming in her throat as she recalled the conversation she'd overheard. She hadn't told anyone about this yet—not even her sisters. "I heard him telling her that if they couldn't get enough useful footage, they might pull my episode and replace it with someone else's."

"They can't do that." Evie gasped. "Can they?"

"They sounded pretty serious about it."

"I'm sure it'll work out." It was nice of Evie to say, but she had no way of knowing that. "I'm not an actress or anything, but I did take drama last year, and I wasn't half-bad at it. Maybe it'll be easier if instead of thinking about how you're putting *yourself* out there, you pretend like you're playing a part. Don't be yourself—be a character."

"Be a character instead of myself," Savannah repeated. It sounded strange, but wasn't that what she'd done in real life when she'd first moved to Vegas? And she'd been okay at it then. "I'll try that. Anyway, I hear a car coming down the driveway. It's probably Grandma. I have to go, but I'll see you Friday!"

"See you then!"

Savannah shoved her phone in her back pocket and walked into the house, praying Grandma could help them make peace with their mom before the Thanksgiving meal tomorrow.

chapter 22: *Courtney*

The Thanksgiving meal went better than Courtney had hoped after Mom and Peyton's fight yesterday. Once Grandma had gotten back from dinner last night, she'd helped them smooth things over and convinced Peyton to stop with the instigating for the rest of the holiday. And the entire time their mom had been locked in her room, she was doing yoga. It apparently helped her relax by "getting rid of negative energy and focusing on being mindful in the present." Whatever that meant. All Courtney cared about was that it worked.

After the meal, Aunt Sophie went to her room to go to sleep, and the rest of them gathered in the living room to watch a movie. They weren't past the black-and-white part of *The Wizard of Oz* when Courtney's phone vibrated—a call from Brett.

Her heart fluttered. In the weeks between Halloween and now, they'd been spending more time with each other—as friends—but it was getting harder to deny the pull between them. Since arriving in California, Courtney hadn't stopped wondering what he was doing back in Vegas, hoping he was also thinking of her. He must have been—why else would he be calling?

"I'm going to take this." Courtney pointed at her lit-up phone and excused herself from the living room. It was too chilly to go out on the deck, so she let herself into Grandma's room, since it was the closest to the living room, and shut the door behind her.

She took a second to calm her racing heart, then answered the phone and pressed it to her ear. "Hey," she said, trying to sound relaxed and not act all giddy just because Brett had been thinking about her enough to call.

"Hey back." She could hear the smile in his voice, which made her smile, too. "How's everything in California?"

She played with her key necklace, thinking about the blowup at dinner yesterday. "About as well as could be expected, I guess."

"That bad?"

She told him the basics of what had happened. "Things are still shaky between Mom and Peyton, but at least they're being civil. For now."

"Sounds rough," he said. "I'm glad they called a truce for Thanksgiving."

"Yeah." She paced in a circle. "Anyway, how's everything going in Vegas?" Brett was spending the holiday with his dad's side of the family. He didn't talk about his dad much— she had a feeling he got along better with Rebecca.

"Same as every year," he said. "Everyone asking the same typical questions. Anyway, I'm still at my dad's and people will notice if I'm gone for too long, but while I was here I had an idea."

"About what?"

"What we talked about on Halloween," he said. "About your records. We know searching through Adrian's files to find whatever secret you think he's keeping from you is impossible."

"Right..." She doubted he'd figured out a way around Adrian's security—they would have more luck stealing the crown jewels.

"But we have this tradition on my dad's side of the family where every Thanksgiving, we go through family albums and scrapbooks and stuff that's stored away for the rest of the year to remind us of everything we're thankful for. It got me thinking—if you think your parents are hiding something about when you were younger, maybe you'll have better luck discovering it at your grandma's house than in Adrian's office."

"Let me get this straight." Courtney stopped pacing. "You want me to snoop through my grandma's stuff on the slim chance that I might find something that reveals whatever my parents have been hiding from me?"

"It's not slim," he said. "You spent time at your grandma's growing up, right?"

"Right..."

"Was there a spot in her house she didn't want you and your sisters looking through?"

Courtney couldn't imagine snooping around Grandma's room, but just in case, she locked the door. "Her closet," she said. "She hated when my sisters and I played dress-up with her clothes and shoes."

"That sounds like a good place to start."

"I'll look, but Grandma just moved," she said, opening the door to the closet. It was a walk-in—much bigger than the closet in Grandma's old apartment. "Even if she'd been hiding something in there, she could have put it anywhere in the new house. All I see in here are clothes, shoes, photo albums and some boxes that are so high up I would need a ladder to reach them."

"Boxes are a great start," he said. "Are there any ladders or step stools, or something in your Grandma's room you could use to reach them?"

"Don't you think we're going overboard?" Courtney sighed, although she did check the room. There were no ladders or step stools—the only thing she could use to step on was the antique wooden trunk at the foot of the bed. And that would be too heavy to drag anywhere.

Then a memory hit her.

Courtney was young—four or five years old. She was playing hide-and-seek with her sisters at Grandma's apartment while they were waiting to eat dinner. It was Peyton's turn to seek, and Courtney was excited because while she'd been searching for her sisters the round before, she'd thought of the best hiding spot.

Peyton turned to the wall, covered her eyes and counted. Courtney hurried to Grandma's room. Savannah followed at her heels, always trusting that Courtney's ideas for hiding spots were the best.

"Where should I go?" Savannah took her thumb out of her mouth to ask.

"You go into Grandma's closet and hide behind her clothes," Courtney said. "I have a better idea, but only one person will fit."

"No fair." She pouted. "I want the better hiding spot."

"It's my idea, so I get it," Courtney said. "Go in the closet before Peyton starts looking for us."

Savannah did as Courtney said. Once the door to the closet had closed, Courtney walked to the trunk at the foot of Grandma's bed and smiled. It was just big enough for her to fit inside. Peyton was never going to find her.

She took the decorative clay bowl off the trunk and placed it next to the bed. Hopefully Peyton wouldn't notice it was missing. Now for the hardest part—taking off the glass top. She gripped it tightly and tried to ease it off the edge, but it was heavier than it looked, and crashed to the wooden floor.

She backed away, panicked. If she broke it, Grandma would put her in time-out for sure. Maybe if she got in real quick she could hide from getting in trouble. She hadn't noticed the lock on it until then, but luckily the hinged lid slid up without a key....

And Grandma shut it closed so fast it was a miracle Courtney's fingers didn't get smashed.

"What are you trying to do?" Grandma's eyes blazed, and she hurriedly arranged the glass and the clay pot back on the trunk.

Courtney backed away, her eyes on the floor. She couldn't answer for fear of bursting into tears. Savannah emerged from her hiding spot in the closet, and Peyton wandered into the bedroom, asking what was going on.

"We were playing hide-and-seek and I thought it would be a good hiding spot," Courtney finally managed to say.

"Never try that again." Grandma's voice was stricter than Courtney had ever heard. Courtney's lip quivered, and Grandma must have realized how much she'd scared her, because she lowered herself to the floor so their eyes were level. "If you had gone in there and closed the lid, you might have run out of air and suffocated to death before anyone found you. And then there are all those spiders..."

"Spiders?" Courtney shivered as she imagined eight tiny legs crawling over her skin.

"Lots of them." Grandma nodded. "They bite, too. That's why I keep the trunk closed. Do you promise not to open it again?"

"Yes." Courtney trembled at the thought of letting out all those spiders. "I promise."

Then Grandma told them the cookies were ready, and that they could each have one before dinner. In less than a minute, the trunk with the spiders was forgotten.

And they had never tried to open it since.

"Courtney?" Brett's voice brought her back to the present. "Did you find something?"

"No," she said. "But I have an idea. I'll have to put the phone down to look, and if I'm wrong—which I probably am—I have to go back and watch the movie with my family before they wonder why I've been gone for so long. So let's hang up for now, and I'll call back if I find anything, okay?"

"All right," he said. "If you don't find anything, keep looking the rest of the weekend. You have a much better shot finding something there than here."

"I will," she said. "Thanks for thinking of me and trying to help. And Happy Thanksgiving."

"You, too." His voice sounded so sweet, and she wanted to keep talking to him, but she forced herself to hang up.

Now to get to business. She jiggled the handle to the door, double-checking that it was locked. Once sure no one could barge in, she removed the display items from the top of the trunk. The ancient wood was cracked and peeling in places. It had looked huge and looming when she was four years old, but it was only the size of a coffee table, just taller. Now that she was older and stronger, the glass top came off easily, and she placed it on the floor, making sure to be quiet.

Time for the scary part. What if there really *were* spiders in there? She shivered at the thought. She would just open the top quickly and peek inside, not allowing the spiders enough time to escape.

She placed her hands on the sides of the lid and took a deep breath. But when she tried to pull it up, it didn't move. She tried again, and nothing. The lid wasn't budging.

She glared at the black metal lock. Yes, she'd known it was there, but when she was four years old, it hadn't been locked. She'd assumed it would still be unlocked now. But apparently, Grandma was serious about keeping people out of that trunk. If she'd gone to the trouble to lock it, it had to be for a more important reason than making sure the spiders didn't get let out.

Courtney sat in front of the trunk and sighed. Now that she was locked out, she wanted to see what was in it more than ever. There had to be a solution.

Picking up her iPhone, she Google searched "how to pick a lock." In movies, lock picking looked simple—a girl would take a pin out of her hair and use it to break in. But according to Google, it wasn't that easy. She could use a paper clip, but she also needed a tension wrench, or pliers or a specific screwdriver—none of which she knew where to find, or what they exactly were.

She read over the articles, playing with her necklace as she wracked her mind for ways to improvise. But it was more complicated than she'd anticipated. She tossed her phone to the ground and ran her fingers through her hair. This was hopeless.

Then she looked down at her necklace—the antique silver key Grandma had given her for her last birthday. It had been her great-great-grandmother's. And the trunk, with its peeling wood, could be from around that time, too. What if…?

Courtney undid the clasp of the necklace and held the key up to the lock. It looked like it could fit.

There was only one way to find out.

Not expecting anything, she shoved the key into the lock—it slid in perfectly. She turned it, and her heart jumped at the click. She was in.

She put the necklace back on, and then placed her hands on both sides of the trunk, steadying herself and taking a deep breath. This was it. Whatever was in there—whatever Grandma had yelled at her for almost finding when she was four—had to be important. It had to be *private*.

Courtney chewed on her lower lip. She shouldn't be doing this. But if Grandma had given Courtney the key, it meant she wanted her to find it, right? So she wasn't snooping?

That had to be right. Besides, she was too curious to turn back now.

She inched the top up slowly. The trunk smelled like dust and mildew—she had to breathe shallowly to keep from sneezing—and the hinges squeaked when it moved. Courtney wouldn't have been surprised if the last time it had been opened was when she'd tried to hide in there when she was four.

She didn't want to open it all the way without checking for spiders, so she used the flashlight app on her phone to do a preliminary search. Not a spider in sight. Her muscles relaxed, and she lifted the lid all the way. The trunk was empty, except for one lone item on the bottom—it looked like a children's picture book—and it was facedown. She reached inside and lifted it out of the trunk, flipping it over to see the front.

It was pink with white polka dots, and it said *Britney and Courtney,* with the *B* and the *C* blown up extra big. Courtney would have thought it had something to do with her, but who was Britney? A family member on Adrian's side whom her mom didn't want her to know about? But Adrian didn't have any siblings, and his parents had passed away in a car accident years before Courtney and her sisters had been born. Curious, she opened the cover.

And the world quaked around her.

Because inside the book was a photo of herself as a baby, in the hospital, in her mom's arms after being born. She'd seen this picture in her baby book. But apparently the picture she'd seen had been cropped, because in the photo she was looking at now, Adrian stood next to her mom—holding another baby. One that was identical to her.

Courtney's stomach swirled, nausea creeping up her throat. This couldn't mean what she was thinking.... They wouldn't hide something that huge from her. They *couldn't*. There had to be another explanation.

She held her breath and turned the page, hoping to find answers.

The next photo was of two babies—both of them looking exactly like her—in side-by-side hospital cribs. One of them was a photo she'd seen before, because the label near her feet said her name, Courtney Diamond, followed by her measurements. But the other crib must have been cropped out of the picture she'd seen. The one of the baby that looked *just like her,* matching pink outfit and all, except the name at her toes said Britney Diamond.

A baby identical to her. In a hospital crib next to hers. With the same last name.

It could mean only one thing.

Her chest caved in, collapsing around her lungs, her heart racing so fast that the world spun around her. How was this possible? If she'd had a twin sister, she would have known. Her mom would have mentioned her, Grandma would have mentioned her.... She couldn't have gone through her entire life without knowing something so important. She gripped the book so tightly that her knuckles turned white, her eyes glued to the photo. Even if Britney hadn't survived past infancy—which was possible, since Courtney had been a preemie—someone would have told her.

But as she thumbed through the pages, it became clear that Britney hadn't passed away soon after birth. She'd been by Courtney's side for *months*. There were photos of them going home to a beautiful house in the suburbs, with Mom and Adrian smiling as they carried them inside. Pictures of them on both sides of Peyton, who wasn't even one year old yet herself. Pictures of them taking their first bath, of them in their cribs in what Courtney guessed was their room, of them sucking on matching pacifiers, and loads more. Some were photos Courtney had seen before—although Britney had been cropped out—and some were ones she hadn't, likely because the babies were too close together.

Then, when they were around seven months old, the photos stopped.

The rest of the pages were empty.

Courtney didn't know when she'd started crying, but the tears that had been streaming down her cheeks came out full force as she looked through the photos again, her heart pounding as she grieved for a sister she'd never known. And not just any sister. A *twin* sister. Why had no one told her? Were they going to let her go her entire life not knowing? Why would someone do that to someone they loved?

She cried so hard that her stomach couldn't take it any longer, and she ran into Grandma's bathroom, collapsed in front of the toilet and lost her entire Thanksgiving meal. She wasn't sure how long she stayed there, but once sure her stomach was empty, she forced herself to the sink and rinsed her mouth with Grandma's mouthwash.

Her red-eyed reflection was a haunting reminder of the twin sister she'd lost—the sister who, if she were alive today, would have looked just like her. What had happened to Britney? Was she still alive, growing up with another family somewhere, unaware of her biological parents and sisters? Or—and Courtney suspected this was more likely—had something happened to take her away from this life before her first birthday?

Courtney's head spun with the possibilities, and she glared at her reflection. An hour ago she'd been enjoying the Thanksgiving meal with her family. Now her world was shattered. She swallowed, grimacing at the remaining taste of bile in her throat, and took another swig of mouthwash. Had these past moments really happened? But the baby book splayed on the ground confirmed that, yes, it had. She wasn't sure what to think, what to do.

There was one thing she did know—she needed answers, and she needed them *now*.

She picked the baby book off the ground and marched into the living room where Mom, Grandma, Peyton and Savannah were in their same spots watching the movie. So relaxed...so *normal*.

"We thought you were never coming out of there," Savannah said. "Didn't you get my texts? Or were you too busy talking to whoever had called to look at them?" She smiled, so carefree, her eyes shining with the unspoken words that she hoped to hear all about this mystery caller later.

It felt like hours since Courtney had talked to Brett. And she must have left her phone on the floor, which was why she hadn't seen Savannah's texts.

But none of that mattered right now.

She held the baby book in front of her, the cover facing outward. "Does anyone want to tell me what this is about?"

Her mom took one look at the book and paused the movie. "Is that what I think it is?" she asked Grandma, her voice filled with anger. But apparently the question was rhetorical, because she continued before Grandma could respond. "I told you to get rid of that. You *swore to me* that you got rid of it—that it was gone forever. So how the hell is she holding it?"

"I know what I told you, Donna," Grandma said to their mom. "But I lied."

"How could you?" Mom reared her arm back and threw the remote at the coffee table with so much force that it bounced off the wood and onto the rug. The back of the remote popped off, the batteries rolling out. They all stared at it until the last battery was still, except for Mom, whose eyes burned as she looked at Grandma, waiting for an answer.

"You know I disagreed with your decision," Grandma said, surprisingly calm in contrast to Mom. "I couldn't throw away all evidence that she'd existed. I didn't want you to regret it and have nothing to remember her by."

"What are you all talking about?" Peyton looked back and forth from Courtney to Grandma and Mom. "What's so important about that book?"

"Did you open it?" Grandma ignored Peyton, the question directed at Courtney.

"Of *course* I opened it," she said. "I saw everything. How could you keep this from me?"

"Why don't I, you and your mom go back into my room to talk about it?" Grandma got out of her chair and picked up the remote, placing the batteries back inside. "Peyton and Savannah can continue watching the movie."

"No." Courtney stood her ground. "She was Peyton and

Savannah's sister, too. Whatever you're about to tell me, they deserve to hear it." She sat on the couch between Savannah and Peyton and placed the book on her lap. Her face burned, and she glared at Mom, who was staring blankly at the wall. Why wouldn't she *look* at her?

"I can't do this right now." Their mom stood up, her gaze darting around the room like a wild bird trapped in a cage. "You never should have found that, Courtney." She shook her head, stumbling backward. "I need to get out of here."

"You're staying right here." Grandma's voice was stern, and their mom froze. "You've lied about this for long enough, Donna. I've always said you couldn't keep it up forever. Now it's time for you to tell the truth."

"But I'm not ready yet." She sounded like a ten-year-old, and tears glimmered in her eyes. "It's not the right time."

"There's never going to be a right time for this conversation," Grandma said. "But it has to happen, and since Courtney has seen the book, it has to happen *now*. You've run away from the past for too long—first with moving back to Fairfield after the tragedy, then with the drinking. Now you say you're starting fresh, but you'll never be able to do that if you keep this secret buried. Don't you think your girls deserve to know the truth?"

"I don't have much of a choice, do I?" She glared at Courtney—as if *Courtney* had done something wrong—and fell back into the armchair.

While this was all going on, Peyton and Savannah had browsed through the contents of the book. Peyton was cursing up a storm, her eyes livid. Savannah was speechless, and she grabbed on to Courtney's hand, gripping so tightly that Courtney's fingers went numb.

"How did you find this?" Grandma asked in her gentle way that made anyone want to confide in her.

Courtney told them everything: how she suspected everything she'd been told about the kidnapping didn't add up, and that whenever she asked about it, she felt as if no one was being honest with her.

"With no one telling me the truth, I had to find it out myself," she said. "I was in Grandma's room and remembered how she forbade us from opening her trunk. I figured it couldn't hurt to see what was in there, and that's where I found the book." Her chest tightened, the tears pouring down her face. She purposefully left out the part about her key necklace unlocking it—she didn't want to give Mom another reason to get angry at Grandma. "Was there ever a kidnapping?" she asked. "Or was that a story you all created to hide whatever happened to Britney?" It was the first time Courtney had said her name out loud, which made this devastatingly real. How could her family—people who claimed to *love* her—hide something this huge from her and her sisters?

She would never see them the same way again.

Grandma pursed her lips and looked at Mom. "Do you want to tell her, or should I?"

Mom stared at the ground, her expression blank, and Courtney knew she would take the coward's way out and make Grandma do it. But then she straightened her shoulders and met Courtney's eyes. "I'm the one who wanted to protect you from the truth," she said. "So I should tell you what happened."

She was really going to twist this around by claiming that instead of "lying" she was "protecting her from the truth"? Courtney clenched her jaw and gripped the book more tightly. But she nodded, needing to hear this. At least her sisters were on either side of her, silently letting her know that whatever their mom told them, they were in it together.

"As you saw in the baby book, you were born a twin." Their mom's voice was small, each word a struggle. She picked at her cuticles, and her lips trembled, but she managed to continue, "Courtney and Britney. It was an early delivery, and while you had to stay in the hospital for longer than normal, you were both beautiful and perfectly healthy. Your father and I brought the two of you home, and we were so happy. I got pregnant again two months later, and our life seemed perfect. It was easy to forget about the dangers that come with Adrian's business and try to be a 'normal' family. But we got too comfortable, because as Adrian told you, when you were six and a half months old, you were kidnapped while your nanny was taking you out for a walk."

"It wasn't just me she was taking out for a walk, was it?" Courtney asked, gripping Savannah's hand harder. "Britney was there, too."

"Yes." Mom wiped away a tear. "She was." Her chin quivered, and she looked unable to continue without bursting into tears, so Grandma got them all glasses of water from the kitchen. After a few sips, she regained control. "It happened within a few hours. I was out with my friends, and I had no idea anything was wrong. Adrian only called to tell me to come home after you were safe."

"But what happened in those few hours?" Courtney prodded. "How did Britney…" She swallowed, unable to say the word she was thinking out loud. "What happened to her?"

"The man leading the kidnapping was already on the run for previous crimes, so he had nothing to lose." Mom's eyes were far away, as if she was seeing it happen in front of her. "All he wanted was enough money to flee the country and be financially secure for the rest of his life. He 'took care of' your nanny, then called Adrian to let him know that he had the twins and how much cash he wanted as ransom. But to make sure the authorities didn't get involved, he..." She shook her head and buried her face in her hands, breaking into gut-wrenching sobs.

Grandma joined her on the armchair, put her arms around her and rubbed her back. "Do you want me to tell them the rest?"

Their mom squeezed out a small "Yes."

Grandma took a deep breath, met Courtney's eyes and continued, "The kidnapper didn't want Adrian to get the authorities involved, so he took Britney's life while he was on the phone with him." Her arm was still wrapped around their mom, who cried harder when the words were spoken out loud. "He said if Adrian didn't do as he wished, the other twin—meaning you, Courtney—would meet the same fate. So Adrian followed his instructions perfectly, delivering the cash where asked.

"Once the cash was received, the kidnapper told Adrian where to go to find you. Adrian hoped the kidnapper had lied about what he'd done. But while both of you *were* in the car, you were healthy and safe, and Britney was already gone. So while Adrian was grieving over his daughter, that awful man used the money to flee the country, and he hasn't been heard from since."

"I never forgave Adrian for what happened," their mom finally whispered, lifting her head to reveal her tear-stained face. "And he never forgave himself. He should have made sure you were guarded enough to prevent what happened. It was his fault, and he knows it. If he'd been more careful, Britney would still be here today."

Courtney's stomach turned inside out. If she hadn't been sick earlier, she would have thrown up in the middle of the living room. "Oh, my god." Her voice caught, and she looked at Grandma and Mom as if they were strangers. "I had a *twin sister.* No matter how guilty you and Adrian felt about what happened to her…how could you keep that from me?"

"From *all* of us," Peyton said. "This might affect Courtney the most, but Britney was our sister, too. You had no right to keep her memory from us."

"I knew it was wrong," their mom said. "But if I told you about her, I would have had to tell you about Adrian, too. And he was the reason the kidnapping happened in the first place, so I couldn't let him be in your lives. He didn't argue with me when I cut him out. And luckily this all happened before the internet blew up, so he arranged for all traces of our connection to be removed from the web. We could leave his awful world and live in peace."

"But you still haven't answered my question." Courtney clenched her fists, anger flooding her veins at the sight of her mom, at the thought of her lies. "How could you live with yourself knowing what you were keeping from us? How could you get through each day without being consumed by guilt?"

"I couldn't." She shrugged and studied her hands. "That's why I drank. Alcohol numbed it all, so I didn't have to think about it." She paused to sip her water. "But try to understand—when was a 'good time' to tell you? When it happened, you and Peyton were too young to remember, and Savannah hadn't been born yet. I couldn't think about Britney without being overcome by grief, so I buried her away. Years passed, and I *wanted* to tell you the truth, but there's never a good time to turn your daughters' worlds upside down."

"So you were going to keep her from us forever?" Savannah asked.

"That was never my intention."

"But you wanted Grandma to get rid of the baby book, and you threw out everything else of Britney's." Courtney wasn't sure if the last part was true, but she'd never seen anything that could have belonged to her twin. The guilt in her mom's eyes when she said it let her know she was right. "You threw her memory away and pretended she never existed. If your intention wasn't to keep her from us forever, you never would have done that."

"Stop attacking me!" She slammed her palms against the arms of the chair and glared at them, her face red. "You have *no idea* what this was like for me. I don't blame you for hating me for this, but I did what I thought was the best for the three of you."

"What you did was wrong." Courtney's voice was hard. She was *not* letting Mom pull a "poor me" routine. *Nothing* could validate what she did. Nothing.

"I guess this explains why my baby book was never as filled up as Peyton's and Savannah's, and why sometimes when you looked at me, you got sad for no reason, as if I'd done something wrong." She was glad when Mom shrank away from her—glad to see how every word made her face twist in guilt. "It's because seeing me reminded you of *her,* didn't it? Of what Britney would have looked like if she'd had the chance to grow up."

Her mom refused to meet her eyes, which was all the proof Courtney needed. How could this be happening? Her mom had looked at her every day and hadn't told her about this huge part of herself—an identical twin sister—whom she'd never known.

Courtney would never forgive her for this.

"I can't look at you for a second longer," she said, not caring that her words caused her mom to start sobbing again.

She grabbed the baby book and stood to face Peyton and Savannah, who watched her closely, waiting for her next move.

"Let's call the airport and tell them to get the plane ready. We're leaving tonight."

chapter 23: *Peyton*

They got back to the Diamond late Thursday night and found Rebecca pacing in their condo. Her hair was a frizzy mess, as if she'd been pulling at it, and her forehead was creased with worry.

"Your grandma called and told me everything," she said. "She thought I would be the best person to break the news to Adrian. He's arranged to fly back early from Macau and should be here by Saturday morning."

"And I thought by coming back here I could get *away* from people who've been lying to me," Courtney said, each word filled with so much anger that she sounded nothing like herself. "I'm not sure if what Adrian did was better or worse than Mom. She lied to us every day, but he cut himself out of our lives completely. I hate them both."

Peyton had never seen this side of Courtney before, and she had no idea how to make her feel better, because she was fuming, too. Yes, Britney had been Courtney's twin, but she was also Peyton and Savannah's sister. A sister they would never know. Because she had died. No, not died. Because she'd been *murdered*.

None of it felt real, but Courtney had the pictures to prove it.

"So you knew about all of this, too?" Savannah sounded helpless as she asked Rebecca.

Rebecca ran her fingers over her long strand of pearls and nodded. "My ex and I were friends with Adrian and your mom when everything happened, so I've known for years. When Adrian and I started dating again, he made me promise not to say anything. He still blames himself for what happened. I've told him repeatedly that he needs to tell you the truth, but he refused, claiming he's already thrown so much at you, and he didn't think you were ready yet."

"It would have been better for him to be honest with us when we first got here than to have found out this way," Peyton said.

"I agree," Rebecca said. "I wish I could have told you myself, but it wasn't my secret to tell. I'm so sorry. But you deserved to hear it from your parents. And while I know you might not believe me, I think Adrian was going to tell you soon."

"Now we'll never know, will we?" Courtney hugged the baby book close. She hadn't let it out of her sight since she'd found it. "I'm going to my room—I need to be alone."

"Let us know if you need anything?" Savannah asked.

Courtney nodded and hurried away, slamming the door behind her.

"Should we go in after her?" Rebecca looked worriedly at where Courtney had disappeared.

"No," Peyton said. "She hasn't been herself since finding out, and I know how Courtney is—she needs time alone to process everything. She'll talk when she's ready."

Rebecca wrung her hands together and resumed pacing around the living room. "I knew nothing good could come from Adrian keeping this from you," she said, stopping to face Peyton and Savannah. "How are the two of you holding up? You both seem to be handling this better than Courtney."

"I'm pissed that Mom and Adrian kept this from us. And Grandma, too." Peyton flopped onto the living room couch, glad to be back in the condo after the day from hell. "I know I was too young when it happened, but I feel like I should remember her. Instead I have nothing."

"You weren't even one when it happened." Rebecca sat on the opposing couch. "Remembering anything from that age is impossible."

"And I have no idea what to say to Courtney," Savannah said, situating herself next to Peyton. "This is awful for us, but the worst for her. If none of this had happened, she would have a twin sister. She'll never have that, and she didn't even know until now that it was something she should miss."

"This isn't going to be easy to get through," Rebecca said. "The three of you have dealt with a lot, and I know Courtney's always been there for you. But when she's ready to talk, you need to be strong for her. And I hope you know that I'm here for you."

"Thanks," Savannah said. "And this might sound strange, but even though I've seen the pictures and heard the story about what happened, none of it feels real yet. It's like Britney never existed, even though I know she did. Maybe it's because I was never alive at the same time as her.... I don't know."

"Maybe," Rebecca said. "But I hope that when Adrian gets back on Saturday morning, you listen to what he has to say. He's carried so much guilt with him. He feels responsible for Britney's passing."

"Her murder, you mean," Peyton said.

"I was trying to word it more sensitively." Rebecca fidgeted with her engagement ring, her cheeks turning red. None of them said anything for a few seconds. "Anyway, are you girls hungry? We could order up dinner or dessert."

"I'm still full from Thanksgiving dinner," Peyton said. Had it really only been hours since she, her sisters, Grandma, Mom and Aunt Sophie had sat around the Thanksgiving table, surrounded by more food than they could finish?

"I'm just going to go to sleep." Savannah covered her mouth and yawned. "It's been a long day, and I'm tired."

"All right." Rebecca stood up and straightened nonexistent creases off her pants. "Brett's staying with his dad over break, but he knows the three of you came back early, and he asked me why. Now that the truth is out, I have to tell him. But this is a family matter, so I'll make him promise not to say a word to anyone."

"Courtney should be the one to tell him," Peyton said. Although Courtney had been ignoring his calls and texts since everything went to hell that afternoon. Brett had even texted Peyton and Savannah to ask what was going on, but Courtney had told them not to reply. And Peyton had listened. She'd never seen Courtney shut down like this before, so she didn't know what else to do.

"He said he's called and texted her, but she hasn't responded," Rebecca said. "I know my son, and if he's determined for an answer, he won't give up. Courtney clearly isn't ready to talk, so it's best if I handle this."

"Okay," Peyton said, although she wasn't sure about that. Despite Courtney swearing that she and Brett were only friends, Peyton didn't buy that she didn't have stronger feelings for him. But Rebecca and Adrian were so on edge about Courtney and Brett getting *too* close, and Peyton didn't want to say anything that might get her sister in trouble. She was devastated enough as it was.

"If you girls need anything, no matter what time it is, you can come to my condo to talk," Rebecca said. "And I truly am sorry you had to find out this way."

"Thanks." Peyton didn't know what else to say. It wasn't Rebecca's responsibility to have told them the truth—it was their mom's and Adrian's.

Once Rebecca left the condo, Peyton turned to Savannah. "Are you really going to bed, or did you just want Rebecca to leave?"

"I'm really going to bed." Savannah yawned again. "Today's been exhausting. But I like Rebecca, and it was nice of her to be here for us when we got back. I truly believe she wanted Adrian to tell us the truth from the start."

"Maybe." Peyton didn't disagree, but she didn't feel like admitting it. She supposed Rebecca was nice—in a prim and proper type of way. But she didn't want to have heart-to-hearts with her.

"I wish I could say something to Courtney to make her feel better." Savannah glanced hopelessly at Courtney's room. "She's so angry, and it scares me. She's always been the one who can handle anything, you know?"

"I know," Peyton said, and even though she felt the same

as Savannah, she had to say something to make her sister feel better. "But even Courtney isn't perfect. Give her time. This is a huge shock to all of us, but it's the hardest for her. Once she gets some rest tonight, she'll be ready to talk tomorrow."

"I hope so," Savannah said. "I hate seeing her like this. She's such a good person, and she deserves better."

"Have you looked around?" Peyton laughed and held out her arms. "We have so much more than any person 'deserves.'"

"That's not what I meant," Savannah said. "Trust me, I've appreciated every second since we've gotten here. But I wish we had two parents who loved each other and who loved us— who spent time with us and were honest with us. I saw that picture in the baby book of Mom and Adrian taking Courtney and Britney home from the hospital, and I thought, 'That could have been our life.'" Her eyes glistened, and she blinked a few times, swallowing back tears. "Instead, Mom's a lying alcoholic disaster and Adrian never has time for us."

Peyton rested her chin in her hands. "The kidnapping screwed everything up, didn't it?"

"Yeah," Savannah said. "It sucks."

"But that's just the way things worked out," she said. "Even if the kidnapping had never happened, who knows how things would have ended up for Mom and Adrian? Divorce happens all the time. And just because they looked happy in pictures doesn't mean they actually *were* happy, or that everything would have been perfect for them."

"But they would have had a shot," Savannah said. "And they wouldn't have lied to us about everything. I hate not being able to trust them."

"No matter what, you have me and Courtney, and you can trust us with anything," Peyton said. "You know that, right?"

"Yeah." Savannah nodded. "Evie used to brag about being an only child. And sure, most of the time it was annoying that me, you and Courtney had to share a bedroom and bathroom, but Evie's bragging never made me jealous. Because I don't know what I would do without you guys. I guess that's why it scares me that Courtney's shutting us out."

"She'll come around," Peyton promised. "She just needs time. You know that when Courtney thinks, she likes to do it alone."

"Yeah," Savannah said, rubbing her eyes. "But I really am tired. See you in the morning?"

"See you."

She left, and Peyton was alone in the living room, staring out the floor-to-ceiling windows overlooking the lit-up Vegas Strip full of partying tourists. It didn't feel right for everyone to be having fun when Peyton had a fresh hole in her chest for the sister she hadn't known existed until this afternoon.

She wanted to talk to someone, but who? Not Rebecca, even though she'd offered. It was nice of her, but Peyton still didn't feel like Rebecca "got" her. She hadn't kept in touch with anyone from Fairfield, because while Peyton had had fun with her friends while she'd lived there, she'd never opened up enough to have a strong bond with them, like the bond Savannah shared with Evie. And while she had acquaintances from Goodman, she wasn't close enough to any of them to share something so personal.

There was only one person who knew her well enough to listen and maybe care, and that was *if* he hadn't known about Britney and had been lying to her, too. So Peyton went to her room, freshened up and left the condo. Even though it was nighttime, she kept her sunglasses on, since her eyes were red and puffy. She hadn't bothered reapplying her black eyeliner, in case she started crying again.

Jackson, Teddy and Carl were waiting in their usual spots in the hall. Peyton was glad to have caught them before the night guards took over their shift. Luckily their guards adjusted their schedules in accordance to Peyton and her sisters', so they also got to sleep in and stay up late on weekends and vacations.

"You guys don't get holidays off?" she asked, shutting the door to the condo.

"We were supposed to get Thanksgiving off, since Mr. Diamond hired local guards in California for your visit, but we were called into work when you and your sisters returned to Vegas early," Savannah's guard, Carl, told her.

"We don't mind, though," Teddy added. "Adrian makes it well worth it, and we get plenty of vacation days."

"Sorry about that," Peyton said. "We didn't mean to ruin your Thanksgiving. But we had a family emergency."

Carl assured her it was okay, and she headed to the elevators. Jackson, of course, was right behind her.

The doors closed, and he watched her, concerned. "What's going on?"

"A lot of shit went down at my grandma's." Peyton's eyes watered as she replayed the scene, and she was glad she was wearing sunglasses. "I know you always tell me that we have to have a professional relationship, but I need someone to talk to, and you're the first person who came to mind."

"So you came out tonight to hang out with me?" He didn't sound like he loved the idea, but he didn't sound like he hated it, either. "You know I can't do that, Peyton. Too many people at the Diamond know who we are to risk being seen socializing. Remember when your classmate took that picture of you talking with your teacher?"

"How could I forget?" she said. "But something big happened, and I need a friend. Isn't there somewhere we can go to talk?" For emphasis, she pushed her sunglasses to her head. With red eyes and no makeup, she felt exposed, but it was all she could do to show him how serious she was.

His eyes flashed with compassion. Apparently she looked as disastrous as she felt.

"Tell your driver to take you to the Imperial Palace," he said. "When you get there, keep your sunglasses on. I'll be right behind you."

When Peyton arrived at the Imperial Palace, she understood why Jackson had picked it. The Japanese-themed building was dinky compared to the other glamorous hotels on the Vegas Strip. The inside was all muted browns, with low ceilings and worn carpets, and it smelled like dust and stale cigarette smoke. No one would think Peyton Diamond, daughter of Adrian Diamond of Diamond Resorts Worldwide, would spend her time there.

She walked into the lobby, keeping her sunglasses on. Jackson's Town Car had followed her Range Rover, and he got out after her. But what she hadn't expected was that he had changed. Instead of wearing his bodyguard suit, he was in a forest-green T-shirt that he could have worn to the gym. He still had on his black dress pants (which looked a little silly with the T-shirt), but out of his uniform, he looked younger than ever.

"What happened to your suit?" Peyton asked.

"I always wear a T-shirt as an undershirt in the winter," he said. "And since we're trying to stay under the radar, I ditched what I could of the suit in the car. On the way back to the Diamond, I'll put it back on again."

"You look more comfortable in a T-shirt," she observed. Plus, it brought out the green in his hazel eyes.

"I never was a suit-and-tie type of guy," he said. "When I guarded you in California, I wore street clothes, and I preferred it to what Adrian has us wear in Vegas. But it's worth putting up with for the job."

Peyton nodded and looked around the Imperial Palace, which was packed with people in their twenties and thirties drinking beer and gambling. "Where did you want to go in here to talk?" she asked. "I was hoping somewhere private… like a room?"

Frustration mixed with what Peyton thought was desire twisted in Jackson's eyes. "You know I won't do that," he said. "But there's a place where we can talk without people paying attention to us."

"All right," Peyton said. It was worth the try. "Lead the way."

She followed Jackson up two escalators to the third floor, with a sign overhead announcing that they were entering the Imperial Palace Karaoke Club. But she didn't need the sign to tell her that—the off-key singing was proof enough.

The bar was packed, most everyone clustered up front to watch the karaoke performance. Every small, round table had a pitcher or two of beer in the center, and people browsed the karaoke binders, deciding what song they wanted to sing (or butcher, as was currently happening onstage.)

"*This* is where you thought to go for privacy?"

"Let's sit over there." He pointed to a table in the back corner, and they sat kitty-corner, their legs so close that one small movement would make them brush against each other. "No one would expect you to come here. Plus, everyone's too focused on the stage to pay attention to us in the corner, and it's not as loud as a club, so we can talk without having to yell. Just keep your sunglasses on, and no one will recognize you."

The waiter took their drink orders—Peyton asked for a pitcher of beer, since that seemed like the thing to do here, and she was stressed, so it would help her relax. The fake ID she'd gotten last summer was scannable, so it proved no problem. Jackson, of course, ordered a Coke. But when the waiter delivered the beer pitcher to the table, he left them with two cups.

"You're really going to drink all of that yourself?" Jackson pulled his Coke closer, leaving his beer cup turned over.

"After the day I've had, you would, too." Peyton poured her cup to the rim. "But, no, I'm not going to drink the whole thing. The pitcher was just so cheap, so I figured, what the hell?"

"I'm guessing something serious happened for you and your sisters to come home early."

"You have no idea." Peyton gulped her beer and placed it on the table. "I know you've seen my files," she started. "But have you seen the files for Courtney and Savannah, too?"

"Yes," he said. "Although I can't tell you what's in them. I'm under a confidentiality contract."

"I understand," she said. "But could you tell me what's *not* in them?"

He watched her closely, as if contemplating the question. "It's hard for me to say without knowing what you want to ask. But…you're free to ask whatever you want."

That must be his cryptic way of telling her to go ahead.

She might as well start with what she'd come here for. "Did Courtney's file say anything about Britney?"

His eyebrows scrunched—he seemed genuinely confused. "No." He shook his head. "I don't remember a Britney in Courtney's file. Why?"

Peyton breathed out in relief. "She's definitely not someone you would have forgotten. Britney was Courtney's twin sister."

Jackson's expression went from shock to confusion to disbelief. "Courtney doesn't have a twin sister," he finally said. "Something that huge would be in her file."

"Unless Adrian was determined to keep her secret."

"Why would he want to do that?" Jackson scratched his head, as if he could figure it out by thinking hard enough.

"This afternoon, Courtney found her baby book at Grandma's house," Peyton said. "Except it wasn't just for her, but for her and *Britney,* who was her twin."

From there she told him everything—from Courtney storming into the living room with the book in her arms, to Mom and Grandma telling them the truth about what had happened to Britney, to them flying back to Vegas. "Now Courtney's locked herself in her room, and she and Savannah need me to be the strong one, but I'm just as angry and confused as they are, and I didn't know who to talk to," she finally finished. She'd started crying sometime in the middle of the story, and the tears were fogging up her sunglasses, so she pushed them to her head and wiped her eyes.

"Wow." Jackson flipped his cup right side up, poured himself some beer and took a long swig. Peyton had never seen him drink on the job before—well, she'd never seen him drink at *all* before. "I promise I never knew about this. I can't believe they would keep something like that from you. And from Courtney…" He shook his head. "I can't imagine what this must be like for her."

"It's so strange to think about.…" Another tear trickled down Peyton's cheek, and she didn't bother wiping it away. "We had another sister, and if the kidnapping hadn't happened, she would be here today. Obviously she would look like Courtney, but would she be similar to her, or different? What would her relationship be like with me, and with Savannah? Britney being alive would change *everything*. I just wish I knew how."

"And I wish I had the answers for you," Jackson said, brushing the tear off her cheek. His eyes were so intense, as if he could see into her soul, and her heart thudded with how there were only inches between his face and hers. She wanted to close the space between them, but she'd kissed him twice already, and both times he'd pushed her away. She was done throwing herself at him and getting nothing back. It hurt too much.

But then he leaned toward her, his lips dangerously close to hers—so close that she could feel his breath on her cheek. She lifted her chin and closed her eyes, but instead of the kiss she'd expected, he rested his forehead against hers. He stayed like that for a few seconds, and her blood pumped faster, waiting for him to give in. But he pulled away and took a deep drink of his beer, as if it could cleanse his mind of whatever had just happened between them.

She crossed her arms and watched him, her eyes hard. He owed her an explanation.

"This can't happen," he said, running his hands over his short hair. "I'm sorry, Peyton. I want to be here for you, but the way that I *want* to be here for you and that I'm *allowed* to be here for you are too different."

Peyton arched an eyebrow—that was the most up-front he'd been with her in a while. "So you *do* have feelings for me?" she asked, although her voice wobbled, ruining any attempt at sounding confident.

"If I did, it wouldn't matter, because nothing could come of it."

"That's not true." She tried to swallow away her tears, but her eyes heated up again, and once more, they came pouring out. Why was she *crying* so much? She never cried. She hadn't even cried when she'd learned Mom was going to rehab. She wiped her tears away and slid her sunglasses back over her face, as if they could hide her from the world.

"I'm sorry, Peyton." Jackson reached forward to place his hand on top of hers, but then he pulled away, which only made her feel worse. "I didn't mean to make this harder for you."

"You didn't make it harder for me." She sniffed. "I needed someone to talk to. You're the only person I trust to keep this secret and who cared enough to listen. My sisters are looking to me to be the strong one. Clearly I can't talk to Grandma or Mom, and Rebecca says she's there for us, but she doesn't know me at all. Besides, her loyalty's with Adrian."

"I know you're not fond of Rebecca, but it might not hurt to give her a chance," Jackson said. "I don't know her well myself, but it seems like she wants to be there for you and your sisters."

"That's what Savannah says, too." Peyton shrugged. "But Adrian's still first for her. He's in the wrong here—he and Mom and Grandma—but Rebecca loves him and will defend him in the end."

"She will," he agreed.

"But here's what I don't understand," she said. "Why are

you so insistent that nothing could come from whatever's going on between us? I feel it, and you pretty much told me you feel it, too. There has to be some way we can make it work without Adrian finding out. After all the lies he's told me and my sisters, I wouldn't even feel bad about it."

"It still doesn't make it all right to go behind his back," Jackson said, and Peyton's heart sank. "If we were going to be together, I wouldn't want to hide it. You deserve better than that. Besides, Adrian's your father, and he's my employer. If we got found out—and we *would* get found out—the consequences for me would be severe. You might get grounded. I would get fired. Adrian Diamond is a powerful man, and with that on my record, I would be blacklisted for any future employment. Add on top of that you being a minor, and who knows how much trouble I would be in."

"So basically, being with me could destroy your life."

"Yes." He clenched his jaw, his eyes pained, and Peyton realized how unfair she'd been by throwing herself at him. How had she not put herself in his position until he spelled it out for her? He must think she was a selfish brat.

"I'm sorry," she said, since it was all she could come up with to say. "All I knew was how much I liked you. The only people I've ever trusted before were Grandma, Courtney and Savannah, but for some reason, I've trusted you from the moment we met. You understand who I am, and you *like* who I am. Or at least, I think you do."

"Of course I like who you are." He smiled for the first time since they'd sat down. "You're stubborn, tough, honest and you'll do anything for the people you love. Those are amazing qualities. I might not agree with all your decisions, but I admire how you go after what you want, no matter what. Do you think I would have put up with your troublemaking otherwise?"

Tears rose in her throat again, and she smiled, although it was bittersweet. How had he gone from saying that they couldn't be together to saying the nicest things to her ever?

"It's hard to tell sometimes," she finally said. "But I'm glad you were honest with me—about everything. I guess I never thought about how serious the consequences could be for you because I didn't *want* those consequences to exist. Hearing you say it out loud made me realize how real they are. And there's no way in hell I would let you lose your career because of me. So I'll stop pushing you, I promise."

"Thank you," he said, although his voice was tight, his eyes sad. "But I hope you realize that a lot of your feelings for me are because you were forced to have me in your life and let your guard down around me. You knew I knew the details of your life from day one, so you didn't bother hiding anything. If you open yourself up like that for someone else, maybe you'll feel the same way for them, too."

"I doubt it," she said, amazed by how he made it sound so easy. "Trust takes a long time to earn. And usually it's never deserved at all."

"There are people out there worth trusting," he said. "They might be rare, but they exist. And you're never going to get to the point where you trust someone if you don't let your guard down to begin with. I know you will someday. But for now, I hope you know that I'm sorry."

"Why are you sorry?" she asked. "None of this is your fault."

"You didn't let me finish," he said. "I'm sorry it has to be like this between us. It might not always be this way, but at least for the next few months, until you turn eighteen, we can't change our situation. I just hope we can be friends."

Friends. She wanted more than that, but she refused to let Jackson ruin his career—and possibly his life—for her. So, being friends would have to do for now.

They finished their drinks, and for the first time, they were able to talk freely. Yes, she had feelings for him—those couldn't disappear overnight—but being around him was no longer a battle of who would give in to the other first. And despite the terrible things she'd learned earlier that day, talking with Jackson made her feel not quite as awful anymore. As if her life hadn't just been torn apart by more lies.

But she knew it would all come crashing down again once Adrian got back to Vegas.

chapter 24: *Madison*

MR. ADRIAN DIAMOND
AND
MS. REBECCA CARMEL

INVITE YOU TO JOIN US AS WE CELEBRATE

the sixteenth birthday of

Savannah Diamond

Saturday, December 13th

7:00 p.m. — midnight

ABANDON NIGHTCLUB

THE DIAMOND RESIDENCES

SOUTH LAS VEGAS BOULEVARD

LAS VEGAS, NEVADA 89109

RSVP TO REBECCA@DIAMONDLASVEGAS.COM

FESTIVE ATTIRE
*The celebration will be featured on the television show
My Fabulous Sweet Sixteen, so dress appropriately.
If you give consent to be on the show, please fill out the
enclosed waiver (or have your parent/guardian fill it out
if you're under eighteen) and present it at the door.

"Did you girls get invitations to Savannah's Sweet Sixteen?" Madison asked Kaitlin and Tiffany over lunch at Nobu in the Hard Rock, their favorite sushi restaurant. Her friends had reached out to her on Thanksgiving—they felt guilty for ostracizing her since Halloween—and now they were getting sushi like old times. Well, not exactly like old times, since the fourth person in their core group, Larissa, was missing from the table. But it was close enough.

"Yep." Tiffany finished off her last piece of sushi. "How cool is it that it's going to be on *My Fabulous Sweet Sixteen?* I bet Savannah's so excited."

"Your parents signed the waiver?" Kaitlin asked.

"Of course," Tiffany said. "I think my mom's more excited about the television show than I am. And she's not even going to *be* there."

"Did your parents not sign it?" Madison asked Kaitlin.

"Nope." Kaitlin rolled her eyes. "They don't want my face on national television. I just don't want to have to stand on the sidelines while the exciting parts of the party are being filmed."

"I'm sure it won't be a big deal," Madison said, trying to reassure her, even though she would have been annoyed if her parents had refused to sign her waiver. Not because she cared about being on TV—she didn't—but because she liked making her own decisions.

They chatted about what they were thinking of wearing and ordered dessert to share. *Only one or two spoonfuls,* Madison told herself. She'd lost most of the weight she'd gained and didn't want to blow it on dessert. But it felt good to be out at lunch with her friends. Keeping herself from telling them about Adrian being her biological father was still a struggle, but after spilling the secret to Oliver, it wasn't as hard as before.

And while she did plan on following through with her promise to Oliver and telling her parents that she wanted to confront Adrian, she hadn't gotten a chance yet. She hadn't wanted to bring it up on Thanksgiving and ruin the holiday, and they'd left for work before she'd woken up this morning. Tonight they were going out on a date…so she would wait until tomorrow.

Her neck muscles tightened at the prospect, and she tried to relax so that she wouldn't get a migraine.

The waitress placed their dessert on the table, and then Kaitlin focused on Madison, her eyes more serious than they'd been for the entire meal. Madison knew that look: Kaitlin was about to tell her something she didn't want to hear.

She braced herself for whatever was coming.

"We have to tell you something, and you're not going to be happy about it, but please, hear us out," Kaitlin started.

"Okay…" Madison put down her spoon; the anticipation

for whatever they were about to tell her had killed her appetite. Not like that was a bad thing. "What is it?"

Tiffany pulled her thick dark hair over her shoulder. "We know you and Larissa haven't been getting along well recently, and we want to help fix things between you two," she said. "We've all been such good friends for so long, and this will all be better once both of you talk about it." As always, Tiffany was completely genuine. But this meal had been going fine without Larissa. Whatever they had planned would surely ruin that.

"I don't know," Madison said. "Larissa accused me of some pretty awful things on Halloween, and as far as I'm aware, her opinions haven't changed."

"But the four of us have been best friends for years," Tiffany said. "Sure, the two of you clash sometimes. But you always get over it."

"I know." Madison shrugged. "But this is different. She accused me of sleeping with Oliver, called me a selfish lying bitch, turned my friends against me and hasn't even apologized. I can't just 'get over' that."

"We understand." Kaitlin nodded. "And I don't want you to take this the wrong way, because we love both you *and* Larissa, but—*did* you sleep with Oliver?"

"No!" Madison shook her head. "I thought you both knew me better than that. Which is why I couldn't believe you sided with Larissa these past few weeks."

"We didn't 'side' with Larissa," Kaitlin said. "We just felt like you were avoiding us. Even before the fight you had with her, you ignored us when we reached out to you. But Larissa still wanted to go out, and since we're friends with both of you, we ended up spending more time with her. It wasn't intentional."

"I know." Madison stared at her water glass, wishing she could tell them *why* she'd been distancing herself. But the more people she told, the more chance of someone spilling it before she talked to Adrian. "I've just been really stressed out recently," she said. "I didn't mean to make both of you feel like I didn't care about hanging out anymore."

"We know that, but we also felt hurt that you were shutting us out," Tiffany said. "It seems like this is all a big misunderstanding. That's why—"

"You two didn't tell me *she* would be here," Larissa said from behind Madison's chair. Madison turned around, and sure enough, Larissa was standing there with her arms crossed and a sneer on her bright pink lips.

"They didn't tell me you were coming, either." Madison picked up her purse. "But don't worry, I'm on my way out." She looked at Tiffany and Kaitlin, willing herself not to get irritated at them in the middle of the restaurant about how they didn't warn her Larissa would be here. "Let me know how much I owe you for lunch, and I'll pay you back on Monday."

"Don't go," Kaitlin said. "Can't you both sit down, so we can talk?"

"Was this what you were trying to tell me?" Madison asked. "That you were going to hold a friend-tervention?"

"We just want you to work this out," Tiffany said. "The only way we could think to fix it was for both of you to have an in-person conversation, with me and Kaitlin here to help."

"This is more than a 'misunderstanding.'" Madison narrowed her eyes at Larissa, who annoyingly made herself comfortable in the fourth seat at their table. "You accused me of sleeping with Oliver, and when I told you I didn't, you refused to believe the truth."

"The 'truth'?" Larissa scowled. "I saw the way you and

Oliver were looking at each other on Halloween—like you wanted to rip each other's clothes off and go at it then and there. You two are together *all the time* nowadays. How could I not think you're sleeping together? If you weren't, you would have tried harder to get me to believe you. But you left and avoided me, so I know I was right."

"Or *maybe* there's more important stuff going on in my life than worrying about you thinking I slept with Oliver when I honestly told you I hadn't," Madison said. "You can't wrap your mind around the fact that I have bigger things going on, and that I'm not wasting energy trying to make you feel better because you're jealous of my friendship with Oliver."

"What sort of things?" Tiffany asked. "I thought you knew you could talk to us about anything."

"It's personal stuff." Madison willed them to understand. "Family stuff." It sounded so lame. But she couldn't explain *why* the secret was so huge without revealing the truth, and she would never want Larissa, Kaitlin and Tiffany to know before Peyton, Courtney and Savannah.

"See?" Larissa rolled her eyes. "This is what I mean. What's so huge that you're going to such lengths to keep it from your best friends?"

"Trust me, you would understand if you knew," Madison said. "But I can't tell you because more people are involved than just me. Hopefully I'll have it worked out soon, and then I promise you'll all be the first to know."

"Sure," Larissa said. "But I bet you've already told Oliver, haven't you?"

She froze, and that split-second pause was enough to give her away.

Larissa arched an eyebrow. "I'm right, aren't I? You *did* tell Oliver."

Madison took a deep breath, contemplating how to approach this without lying, while also making sure not to make things worse with Larissa. "It was only recently," she said. "After you *wrongly* thought Oliver and I had slept together and made sure our friends ostracized me. He was the only one there for me, and I needed someone to talk to."

"Tiffany and I were trying to be there for you, but you pushed us away," Kaitlin said. "Why would you talk to him and not us?"

"It wasn't anything personal." Madison leaned back in her seat, knowing how bad this sounded. Because, yes, Kaitlin, Tiffany and even Larissa were her closest friends. But Oliver was her *best* friend. He had been since lower school. There was no one she trusted more than him. "He's the only one who knows, and he only got it out of me after a few glasses of wine."

"And you expect us to believe you're not sleeping with him?" Larissa said. "I'm not an idiot, Madison. It's pretty clear what's going on here. 'He only got it out of me after a few glasses of wine'? Really? What *else* did he get out of you after those glasses of wine? Or, should I say, what did he get *in* you?" She snickered, as if that were the most brilliant comment ever.

"It sounds bad when you put it that way," Madison said. "But I swear I haven't slept with Oliver. You girls know me better than that."

"Do we?" Larissa asked. "Because recently it feels like I don't know you at all, and I know Kaitlin and Tiffany agree. Do you really want us to believe you and Oliver are just friends?"

"Yes," she said, although it came out shaky. Because friends don't make out in bed, or take off each other's shirts…or wonder if one of them *should* lose their virginity to the other. But she couldn't exactly say that right now. "And while I shouldn't have told *anyone* about what's been going on with my family, he gave me good advice. When I follow through with it—and I will soon—I'll tell you everything. But the other people involved deserve to hear the truth directly, not through the grapevine. I swear it's not about any of you, and that I wasn't keeping it from you because I don't trust you." Well, she trusted Kaitlin and Tiffany…but Larissa was known for not keeping her mouth shut about anything. "It's just not my place to tell."

"How long have you been keeping this big secret?" Tiffany asked.

"Since the end of September."

"Which was when you stopped hanging out with everyone." Kaitlin clasped her hands on the table, looking worried, not upset. "And you waited until *a few days ago* to talk to someone? You've been keeping it to yourself for two months?"

"Yep." She shrugged, trying to make it seem not as awful as it had been. "It's been a sucky two months, and I didn't mean to push you all away. But knowing something so huge and not being able to talk about it is hard."

"So you stopped coming out at all," Kaitlin said, and Madison nodded, since, as pathetic as it was, she was right. "What did you *do* with all that extra time?"

"I've seen every episode of *Downton Abbey, The Vampire Diaries* and now I'm on season fourteen of *Big Brother*."

"That was a good season," Larissa said.

"Don't tell me what happens!" Madison covered her ears. "I'm hoping Dan wins, but I don't want to know before I get to the finale."

"Fine, fine." Larissa laughed.

Tiffany looked back and forth between the two of them and smiled. "Does this mean we're all friends again?"

"Do you believe me that I didn't sleep with Oliver?" Madison asked Larissa.

"As long as you know that I was never jealous—you were right that I'm over Oliver and am dating Harrison now," she said. "I only said that stuff on Halloween because I *did* have a thing with Oliver over the summer, and you knew about it. I really thought you'd slept with him, and that you were hiding it from me because you'd been sleeping with him since before things had ended with us, so I was angry. But I guess I was wrong."

"Thanks," Madison said, surprised at Larissa's honesty. That was as much of an apology as she would get from her. Although she did feel guilty, because while she wasn't *sleeping* with Oliver, she didn't see him only as a friend anymore, either.

"I'm sorry for disappearing like I did," she said, deciding she would tell them about her feelings for Oliver once she worked them out herself. "These weeks without you all have sucked."

"We were starting to think you would never come back to us!" Larissa smiled.

"I knew once we sat down and talked we would be back to normal," Tiffany said. "That's how my sisters and I work out our fights. And the four of us have been friends for so long, we're pretty much as close as sisters."

Tiffany had no idea how close that hit to home. Because once Madison told her parents she was done keeping this secret for them, everyone—most important, the Diamond sisters—would finally know the truth.

www.campusbuzz.com

Peyton Diamond's New Man?!

Posted on Friday 11/28 at 2:37 PM

Did anyone see the pictures of Peyton Diamond floating around the internet of her getting cozy with that hottie at Imperial Palace last night over a pitcher of beer? Some girls were in town for Thanksgiving break and Tweeted the pictures, but NO ONE can figure out who he is!!! All we know is that he's way too hot to be in high school...

Disclaimer: I don't go to Goodman—I'm one of the girls who took the pictures—but my friends and I found this message board and figured it might be the right place to ask!!

1: Posted on Friday 11/28 at 2:59 PM

You came to the right place, but it would help if you posted a link to the pictures.

2: Posted on Friday 11/28 at 3:10 PM

DUH-SKI! CLICK HERE for the pics!

3: Posted on Friday 11/28 at 3:13 PM

"Duh-ski?" Who the hell talks like that? If it wasn't obvious you don't go to Goodman before, it sure is now.

4: Posted on Friday 11/28 at 3:39 PM

whoever that guy is, he doesn't go to goodman. and you're right that he looks older than high school.

5: Posted on Friday 11/28 at 4:03 PM

I've seen him around before! He was hanging at Myst. Maybe he met Peyton there?

6: Posted on Friday 11/28 at 4:35 PM

OMG I know who that is (although I can't tell you how, so you'll have to trust me on this) — he's her BODYGUARD! How scandalous...

chapter 25: Savannah

Savannah woke on Saturday morning to dishes clanging and the sweet smell of pancakes, cinnamon rolls and eggs. For a moment she felt like she was in her old bed, in the room she'd shared with her sisters in their apartment in Fairfield. Courtney had always cooked breakfast on Saturday mornings. There weren't many things Savannah missed from that apartment, but Saturday morning pajama breakfast was one of them.

Savannah freshened up and made her way to the kitchen. As she suspected, Courtney hovered over the stovetop, spatula in hand. This was the first time her sister had emerged from her room since Thursday night—not counting when she'd answered the door for room service. Savannah had knocked last night to check on her, but Courtney had yelled at her to go away, so she did.

"Does this mean you're feeling better today?" Savannah asked, hoping for a yes.

"I was going stir-crazy, and I woke up early this morning, so I went to the store to get breakfast ingredients," Courtney said as she flipped a pancake. That explained why she was in jeans and a T-shirt instead of pajamas. "Can you believe we've gotten so used to room service that we didn't have pancake batter and eggs around here?"

"It smells delicious." Savannah opened the cabinet and pulled out three plates to set the table. Back home when Courtney cooked, it was Savannah's job to set up and Peyton's job to clean. Their mom would join them if her hangover wasn't bad, but usually it *was* bad, so Savannah would make her a big cup of ice water and leave it on her nightstand.

Savannah placed their drinks at their place settings—orange juice for herself, chai tea for Courtney and coffee for Peyton. Right on cue, Peyton strolled into the kitchen, still in her pajamas, her long hair pulled back in a messy bun.

"Good morning!" Courtney called over her shoulder as she whisked a bowl of eggs.

"Morning," Peyton mumbled, looking quizzically at Savannah. She checked to make sure Courtney was focused on the eggs, and whispered, "Does this mean she's doing better?"

"I heard that," Courtney replied, surprisingly bubbly. "And I don't know. But I was tired of sitting around in my room trying to study for the SATs and read but not being able to focus. Then I thought about our old breakfasts, and how cooking helped me de-stress, and I figured I could try it. Savannah, can you get the cinnamon rolls out of the oven?"

Savannah shrugged at Peyton and did as Courtney asked. Her mouth watered at the sugary smell of the cinnamon rolls, and it took all of her effort to resist eating one as she spread the frosting on top.

They sat down to eat, and Savannah gathered pancakes onto her plate, unsure what to say to Courtney. Her sister was so chipper that she didn't want to mess that up. Instead, she doused her pancakes in syrup and took a bite. "These are amazing," she said, the food not even halfway swallowed yet.

"As good as the pancakes at the Grand Café?" Courtney asked.

"Better," Savannah lied. It was impossible for a pre-made mix from the grocery store to be better than the pancakes at the Grand Café.

"Sure they are," Peyton said, eating a forkful of scrambled eggs. But Peyton was a weirdo who didn't like sweet carbs for breakfast—no pancakes, waffles or French toast—so her opinion didn't count.

Courtney took a cinnamon roll with extra frosting. Normally Savannah would have reminded her that the ones with extra frosting were hers, but this morning she said nothing. She didn't want to risk sending Courtney back into her bad mood.

Peyton chased down her eggs with her coffee. "Does this sudden good mood mean you're not mad at Mom and Grandma anymore?" she asked Courtney. "Because I sure hope not. They deserve us being angry at them."

A shadow passed over Courtney's eyes. "Trust me, I'm more than mad at them," she said. "Mostly at Grandma. Mom's always hidden from her problems, but Grandma was the one we could trust, and she put Mom's twisted lies first. I'll never forgive her for it."

Savannah shrank at Courtney's anger. "I think Grandma wanted us to know, but she wanted Mom to tell us. Then it must have gone on for so long that they didn't know how to do it. I mean, obviously what they did was wrong," she added.

"I'm just trying to understand what could have been going through their minds."

"Stop being so nice." Peyton stabbed her fork into her eggs. "Mom should have told us when we were old enough to understand. She didn't because she's a coward. She hides from the truth by lying, she hides from her guilt by drinking.... We have every right to never forgive them for this."

Savannah looked away from Peyton and finished her orange juice. Yes, she was angry at Mom and Grandma, but she couldn't *never* forgive them. Wasn't that too extreme? Especially since Mom truly wanted a fresh start, now that she was out of rehab. Savannah would feel horribly guilty if their mom started drinking again, all because they wouldn't let her back into their lives. Besides, they were family. They had to forgive each other eventually.

"I wouldn't go as far as never forgiving them, but I do need a break from them," Courtney said. "So if you both wouldn't mind, I'd like you to support me by standing by me in this."

"One hundred percent," Peyton said. "Whatever you need." She looked at Savannah, as if waiting for her to repeat her words.

But as much as Savannah wanted to…she couldn't.

"You don't want us to speak with Mom and Grandma?" she asked Courtney.

"More like take a break from speaking with them," Courtney said. "It won't be for forever. I wrote Grandma an email last night telling her that I needed space from her and Mom while I worked through this, so she won't worry when I don't pick up her calls. I don't know how long I'll need, but the lies, and finding out about Britney…" Her voice cracked, and she sipped her tea. "It's too much. I can't think of either of them without getting so *angry*. So if the two of you could back me up by also taking space from them, it would mean a lot. Anyway, Britney was your sister, too. Yes, she was my twin, so it's different for me, but you have as much of a right to be angry at Mom and Grandma as I do."

It was definitely wrong of Mom and Grandma to keep Britney secret. But Savannah hated the idea of not speaking to them—especially since Mom was doing better than she had in years. But Courtney rarely asked anything of her. She had to do this for her sister.

"Okay." Savannah started on a cinnamon roll, even though she was full from pancakes. "But what about Adrian? He also kept the secret from us."

"I'm angry at him, too," Courtney said. "But it's different. Mom and Grandma knew us for our whole lives. Mom was there with us *every day*. Adrian just met us a few months ago, and he's so busy that he still doesn't know us well. Which isn't an excuse, and we'll see what he has to say to us when he gets back, but I can't help it—I'm angrier at Mom and Grandma. They owed it to us to tell us. But they didn't, and I don't know if I'll ever get over it."

Savannah spread icing onto the gooey inside of her cinnamon roll and nodded, although mentally she was a jumbled mess. Courtney wouldn't expect her to never forgive Mom and Grandma—right?

"Everything that's happened made me realize that we're the only ones in our family we can trust," Courtney said. "I know both of you have my back, but we have to be here for each other no matter what, and be honest about *everything*. Okay?"

"Of course," Savannah said, since she'd always known her sisters were there for her. But did they feel like she was there for them? Last night when she'd knocked on Courtney's door and Courtney had yelled at her to go away, she'd listened. She'd been scared to see her sister helpless and vulnerable, and she hadn't wanted to say the wrong thing and make everything worse.

"I'm sorry I didn't try harder to check on you yesterday," she said to Courtney.

"You *did* try." Courtney managed a smile, although it didn't reach her eyes. "I yelled at you to leave me alone. I can't blame you for listening, since I wasn't very nice about it."

"But I shouldn't have given up that easily," Savannah said. "If I'd been the one refusing to come out of my room, you and Peyton would have broken down the door, with cookies or ice cream to help me feel better. And if I wasn't ready to talk about whatever was bothering me, you would have talked with me about something else to distract me."

"Yeah, that's probably how Courtney would have handled it," Peyton said. "But you're not Courtney. You're you. And I was no better. When I knocked and was yelled at to go away, I told her to come to my room if she wanted to talk, then watched movies all night without trying again."

"It shouldn't have been like that," Savannah said. "Courtney's always held things together, but when she needed us, we froze up."

"You both know I'm still sitting here, right?" Courtney asked with a small laugh.

"This was the one time we had to be there for you, and we sucked," Savannah said. "Even now, you're making breakfast and fixing things, when it should be the other way around."

"Yeah," Courtney agreed. "But I shouldn't have pushed

you away. Yes, I needed space, but you're both affected by what we found out, too. I should have said *something* besides yelling at you to leave me alone. Instead I was only thinking of myself. I'm sorry."

"Don't try turning this around," Peyton said. "Yes, this hurts us, too, but it's worse for you. We should have been there for you yesterday, and we blew it."

"It was just so strange to see you like that." Savannah pushed the mushy remainder of her pancakes around on her plate. "I didn't know what to do. But you're right. We have each other no matter what. It's just…I've never felt like either of you have needed *me* before. You're both so strong and confident and know how to handle everything. I've always felt clueless and stupid in comparison."

"You're not clueless *or* stupid," Courtney reassured her. "You're lucky. You have two sisters who love you and will do anything for you."

"And I love both of you and will do anything for you," Savannah said. "I wasn't good at showing it yesterday, but from now on, I will. I promise. But we did do what you asked and didn't let Brett inside. I felt awful about that, too, especially since he tried a few times. He sounded so worried about you."

"He did?" Courtney sounded more vulnerable than ever.

"Yeah," Savannah said. "I know you don't want to break the rules or whatever, but he really cares about you. And the two of you have so much in common. If you have feelings for him, what can it hurt to let him in and see what happens?"

Courtney swallowed and sipped her water, as if she were too choked up to respond. Peyton opened her mouth as if she were about to say something, but before she had the chance, the sound of a key card entering the slot came from their door.

Savannah's stomach flipped, suspecting who it must be, and she jerked her head to look at the entryway.

Adrian stepped inside the condo.

chapter 26: *Courtney*

Courtney crossed her arms and glared at Adrian. She'd known he was coming back this morning, but did he have to interrupt breakfast?

"I was going to order us some breakfast, but I see you beat me to it." For someone who didn't talk loudly, it was amazing how Adrian's voice filled a room.

Courtney tensed. She was so angry, she didn't know where to start. So she just stared at him. Waiting. Her sisters followed her lead.

He cleared his throat. "Obviously we have a lot to discuss," he said. "How about we all sit down in the living room?"

Courtney nodded and walked toward the living room, Savannah and Peyton behind her. They claimed one couch, and Adrian took the one across from them, the sleek coffee table a barrier between them. Now that he was closer, Courtney noticed the puffy dark circles under his eyes. Good. He deserved to lose sleep over the secret he'd kept from them.

"I'm surprised you didn't bring Rebecca with you for 'moral support.'" Peyton's voice dripped with sarcasm.

He leveled his eyes with hers. "Given the situation, I wanted to talk with the three of you alone."

"And you're not going to hurry off to some important business meeting after only five minutes?"

"No." He sat straighter, his voice strong and confident. "I have no meetings on my schedule today, since I wasn't supposed to get back from Macau until tomorrow night. The three of you have my undivided attention."

Peyton nodded, and it was the first time Courtney had seen her older sister approve of anything Adrian did. Then again, this was the first time Adrian had reached out to them without having to be somewhere soon, or for public show.

"After Rebecca called and told me what happened, I arranged to come home immediately." He sat stiffly, his hands clasped tightly together. Then he looked straight at Courtney and said, "You shouldn't have found out that way."

"No, I shouldn't have." She pushed her chin up higher, not breaking eye contact. "Although it sounds like everyone would have preferred that I'd never found out at all."

"It's more complicated than that," he said. "After everything happened, your mother and I were a wreck. She blamed me, and I blamed myself. I *still* blame myself. You see, we got too comfortable in our gated community. The entrances were guarded at all times, and we felt as though when we were behind those gates, we could live like any other family. I should have known better, but it made your mom happy, and I wanted her to be happy. So I lowered our security while we were in the neighborhood. The park your nanny took you to that day was inside the community. But the gates didn't stop the kidnappers."

"I understand what happened." Courtney dug her fingernails into her palms. She'd cried so much in the past two days that no tears were left. "But I don't understand how you and Mom thought it was okay to keep this from me, Peyton and Savannah. Britney was our sister. She was my *twin!* And you just...didn't think I should know she existed?"

"Not discussing Britney was your mom's way of handling her grief," Adrian said. "As was moving away from me, and keeping the three of you out of my life."

"Come on." Peyton rolled her eyes. "We know how much power and influence you have. You could have been in our lives if you'd wanted to."

"You don't understand." Adrian slammed his hand down on the couch, and Courtney jumped back. "Because of me, one of my daughters was *murdered*. I felt like I'd killed her myself, seeing how negligent I was with our personal security. The three of you being around me would have put you in danger, and at the time, I couldn't deal with that."

Everyone was silent, as though waiting to see who would be first to crack.

"You do know where we lived with Mom, right?" Savannah asked quietly. "How dangerous the neighborhood was?"

"Of course I do." Adrian looked at Savannah, and his eyes softened. "Which was why you were guarded at all times. Your top-of-the-line trained guards could protect you against petty street thieves. But what made you safe was your anonymity. If no one knew you were my daughters, you wouldn't be at risk for a repeat of what had happened. It was the hardest decision I've ever had to make, but I was clouded with grief and guilt. And your mom and grandma had no problem going along with it."

"So you stepped out of our lives forever." Peyton's voice was eerily calm.

"Not forever," he said. "You're here now. And now you know the truth—you know just how dangerous your connection with my world can be."

"You told us most of this when we got here, minus the part about Britney," Courtney said. "But I knew something was off. You got me back safe, so I didn't get why you felt so guilty that you cut yourself out of our lives. It makes more sense now that I know the truth. I don't think it was right, but I understand a little bit better. But I will never understand how you and Mom kept Britney's memory from me—from *us*—and thought for one second that it was okay."

"I know." Adrian took a deep, pained breath, and placed his hands on his thighs. "I thought your mom would tell you once you were old enough, but she never did. Of course, I expected her to make up a story about why Britney was no longer with us, but I thought you'd have at least known she'd existed. Then when you came here, your grandmother told me the three of you knew nothing about her. And there were so many changes going on in your lives that I couldn't throw one more thing at you. Rebecca wanted me to tell you everything—she said it was what I had to do to earn your trust—but I didn't, and it was a mistake."

Courtney couldn't believe it. Was Adrian admitting he was wrong?

"So you would have told us eventually?"

"I like to think so," he said. "But now I know why Rebecca wanted me to tell you everything from the start. When you're keeping a secret, it gets harder to come clean every day, until you wonder if it's better to bury the truth completely. But it wasn't better. It only made it worse."

Learning about Britney's death left a hole in Courtney's heart that she'd never known existed until two days ago. Before, she'd been generally happy. She loved Peyton and Savannah, and having such wonderful sisters had always been more than enough for her. Was she betraying Britney's memory by having felt that way? Should she have felt something missing in her life—should she have known she was supposed to have had a twin?

But she'd always known something was off. Her baby book had been sparse compared to Peyton's and Savannah's, and she'd never lived up to her mom's expectations no matter how hard she'd tried.

"Despite how much it hurts, I would rather have known the truth," she said.

"I know." Adrian cracked his knuckles. "I'm sorry. If I could go back to the day the three of you got here, I would tell you everything from the start. But that's not possible."

"No, it's not." Courtney shook her head, unsure where they could go from here.

"I don't expect you to forgive me immediately," he said. "But I want a second chance. Since you moved here, I haven't been accessible, and I plan on changing that. I was hoping that from now on, every Sunday afternoon could be official father/daughters time. The four of us spending time together so we can get to know each other. Does that sound like something you would want to do, too?"

Courtney bit her lip, unsure what to say. If she said yes, it might come across as her forgiving him, and she wasn't there yet. But he'd apologized, and he was trying, so that had to count for something.

She looked at her sisters for a hint of what they wanted. Savannah's eyes were huge, as if she wanted to say yes. Peyton studied the chipped black polish on her nails, as if she didn't care either way. Which was surprising—she expected Peyton to have a sarcastic retort.

"That's a nice idea," Courtney finally said. "We could try it and see how it goes."

"Yes." Savannah bounced her knees, looking like she was about to pop right off the couch. "I would definitely like to do that."

"And does it sound good to you, Peyton?" Adrian asked.

"Sure." Peyton shrugged. "I guess that sounds fine."

"It's settled, then." He smiled for the first time since seeing them this morning. "Tomorrow will be our first father/daughters day. Is there anything particular you'd like to do?"

"I don't know." Courtney hadn't had any time to think about it. "What were you thinking?"

His eyes glinted. "Have you ever been to the Grand Canyon?"

"Considering that before moving here, we'd never left California, what do you think?" Peyton asked.

"It's one of the seven natural wonders of the world, and it's nearby, so it's something you should see," he said, ignoring Peyton's snark. "We can take the helicopter to the canyon, fly over it so you can see it from above, touch down at the bottom for a picnic lunch, take a boat ride down the Colorado River and be back to Vegas in time for dinner."

"It'll be just the four of us?" Courtney asked.

"Along with our pilot and a bodyguard," Adrian said. "But besides them, yes. It will only be the four of us."

"All right," Courtney said. "That sounds like a great idea."

"Glad you approve," he said. "I'll meet you here tomorrow at nine?"

"A.m.?" Peyton's eyebrows shot up in horror.

"Yes." Adrian chuckled. "I think you'll survive. You might even have fun."

"Thank you for doing all of this," Courtney said. "All Mom did was defend what she'd done and try to make it seem like she wasn't in the wrong. But that made it worse. So even though there's no way to make this all better, and I hate how everyone lied to us for so long, I do appreciate your apology."

"I'm happy to hear it," Adrian said. "And I'm looking forward to tomorrow."

"Me, too," Courtney said, surprised by how much she meant it. "But I was planning on spending tomorrow studying for the SATs, so I better get started now instead."

Despite her world being turned upside down by learning about Britney, she couldn't ignore her schoolwork, especially since her PSAT score hadn't been what she'd wanted. She was only in the ninety-fifth percentile, which wasn't high enough to qualify for the National Merit Scholarship. It was frustrating to find out, but if she studied hard enough for her SAT and boosted her score, there would be other scholarship possibilities.

She should also talk to Brett at some point, but she wasn't ready yet. She felt more vulnerable than ever, and she was terrified of what would happen if she were around him. She wouldn't have the strength to fight her feelings. What if she did something that she ended up regretting?

It was too much stress on top of everything else that had happened in the past two days.

"And I need to practice some songs to figure out which one to record next," Savannah said. "My fans have been asking for a new video all week. I still can't believe I have *fans*. How cool is that?"

"Very cool." Courtney smiled, happy to see Savannah's dream coming true.

"I'm glad the two of you have things to do, because I need to have a conversation with Peyton," Adrian said.

"Why?" Peyton laughed. "Am I in trouble?"

Adrian's expression revealed nothing. "We'll discuss it in private."

Peyton's smile disappeared, and she picked at her black nail polish.

"I'm going to my room now to study," Courtney said, giving Peyton a look that meant *You better tell me what this is about later.* Then she remembered they hadn't cleaned up from breakfast. "But first, Savannah and I will clean up the kitchen." Cleanup was normally Peyton's job, but since Peyton would be busy, Courtney would take one for the team. She didn't want the dirty dishes sitting around for too long. Yuck.

"Do you want to talk in your room, or in my condo?" Adrian asked Peyton.

"My room, I guess." She fidgeted and looked at the floor. Either she had no idea why Adrian wanted to talk to her, or she suspected he'd found out about something he shouldn't have. She looked at Courtney for help, but all Courtney could do was shrug and send her good luck vibes.

Peyton followed Adrian to her room, the door shutting behind them.

"I wonder what that's about," Savannah said.

"I have no idea." Courtney stacked the dirty dishes and brought them to the sink. "But I can't wait to find out."

chapter 27: *Peyton*

Why did Adrian need to talk to her alone? Did he know she'd kissed Hunter? Was he upset about her decision not to apply to college? Peyton's stomach felt hollow, like it had that one time last year when a friend in Fairfield had dared her to swipe nail polish from a store and she'd been caught and forced to give it back. She wrapped her arms around herself and waited for Adrian to start the conversation.

"Do you mind if I sit?" He motioned to the swivel chair at her desk.

"Sure." She sat on the edge of her bed and crossed her legs, trying not to pick her nails or do anything that might give away guilt for whatever he thought she'd done. "So, what's up? I'm not in trouble, am I?"

"There are a few things I want to talk with you about," he said.

"Great, I am 'in trouble,'" she said, sitting straighter when he didn't deny it. "You're fucking kidding me. I don't even know what I did."

"No, I'm not 'kidding you,'" he said. "And I would like for you to stop using language like that. It's not classy, and it makes you sound much less intelligent than you are."

"Yeah, right." Peyton rolled her eyes. "I get pretty much all Cs. And I'm not even in AP classes. I'm not putting myself down—I know I have a lot going for me—but book smarts isn't one of them. So I hope this isn't about my grades."

"Your grades are definitely a concern." Adrian leaned back in the chair. "Along with how you *are* putting yourself down right now. You don't realize your potential."

Peyton clenched her fists. Could he have sounded any cornier? "If you're going to try to force me to fill out college applications, forget it," she said. "Sitting in class all day is my own personal hell. There's no need to put myself through it for four years more than necessary."

"This isn't about college applications," he said. "Your astronomy teacher called over break to discuss you."

"Why?" Peyton asked. Ms. Mandina weirdly seemed to like her, and Peyton didn't think she was failing her class.

"She told me you've been getting Cs on your tests, and she thought you could do better," he said. "Then she told me that she cornered you after class and forced you to sit down with her during a few lunches for individual tutoring sessions, and how quickly you picked up on concepts in a one-on-one scenario. She finished grading the test you took before Thanksgiving break. You got an A."

"No way." Peyton shook her head. She hadn't gotten an A on anything since elementary school. "I didn't even study."

"Apparently the tutoring sessions were enough," Adrian said. "I put in a call to the school, and found out that you have

Bs in history and English, too, which isn't great, but it's better than the Cs you barely had in the same subjects at Fairfield High. So, tell me why you chose to stay at Goodman, instead of switching to public school after two months."

He *had* noticed how she'd dropped the public school thing.

She supposed there was nothing she could do but tell the truth. "Because school sucks no matter what, but the small class sizes at Goodman aren't quite as torturous as the huge, boring classes in public school."

"Right." He nodded. "And tests at Goodman aren't timed, right? If it's not completed by the end of the class period you have to come back during lunch or after school to finish?"

"Yep." Peyton's cheeks heated. She'd had to do that more times this semester than she cared to admit. At Fairfield High, tests were turned in at the bell—finished or not—and not finishing her tests on time was part of the reason behind her bad grades.

"I have a feeling you're not going to like what I'm going to say next," Adrian said. "But before getting upset, please hear me out and take what I'm saying into consideration."

"Okay..." She bounced her legs. That was never a good way to start a discussion.

"Ms. Mandina has a brother with Attention Deficit Disorder—ADHD—so she knows a lot about it. She thinks you show signs of having it, too."

"No way," Peyton interrupted. "I don't have a *disorder*. I'm not the best in school, but that doesn't mean there's something wrong with me."

"No one's saying there's anything wrong with you," Adrian said. "A better way to think of it is as a learning *difference*. Some of the best, most creative thinkers in the world—like Albert Einstein and Walt Disney—are thought to have had ADHD.

It isn't a 'disorder' as much as a unique way of thinking that doesn't conform with the traditional school system."

"Now you're an expert, too?"

"I researched it on the plane home from Macau. Having to sit still in a large class while listening to a lecture is a hard way for a student with ADHD to learn. That could be why in the smaller classes at Goodman, where class is discussion-instead of lecture-based, and with individual attention from your teachers, your grades are improving from what they were at Fairfield High. It also explains why you're not as bored in class."

"I'm not convinced, but even if I *do* have ADHD, then what?" Peyton asked. "It sounds like school still wouldn't be a good place for me, especially since in college the classes are bigger than they are in high school."

"That's not necessarily true," he said. "There are many smaller colleges around the country that have classes similar to what you have at Goodman. But we don't need to get ahead of ourselves. My primary concern—and Ms. Mandina agrees with me—is to get you tested for ADHD or any other learning differences. It's a two-day test, and you're scheduled for Monday and Tuesday."

"But I have school."

"You'll miss those two days," Adrian said, as if it didn't matter. "You'll get caught up. It's more important to get this figured out."

"Okay." Peyton wasn't going to protest missing two days of school. "Is that all you wanted to talk with me about?"

Maybe she'd been wrong to assume that she was in trouble.

"No," he said, and then he took his iPhone out of his pocket, tapped on the screen a few times and held it out to her.

She looked down at the screen and froze. On it was a photo

of her and Jackson from Thursday night, when they were at their corner table at the Imperial Palace Karaoke Club. It was pixelated, clearly taken from across the room, but sharp enough for the two of them—and the pitcher of beer they'd both drunk from—to be identifiable.

They sat close to each other, their heads bent in conversation, her sunglasses covering most of her face. She scrolled down to the next photo. Her sunglasses were off her face now and on her head, making it unmistakably *her,* and Jackson's hand was on her cheek. She scrolled down again and saw a picture of Jackson resting his forehead against hers, their lips nearly touching.

Peyton's chest tightened. She'd promised Jackson she would back off, since she couldn't stand the thought of getting him in legal trouble because of her. But any possibility of passing off their relationship as a friendship disappeared with that final photo.

"Where did you get these?" she asked, her voice trembling.

"Where I got them doesn't matter," Adrian said. "But needless to say, I've dismissed Jackson from my service. From now on, you will have a new—much *older*—bodyguard, so there is no chance of this happening again."

What? Peyton's brain felt fuzzy, and she couldn't focus on anything but replaying those words, praying this wasn't happening. Had Adrian really said that he'd "dismissed Jackson from his service"? As if it wasn't a big deal?

She had to fix this. She wasn't sure how, but she had to.

"It's not what it looks like." Her hand shook as she handed Adrian back his phone. Would Jackson's fears come true and he would never find another job again? If that happened…it would be her fault. She would have ruined his life.

"Do you care to explain how this 'isn't what it looks like'?"

Adrian asked. "Because I fail to see how it can be anything else."

"Because I'm the one at fault." Peyton picked at a hangnail, biting the inside of her cheek when she ripped it to the blood. "Not Jackson."

"You're seventeen," Adrian said. "Jackson is twenty-three. Legally, he's the one at fault."

Peyton's heart pounded. "You're not going to get him in legal trouble, are you? Because nothing more than what you see in those pictures happened, I swear it."

"No," he said, and Peyton breathed out in relief. "I wouldn't do that to him. But as I said, I've released him from my service, and you will not see him again."

"But you have no idea what happened," she pleaded, her eyes filling with tears. She hated getting personal, but she had to now, for Jackson. "Those photos were from the night we found out about Britney. Courtney was a wreck, everything was falling apart and I didn't know what to do. So I went to Jackson. He was the only one who was truly there for me, who I felt comfortable talking to. But he told me there couldn't be more than a professional relationship between us. He explained why, and I agreed with his points. So you can't fire him because of this."

"He already told me all of that," Adrian said. "However, that doesn't change my decision. The relationship between the two of you crosses the line of what's appropriate. You will have a new bodyguard, and you will be grounded for a month."

"Grounded?" she repeated, her mouth dropping open. "What does that even *mean*? Stuck in my room...stuck in the condo...stuck in the Diamond? It's a pretty broad term."

"Stuck in your *room?*" he said, baffled. "I would never be that extreme. But for the next month, you'll come straight home after school. You won't be going out with friends on school nights or weekends. You can go to the restaurants in the Diamond with your sisters, and you can go to the gym, but no pool. All other outings will be family activities, like the trip to the Grand Canyon tomorrow and Savannah's birthday party. Your new bodyguard will be informed of these rules. If you break them, you'll be grounded for longer. And you won't be seeing Jackson again—not while you're grounded, and not afterward."

"You can't do that," Peyton said. "Like you said, Jackson doesn't work for you anymore. So if we want to see each other, why can't we?"

"I actually *can* do that, because he's too old for you." Adrian's eyes were hard. "Besides the fact that it's illegal for the two of you to be involved with each other, he's twenty-three, has graduated from college and is working in the professional world. You're seventeen and still in high school."

"The age difference doesn't matter," Peyton insisted. "Besides, aren't you a few years older than Mom?"

He pressed his lips in a firm line. "Your mom was in college when we met, not high school."

"A few years can't make a big difference."

"A few years *does* make a big difference. And you can fight this all you want, but it won't change the law."

"I'll be eighteen in a few months." She crossed her arms and held her gaze with his, waiting to see how he would argue against *that*. "Will you give Jackson his job back after my birthday?"

"It doesn't matter how old you are—you can't be in a relationship with your bodyguard," he said, his voice clipped. "Your bodyguard's job is to watch and protect you—he must be aware of your surroundings at all times. He can't do that if he's distracted by his feelings for you."

Peyton opened her mouth to protest, but Adrian held his hand up to stop her.

"Take the pictures from Thursday night as an example," he continued. "If Jackson had been doing his job and not been focused on the conversation he was having with you, he would have been aware of the people taking photos of you and put a stop to it. Those pictures aren't only evidence of an inappropriate relationship, but of *why* a relationship with your bodyguard stops him from effectively doing his job."

Peyton's throat tightened, her eyes filling with tears, and she blinked a few times to will them away. "Nothing happened between me and Jackson." She balled her fists by her sides, frustrated by the feeling that this was an argument she couldn't win. No matter what she said, Adrian wouldn't believe her. All she could think to do was repeat what she'd already told him and hope he would understand. "Jackson knows what a risk it would be. Thursday was a rough day, and Courtney and Savannah were going through a lot, too, so he was the only person I could talk to. He helped me—he was *there* for me. He shouldn't get fired for that."

"You could have talked to Rebecca," Adrian said. "She told me she made sure you and your sisters knew she was there to listen."

She crossed her arms. "It's not the same."

"I wish you'd give Rebecca a chance," he said. "But my decision about Jackson is final. I saw the pictures. Beyond his relationship with you being unprofessional, he was drinking with you. That behavior is unacceptable, and it won't be tolerated."

Peyton sniffed and swallowed back more tears. Because she

wanted to change Adrian's mind, but Jackson *was* drinking beer with her in those pictures. She couldn't argue otherwise.

"I know you're upset with me, but I hope you can put this aside tomorrow when we go to the Grand Canyon," Adrian said. "I meant what I said about wanting to get to know you and your sisters."

There was no way Peyton was forgetting this. She would be reminded every time she saw her bodyguard and it wasn't Jackson. But how could she argue against the two of them drinking together? There was photographic evidence. So she said okay—mainly because she needed to think and couldn't do that with Adrian in her room reminding her how badly she'd screwed everything up—and he finally said he would see her tomorrow and left.

The door closed, and she picked up her phone to text Jackson.

Adrian told me everything. I'm sooo sorry...I never meant for this to happen :(I tried to change his mind, but he wasn't budging. I wish there was more I can do. Just please text me back and let me know you're okay??

She pressed Send and stared at her phone, waiting for his response. But there was nothing.

Before she could text him again, her door flew open and Savannah jumped onto the bed, followed by Courtney, who situated herself in the chair Adrian had just vacated.

"What was that about?" Courtney asked.

"Make sure to tell us everything," Savannah added.

Peyton just wanted to text Jackson again, but her sisters looked like they were going to explode from curiosity. So she gave them a rundown on the conversation—from her possible ADHD to Adrian showing her the pictures of her with Jackson to what had *actually* happened between her and Jackson to her current status of "grounded" and his of "fired." All because of her.

"Wow," Courtney said when she was done. "I knew you were attracted to Jackson, but I had no idea anything had actually *happened*. How could I not have seen it until now?"

"I know." Savannah splayed out on the bed, balancing her chin in her hands. "How could you not have told us?"

"It's only been a few intense conversations and two kisses, and he pushed me away pretty quickly both times." Peyton sniffed and looked at the ceiling, willing herself not to replay the scenes with Jackson in her mind. Because then she might lose it again, and she'd cried enough in the past week to last an entire year. "I didn't want to risk telling *anyone,* because then there would be a higher chance that Adrian would find out and fire him. Which didn't matter, since that's what happened anyway."

"But you didn't even trust me and Courtney?" Savannah sounded betrayed. "You know we wouldn't have told anyone."

The hurt in her voice made Peyton feel guiltier than before. "I know," she said. "I'm sorry."

"You know what I think?" Courtney said, and both Peyton and Savannah looked at her to continue. "The three of us need to get better at not keeping anything from each other. There have been so many secrets since we moved to Vegas, and it needs to stop. To prove it, I'll tell you something I've kept to myself until now—I still have feelings for Brett." She held her head high and straightened her shoulders, as if that was some big confession that was going to majorly shock them.

"Really?" Peyton faked surprise, and laughed. At least Courtney's "shocking" confession had taken her mind off

Jackson, even if it was for only a second. "Of *course* I know you have feelings for Brett. It's written all over your face every time you're around him. And he was so devastated when you shut him out these past few days."

"I still think you should go for him," Savannah said. "You and Brett are perfect for each other. It's been obvious since the moment you met him at that first dinner and the two of you wouldn't stop talking. And he's a really good guy—he helped me with my videos for YouTube without thinking twice about it. He's never said anything to me about you, but his eyes light up every time I say your name."

"Do they really?" Courtney asked.

"Yep." Savannah smiled. "Just like yours are right now."

"We do get along really well." Courtney sighed. "But Rebecca talked with me about it, and she made good points about why it would be unwise for me to date him, given the situation."

"Fuck the situation," Peyton said, which made both Courtney and Savannah laugh. "Better to see what could happen between you two than to look back and wonder."

"Maybe." Courtney's cheeks turned red. "Anyway, Savannah, it's your turn. Pick something you've been keeping to yourself and share it."

Savannah rolled over and stared at the ceiling. "I can't think of anything," she said. "I mean, there's one thing, but it involved Peyton, too...."

Courtney's eyes darted to Peyton. "What thing?"

Peyton had a sinking feeling where Savannah was going with this.

"The thing that happened at the pool last month?" Savannah looked at Peyton, her voice shaky. "With Oliver and Madison?"

"Why am I getting the feeling that this is something I should know?" Courtney asked. She watched Peyton expectantly, with the determination in her eyes that meant she wouldn't give up until she got answers.

"All right." Peyton sighed and ran a hand through her hair. She might as well get this over with. "I wasn't going to tell you because you'll take it the wrong way and it's not a big deal anymore, but here it goes. Remember the week we moved here, when Ellen Prescott had Oliver ask you to that charity event when we were at dinner at the Gates?"

"Yeah." Courtney nodded. "How could I forget?"

"Well, I was pretty pissed when that happened, because I hooked up with Oliver the first night we moved here."

Courtney shot up in her chair. "You had *sex* with Oliver?" she said. Peyton nodded, her cheeks heating up. "Why didn't you say anything? Especially after he asked me out. You know I would have told him no way if I'd known." She glanced at Savannah. "Did she tell you?"

"Not when it happened," Savannah said. "I had no idea until last month."

"I was going to tell you after dinner, but you went straight back to the condo, so I figured I would wait until the morning," Peyton said to Courtney. "At Luxe, I told Oliver you wouldn't go out with him after I told you what had happened between us."

"You were right," Courtney said. "I would have told him to forget the dinner. But you never told me. Don't you think I should have known?"

"Yeah, you should have." Peyton picked at her nail polish. "But then I told him that even if I *didn't* tell you, you still wouldn't go for him because he's not your type. He's so conceited that he saw that as a challenge. He told me that if I was right, and you didn't go for him without me telling you what had happened between us, I could ask him to do any one task I wanted."

Courtney pressed her lips together. "And if you were wrong?"

"I knew I wouldn't be wrong." She tried to sound confident, even though her hands were shaking. "Oliver is everything you hate rolled up into one person."

"But if you were," she pressed. "Then what?"

Peyton looked at the floor, unable to meet her sister's gaze. "Then I would have to do any one task he wanted."

"*And* you would have gotten yourself into a huge mess, because I would have been interested in a guy who had slept with you earlier that week." Courtney gripped the armrests of the chair, her eyes swirling with anger. "You made a bet on my emotions. How could you think that was okay?"

"But I knew it wouldn't get to that, because you would never go for Oliver," Peyton said, although her reasons were sounding weaker by the second. "And I was right. You put him in his place when he tried to kiss you. I was actually surprised he tried at all, since I doubt you were giving him signals that you wanted him to, but he was probably too drunk to notice."

"I can't believe this." Courtney's face paled. "I wouldn't have been in the car with him while he was drunk at *all* if you'd been honest with me from the start. It's a good thing he only tried to kiss me. What if he'd tried more than that? What if Oliver wasn't the type of guy who took no for an answer? Did that cross your mind?"

"Oliver's an ass, but he's not *that* bad," Peyton pleaded, wishing Courtney would calm down. "So many girls want to hook up with him that he hardly needs to force anyone.

Plus, his parents are close with Adrian. He would never do anything that serious to mess that up."

"But you'd only known him for a few days," Courtney said. "You couldn't have been sure. I'm your sister—I should have come before some stupid bet. And then you let me go out with him *again,* to the grand opening? How could you not say anything to me?"

"You said you told him you weren't interested in him, and that you were going as friends," Peyton reminded her, although she knew it sounded lame.

"We were *supposed* to go as friends," Courtney said, her voice escalating in volume. "Until he tried forcing his tongue down my throat in the middle of the dance floor. Luckily Brett stepped in. And where were you? Oh, yeah, dancing with strangers on the second floor. Were you *ever* going to tell me about you and Oliver? Or were you going to pretend like it never happened?"

"I don't know." Peyton couldn't meet Courtney's eyes, because she knew the real answer: she probably wouldn't have mentioned it. "When I talked to Oliver at Luxe, he was a total jerk. He made it clear he wasn't interested in me and that we were never going to hook up again. I'm not gonna lie—it hurt. I left the club right afterward. I guess I wanted to leave it all in the past. Then I won the bet, and I figured I could use it to get back at him." But when said out loud, it sounded pathetic. Bitterness rose in her throat, and she glared at Savannah. "Why did you bring this up?"

Savannah looked down at her hands, playing with her bracelets. "Because we were confessing secrets and starting fresh," she said, her voice small. "I'm sorry."

"This isn't Savannah's fault," Courtney said, each word full of anger. "This wouldn't have happened if you'd put your loyalty to me before your stupid bet. I can't imagine that *anything* you could have asked Oliver to do was worth betraying me."

Finally—a point where Peyton could defend herself. "Actually, what I ended up asking him to do helped all three of us."

From there, she recounted everything: Madison taking that picture of her with Hunter at the Lobby Bar, the same picture showing up on the nasty forum post that had attacked all three of them, to the conversation she and Savannah had with Oliver at the pool, where she told him that his task was to take Madison's virginity.

"Once it's done, I'm going to tell Madison everything—about how Oliver only slept with her because of a bet, and that it should teach her to stop messing with us," she said. "I wouldn't be surprised if Madison is behind the pictures of me and Jackson getting out, too. That girl seriously has it coming to her."

"That is the most twisted, convoluted plan I've ever heard," Courtney said once Peyton was finished. "You don't know if Madison wrote that post. Yes, it's suspicious since you saw the picture on her phone, but are you *positive* it was her?"

"Who else could it be?" Peyton looked at Savannah for backup, but Savannah bit her lip and shrugged, not seeming as convinced anymore.

"Anyone!" Courtney threw her hands in the air. "You didn't delete the picture immediately after Madison took it, and clearly, since it showed up online, it was never truly deleted. You're so sure she backed it up somewhere else. But what if, instead of backing it up, she sent it to her friends before you approached her? Then those friends could have sent it to their friends, and so on. Yes, Madison *took* the picture, but you can't know who wrote that post."

"But Madison hates us." Heat rose in Peyton's chest—

Courtney was making her feel like an idiot. She'd been *so* sure it had been Madison. She *still* thought it was Madison. "I guess that all could have happened, but everything points to her being the one who posted it. And even if she didn't, Madison and Oliver aren't exactly saints. Or did you forget how Madison humiliated Savannah over the summer by making out with Damien at Luxe, and how Oliver made that bet to try sleeping with all of us?"

"I never said I liked either of them," Courtney said. "But what you're doing is worse than anything they've done to us. Even if Madison wrote that post—and I agree that, from what you told me, she looks guilty—no one deserves to lose their virginity because of a bet. That's something that will stay with her forever. Just, please, tell me she hasn't given in to sleeping with him yet."

Peyton felt like the room was closing in around her, every muscle in her body numb. All her doubts had been summed up by Courtney in a few sentences. Which, Peyton supposed, was why she'd kept this from her sister to begin with. She knew Courtney would force her to face how horrible this thing was she'd asked—well, more like blackmailed—Oliver to do to Madison. Tears rose in her throat, and she had to swallow a few times to make them go away. This combined with how awful she felt about getting Jackson fired was too much at once.

But at least she might still be able to make this right.

"Last Oliver told me, he was close, but I don't think it's happened yet," she said, picking one last huge flake of polish from her thumbnail, so it was now completely bare. "He would have gloated to me if it had."

"Then you need to text him right now that the bet is off."

"Just like that?" Peyton asked. "Maybe there's something else we can get him to do. Something that would help Jackson." Her heart leaped at the possibility. Adrian seemed set on his decision, but maybe… "We could see if Oliver could convince *his* dad to hire Jackson, so he wouldn't be blacklisted and left without a job. It wouldn't be the best solution—obviously I would rather Jackson be my guard again—but at least I'll have done something to fix this mess."

"Come on, Peyton," Courtney said. "I know you want to help Jackson, and I agree that Jackson's a good guy who doesn't deserve to have his career ruined because of what happened, but this isn't the way. Blackmailing Oliver into helping you do *anything* is just going to lead to trouble. You need to put an end to this. Now."

Peyton hated thinking about how pleased Oliver would be when she called off the bet with no explanation why. But she felt guilty enough about *asking* Oliver to take Madison's virginity…. How awful would she feel if he went through with it? She would have to live with that forever. And if she wanted Courtney to forgive her for making a bet about her instead of telling her the truth, Peyton had to do this.

She picked her iPhone up off her nightstand, and her chest panged when she saw no reply from Jackson to her earlier text. Maybe he hadn't seen it yet. That had to be it. Because she was driving herself crazy wondering if he was okay, and the thought that he'd seen the text and ignored it crushed her. She wanted to reread the message she'd sent and figure out if she'd said something wrong. See if there was something more she could say to get through to him.

But Courtney was waiting, so she opened her conversation with Oliver and started typing.

Change of plans—the bet's off.

Her phone buzzed seconds later. She hoped the text was from Jackson, but of course it was Oliver.

Are u talking about what me, u and Savannah discussed at the pool last month?

What other bet would I be talking about? It's off. You don't have to sleep with Madison, and I'm not going to ask you to do something else instead.

And the pictures Savannah has of me from that party?

Won't be posted.

Should I ask why…?

She tossed the phone behind her, not bothering to respond. "Done." She looked at Courtney, wanting her sister to forgive her and forget about this mess. "Are we okay now?"

"No." Courtney crossed her arms. "I still can't believe you made a *bet* about me. Hearing about that, combined with all that's happened in the past week… It's too much. I need some space."

Then she got out of the chair and left Peyton's room.

The door to Courtney's room slammed shut, and Peyton turned to Savannah. "I can't believe you brought that up," she said. "Everything would have been fine if you hadn't."

Savannah played with the ends of her hair. "We said no more secrets. And that was a big secret. I didn't think Courtney would get *that* upset—I thought Madison was behind that post as much as you did—but it seemed like something she should know. I'm sorry. But none of us ever stay mad at each other for long. She'll get over it in a few days."

"Maybe," Peyton said, although she wasn't sure. So many secrets had been thrown at Courtney recently, and she was worried about how her sister was handling it. But she *did* feel relieved that Courtney and Savannah knew about Jackson.

Now she just needed him to text her back so she could hear from him that she hadn't messed up his life.

chapter 28: *Madison*

It had been one week since Madison was supposed to have confronted her parents about Adrian, and she still hadn't worked up the courage to do it. She'd tried last weekend, but right after she'd sat down with them, her mom had started talking about how she was concerned about Madison's diet and had scheduled her a weekly appointment with a nutritionist who would come to their condo. Which was annoying, but it was better than a psychiatrist, so she'd agreed to it. After that conversation, Madison had chickened out about what she really wanted to talk with them about.

But she couldn't put it off forever. She paced around her room, a cup of ice water in her hand, running through what she planned on saying. She had to do this now. It was Saturday afternoon, and her parents were both in the library. It was the perfect timing.

So why was she hesitating? She reminded herself of one of her mantras: once you find the right thing to say—and there's *always* a right thing to say—you can get whatever you want.

But what was she going to accomplish? She couldn't force Adrian to want to be in her life.

Still, as much as Madison had disliked the Diamond girls when they moved into town, they deserved to know that they had another sister. And she deserved a chance to get to know them.

If she was going to have this conversation with her parents, she needed to look presentable. She studied her reflection in her full-length mirror. Her skinny jeans and black knit sweater looked fine, and she ran her straightener through her hair and put on enough makeup to look natural but not overdone. She took a deep breath and stared straight into her eyes, trying to look mature, capable and confident. She could do this.

It didn't stop the beginning of what would escalate into a throbbing headache from creeping up the back of her neck. She opened a drawer, took out two Excedrin migraine tablets and swallowed them with her water. *Now* she was ready.

She marched into the library, and her parents were exactly where they'd been half an hour ago—her mom reclining on the sofa reading a novel, her dad in the big armchair with a science journal. They looked so relaxed and unprepared for what Madison was about to throw at them. But no more excuses. She was doing this.

"Do you guys have a few minutes?" she asked.

"Of course." Her dad laid the science journal on his lap. "Do you need help with your homework?" That was one of the things she and her dad bonded over—him helping her with her science and math homework. His being the lead neurosurgeon at the top hospital in the state was advantageous that way.

"Actually, I need to talk to both of you about something important," she said, sitting in the only open chair in the room—the one behind the wooden desk.

Her mom sat up on the couch and marked the place in her novel. "Is something wrong?"

Madison's throat dried, and she sipped her water. "I've been thinking a lot about what happened," she started. "And I'm going to tell Adrian that I know."

"What?" Her dad sat straight up in his chair, the science journal sliding onto the floor. "You can't be serious."

"We agreed when we told you the truth that it would stay between us," her mom added.

"I know." Madison looked at both of them, begging them to understand. "And I'm glad you were honest with me. But by doing so, you made me a part of keeping this secret, and I can't live with that anymore. It's been tearing me apart."

"But Adrian already *knows* everything," her mom said softly. "This is the way he wants things to be. You know that."

"True." Madison nodded. "And after all these years of him not wanting to be in my life, he'll never be anything more than a sperm donor to me." She looked at her dad, her throat constricting. "I'm not over how you lied to me—I don't think I'll ever be over it—but you're my dad and I love you. Nothing will change that."

"I love you, too, sweetheart." He smiled. "But if you mean what you said, why do you want to confront Adrian?"

"Because this is bigger than just us," she said. "It also involves Peyton, Courtney and Savannah. They're my *sisters,* and they've been lied to, as well. They should know the truth. I don't know how happy they'll be about it, since I'm not exactly friends with them, but we deserve a chance to get to know each other. As sisters."

"I understand why you feel that way," her mom said, playing with the cover of her paperback. "But shouldn't we sit down with a professional to talk about it first? Look at all the options and consider what's best for us as a family?"

Madison crossed her legs and leaned back in the chair. "What are you afraid of happening if I tell him?"

"You don't get it." Her mom sighed. "Don't you value your dad and I—your *real* family—who've raised you and given you everything? I know we work a lot, and it keeps us away more than some of your friends' parents, but we love you and we'll do anything to help you succeed and get what you want in life. We're so proud of you, and your future is so bright. Your dad and I have worked hard for the three of us to be happy. If you go through with this, and if it goes public, all of that will change. Is that really what you want? Aren't you grateful for what you have...for what *we* have?"

"That's why it's taken me so long to say anything. I don't know how this will change things, and that scares me," Madison admitted. "You know I've always been happy. Yes, sometimes I complain about you guys constantly working, but you're doing what you love, and you always make up the time on our family vacations. I may not always show it, but I know how lucky I am. It's why I want to intern with Doctors Without Borders someday—so I can give back after everything that's been given to me.

"I know that telling the truth to the Diamonds will change our family. And I have no idea if that change will be better or worse. But I can't—I *won't*—keep this secret anymore. I'm going to tell Adrian, and I came in here to tell you because I love both of you and don't want to go behind your backs. You trusted me, and I appreciate that, but this secret is bigger than just us. I'm not asking for your permission to tell Adrian. I'm asking for you to stand by my side when I do."

Her parents stared at her and then at each other, as if they were communicating without talking. Madison fidgeted, swinging the chair from side to side. This could either go really well, or really badly.

"You're serious about going to Adrian with or without us?" her mom finally asked.

"Yes." She kept her voice firm and held eye contact. She needed to make it clear that she wasn't backing down.

"Your dad and I need to discuss this in private," her mom said. "We'll go to the bedroom to talk. It shouldn't take long. Wait here."

Her dad stood up, picked the science journal up from the floor and placed it on his chair. "That was well said," he told her. "Have you considered going into law?"

"Ugh." Madison scrunched her nose. She liked science and facts. Reading long legal textbooks would be the worst kind of torture.

"Just kidding." He laughed. "We'll be back in a few minutes. Sit tight, okay?"

She played around on her phone, trying to distract herself from thinking about what her mom and dad were saying in their room. Larissa and Kaitlin had posted a picture of themselves at the pool, and Madison commented, saying how it looked like they were having a blast and she wished she could be there. Then her phone buzzed with a text from Larissa.

saw ur photo comment—come join us!! we're at my club

Can't...too much homework. Tomorrow?

definitely! :)

Finally her dad walked back into the library. Madison placed her phone down, anxious to hear the outcome of the conversation.

"Mom called Adrian to give him a heads-up," he said. "She's on the phone with him now."

"Adrian's going to be angry that the two of you told me, isn't he?"

He settled back into his chair and kicked his legs up onto the ottoman. "To tell you the truth, I have no idea what Adrian's reaction will be. Back when he decided not to be in your life, he had very personal reasons for doing so. He didn't feel fit to be a parent, and at the time, he probably wasn't. Now that Peyton, Courtney and Savannah have moved in with him, that may have changed. But, Madison, I hope you know that no matter what genetics say, I'm your father, and I love you, and no biology is going to change that. Okay?"

"I know that, Dad." Madison's throat thickened, and she blinked away tears. "I love you, too. I would never want Adrian Diamond to try and take your place—he never *could* take your place. I meant what I said about this not being about Adrian. It's about Peyton, Courtney and Savannah. My *sisters.*" The word felt strange and foreign, but it's what they were. It needed to be acknowledged. "Adrian chose not to be in my life. But they were never given a say."

"I know," he said. "Your mom and I respect that you feel that way, which is why we're standing by you now."

"Thank you," Madison said, meaning it. She didn't want to be angry at her parents forever.

Finally her mom came back into the library. Her face was pale, and she sat back down on the sofa, staring at the phone in her hand like it was a ghost.

"What happened?" Madison asked, her heart racing.

She swallowed and finally met Madison's eyes. "Can I have some of that water?"

"Sure." Madison brought the water to her mom and joined her on the couch. "Dad told me you talked to Adrian."

"Yes." She sipped the water, which put some color back into her face. Once composed, she continued. "I told him everything, and asked him to come over to talk to you."

"And?" Madison leaned forward and held her breath. After all these weeks of knowing Adrian was her biological father but not being able to say anything, he finally knew that she knew. She wouldn't have to keep the secret anymore. It was exciting and terrifying at the same time.

"He said that now wasn't a good time."

Madison's chest sunk. "So, when *is* a good time? Tonight? Tomorrow? Next week?"

"Longer than that." Her mom sighed, and Madison could tell that whatever was coming next wouldn't be something she wanted to hear. "Peyton, Courtney and Savannah are going through a lot right now. They just had something big thrown at them, and they're having a rough time dealing with it. Adrian wants to give them time to adjust."

"How long do they need?" Madison narrowed her eyes. "Days? Weeks? *Months?*"

"He didn't give a time frame," she said. "Just that he would let me know when."

"And what about me?" she asked, her voice cracking. "Does he care that I know he's my father?"

"I thought you considered him to be only a 'sperm donor'?" Her mom held her fingers up in quote signs as she repeated Madison's words.

"I know." She swallowed. "But I guess I thought that once he knew I knew, he would at least want to talk to me."

"He *will* talk to you," her mom insisted. "This came as a shock to him, that's all. Give him time to figure out how to handle it."

"How to *handle it?*" Madison was practically yelling now. "I'm a person, not an 'it.' And I can't keep this secret anymore. I know moving here is a big adjustment, but I've seen Peyton, Courtney and Savannah around school. They're adjusting fine. I think they're ready to find out the truth."

"They might have been fine the last time you saw them at school," her mom said. "But the incident Adrian's referring to happened recently—over Thanksgiving break."

"What happened?" Madison asked. "What's so big that it left all three of them such a mess?"

"It's not my secret to tell…."

"Enough of this," her dad said. "Madison deserves to know as much as those three girls. So, if you don't tell her, then I will."

"Fine," her mom said. "I would have preferred for Adrian to tell you this himself, but he's insistent that we wait, and I'm done keeping secrets."

"Okay…" Madison pressed the pads of her fingers together, ready for whatever was going to be thrown at her next.

And then her parents told her about Britney.

www.campusbuzz.com

Savannah's friend?
Posted on Friday 12/12 at 3:29 PM
Who was that girl shadowing Savannah Diamond around school today? All the senior guys were talking about how hot she was and how they were going to try to get with her this weekend. I saw her once or twice, and I guess she was unique looking, but she didn't seem all that special.

1: Posted on Friday 12/12 at 3:36 PM
That was Savannah's friend Evie! She was at the first volleyball game earlier this season, but she didn't talk to many people. They were best friends in their school in California, and Evie's in town for Savannah's birthday party tomorrow night. She was nice, and she seemed fun, but I also don't know why all the guys were so into her...

2: Posted on Friday 12/12 at 3:43 PM
how could you not notice that ass and those tits?!

3: Posted on Friday 12/12 at 3:51 PM
hell yeah! thinking about getting my hands on those got me hard in class

---

4: Posted on Friday 12/12 at 4:06 PM
haha were you the tool jacking off in the bathroom?

5: Posted on Friday 12/12 at 4:09 PM

You guys are such pervs.

6: Posted on Friday 12/12 at 4:25 PM

Don't get your hopes up, cause she was eyeing up Damien Sanders all through lunch...

7: Posted on Friday 12/12 4:41 PM

I guess Savannah and Damien are over?

8: Posted on Friday 12/12 4:59 PM

Over? They apparently hooked up a few weeks ago, and now they spend a bunch of lunch blocks every week in the recording studio while Savannah records her YouTube videos. Sounds more like Evie's secretly crushing on her best friend's kind of boyfriend!!!!

chapter 29: *Savannah*

"Peek over the magazine, gossip for a few lines and make sure to *ignore* the camera. Pretend we're not here. Take two!"

Carson and the rest of the crew from *My Fabulous Sweet Sixteen* always gave Savannah those same instructions—pretend we're not here!—but it was hard when the camera men, lighting men and director were surrounding her to get the perfect shot. Luckily Evie's advice had been helpful, and once Savannah pretended she was playing a part instead of being herself, she'd improved enough that they had sufficient footage to work with. Since her improvement, the cameras had been *everywhere* this week. And even though Savannah had chosen her dress last month, they went back to the store with her, Rebecca and her sisters so they could reenact the "finding the perfect dress" scene that she'd messed up when it had actually been happening.

Now the stylists in the Diamond Salon pretended to do final touches on Savannah and Evie's pedicures, while they tried to make this "gossip session" look realistic.

Evie tilted her head in what she probably thought was her best angle for the camera, and said, "This is going to be the best party *ever*."

"It's going to be the perfect night." Savannah widened her eyes, since she tended to squint when the light shone in her face. "I can't believe it's happening tomorrow."

"You're going to look absolutely amazing." Evie scooted forward and raised her eyebrows in a way that was kind of cartoonish. "Are you sure there's no one special you have your eye on?"

"Well, there might be someone…." She placed the magazine down on her lap and leaned across the gap between their chairs, cupping her hand around Evie's ear as if they were sharing a secret. The microphone wouldn't pick up this part, so she whispered, "Some guy got so hot staring at your boobs today that he jacked off in the school bathroom," which sent Evie bursting into giggles. Savannah started laughing, too, since Evie's laughter was contagious.

"Are you *serious?*" she said once she got a hold of herself, her cheeks bright red. Savannah nodded, which started them laughing some more.

"And…cut!" Carson said. "Perfect. That's a wrap for the day."

"Great." Savannah dropped the magazine on the end table. They'd been bombarded with the cameras after school, and she was dying to talk with Evie in private about her day at Goodman before they went to dinner with Evie's mom.

When they got back to Savannah's room, Evie collapsed onto the king-size bed. "Are your days always so exhausting?" she asked, sighing dramatically.

"It's the cameras," Savannah explained. "Without them here, everything's normal, but this week has been crazy."

"Normal?" Evie sat up and looked at Savannah like she'd gone mad. "You live in a penthouse in one of the most glamorous hotels in the world, and your YouTube videos are making you an internet celebrity. How can your life ever be *normal?*"

"It wasn't at first." Savannah plopped down next to Evie and leaned against the mountain of pillows. "Over the summer, it felt like a fairy-tale dream. But then school started, and it's been the same routine of waking up early, sitting through classes, going to volleyball practice, getting home, doing homework and then doing social media stuff on Twitter and Facebook. And you know how at Fairfield caring about school is considered not cool?" she asked, and Evie nodded. "Well, at Goodman, people think you're a loser if you *don't* care about doing well. So I've had to try harder. I'm not getting straight As or anything, but I'm getting pretty steady Bs and B-pluses."

"I was pretty lost sitting in your classes today," Evie said. "You're doing way more advanced stuff than I am this year, and everyone in your school seems so *smart.* They really get into class discussions."

"That's what happens when a huge chunk of your final grade is based on participation," Savannah said. "We have to do our readings and come prepared to talk. Or else the teacher will call on you randomly, and if that happens and you don't know the material, it's *so embarrassing.* I learned that the hard way the second week of school."

"What happened?"

"Just a mix-up in Spanish class about the word for *foreign country.*" She shrugged. "I'll never forget what *país extranjero* means again."

"Enough about your classes," Evie declared. "We need to

talk about the *guys,* and how there are so many *hot ones* at your school!"

"Yeah, there are," Savannah said. "Although I've been so busy recently that my guy life has been nonexistent."

"Really?" Evie sounded surprised. "Because it sounded like you and Damien have been spending a lot of time together, with the way he's been helping you record videos for You-Tube."

"We're just friends," she said, trying to keep her voice steady. If Damien saw her as more than that, he would have done something about it by now. But he hadn't, and Savannah was doing her best to accept it. Being friends was better than nothing, right? And he'd been a great friend to her. She might have deleted her YouTube channel if it wasn't for him. He was the reason that she was where she was now.

"So what you said during the video shoot about having your eye on someone was made up?"

"Yep," Savannah lied. "That was for the cameras. I'm so busy filming for the show and with my YouTube stuff that I don't have time to be interested in anyone. Seriously. There hasn't been anything more than friendship between me and Damien in months."

Maybe if she kept saying it, she would believe it. And she didn't want typical Evie advice on how she should flirt with Damien and *make* him interested. She couldn't force him to return her feelings. If he didn't see her that way, then he didn't see her that way. End of story.

"I'm glad to hear it," Evie said. "Because during lunch today I felt a connection with him, but I didn't want you to be upset if you still had feelings for him."

"Oh." Savannah's breath whooshed out of her, as if she'd

been punched. She hadn't forgotten about that moment Evie and Damien had had at Jackie's party. "Okay."

"What?" Evie's eyebrows shot up.

"It's just..." Savannah searched for a reason to explain her less-than-enthusiastic response. "He lives so far from you. Even if you felt a 'connection' with him, you don't think anything will happen, right? Because, no offense, but Damien's not the long-distance-relationship type of guy, especially with someone he's only known for a few days. He's actually kind of a player."

"I'm not looking for a *relationship*." Evie tossed her hair over her shoulder. "I just want to have fun with him while I'm here."

"And by 'fun' you mean..."

"I want to have sex with him."

"No way." Savannah's jaw dropped. "I can't believe you lost your virginity and haven't told me!"

"That's because I haven't lost it yet." She smiled mischievously. "But I want to this weekend." Savannah opened her mouth to protest, but Evie cut her off. "You have *no idea* what it's been like at home. Everyone's had sex already, and I'm the only one who hasn't, so it's best to get it over with while I'm here. What happens in Vegas stays in Vegas, right?"

"Don't you want your first time to be meaningful?" It sounded lame, but Savannah didn't care—the image of Evie and Damien together made her want to punch something. "With someone you trust and who cares about you? I'm not saying you should be soul mates or think you're going to marry the guy someday, but you barely *know* Damien."

"Which makes it so much easier," Evie said. "Once we get started I'm guessing he'll realize I was a virgin, and maybe it'll be embarrassing, but at least I can get back to Fairfield and no one will know any differently. I finally won't have to pretend I'm not a virgin anymore."

"Hold up." This was getting more twisted by the second. "You're not going to tell Damien you're a virgin before you try to have sex with him? And you told everyone at school that you're *not* a virgin?"

Evie bit her lip and focused on the bedspread. "Maybe…"

"Who did you say you lost it to?"

"A guy from Vegas the last time I visited you," she said quickly. "No big deal. But now there's this guy I like from one of my classes, but he thinks I'm not a virgin, and if I have sex with him he'll realize I was lying and then *everyone* will know I've been lying." Her eyes teared, and she looked so desperate. "The only way for me to fix this is to get it over with while I'm here. When I get back home I won't be a virgin anymore, and no one will know that it happened now and not a few weeks ago."

Savannah shook her head. This situation was so typically *Evie*. "You really want to just 'get it over with'? You don't care at all who it's with?"

"I don't buy into that whole 'first time being special' crap," Evie said. "From what the girls on the volleyball team told me, the first time hurts and really sucks. So, yes, I want to get it over with, here in Vegas, with Damien. At least you're friends with him and trust him. It's better than losing it to some random guy."

"Yes, I'm friends with him and I trust him," she said. "But you can't tell him you've had sex before, and then, once it's in, be like, 'Surprise! Just kidding! You're actually my first!'"

"Why not?" Evie asked. "I'm not going to *tell* him I've had sex before. I just won't tell him that I *haven't*."

"But it's still lying!" Savannah dropped her fists onto the

bed. After her family not telling her and her sisters about Britney, she knew that *not telling* someone something was as bad
as lying. "And what if Damien doesn't *want* to take your virginity? Don't you think he should know if he's your first?"

"I'd be having sex with him." Evie laughed. "I can hardly
imagine a guy complaining about that. But if it bothers you
that much, I won't do it."

"Really?" Savannah relaxed for the first time since this
conversation started. "Just like that?"

"Well, I won't do it with Damien," she said. "Since I can
tell it bothers you. Half of my saying all that was to see if
you're *really* okay with just being friends with him, and I can
tell you have feelings for him."

"I'm not sure what's going on with me and Damien, but
it would definitely sting to see you with him," she said, surprised by Evie's sudden insightfulness, but grateful at the same
time. "Thank you for backing off."

"Of course," she said. "But I'm serious about wanting to
lose my virginity while I'm here. So if Damien's not an option, do you have any suggestions?"

Savannah still thought what Evie was considering doing
was a mistake, but she knew her best friend—once she set
her mind to something, she didn't give up. And Savannah
had given her opinion. What happened next was up to Evie.

"For the record, I think this plan is super messed up," she
said. "But do you remember that guy who stopped by our
lunch table today to introduce himself? Oliver Prescott…?"

chapter 30: *Courtney*

The past week had been nonstop busy with the camera crew following Savannah around for *My Fabulous Sweet Sixteen,* and they wanted Courtney and Peyton in a lot of the scenes, too. It was exhausting. Courtney was glad to finally be by herself in her room, and she would be happy if she never saw a camera again.

She walked to the floor-to-ceiling window and gazed out at the lit-up Strip below. With how busy it had been during the past week, she hadn't had much time to herself, but that didn't stop her from thinking about Britney. Courtney hated that she would never know what Britney would be like if she were here now, so she'd created a version of Britney in her mind. She imagined that, like her, Britney would be smart, ambitious and would do well in school, but that she would also be outgoing, free-spirited and daring. She would bring out those qualities in Courtney, and Courtney would be the calming force in her wilder twin's life. They would balance each other perfectly.

She looked out at the stars, knowing it was pure luck that she was the one here now. What if in another universe it had been Courtney who was killed, and Britney was alive, looking out her window, wondering about the twin she'd never known?

Gazing at the stars reminded her—the Geminids meteor shower was peaking tonight. The best place to view it would be out in the desert, away from light pollution. But Savannah was busy with Evie, Peyton was grounded and Courtney didn't want to venture out there by herself. The next best plan was to go to the rooftop pool and hope to catch a few. The rooftop pool should be empty now, since they stopped serving drinks and food after ten, so the late-night partiers moved to the main pool. Plus, it was nighttime in December, and it was cold.

Courtney opened the door to the rooftop and walked into the cool desert air. People chatting and cars honking echoed from the Strip below, although her view of the pool was dark and still. The walls around the edges of the building rose so high that the sounds of busy nightlife seemed like a different world.

She thought she was the only one up there, but then she saw movement from a lounge chair in the back.

"Courtney?" asked a voice she recognized as Brett's. Her heart leaped. She hadn't spoken more than a few words to him at school, not wanting to talk about Britney with so many people around. Then, after school was busy with the camera crew for the show, and she had homework…. Truthfully, she'd been avoiding him. Because she was scared to truly talk to him. Scared that they were reaching a turning point in whatever was going on between them, and she wouldn't be able to hide her feelings from him anymore. She wasn't sure she was ready for that—especially with everything that had been on her mind about Britney.

She was also ashamed that it had been Rebecca who had told him about Britney, and not her. He'd encouraged her to dig deeper to find out the secret, and she hadn't had the strength to tell him about her discovery herself. He'd deserved to hear it from her, and she'd shut him out.

But by some twist of fate he was here, and she would never forgive herself if she walked away from him now.

"Hey." She moved toward him, trying to act normal, and sat on the chair next to his. "What are you doing up here?"

He smiled and leaned back in his chair. "I could ask you the same thing."

"There's a meteor shower tonight," she said. "The Geminids. I was going to try to watch, but there might be too much light pollution from the Strip. I was hoping that being high up would give me a chance to see a few."

"That's why I'm here, too," he said. "The Spacedex Facebook page said it was the best night to check them out."

Courtney tilted her head. "You follow Spacedex?"

"I do," he said. "I'm guessing that you do, too?"

"Yeah." She nodded. "I always wanted to catch a meteor shower when I was living in California, but I was so busy that I didn't have time. Then I missed the Perseids in August, so I figured I would *try* to see the Geminids. They're not supposed to be as good as the Perseids—which are the best of the year—but they're close."

"Wow," he said. "You know a lot about meteor showers."

"Just the basics." She shrugged. "I find the night sky fascinating. Each of the hundreds of billions of stars in our galaxy is a sun, possibly with a solar system around it, with planets that could have life. And then there are hundreds of billions of galaxies in the universe.... It's mind-blowing. I don't see how a person could look at the stars and not be in awe of how small they are compared to the universe, and the endless possibilities of what could be out there."

"It is truly mind-blowing," he agreed. "Those numbers are beyond what anyone can fully comprehend. So I'm going to assume you believe in aliens, too?"

"How could I *not?*" she said, eyes wide. "With numbers like those, it's improbable to assume we're the only ones out there. But they could have existed a long time ago, or way in the future. I doubt I'll live long enough to see it if—or when—we make contact."

"With cryonics, who knows what we'll be alive long enough to see."

"With *what?*"

"Cryonics," he repeated. "The idea that people can be frozen at the moment they're considered dead by current definition, then healed in the future, when technology has advanced beyond what's available today. It's something Adrian—and now my mom and I—believe in. Ask him about Alcor. I'm sure he'd love to talk with you about it."

"Alcor," she repeated, so she would remember later. It sounded like something from science fiction novels—not something that could happen in real life—but she loved learning about new things. She did her own research before believing anything, but she liked to be open-minded. There was always something to learn from listening to and understanding people's viewpoints. "What does that mean?"

"It's the cryonics foundation Adrian supports," he said. "It's named after a star." With that reminder, they turned their eyes up to the night sky, just as a meteor zoomed overhead.

It was gone in a flash—so quickly that Courtney was unsure it was there at all.

"Did you see that?" She pointed at where it had disappeared.

"I did." He smiled, his eyes reflecting the starlight. "First one of the night." They both studied the sky, waiting for another meteor, but all was still. "So…how are you doing after everything that happened over Thanksgiving?"

Everyone who knew referred to it in a similar way—"what happened over Thanksgiving," "the Thanksgiving incident" or "your discovery at Grandma's." No one wanted to say Britney's name out loud.

"Honestly, I'm not sure," she said. "It's a lot to process. I'm angry with my mom and Grandma most of all. I haven't forgiven Adrian either, but it's different with him, since he didn't live with me for all those years and lie to my face every day. Besides that, I guess there's nothing I *can* do, other than move forward. But it's hard, knowing I had a sister—a *twin*—who I'll never know. I can't stop wondering what she would have been like if she'd lived. What *I* would have been like if she'd lived."

"I can't imagine how that must feel."

"It's awful." She stared up at the stars, as if they held the answers. "But Adrian's really trying to make things right between us. He took me and my sisters to the Grand Canyon, and we had a great time. And while he meant well, and he seems to want to keep doing these father/daughters Sunday activities, I wish he'd told us about Britney when he first told us about the kidnapping."

"For what it's worth, my mom keeps telling me how terrible Adrian feels about it, and that he regrets not telling you everything the day you moved here," Brett said. "I know that doesn't change anything, but despite the secrets, I don't think he's a bad person. My mom wouldn't be marrying him if he were."

"I know," Courtney said. "And I don't think anyone kept this from me and my sisters because they *wanted* to hurt us. But they—my mom, Grandma and Adrian—were being so selfish. They didn't tell us about Britney because it hurt *them* to think about what happened to her, and it made their lives easier to pretend she never existed. I hate how they lied for all those years, and I hate how if I hadn't stumbled upon that baby book, they might have kept the truth from us forever."

Brett reached across the gap between their chairs and took her hand in his, sending tingles up her arm and through her body. "I can't say that I've been there or understand how you feel, but I hope you know that I'm here for you," he said, his eyes shining with how much he meant every word. Their hands felt so perfect linked together, as if it was where they belonged. "I've been trying so hard to talk to you for the past week, to see how you're doing. I'm glad you ended up here tonight."

"I wish our parents weren't getting married," Courtney said, surprising herself by her honesty. "It would make this so much simpler."

"Maybe." He kept his eyes locked on hers, the intensity in them leaving her breathless. "Or maybe not. If our parents weren't getting married, I wouldn't have switched to Goodman or live in the Diamond, so we might never have met."

"I like to think we would have."

He leaned forward, as if he were going to kiss her again, and it was as if a magnetic force were pulling them together. His lips were centimeters from hers, but then she remembered everything going on in her family, and how she was stuck in the center of it all, and it was too much.

She dropped her hand from his, her skin feeling cold where Brett's fingers had been. The disappointment in his eyes left her heart feeling empty.

"I'm sorry," she somehow managed to say, since she had to say *something*. "I care about you a lot, but I just can't. Not right now, with everything going on with the family. It's all so confusing, like I'm being pulled in a million directions, and I don't know what to feel about anything anymore. I can't complicate everything more than it already is."

"Have you ever thought that you're stressing yourself out more by not allowing yourself to be honest about your feelings for me?" he asked. "Haven't you ever wanted to put yourself first and focus on what *you* want? To do what feels right instead of what people tell you is right?"

"I think about it constantly," she said. "But what if we try to make it work, and it ends terribly? It won't be like a normal relationship where both people move on with their lives. It would be a million times harder, because we'll be family. We'll both end up getting hurt."

"But what if it *could* work between us? Won't you regret never letting yourself find out?"

"Maybe." She pulled her legs toward herself and wrapped her arms around them. "I don't know. Everything's been so crazy with all that's been going on that I don't know what to feel about anything anymore. I just... I need time to think about it."

"I get it." He nodded. "This is a hard time, and I'll stop pushing you. But I'm glad you're here with me now. Let's just enjoy the meteor shower, okay?"

She said okay, and they both leaned back in their lounge chairs, staring up at the stars. He made a good point—did she want to look back to this part of her life and wonder *what if* when it came to Brett? And then, because she'd been thinking about her a lot recently, she wondered…what would Britney have done in this position?

She would never know for sure, but the daring twin she'd created in her mind would stop worrying about the what-ifs and follow her heart.

chapter 31: *Peyton*

Being grounded sucked.

It had been two weeks, and the only time Peyton was allowed to leave the Diamond was for school and "official" family outings. At least she was allowed to go to restaurants in the hotel with her sisters. Otherwise she would have gone stir-crazy. And while this past week had been more exciting because of the camera crew following Savannah, Peyton didn't know how she was going to last another two weeks. At least she had Savannah's Sweet Sixteen tomorrow night. Besides that, she'd been reduced to watching reality show marathons while everyone else was out having fun. She'd even been so bored that she'd taken a practice test from the SAT book Courtney had put in her room. Pathetic.

But the worst part about the past two weeks was that Jackson had only sent her one text message:

Hi, Peyton. Thanks for your message. I'm spending a few weeks with my parents in Omaha, figuring out what to do from here. I think it's best that we take some space from each other. Hope all is well. --J

It was so formal, and reading it had crushed her. She'd texted him back, asking him to just *talk* to her, but she'd gotten nothing. It was like everything that had happened between them—every moment, every connection—had never existed. Her heart hurt, like her chest had collapsed around it and shattered it into a million tiny pieces. Every time her phone buzzed, she hoped it was Jackson, saying he didn't need "space" anymore, but it never was.

He must hate her. He probably blamed her for his getting fired. And it *was* her fault. If she hadn't been so pushy and had just let him do his job, none of this would have happened. Now she was staring blankly at the open SAT book, feeling sorry for herself and wishing she could go back in time and fix her mistakes.

So when Courtney knocked on her door a little after midnight and asked if she wanted to grab a late-night snack at the Diamond Café, Peyton jumped at the invitation. They each got the Diamond Signature Hot Chocolate, along with a ginormous slice of red velvet cake to share, and situated themselves at a table in the back corner.

"You were out late tonight." Peyton stabbed the cake with her fork and shoved the bite in her mouth. The red velvet was truly heaven in a dessert.

Courtney stared at where Peyton had attacked the cake, carefully cut it in half, and put the untouched piece on her plate. "I went to the rooftop pool to watch the meteor shower."

"By yourself?" Peyton frowned that she hadn't been invited. Watching a meteor shower was hardly her idea of a fun Friday night, but with needing her sisters as escorts for the next two weeks, it was better than sitting in the condo watching reruns of *America's Next Top Model*.

"I needed time to think, so I *wanted* to go by myself." Courtney took a sip of hot chocolate, her cheeks turning red. "But when I got to the roof, Brett was already there."

"And running into him just *happened* to be a coincidence?"

"It was a total coincidence," Courtney said, and then she told Peyton every detail of the conversation she'd had with him.

"And you left it that way? With you having to 'think about it'?" Peyton forced herself to slow down eating, since while Courtney had been telling the story, she'd nearly finished her half of the cake.

"Was that wrong?" she asked. "He was disappointed, but I was being truthful. I do need time to think about it."

"But you two really are perfect for each other," Peyton said. "You should at least see what happens. If it all goes to hell and it doesn't work out, you know Savannah and I have your back."

"I know." Courtney sighed. "But Adrian and Rebecca were clear about not wanting me to get involved with Brett. They have good reasons for it, and I would hate to disappoint them."

Peyton nearly choked on her hot chocolate. "After Adrian lied to us about Britney, you're *still* worried about disappointing him? If I were you I would go for Brett just to piss him off."

"I've actually been thinking about it," Courtney said, and Peyton nearly dropped her mug. "Not the part about dating Brett to piss Adrian off. But about acting on my feelings for him. I understand what Brett means about not wanting to look back and regret never knowing what could have happened between us, and I don't want to make a mistake like that."

"That's more like it." Peyton smiled and clicked her mug with Courtney's.

"Anyway," Courtney said. "Were you doing an *SAT practice test* when I came into your room?"

"I was bored." Peyton shrugged. "I still don't want to go to college. But I had nothing else to do."

"Is the ADHD medicine helping your score?"

"I don't know," she said. "I never tried to take it without the Adderall. My score isn't as good as yours, but it's not terrible, either. Don't get any ideas, though. I'm only doing this because I have nothing better to do while I'm stuck in the condo."

"And school isn't as torturous for you with the Adderall, right?"

"I'm never going to love school like you do," Peyton said. "But with the medicine, it's not *as* hard to stay focused. My mind still wanders, but not as much, and I don't want to jump out of my seat after only fifteen minutes of class."

"That's good." Courtney nodded, and ate a few more bites of her cake. "So, I'm guessing you haven't heard anything more from Jackson?"

"Nope." Peyton touched the button on her iPhone to make sure there were no missed messages. There weren't. "I texted him back, asking him to let me know when he was ready to talk, but he hasn't replied. I keep making excuses for him— maybe he didn't get the text, maybe there's something wrong with his phone, maybe he has a new phone and I should try to send him a Facebook message instead, or that I should simply demand to know how long he needs 'space.' Every day it's a struggle not reaching out to him, but I stop myself. I refuse to be pathetic about it."

"It's hard," Courtney said, staring at her cake as if she were thinking about something else. "Wanting to be with some-one you can't have."

"Yeah," Peyton agreed. "It sucks hard-core. But here's the big difference between our situations—Jackson's not inter-ested in me anymore because I screwed up his life. But Brett's interested in you. He cares about you so much—you should have heard him banging on the door the day after Thanks-giving, begging for a chance to talk to you. It took a lot of self-control for Savannah and I to refuse, and we only did it because we were worried you would rip our heads off if we didn't give you space."

"I wouldn't have ripped your heads off," Courtney said. "But I really did need space that day."

"I get that," Peyton said. "And I get how much it sucks to want to be with the one person you can't have. But while Brett's being open and honest with you about his feelings now, he's not going to pine away for you forever. If you want any-thing to happen between you two, it's up to you to do some-thing about it."

chapter 32: *Madison*

Tomorrow was Savannah's big Sweet Sixteen party, and most of Madison's friends had gone to Myst to start off the weekend celebrating with Savannah and her redheaded friend from California. Everyone had been so nice to Savannah recently—probably because they were hoping for airtime on *My Fabulous Sweet Sixteen*. It was pathetic.

So instead of tagging along with them, Madison was reading under her favorite statue in the Lobby Bar—the gold one of the woman turning into a tree. It was comforting, as if the lady in the statue was watching over her. She reached the end of a chapter and looked up just in time to spot Courtney and Peyton walking by, holding a takeaway bag from the Diamond Café. Courtney's eyes met hers, and while they weren't friends besides that one conversation in the tutoring center, Madison waved. She couldn't be mean to the Diamond girls anymore.

From the way Courtney angled her body toward Madison and Peyton angled hers toward the elevators, they must have been debating coming over and saying hi. Courtney apparently won, because they headed in Madison's direction. Peyton scowled, as if she wanted to be anywhere but there.

"Hey." Courtney glanced at the book in Madison's lap. "That's a good book. One of my favorites."

"Everyone's been talking about it, so I figured I should give it a try," Madison said. She wasn't a huge reader—she normally preferred hanging out with friends—but she did read the popular books that were being turned into movies. "It's good so far."

Courtney looked up at the statue. "Do you normally read here?"

"Occasionally," she said. "This is my favorite place in the Diamond. I love the statue."

"The story of Daphne and Apollo is one of my favorites."

"What?" Madison had no idea what Courtney was talking about.

"That tree is a rendition of Daphne." Courtney motioned to the golden statue, whose arms and legs turned into the branches of a tree. "In Greek mythology, the god Apollo was struck with a gold arrow that caused extreme lust, and the water nymph Daphne was struck by a lead arrow that made her hate romance. Apollo chased after Daphne, and she ran from him. When she'd run so much that she couldn't continue, she begged her father—a water god—for help. Water gods have the power of transformation, so he turned her into a laurel tree. But Apollo still loved Daphne, and since he couldn't be with her, he cared for her as a tree. That's why the laurel wreath is a symbol of Apollo."

"You knew all that off the top of your head?" Madison asked.

"I like Greek mythology," she said. "When I moved here and saw the statue, I refreshed my memory on the story."

"Okay." Madison picked her book back up. She didn't *hate* talking to Courtney, but being around her and Peyton made her skin feel tight, as if the secret were trying to force its way out. She wanted to keep her distance until Adrian's big reveal.

Courtney played with her hands, as if debating saying more. "So this is kind of awkward, but we have to ask you," she said. "You didn't post those pictures of Peyton with Hunter and that video of Savannah botching that song at that party on the Campusbuzz forum, did you?"

"This again?" Madison didn't get it—why did people think she wasted time posting that crap? "First Oliver asked about it, and now you. No, I didn't write that post. I checked it out after Oliver mentioned it, but I swear I didn't write it. I wasn't even at that party when Savannah sang that song."

"But you took that picture," Peyton said. "The one of me and Hunter at the bar. I saw it, and I deleted it from your phone. I know you remember."

"Of course I remember," she said. How could she forget? Especially since that strong (and very sexy) bodyguard of Peyton's had forced her to enter her password on her phone. "But by the time you deleted it, I'd already texted it to a friend. Sorry."

All right, maybe it was more like *two* friends. Because Larissa had insisted she have a copy, too.

"Why would you do that?" Peyton's eyes raged, and she took a step closer to Madison.

"Because you were having a drink with our hot new English teacher, and one of my friends had been talking about him since school started, so I shared the picture with her," she said, backing into her seat. That had all happened before she'd found out the Diamonds were her sisters. She never would have taken the picture if she'd known. But she couldn't tell Peyton and Courtney that, since this wasn't the time or place for that conversation, and she'd promised her parents she would wait until Adrian was ready. "I didn't mean for it to go public, and I didn't write that post."

"Sure you didn't." Peyton rolled her eyes.

"You don't have to believe me, but it's the truth."

Peyton glared at her, but Courtney placed her hand on her arm, which stopped whatever retort she was about to say next. "We have to head back," Courtney said. "Sorry to ask you about all of that, but we had to know. Bye, Madison."

They headed to the penthouse elevators, and Madison watched them until they turned the corner. She returned to reading her book, but she didn't get far before her phone buzzed with a text message. It was from Oliver.

are u coming to myst?

No. I'm trying to keep my distance from the Diamond girls, and I know everyone's fawning over Savannah and her little friend tonight.

yeah they are. it's lame. u in your condo?

Nope. Lobby Bar. Near the statue of Daphne turning into the tree.

on my way

Then he followed it up with another text.

when did u name the statue?

I didn't name her—the statue is from a Greek myth. That's her name. See you soon!

She placed the phone down and fidgeted in her seat. She hadn't seen Oliver outside of school since they'd kissed over Thanksgiving break—mostly because she had no idea what was going on between them, and she was scared to find out. Would things be weird? Because she had no idea if her feelings for him were real, if his feelings for her were real or if the spark between them was because she was stressed with everything going on and he'd been there for her. Plus, she'd never *considered* dating Oliver in the past because he was a player. Why would he change for her?

Whatever had happened between them had most likely been an in-the-moment thing.

It didn't take long for him to join her in the Lobby Bar. He was wearing his usual clubbing attire—dark jeans and a black button-down top—and his eyes were unfocused and glassy, like he'd had too much to drink.

"Was Myst not fun tonight?" she asked. It wasn't even one in the morning, and Oliver usually stayed out until at least two on the weekends.

"Everyone was sucking up to Savannah because of her Sweet Sixteen," he said. "Other than that, it was the same as always. But I was hoping to see you there."

He sounded so genuine that Madison's stomach flipped, and she had to look away, hoping he wouldn't notice the flush in her cheeks. She sipped her water, buying time to collect herself. "I wasn't in the mood for the club scene tonight," she said, trying to act unfazed. "Plus, Savannah's friend Evie seemed annoying when she was shadowing Savannah around school today. The last thing I wanted to do was pretend like I cared about getting to know her."

"Speaking of Evie," Oliver said, a mischievous glint in his eyes. "Want to hear a funny story?"

"Sure." Hopefully he wasn't ogling Evie like every other guy at school. Madison didn't get it. Yes, Evie was curvy in those places guys liked, but her face was caked with foundation and she wore glitter eyeliner to school. Seriously, who did that?

"At Myst, I was hanging out with our friends at Savannah's table, and Evie couldn't keep her hands off me," he started. "She's not my type, but I didn't want to embarrass her in front of everyone, so I went along with it."

Madison tensed at the image of Evie's hands all over Oliver, and she curled her lips in distaste. "If she's not your type, why didn't you tell her to back off?"

"Come on, Mads," Oliver said. "I didn't think she meant anything by it. Then Savannah cornered me and told me that Evie's a virgin, and she wants to sleep with someone while she's in Vegas. And apparently Evie had picked *me* for this task. She didn't plan on telling me she was a virgin, but Savannah wanted me to know before anything happened, and she didn't want me to tell Evie that she'd told me. Stupid girl drama."

"So what'd you do?" Madison's chest tightened at the idea of Oliver taking Evie's virginity. Or was she just upset about the thought of Oliver sleeping with *anyone* after their kiss over Thanksgiving?

"I told Savannah to send Evie someone else's way."

"Really?" Madison's eyes widened. "Why?" It couldn't have been because of her. Could it?

"Because she's a virgin." He shrugged. "I don't want to get involved with that."

"What about that bet you had about sleeping with all three

Diamond sisters?" Madison asked. "Two of the three of them are virgins—at least, I'm *assuming* Courtney is—and you didn't have a problem with it then."

"Let's just say it's a new policy of mine."

"So you would *never* sleep with a virgin?" she asked. "Even if that person meant a lot to you?"

"Never say never." He smirked. "I did wish Evie the best of luck, but taking someone's virginity isn't something I would do lightly anymore."

"Good," Madison said, feeling like she could breathe again. "Maybe you're finally growing up a little."

"Crazier things have happened," he said. "But the hottest girls usually aren't virgins, so it makes the selection process easier."

"Jerk." Madison kept her tone light, but inside she was on fire. Did Oliver not think she was hot?

"Of course there are always exceptions." His eyes focused on hers, making her forget to breathe again.

Was he talking about her? Did she *want* him to be talking about her?

Yes, she realized. She did.

"So, tomorrow night," he said. "Who are you going with to Savannah's party?"

"I was planning on meeting up with the girls when they get here and going into the party together," she said, since the only reason Kaitlin, Tiffany and Larissa were invited was because her mom had insisted Rebecca include them. Madison had told her it wasn't necessary, but her mom had been worried about her being around the Diamond sisters without her friends by her side. So she'd pulled strings and made it happen. "Why?"

"Because I was thinking we could meet here for drinks first, and then go to the party together."

She froze, and time felt like it stopped moving. Was Oliver asking her on a *date?* Or maybe he was just asking because he knew the only reason they were invited was because their families were on Adrian and Rebecca's guest list, and not because Savannah wanted them there.

He watched her closely, and she could have sworn she detected panic in his usually confident gaze. "We could invite your friends, too, if you'd like," he added. "The adults will probably be watching what we're drinking at the party, so it makes sense to pre-game."

"We don't have to invite them," Madison said quickly. "I would rather it be us two. It's Savannah's party, and being around the Diamonds will be stressful for me, and I might want to vent or whatever. You're the only other person who knows the truth, so it's best that it's just us. I'll see the girls in the actual party. But before the party, I would rather be with you."

It was a good reason to not invite anyone else along on what *might* be a date—right?

"So we'll meet here at six tomorrow?" he asked.

"Sounds perfect."

She didn't know if it was officially a date, but she wanted it to be. Could she and Oliver take their friendship to the next level? And if they did, would she *mean* something to him, or would she be another girl he grew sick of and tossed to the side?

She would never know if she didn't take the risk.

www.campusbuzz.com

Happy Sweet Sixteen, Savannah!
Posted on Saturday 12/13 at 10:47 AM
The big day is finally here—Savannah Diamond's Fabulous Sweet Sixteen! Everyone there (including me, of course) will be one of the first to see the new Abandon Night-club, since it hasn't officially opened yet. It's going to be the best Sweet Sixteen party of the YEAR.

1: Posted on Saturday 12/13 at 10:59 AM
Did Savannah invite everyone from school? From the way everyone's been talking about the party, it sure seems like it!

2: Posted on Saturday 12/13 at 11:10 AM
She didn't invite everyone :(

3. Posted on Saturday 12/13 at 11:27 AM
I'm on the volleyball team with Savannah, and she told us how she invited people. She couldn't invite everyone from school because Adrian and Rebecca are inviting family and friends as well, and there are limits on how many people can be in the club, especially with all the activities they're setting up to entertain us all night.

So it's basically like this: she invited everyone on the volleyball team, all of the sophomores and friends of hers from the other grades. Then Peyton was allowed to invite a few seniors, Courtney invited a few juniors, and Adrian and Rebecca invited the kids of their friends. (Like Madison and Oliver. Which is so stupid because everyone knows Savannah doesn't like them, but whatever. That's what happens when your family is connected.)

---

4. Posted on Saturday 12/13 at 11:46 AM
so freshmen had no chance of an invite?

---

5. Posted on Saturday 12/13 at 11:54 AM
Not unless you're on the volleyball team or your parents are family friends with Adrian and Rebecca! Don't feel too bad about it — only a handful of freshmen were invited.

---

6. Posted on Saturday 12/13 at 12:21 PM
i heard a surprise guest will be there tonight! anyone know who it is??

---

7. Posted on Saturday 12/13 at 12:41 PM
The theme of the party is MUSIC, so probably a big music star! The Diamonds definitely have the connections to make it happen. One thing is for sure...tonight is going to be EPIC.

See you there!

chapter 33: *Savannah*

"And now let's give a big welcome to the reason we're all here, the birthday princess herself, the one and only Savannah Diamond!"

The double doors flew open, and Savannah made her grand entrance, carried in an extravagant litter like the ancient queens of Egypt, with colorful silk pillows surrounding her. The litter required eight men to hold her up—but the hired dancers were so strong that they made it look effortless. Everyone cheered as she passed, and she waved back, as if greeting her royal subjects. She spotted Nick and waved to him, so that he'd know how glad she was that he'd made it out. Damien was also in the front, and he smiled so radiantly at Savannah that her heart felt like it was about to burst. Their eyes connected, and for those few seconds, it was like everyone else in the club disappeared.

"Savannah's wearing Dolce & Gabbana, and if you want to copy her look, be prepared to shell out a hefty $6,800," the host of *My Fabulous Sweet Sixteen,* Jillianne Powells, said to the camera. Savannah forced her gaze away from Damien's and fluffed her white-and-black lace dress, smiling for the camera as instructed.

She reached the stage, where her family (who had been previously introduced) was standing. The men placed the litter down and Savannah stepped out to join them. Her sisters looked amazing—Courtney in a short red Valentino dress that flounced when she twirled, and Peyton in a tight leather number by Alexander McQueen. Adrian, Rebecca and Brett were there, as well. The only people missing were Mom and Grandma. Savannah's chest tightened at the thought of them, and how, in respect for Courtney's decision to take space, they still hadn't talked after the fight over Thanksgiving.

But they would work things out soon. For now, she wanted to enjoy her party.

"Let's give another round of applause for Savannah Diamond and the Diamond family!" the DJ said. Then an upbeat song came on, and the dancers pulled the guests to the center of the action to get the party started.

The dancing continued until dinner was served, although Savannah could barely eat her filet since she'd had so many appetizers earlier. (The lobster macaroni and cheese in martini glasses was positively *to die* for.) So many people wanted to get five minutes in with her—and the cameras—that she didn't have time to eat dinner, anyway. When one of Rebecca's high school best friends finally stopped talking to Savannah, Jillianne rushed to her side.

"There's a big surprise for you at the end of dinner—in about five minutes—and we have to make sure you're in a good spot for the camera to capture your reaction," she said. "We need the family in the frame," she said louder, and Adrian, Rebecca, Peyton, Courtney and Brett moved their chairs closer to each other. Evie and her mom were the only others at the table, and they had to move aside so they weren't in the scene.

"Did you two know about a surprise?" Savannah asked Courtney and Peyton.

"Rebecca couldn't have made it happen without our input," Courtney said, smiling.

"Once the surprise is announced, you'll be the first person who runs to the stage," Jillianne told Savannah. "Your sisters and friends will follow."

"Okay," Savannah said, barely able to stand still. What was this big surprise, and why was the stage involved? They weren't going to have her sing, were they? Because she would have needed to prepare. She couldn't have another disaster like what had happened at Jackie's party.

Then every light in the club dimmed except for the one shining on the DJ. Savannah held her breath, and took her sisters' hands in hers. The DJ said a few things about how great the party was so far, and how everyone must be having such a good time, but Savannah couldn't focus on what he was saying because she *wanted to see the surprise already.*

Finally, he said, "If you think this party couldn't get any better, than you're in for a treat, because here to perform a few of their hits are your five favorite boys straight from the UK—the one, the only, One Connection!"

The opening riff of their recent single rang through the club, and the five of them ran onto the stage, breaking out into song. Savannah squeezed her sisters' hands, screaming along with every other teen there. One Connection?! Performing at *her* Sweet Sixteen?! This was beyond anything she could have imagined. She was so excited she thought she might hyperventilate, and her sisters pulled her out of her seat and rushed the stage with her, not letting go of her hands through the entire song. Which was a good thing, because she might have fallen over otherwise. Alyssa, Jackie, Brooke and the rest of the volleyball girls were all around them, too, singing along to every word. As was Damien—he was being more chill about it, of course—but he'd gotten to know the songs pretty well when he was working with Savannah on recording the covers.

"The next song is one that Savannah Diamond covered herself on her YouTube channel," Perry Myles said, and Savannah clapped and screamed at how *her name* just came out of *Perry Myles's* mouth. "And we loved her version so much that we're going to take a few seconds to Tweet about it so all our followers can check it out! Right, boys?" They all agreed and took out their cell phones, supposedly Tweeting about Savannah's YouTube cover. "This one's for you, Savannah!"

She jumped up and down, clapping and singing along with everyone around her. Did that *really* just happen? Her channel was going to *blow up* after this. If she'd had her phone on her she would have checked her Twitter, but it was probably a good thing she didn't, because she was able to dance and sing along for the rest of the songs without any distractions.

"And now, we'd like Savannah Diamond to join us on stage so we can sing 'Happy Birthday' to her!" Noel said, holding out a hand to help her up. He and Kayn pulled her onstage— omigod they *touched her arms*—and the DJ rolled the four-tiered topsy-turvy cake with pink, black and white icing onto the stage. The boys of One Connection surrounded her to sing "Happy Birthday," and the crowd joined in, too.

Savannah pulled her hair in front of her shoulders and smiled, hoping everyone didn't realize how awkward she felt when people sang "Happy Birthday" to her. Once the song was over, Perry presented her with a cupcake with a lit 16 candle, and Savannah blew it out. Then he kissed her cheek and smiled, his brown eyes warm as they met hers. She returned his smile, her heart feeling like it was about to pound out of her chest, her skin tingling where his lips had been on her skin. She felt like she'd walked into a dream.

"We'll be hanging around the pool throughout dessert, and look forward to meeting you to sign autographs and take pictures," Perry announced. "Thank you for having us here tonight, and again, we'd like to wish a very happy birthday to the beautiful and talented Savannah Diamond!"

The crowd cheered, and the next few minutes of her friends rushing up onstage to tell her how her party was the best *ever* were a blur. When she finally made it back to her table, she found Rebecca and Adrian sitting there trying all of the desserts available at the dessert bar.

"How did you guys manage to get *One Connection* to be here?" she asked, breathless.

Rebecca smiled. "I'm guessing your sisters were right that they're one of your favorite bands?"

"Yes!" Savannah said. "Thank you both so so so much. This party has been unbelievable. I knew from the planning that it was going to be awesome, but this is beyond what I imagined." She gave Rebecca a huge hug, and then moved on to Adrian, who surprised her by picking her up and swinging her around in a small circle.

"I'm glad you're having fun, Savannah," he said, and Rebecca reached over to hold his hand. "I know everything hasn't been as smooth as you and your sisters would have liked with us getting to know each other, and a lot of that is my fault, but I hope you believe that I only want things between us to get better from here."

"I know that," Savannah said, giddy after everything that

had happened tonight. "And I'm sure my sisters will, too. But can you guys believe that One Connection Tweeted about my cover of their song? You didn't force them to do that, did you?"

"We didn't tell them about your video or ask them to share it online—they must have found it on their own," Adrian said.

"Really?" She squealed and jumped up and down again. "So they really loved it?"

"They really did," Rebecca said.

"Wow." So much energy rushed through her body that she thought she might explode. "Damien's going to be so excited for me—I have to find him and tell him!"

Everywhere Savannah went, people stopped her to chat, so it took forever to get anywhere. Finally, she spotted Damien in one of the back booths...with Evie practically on top of him. Her hand rested on his arm, their faces inches apart. She whispered something to him, and he laughed as if it were the funniest thing he'd ever heard.

Savannah's pulse sped up, and she clenched her fists, her nails biting into her palms. How could they *do* this to her? Sure, Damien might only see her as a friend, but Evie *knew* about her feelings for him. She'd promised yesterday she wouldn't go for him. Why would she betray her like this?

Savannah marched to their table, fire pounding through her veins.

Damien's eyes met hers, and he pulled his arm away from Evie, as if he knew Savannah would be upset by his flirting with her best friend. "Hey, Savannah," he said when she approached. "Can you believe One Connection was here? This is going to be so awesome for your channel."

"Yeah, it will be." She crossed her arms and glared at them. "I wanted to tell you something, but since you're having so much fun together, I guess I'll wait until later."

Or never.

"We were just talking." Evie shrugged and pushed her hair behind her ears. She looked at Damien to back her up, but he didn't notice, because his eyes were locked on Savannah's.

"Evie?" Damien said softly. "Would you mind giving Savannah and I a few minutes to ourselves?"

"Sure." Evie stood up and adjusted her dress, pulling the neckline as low as possible. "I wanted to check out the chocolate fountain, anyway."

Savannah wanted to reach out and strangle her, and she took a few breaths to calm down. "I wanted to try the desserts, too," she said, even though she wasn't sure she could eat one more bite. "I'll meet you there in a few minutes."

"Sure." Evie ducked her head and hurried to the dessert buffet.

"Want to sit?" Damien motioned to the spot next to him—the place that had just been vacated by Evie.

"Only because these shoes are giving me blisters." She took the seat, leaving a gap between them.

"So," he said, his dark eyes watching her intently. "What were you coming over to tell me?"

"Nothing important enough to break up the fun you were having with Evie." She knew she was pouting, but she didn't care. This was *her* party. Evie shouldn't have flirted with Damien knowing Savannah liked him. She must not have given up on her plan to lose her virginity to Damien, after all.

"I think you're taking this the wrong way," he said steadily. "I know you've been busy all night with everyone wanting to talk to you and with the cameras following you around, so I don't blame you for not noticing, but Evie's been having a rough time tonight. She doesn't know anyone, and she looked uncomfortable and lost—like how you looked when you walked into Myst on the Fourth of July."

"I never felt 'uncomfortable and lost,'" Savannah said. But thinking back on it, she knew that wasn't true. When she'd first arrived in Vegas, she'd felt like an imposter, like everyone expected her to be someone she wasn't. She *still* felt like that sometimes. As if the person she used to be—the wide-eyed, insecure girl who hid behind her assertive best friend—would resurface at any moment. "Well, maybe it took me some time to adjust. But *Evie's* not like that at all. She's the most confident person I know."

"I'm sure that back in California, where she knows everyone, that's true," Damien said. "But she was sitting here by herself, looking like she was about to cry. So because she's your best friend, and I know you wouldn't want her sitting miserably in a corner, I came over to see if she was okay. She said she was fine and just needed a break, but it didn't look like that to me, so I chatted with her to keep her mind off whatever was bothering her. Then she started flirting with me. I was going to let her down easy, but you spotted us before I had a chance."

"So…you're not interested in Evie?" Savannah asked hopefully.

"Not romantically," he said. "I only wanted to help her because I know how important she is to you."

"Oh." Savannah's eyes locked on Damien's, and her heart raced.

"Anyway, what was it you wanted to tell me?"

"Right…that." They'd gotten so off-topic that Savannah had nearly forgotten why she'd come over. "I found out that One Connection wasn't asked by Adrian to Tweet about my cover—they did it on their own. How crazy is that?"

"It would be crazy for them *not* to see how talented you are." Damien smiled, which sent her stomach fluttering in a million directions. "Did you know they have over fifteen million followers on their Twitter? And they also each Tweeted about you from their personal accounts, so you've reached even more people."

"Wow," Savannah said, unable to wrap her mind around how many people might have seen their posts. "This is insane."

"Before I came over here to check on Evie, I looked up your YouTube subscriber count," he continued. "It was *ten times* what it was before they Tweeted about you. You're into the hundred thousands, and I bet it's higher now. Your Twitter and Facebook pages are blowing up, too. This could make you famous, Savannah."

"I still can't believe it." She glanced at the stage where the magic had happened moments before. "And this is all thanks to you. Without your help, I never would have gone to the recording studio at school, gathered together a band and made more professional videos. I had *no idea* what I was doing with that stuff. You really helped me get my name out there."

"And I've got more ideas after tonight," he said. "That is, if someone as famous as you is still willing to take advice from me."

"Of course I am!" she said.

He leaned closer, and Savannah's breath caught at the possibility that he might kiss her. But instead, he brushed a piece of hair off her face and tucked it behind her ear.

So much for hoping he might see her as more than a friend.

"We'll sit down soon and talk about ideas," he said, his eyes not breaking contact with hers. "But for now, Evie's standing by herself at the dessert bar, watching us. Maybe you should talk to her?"

"Right." Savannah looked to the dessert area, and sure enough, Evie was alone, staring at them. She turned away, but not soon enough that Savannah didn't catch the terribly sad look in her eyes. "I'll see you later?"

"Count on it." He squeezed her hand, and tingles shot up her arm. Her skin felt warm where he'd touched her, and she tried not to think too much of it as she hurried to meet Evie. She took a deep breath, and the delicious smell of sweets filled her nose, as if she'd stepped inside Willie Wonka's Chocolate Factory. Her mouth watered, and she was tempted to have another chocolate-covered strawberry, even though she was so full she might burst.

"I wasn't sure if you were going to come back here or not," Evie said, looking down and smoothing out her dress. Damien was right—Evie wasn't nearly as confident here as she was at parties in California. How had Savannah missed it?

But it didn't change how she'd gone behind Savannah's back by trying to flirt with Damien.

"How could you go for Damien when you knew I have feelings for him?" Savannah blurted out. "I told you it would hurt me if you tried, but you did it anyway. Why?"

Evie's eyes flashed with guilt, and she twisted her watch around her wrist. "I wasn't planning on it," she said. "But he was being so nice to me, and you were mingling with everyone and filming for that show. You were barely talking to Damien. So I figured if something happened with me and him, it wouldn't be a big deal. I mean, you have everything you could ever want, and you could probably get any guy you wanted now, too. Even the boys in One Connection love you! Perry Myles was flirting with you onstage. That's better than some guy from your school, right?"

"But you know about everything that's happened with me

and Damien," Savannah said. "You knew it would hurt me if you went for him. But you did anyway. How could you go behind my back like that?"

"Like how you went behind my back last night when you talked to Oliver?"

Savannah froze. "How do you know what I said to Oliver last night?"

"I asked him," Evie said, as if this were the most obvious response on the planet. "And he told me that you warned him that I was a virgin so he wouldn't hook up with me."

"Yeah, I did," Savannah admitted, since she was clearly caught. "But only because I didn't want you doing something you would regret."

"It's not your place to make that decision for me," she said. "Besides, I was doing you a favor tonight, too, by flirting with Damien. If he went for me, it would show you where he stood with you, right?"

Savannah's mouth dropped open—had Evie really compared her feelings for Damien to a stupid one-night stand she was trying to have with Oliver? "Don't try turning this around by pulling that crap on me," she said. "I might have believed it back in California, but things are different now."

"You're right." Evie's voice was full of anger. "I've tried pretending everything's still the same, but it's not. Ever since you moved to Vegas, you look different, you act different and you think you're the greatest thing to grace the planet. You've turned into a spoiled heiress brat. I barely feel like I know you anymore."

Savannah took a sharp breath, unable to believe that Evie—her best friend for *years*—had said that to her. "You have no idea what you're talking about," she said. "I spent every second with you that I could this weekend, and you knew tonight was going to be crazy since I have to talk to everyone who came to the party and film for the show. I'm sorry I didn't notice you weren't feeling comfortable, and I'm sorry I ruined your plans for last night, but none of that makes it okay for you to have gone for Damien behind my back."

"There you go again," Evie said. "Making this about you, and acting like you're doing me *such a favor* by inviting me here and giving me a second of time at your party. You think you're so much better than me now."

Savannah clenched her fists—if either of them was acting like a brat, it was Evie. "I get it, you're upset at me." She checked to make sure no one was watching them, and lowered her voice. "But can we talk about this later, when we're in private? I don't want this caught on camera."

"Too afraid that your 'fans' will see you in a bad light?" Evie's chin trembled, and she narrowed her eyes. "Why don't you find the guys from One Connection and talk to them instead? Maybe that'll be better publicity for your YouTube channel. Which, by the way, I don't get why it's such a big deal. You don't even write your own music—you just sing other people's songs."

Savannah's chest heated, and she glared at Evie. "Why are you acting like this?" she asked. "You *know* that I'm a singer, not a songwriter. I've never claimed to want to be anything else. Maybe someday I'll write songs, but singing is what I love. And that's what I'm doing. Before tonight, I thought you were happy for me about the success of my YouTube channel. I didn't realize that you were so…resentful. About everything."

"Whatever." Evie stared blankly at the chocolate fountain, as if she hadn't heard a word Savannah had said.

"Okay." Savannah blew out a frustrated breath. "We obviously aren't getting anywhere with this right now. And tonight's my birthday, so I don't want to fight. So, yeah, I'll go talk to the guys in One Connection, to thank them for everything they did for me. Do you want to come with me or not?"

"I'm going to stay here and have dessert," Evie said. "Go have fun with them."

"I will." Savannah turned away and rejoined the party. Maybe she should have tried harder, and offered to introduce Evie to the One Connection guys. But as awful as she felt for leaving Evie like that, she was also glad she wouldn't have to risk her best friend making a scene.

She would work things out with Evie tomorrow. For now, this was her night, and she was going to enjoy her party.

chapter 34: *Courtney*

Courtney watched Savannah talking with the guys from One Connection, glad that the night had been a success. Adrian and Rebecca were smiling and laughing, Peyton was having a blast partying and dancing, and from where she sat at the "phone case bedazzling station," it seemed like Perry Myles was *flirting* with Savannah. Even though she doubted the international heartthrob was truly interested in her sister, since nothing real could ever come of that, it was kind of him to make her feel special for the night.

"I didn't realize bedazzled phone cases were your style," Brett said, situating himself in the seat next to hers.

Courtney glued another crystal into place, trying to ignore the way her stomach swooped from being so close to Brett. "I didn't think they would be," she said. "But I needed a break from chatting with everyone, and I figured this was a socially acceptable thing to do instead. I'm actually liking how it's turning out, so I think I'll use it."

He examined the swirling blue-and-silver design. "It looks

nice," he said. "If the whole going-to-college-to-someday-work-in-publishing thing doesn't work out for you, there's always cell-phone-case bedazzling."

"Let's hope it doesn't come to that." She pressed another crystal into place and yawned, even though there was an hour left of the party and she shouldn't be tired yet.

"You seem beat," Brett said.

"Between everyone here wanting to chat with me and having to act for the cameras for the show, I'm exhausted," she said. "I'm just glad my sixteenth birthday party's already past, so no one could try talking me into a blowout like this. Savannah might love the spotlight, but I could never do what she's been doing all night."

"You prefer sitting on the sidelines, bedazzling iPhone cases." Brett laughed.

"Hey!" she said. "It's relaxing."

"I'll take your word for it," he said. "So, since big parties aren't your thing, what'd you do for your Sweet Sixteen?"

"Went to school." She took a deep breath, preparing to rehash the day. "Then worked at Starbucks for a few hours. Some of my coworkers stuck a candle in a cupcake and sang 'Happy Birthday' to me. When I got home, Mom was already so drunk that she'd broken a lamp and gotten sick on the living room floor, so my sisters and I spent the rest of the night cleaning up and taking care of her until she passed out."

Brett reached for her hand and gave it a small squeeze, pulling away before she could wonder if it was friendly or meant more. "You deserve better than that," he said. "I'll make sure your next birthday is special."

Courtney's throat tightened. "My mom always managed to do *something* to celebrate Savannah and Peyton's birthdays, but on mine she was always a mess," she said, swallowing away tears. "At least now I know why. It's because it was Britney's birthday, too."

"Of course." Brett nodded, his eyes serious. "This year, we'll celebrate for Britney, too."

"Thanks," she said. "That means a lot."

He glanced over at the pool, where the guys from One Connection were hanging out, and raised an eyebrow. "Is it just me, or is Perry Myles taking a liking to Savannah?"

The two of them were in the same spot near the pool, still talking. Savannah handed her phone to him, he typed something into it, and gave it back to her. Then he took his phone from his pocket, tapped the screen, and Savannah broke into a huge grin.

"Did they just exchange numbers?" Courtney asked.

"It looked that way to me."

"Hmm." She refocused on bedazzling. "I hope she doesn't get her hopes up that anything could happen with him."

"Maybe he likes her," Brett said. "He *did* Tweet about her to his millions of fans. And now he's ignoring everyone else to talk to her."

"Come on." She shook her head, watching Perry and Savannah take a selfie together on his phone. "He's an international superstar. Practically every teen girl in the world is obsessed with him."

"So?" Brett shrugged.

Courtney sighed. Brett was pretty down-to-earth—how was he not getting this? "It's nice of Perry to make Savannah happy on her birthday," she said. "But let's be realistic. Adrian is paying him and the rest of the band a lot of money to make sure she has the best night ever. And on the off chance that he *is* interested in her, what could come from it after tonight?

Celebrities date other celebrities, not normal teens trying to make it through their sophomore year of high school."

"Everyone has to start somewhere," he said. "And Savannah isn't exactly a 'normal teen' anymore—she's an heiress to one of the top hotel moguls in the world. With her family connections, and now the support of One Connection, she has an advantage over other singers trying to make it. Besides, I thought you wanted her to upload YouTube videos and go for her dreams?"

"I did," Courtney said. "I still do. But there's a difference between having a popular YouTube channel and becoming a superstar like the guys in One Connection. She needs to have reasonable expectations."

"I guess." He watched her closely, his eyes piercing her soul. "But it's also important to take chances. It's better to try and fail than to never know at all and miss out on something great."

Courtney's cheeks heated, and she lowered her eyes, focusing on bedazzling the phone case as intensely as a doctor performing brain surgery. Then she set the bedazzling tweezers down, and said, "Are you still talking about Savannah, or are you talking about us?"

"I was talking in general," he said. "It applies to many situations. Ours included."

"Right." Courtney's heart pounded, and she couldn't believe what she was about to say. But it was now or never. "Well, I've thought a lot about what we talked about last night. And I want to see what could happen between us."

"Really?" He sat back, as if he couldn't believe it. "You mean it?"

"Yes."

He took her hands in his and leaned forward as if to kiss

her, sending her heart soaring. But she pulled away and looked around to make sure no one had seen. Luckily everyone was too involved in the party to notice her and Brett at the bedazzling table.

"What's wrong?" he asked, frowning.

"Nothing's wrong," she said. "I just don't think we should be so public about this. At least not at first."

"So you want to be together in secret?"

"Not forever," she said. "But while it's all new, yes. I really believe it'll work between us, and my sisters support us being together, too. But my dad and your mom aren't going to be happy. They'll think we're being irresponsible, and disrespectful to their wishes. So instead of rushing into telling them, let's wait and see how it goes—really solidify our relationship. Then we'll have proof we're making the right decision, and they won't think we're being impulsive."

"What about everything you said?" He held her hand under the table, which sent a thrill up her spine. "About how it'll be too hard on the family and on us if it doesn't end up working out?"

"That's all still true," she said. "But to hell with it. I don't want to look back and wonder what would have happened if we'd given us a chance. And I know now more than ever—you're worth the risk."

"I've always known you're worth the risk."

For the first time in a long time, Courtney knew she was making the right decision. And wherever Britney was now, she had a feeling her sister would be proud.

chapter 35: *Peyton*

In the bathroom at the party, Peyton took a swig of vodka from her flask and emptied what remained into her soda. The staff member standing by the sink to help people wash and dry their hands raised an eyebrow but said nothing. Peyton dropped a fifty into her tip jar.

Since the party was televised, the rules against underage drinking were stricter than usual, but pretty much everyone under twenty-one came prepared by pre-gaming, sneaking in a flask or both. The vodka was just what Peyton needed to smile through chitchatting with Adrian and Rebecca's friends, acting for the cameras, pretending she enjoyed the Top 40 boy band that Savannah loved and to stop her from constantly thinking about Jackson—whom she still hadn't heard from since that final text.

She checked herself out in the full-length mirror and glared at the dress Rebecca had tricked her into buying. Not because she hated it, but because she loved it and knew it looked amazing on her. She'd planned on wearing a dress she already owned, but Rebecca had said that was unacceptable and brought a few dresses up to the condo that she thought Peyton might like—hiding the price tags. Peyton had loved the tight leather dress when she'd tried it on, and only *after* committing to wearing it to the party did Rebecca tell her the dress was by some fancy designer and cost $3,500. Peyton had assumed the dresses Rebecca had chosen for her to try on would be expensive, but *thousands* of dollars for *one* dress? It blew her mind.

Her head buzzed, and feeling sufficiently tipsy enough to rejoin the party, Peyton exited the bathroom. She did a walk around the club to see what everyone was up to, staying close to the walls so that Adrian and Rebecca's friends wouldn't approach her. Luckily most of the parental-aged people were on the dance floor, since the DJ was doing a set of old music for them. Savannah and some of her friends from volleyball were hanging by the pool, squealing over the boys from One Connection. The guys from Goodman—who were less interested in taking selfies with the teen heartthrobs—were gathered around the gambling tables, playing poker and blackjack for charity. Peyton had assumed Oliver would have made a home for himself among them, but strangely enough, he wasn't there.

She headed to the dessert bar—the ice cream waffles looked *delicious*—and spotted Oliver and Madison at a table by themselves, their heads close together as they enjoyed a piece of cake. Oliver's arm was draped around Madison, and she leaned into him, as if they were a couple. They were gazing at each other like they were seconds away from jumping each other's bones.

What the hell? Peyton had told Oliver the bet was off—he didn't have to seduce Madison anymore. Given the way he'd been so appalled when Peyton had given him his task that day at the pool, he should have been glad to go back to being friends with her. But Oliver wasn't the type of person to back down. He was probably trying to prove a point—that he could follow through with his task, even though the bet had been called off.

And while Peyton hated to admit it, the conversation with Madison last night at the Lobby Bar had convinced her that Madison wasn't behind that Campusbuzz post. Unsurprisingly, Courtney had been right. Which frustrated her, but it would have been worse if she'd realized this *after* Oliver had followed through with the plan. But here he was, still making moves on Madison. He was such a jerk.

Shouldn't Madison know what Oliver was up to? If a guy had planned on using Peyton because of a bet, she would want someone to tell her. Even if that someone wasn't a person she liked very much. If Madison lost her virginity to Oliver because of this dare, it would be Peyton's fault. She wouldn't be able to forgive herself for that. And from the way Madison was looking at Oliver as if he meant the world to her, Peyton wouldn't be surprised if she slept with him after the party tonight.

She had to stop this before it was too late.

She grabbed an ice cream waffle from the dessert buffet, strutted over to Oliver and Madison's table and plopped herself down next to them. "This seat's not taken, right?"

Both Oliver and Madison looked at her as if she'd grown a second head. "Go ahead," he said. "We were just about to go outside, anyway."

"Don't leave on my account." Peyton licked some chocolate syrup off her fork. She might be doing this to be helpful, but she would definitely have fun with it and make them both squirm. "Especially since I came over here specifically to talk to you. To both of you," she added, so that Madison would feel included, too.

"Okay..." Madison glanced at the pool and shifted in her seat. "About what?"

"About you and Oliver, of course," she said. "I couldn't help noticing how cozy the two of you looked, and I had to know for myself. Are you guys together now?"

Madison stiffened and shoved her fork into her cake, leaving it there. "I don't see why it's any of your business, but, yes, we came here together."

"Like on a date?"

Madison said, "I suppose you could call it that," at the same time that Oliver said, "Yes." Then they looked at each other and smiled. Peyton somehow refrained from rolling her eyes.

Oliver was so good at getting girls into his bed that he almost had Peyton convinced that his feelings for Madison were real. But Peyton knew better. He was doing this because of her dare, and it would only be a matter of time—hours, from the way their hands were still all over each other—until he conned Madison into losing her virginity to him. What about "the bet's off" didn't he understand?

"Then it's good I came over here," Peyton said. "Because there's something important I need to tell you."

Oliver gave her a warning look. "If I were you, I would think twice before confessing anything drastic," he said. "I can smell the alcohol on you from here, and you wouldn't want to say something you'll regret when you're sober, right? Especially something you know nothing about."

"Come on." Madison glanced pointedly at Oliver's soda. "You're not exactly the picture of sobriety right now, either. Besides," she said, crossing her legs and focusing on Peyton.

"I'm vaguely curious about whatever important thing you need to say to me."

"I think Peyton and I need to talk somewhere in private." Oliver pushed back his chair and stood up, but Peyton grabbed his arm, not letting him leave.

"We don't need to talk anywhere in private," she said. "Sit back down. This involves both you and Madison."

Oliver cursed, clearly sensing he was backed into a corner. "You know not to believe a word she says, right?" he asked Madison.

"I won't know until she says it." Madison pulled him back into his seat. "But I want you to be here with me when she does."

Peyton took a deep breath. It was now or never.

"You're not going to be happy to hear this," she said to Madison. "But you should know now, before you make a huge mistake."

"You have no idea what you're doing." Oliver glared at her, trapped and desperate. But Peyton refused to feel sorry for him. He hooked up with girls only to crush them later, like he'd done to her and tried to do to her sisters that summer. He was getting what was coming to him.

Madison looked at him and tilted her head. "Do you know what this is about?"

He threw back the rest of his drink in one gulp. "I won't know until she tells us what she came here to say," he said. "So get on with it, Peyton. But if it's something you shouldn't be sharing—something that you made sure to *take back* a few weeks ago—trust me, you *will* regret it."

Peyton bit her lip to keep from laughing at Oliver's lame attempt to intimidate her. "Over the summer, Oliver and I made this bet," she started, and despite his protests, she spilled the entire story, up until realizing Madison might not have made that post and calling the bet off.

Madison narrowed her eyes and scooted away from Oliver, refusing to look at him, as if doing so would set her off into a rage.

"But apparently Oliver decided not to listen to me when I asked him to call the bet off," Peyton finished. "Because he's here with you now, after making it clear that day at the pool that the two of you would never be anything more than friends."

"Is that true?" Madison clutched her napkin and looked at Oliver, begging him to tell her that, no, it was a lie Peyton had made up.

"It started that way, yes." He took a breath to say more, but Madison cut him off before he had a chance.

"So it *is* true." She leaned her head back and covered her face with her hands. "Wow. I am such an idiot." Oliver reached for her, but she shrugged him off. "Don't touch me." She lowered her arms, her lips twisted in disgust. "I can't believe that all this time, when you knew everything I've been going through, you were going to use the fact that I was feeling vulnerable to win a stupid bet."

"It wasn't like that." He slammed his hand onto the table and glared at Peyton, his nostrils flared. "Or at least it hasn't been for a while. I said okay when you called off the bet. Tell her!"

"This doesn't involve me anymore." Peyton pushed her food away, the ice cream melted by now. "The two of you can work it out from here. I just saw you looking comfortable together, and thought this was something Madison should know before she does something she might regret."

"It *is* something I should know." Madison nodded, her

eyes glassy, as if she might burst into tears. "Thank you for your honesty."

"You're very welcome." Peyton slid her chair back and stood up. "I'm going to find my sisters. I'm sorry you had to find out this way."

The strangest thing was, even though she still didn't like Madison or want to be friends with her, she absolutely meant it.

chapter 36: *Madison*

Madison watched Peyton walk away, every nerve in her body sparking with anger. The night had gotten off to such a great start. Oliver had met her at the Lobby Bar under the statue of Daphne, and they'd had a drink. Then they'd met up with their friends at Savannah's party, and it had felt like old times, except she was finally realizing that her friendship with Oliver was blooming into something more. She'd even considered getting a room with him after the party.

Then Peyton Diamond had ruined everything.

"A bet?" Her voice cracked, and she forced herself to look at him. Her chest collapsed at the guilt plastered all over his face. "This whole time when you were there for me and I thought there might be something real between us, it was because of a *bet?*"

He was unnaturally still, his hands shoved into his pockets. "It wasn't like that."

"Then what *was* it like?" Her heart ached, desperately hoping for a believable excuse. But Peyton had been clear about what had happened, and Oliver hadn't denied it. He'd been playing her for months. And she'd fallen for it.

She felt like the biggest idiot in the world.

"When Peyton told me what she wanted me to do, I said there was no way in hell—I told her I refused to mess with our friendship," he said, his eyes begging her to trust him. "I asked her to pick something else, or the bet was off. But then she showed me a picture Savannah had taken at a party of me doing a line with friends, and she said if I didn't go along with her plan, she would make the photo public. If my parents saw that picture, it would've been the last straw before sending me to boarding school."

"So Peyton *blackmailed* you into trying to sleep with me." Madison shook her head, the pit in her stomach growing. "This is getting worse and worse. I only have one chance at my first time, and you were going to ruin that moment for me—someone you *claim* to care about—because you were afraid of getting in trouble with your parents."

"I never would have made you do anything against your will." He reached for her hand, but she pulled away. He flinched but continued, "I told Peyton that if it happened, it would only be because you wanted it."

"That still doesn't make it okay." She leaned her head back and sucked in a deep breath. "I would never want to lose my virginity because of a bet. Because someone was *using me*." She shivered, horrified at how close she'd come to letting that happen. "If I hadn't been going through such a rough time, I would have known your feelings for me weren't real. But I needed someone to be there for me, and you swooped in to take advantage of it. If Peyton hadn't come clean with the truth, it would have been a great play."

"It *started* because of a bet," he said. "But it became more than that. My feelings for you aren't fake, Madison. If they were, why did I ask you out tonight, *after* Peyton called off the bet?"

She shrugged. "Because you still saw it as a challenge?"

"No." His eyes burned with intensity. "The bet pushed me to dig deeper into our relationship, and it was the push I needed, because what I feel for you is real. I'm here with you tonight because I care about you, and because I think you care about me, too."

"You care about getting what you want," she said. "That's all you've ever cared about."

His face fell, as if her words had physically hurt him. "You know that's not true."

The sad thing was, she *wanted* him to be telling the truth. But how desperate would she be if she blindly believed him and moved forward as if nothing had changed? "I have no way of knowing that," she said. "I never should have trusted you." She pressed her fingers against her temples, unable to believe how stupid she'd been. "You can't tell anyone what I told you about the Diamonds—about Adrian being my father, and Peyton, Courtney and Savannah being my sisters. Promise me that."

"I promise I won't tell anyone your secret," he said, holding his gaze with hers. "I'll do anything to prove you can still trust me."

"After all this, I don't know if there's anything you *can* do." She blinked away tears, dreading that they would pour out at any moment. Then Oliver would comfort her, and she would melt into his arms. She couldn't let that happen. "Do you have any idea how much you've hurt me?"

"I didn't want to hurt you," he said. "But my feelings for you…they're real, I swear it. You have to believe me, Mads."

She wished she could. But he'd used her. All those times in the past few months when she'd believed he cared…it was a lie. A game for him to take her virginity because he was afraid of getting sent to boarding school. The thought of how she'd almost fallen for it made the dessert she'd been eating churn in her stomach, and she pushed the plate away, the smell of the cake making her feel like she was going to be sick. Or maybe it was being so close to Oliver and being reminded of how he'd played her that was making her feel sick.

"I need to think about everything, and I can't do that with you around," she said. "So I want you to get away from me, and stay away for the rest of the night."

"But if you let me explain some more, maybe it'll help you understand," he said, desperate.

"No." She could barely get the word out. "I don't want to talk to you or see you again tonight."

"Fine." He reached into his pocket and pulled out his valet slip. "There was a house party I was going to check out after this, anyway. Can't hurt to get a head start."

"You're driving?" She must have misunderstood. He'd already finished off most of his flask.

"Of course." He smirked. "I didn't get my license and ask for the Maserati for my birthday so I could have the chauffeur take me everywhere in the Town Car."

"But you've been drinking," she said. "You can't drive."

"I'm fine to drive." He watched her closely, daring her to contradict him. "Besides, it's nothing for you to worry about. You don't care about me."

"Don't be an ass," she snapped. "I'm angry and hurt about what happened, but that doesn't mean I want you putting yourself in danger."

"I'm giving you space." He pushed his chair back and stood up. "Isn't that what you wanted?"

"If you're trying to manipulate me into forgiving you right now, it's not going to work, and your safety isn't worth whatever point you're trying to prove." She made a grab for his valet slip, but he lifted it out of her reach.

"Everything's not always about you." His eyes blazed. "You called me selfish, but you're no saint yourself. I didn't have as much to drink tonight as you think. So back off, and stop telling me what to do." He stormed out of the club.

Her eyes heated, and a tear escaped. Oliver had been there for her through the past few weeks, but none of it had been real. He'd lied to her and betrayed her, just like everyone else in her life.

She looked around at the party guests, having so much fun. Happy, loved, carefree. Why couldn't she feel like that? Instead, her chest was hollow, her heart empty. The tears forced their way out in streams, and she hurried to the bathroom, hiding her face behind her hair so no one could see her falling apart.

She locked herself in the far stall, and finally allowed herself to cry.

www.campusbuzz.com

Oliver Prescott :(
Posted on Sunday 12/14 at 12:23 PM
I don't know Oliver that well, but I heard what happened to him last night. He looked so happy at Savannah's party... it's scary how quickly everything can change. My thoughts are with him and his family in this awful time <3

1: Posted on Sunday 12/14 at 12:35 PM
what happened to oliver???

2: Posted on Sunday 12/14 at 12:47 PM
I don't know the full story, but he got in a car accident after leaving Savannah's party. His friends are writing on his Facebook wall that they hope he pulls through this. It sounds like they're not sure if he's going to make it :/

3: Posted on Sunday 12/14 at 12:58 PM
He got in a big fight with Madison before leaving the party. I bet she feels like a bitch now!

4: Posted on Sunday 12/14 at 1:06 PM
Lay off. You have no idea what happened with Oliver and Madison, and no right to say anything about how she feels. She probably feels awful, and your post isn't helping. Have some consideration.

5: Posted on Sunday 12/14 at 1:18 PM
His family and close friends have been at the hospital all night. No one's saying much other than that they're waiting for more news. It doesn't sound good.

6: Posted on Sunday 12/14 at 1:28 PM
Let's all pray for Oliver...

★ ★ ★ ★ ★

Acknowledgments

First of all, a super major shout-out to Natashya Wilson, my editor at Harlequin TEEN. *Diamonds in the Rough* wouldn't be half of what it is today without your incredible insight and ideas about how to make this book the best it could be. Thank you for pushing me to "torture my characters," and to add more drama and tension throughout the story. Reworking the book was a challenge, but your guidance shaped it in ways I never thought possible, and I'm so proud of the final product!

My agent, Molly Ker Hawn—thank you for answering all my questions and being patient with me! While it's been a year and a half since signing my first book deal, I still feel like a newbie to the industry. You're always there for me whenever I have questions about random things, and to help me get over any bumps that might arise!

My publicist, Dana Kaye—thank you for believing in *Diamonds in the Rough* and taking it on to help spread the word about the series. I'm writing this only a few days after you agreed to take on the book, and I just *know* that Kaye Publicity is going to do a great job with getting the word out. I can't wait to see what happens!

My in-house publicist, Jennifer Abbots—I'm writing this very recently after you joined the Harlequin TEEN team, so welcome to the team! (Although by the time this book is out, you'll have been a part of it for months.) I'm looking forward to working with you to spread the word about the series!

Lisa Wray, my publicist for *The Secret Diamond Sisters*— thank you for all your hard work with getting *The Secret Diamond Sisters* out there. From getting reviews by awesome sites, putting together my blog tour, getting beautiful drawings made that represent the personalities of the sisters and helping with event planning, you've been great!

Erin Craig and the cover design team—another BEAUTIFUL cover that perfectly represents the inside of the book and pops on the shelves! Thank you!

Libby Sternberg—thank you for getting through the copy edits at lightning speed!

There are also TONS of people behind the scenes of Harlequin TEEN whom I've never met, who are part of the process of getting the book out there. So even though we've never met, *thank you,* and I hope to meet you in the future!

Brent Taylor—you have had so much enthusiasm for this series from the very, very beginning, and I will never forget that! I hope you enjoyed *Diamonds in the Rough.* <3

Jackie Bach—your support after the release of *The Secret Diamond Sisters* amazed me. Thank you for going around to bookstores, taking pictures of the book and telling all your friends about the book. But most of all, your support as a fellow writer has been incredible. Thank you for your great advice and for listening to me vent about writerly things. I can't wait for the day when both of our names grace the YA shelves. ☺

Kaitlin and Tiffany—you both know how important you are to me! I hope you enjoyed your characters in this book.

Jackie and Brooke—my teen cousins! You two are awesome, and I always have a blast with you at family events. I hope you liked having your names in the book, and I hope you know that I know you're both much nicer people than the characters named for you! ;) (And Jackie, I hope you enjoyed your house being in the book! I *knew* when I first saw it that people would jump from your balcony into the pool.)

Alicia—you're a great friend, and you were the inspiration for the character of Alyssa. She was originally a supernice girl (like you!), but I ended up changing her entire personality to add drama to the plot. So I hope you enjoy your character, even though she's evolved to be quite different from you!

Devan—you're an amazing friend! We always seem to be on the same wavelength, and thank you for knowing when I need to talk.

Wendy—my freshman-year college roommate, who inspired the character of her name. Your kindness and acceptance of others has always been something I admire!

The YouTube artists who inspired Savannah's story—Emily Harder, Tiffany Alvord, Megan Nicole and Madilyn Bailey. You are all incredibly talented. Everyone go check out their channels! They're fantastic.

My parents, Anne and Richard Madow, my brother, Steven Madow, and my grandparents, Lois and Selvin Madow, and Paul and Phyllis Lichtenstein—THANK YOU FOR EVERYTHING. I couldn't have done this without you. As always, I hope you all enjoy the inside family jokes. And Steven, thank you for the info on Habitat for Humanity!

My amazing Street Team members—you have all been so encouraging and helpful with spreading the word about my books. Thank you for reminding me why I write! Aishah Qazi, Ali Byars, Alice Zheng, Allyson Bright Meyer, Aly Phanord, Alyssa Susanna, Amanda Leigh Morey, Amanda Price, Amanda Welling, Amber Garcia, Amy Halbern, Ana Sana, Anatea Oroz, Andrea Caito, Angela Chen, Annie Lai, Aparajita Basu, Ashley Hopkins, Becca Jayne, Beckie Voigts, Becky Earl, Betsy Diaz, Brooke DelVecchio, Cameron Yeager, Cara White, Carissa Miller, Cary Morton, Catherine Sanchez, Chandra Haun, Christina Madison, Chyna Go, Ciara Byars, Colette Grubman, Danii Calcagno, Darcus Murray, Deena Edwards, Destiny Sparks, Eli Madison, Elizabeth Weibley, Ella Zegarra, Emily Mahar, Emily Nesheva, Emily Rasmussen, Erin Prefontaine, Erin Sawyer, Erin Westlund, Gabbie Johnson, Gabby Matlock, Genissa Daly, Gina Scarcella, Hannah Newlin, Heather Sheffield, Heidi Keil, Hira Mushtaq, Holly A. Letson, Iris Kwakernaat, Ivy Leung, Jackie Wostrel, Jacqueline Bach, Jen Stasi, Jennifer Weiser, Jesselle Villegas, Jessica Recio, Jessica Reid, Jessica Sun, Jessica Woodward, Kaitlin Dang, Kat Colvin, Kat Fleming, Kathy Coe, Kelly Hager, Kendall McCubbin, Kirsty-Marie Jones, Kristen Ana Vazquez, Larissa Hardesty, Lauren Goff, Leanne Maala, Lily Velez, Lis Carcamo, Louisse Ang, Margie Cortina, Marie Landry, Melody Sosa, Michelle Adams, Michelle Minton, Myra White, Natasha Evans, Natasha Vahora, Nicola Wilkinson, Nicole Hackett, Nicole Mainardi, Nicole Miniuk, Nora Deret, Paige Murray, Paola Benavides, Patrice Zurek, Patricia Lopez, Paul E. Petty, Queenielyn Dahilan, Rachel Hoyt, Raizza Mae Cinco, Rebecca Greer, Ren White, Roger McClellan, Saloni Lad, Samantha Panda, Samantha Randolph, Samantha Wallace, Sarah Blackstock, Sarah Brown, Selina

Xu, Sophie Hedley, Stephanie Ehmann, Stephanie Ward, Sue Fabianova, Susan Schleicher, Tabitha Williams, Tanya Sydor, Tiffany Fowler, Valerie Burleigh, and Vi Nguyen.

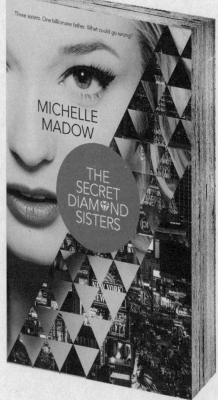

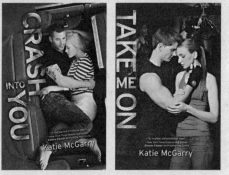

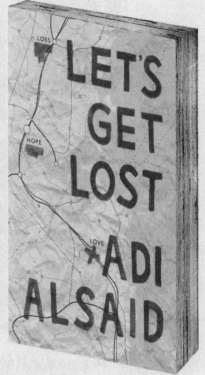

From the *NEW YORK TIMES* bestselling
author of the HALO trilogy,

ALEXANDRA ADORNETTO,

comes the start of a beautiful and
powerful new series.

Chloe Kennedy
has always seen
ghosts. But she's
never been able to
speak to one...
until now. After
meeting Alexander
she must now push
her developing
abilities to their most
dangerous limits,
even if it means
giving the hungry dead
a chance to claim
her for their own.

GHOST HOUSE

Available Now

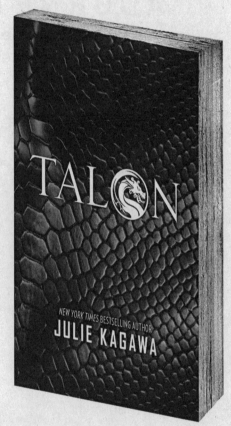